LETTERS FROM JAMES

A High Country Love Story

Ruth Layng

2000

Parkway Publishers, Inc.
Boone, North Carolina

*Although based on stories told to the author by Jennie, and
although some of the characters are real, this is a work of
fiction and a product of the author's imagination.*

Library of Congress Cataloging-in-Publication Data

Layng, Ruth D., 1924-
    Letters from James / by Ruth D. Layng.
        p. cm.
    ISBN 1-887905-23-5
        *1. World War, 1914-1918--Fiction. 2. North Carolina--
Fiction. 3. Letter-writing--Fiction. 4. Young women--
Fiction. 5. Soldiers--Fiction. 6. Ireland--Fiction. I.Title*

PS3562.A958 L448 2000
813'.54--dc21   *00-036718*

Cover design by Bill May, Jr.
Editing, layout and book design by Julie Shissler

Chapter One
Bloody War

James crouched in the muddy water of the trench, his rifle propped beside him, a dented, crusted helmet balanced on his knee. Mud and slime sucked at his heavy wool field jacket and, despite the gripping cold, his brow was slick with nervous sweat.

The Allied barrage raged furiously. Arcing shells from the cannons behind him dumped deadly shards of shrapnel on the enemy lines. On the perimeter of the field of fire, chattering machine guns poured fiery lines of bullets into the darkness and over it all, star shells burst in midair, adding a sense of celebration to the messages of death.

Christ, he was sick of it all; the endless marching that left his feet bloody and blistered and his muscles aching, the lice (filthy buggers), the mud, the gross bloated bodies of dead animals moldering along the roadsides, and the stench that rose in fumes from unwashed bodies, including his own. He'd thought it couldn't get worse and now here he was, sitting in freezing water up to his ass, to meet the Boche head on, to kill or be killed.

He squeezed his eyes shut and muttered to himself. "Steady on, boyo. Just y' blot out the din and the smell of death. Think pleasin' thoughts before y'bloody lose yer blinkin' mind."

The roar of the guns faded and there he was; soaking in a bath, steam rising in tendrils around his ears, his desperate imagination conjuring up the smell of soap. Within reach was a cup of hot tea laced with a tad of whiskey. *Ah, that's better. Tea wi'a touch to banish the shivers and deaden the clamor.*

Pete slid down beside him, his tremendous bulk barely fitting the cramped quarters of the trench. Over the roar of the guns he shouted, "You all right, Irish?"

The spell was broken. James reluctantly opened his eyes. He placed the helmet back on his head, grinned at his friend and thought, *Christ, the lad makes one hell of a target.* He brought his mouth close to Pete's ear. "It's over the top we go soon, bucko." Pete nodded grimly.

One by one the big guns fell silent, the silence more shattering than the cannon fire. Along the trench, wordless soldiers tested gas masks, checked grenades, and affixed bayonets to rifles, awaiting the blare of the klaxon that would send them over the top into no-man's land.

It came ... the shriek of the klaxon.

Pete caught James' hand in a powerful grip. For a brief moment their eyes met and held before they joined the other bodies surging over the lip of the trench. Thick fog swirled and eddied, shrouding the gaping shell holes and tangles of barbed wire that clutched like skeletal hands as they stumbled along. The German cannons began their barrage, sending death out over no-man's land to meet the advancing soldiers.

James and Pete, crouching low, ran, giving little thought to the pitfalls. A shell screamed its approach, forcing them to the ground and they shrank into themselves, hearts thumping with dread. The earth trembled, and falling rocks and debris pelted them. Amidst it all, a scream rose above the tumult and was lost in the fog. *God help the poor sod.*

Pete prodded his shoulder and they stumbled to their feet, resuming the insane rush forward. Another shell burst above their heads, the impact lifting James off his feet. A searing pain ripped through him and he screamed ... or did Pete?

The fog thickened and closed around him.

Consciousness came slowly. When he opened his eyes, darkness smothered him like a blanket; the sounds of bursting shells and muffled machine gun fire were faint in the distance. The advancing troops had left them behind. His mind was muddled as he wondered how long he'd been lying there. *Have to move ... can't... must.* He managed, with great effort, to push his body to a sitting position. Bile rose to his throat and he retched. *Can't stay here, have to move.* "Pete," he called and the sound of his feeble, hoarse voice frightened him.

He rolled over on his hands and knees and his arm collapsed, blood running from his sleeve. The pain dizzied him and bile choked his throat. *Mustn't pass out. Breathe!* But each breath was a knife thrust in his back. *Shallow breaths, that's better.*

The fog was a white swirling ocean, where Pete might be dying. *Have to find Pete.* James pushed himself back up, this time on his good arm, and began to agonizingly grope forward inch by inch and...*Oh God, a body.* It was his buddy, curled into a ball, unmoving.

He sat back on his haunches, shaking his head. The blackness receded and he leaned forward, carefully easing the stress on his arm and shoulder, and pressed his fingers into the side of Pete's neck. Was there a pulse? *Please, God, please...yes, there it was...faint and erratic.*

Was all this blood his or Pete's?

Must get back to the trench...how? The fog was disorienting and Pete's size and weight daunting. *Think, damn it, think.*

Finally he forced himself to stand, rolled Pete on his back, grabbed his friend's collar and began to drag Pete laboriously behind him. Aloud he said, "We'll make it, laddie, hold on. God in heaven, Pete, hold on."

Without conscious thought, he headed back in the right direction and fell into the muddy water of the trench below. Pete's body landed heavily on top of him. Just before he lost consciousness, he heard it. *Surely not...but...yes, there it was again.* From the ravine below, the unearthly song of a nightingale.

$$\boxtimes$$

James came up from a deep, dark place. First, he heard sounds—coughing, moans, quick footfalls, back and forth. Sharp, distinct sounds, like metal on metal. Then the smells—pungent and strong. He struggled to understand, but he was slipping away again...

He awoke with a start. It was daylight and the troubled images that had clouded his sleep slowly faded. Where was he? The last thing he remembered was going over the top, the star shells bursting and then...

The raising of his head sent his arm and shoulder into a spasm of pain, his heart into a frenzied beating as he fell back, fighting nausea.

After a moment or two he raised his head cautiously and despite the pain, a long contented sigh escaped his lips, leaving him giddy with relief. He was in a tent...a field hospital. *He was safe...and Pete? Where was Pete?* Turning his head to the side, he was relieved to find his friend in the next cot, eyes closed, head a white cap of bandages. James wondered briefly how a great hulk of a man such as Pete Sampson could rest comfortably in the narrow confines of the cot.

James turned his attention to his surroundings. He was in a large tent with cots lining the walls. Tables set in a rough circle in the center overflowed with instruments, piles of bandages, bed pans, jars, and bottles. Off to one side, a small wood-burning stove provided just enough heat to ward off the worst of the cold. James curled his toes with pleasure, luxuriating in the absence of heavy army boots.

He was lulled by the heat of the stove, the pillow beneath his head and the warm, clean-smelling blanket snugly wrapped around him. God alone knew the reason they were there. After He sent them into hell, He relented, rescued them and settled them in clean beds free of dirt and lice. With no strength to wonder why, James drifted...and there on the table by his side...was a cup of tea with just a tad...

⊠

"I was just thinking, Pete, the strangeness of it all."

"If you're gonna come up with one of your wise-ass remarks, Irish, you can just..."

"No, no, Pete, I'm serious. You take Edward here," and he nodded at the young man in the cot to his right. "He's from the States, you from Canada, and me from Ireland. Where else in the world would you get a mix like that except in a bloody war?"

Edward was suffering the effects of chlorine gas (or mustard gas as it was more commonly known), his throat and lungs seared.

He reached for his pad, wrote laboriously then held it out to James, who leaned out with his good arm to retrieve it.

James was pleased. "Edward here hasn't felt well enough to communicate these past few days. I'm glad to see he's feelin' a mite better."

Pete lifted himself up on his elbow. "What'd he write?"

James read the note, his face a serious mask. "He wrote, Pete that he has taken a mad fancy to you, and..."

"Oh for Christ sake, Irish..."

James grinned, "All right, all right. Let's see, I think he wants to know where you're from." He looked at Edward and raised his eyebrows. Edward managed a half nod.

The three soldiers were as dissimilar in appearance as they were in background. James was tall, pleasing in looks, with thick auburn hair and clear, grey eyes. Peter, the one you would notice first in a crowd was over six feet tall, well built, blond wavy hair, blue eyes. While ladies gravitated to Peter first, they inevitably ended up in James' company. He was witty and spoke with a soft, rolling Irish accent, which enchanted everyone.

Edward, the youngest of the three, was thin with a narrow face and large, expressive blue eyes. Dora, their nurse, fell over herself mothering him.

"Peter here comes from the beautiful city of Vancouver in the province of British Columbia, Canada and that's where the lad latched on to me when I arrived there from Ireland five years ago. Since then,

I've saved him many a time from the degradation of drink and sinful women."

Peter scoffed. "*Saved* me? Don't you believe it, Ed. James here was green as grass when he came over on the boat. I taught him everything he knows."

James shook his head. "You can see his head is bandaged. The lad is delusional." James became serious. "I've been burning your ears these past few nights about me, me brother Danny and Ireland, Edward, and I don't know a thing about you. If you feel up to writin' on yer pad, tell me something about yourself?"

Edward wrote laboriously.

James reached for the pad. "You're from Zionville, North Carolina?"

Edward nodded and motioned for the pad. When he finished writing, he again handed the pad to James and fell back on his pillow, exhausted.

James read, "You have a farm in the mountains and two brothers and three sisters and do they know." James looked into Edward's anguished face. The boy wiped angrily at his eyes. James said softly, "Aye, laddie, they know. The government surely sent word to them and the best thing you can do for your brothers and sisters is to get well, so you can go back to your farm in the mountains."

Edward began to cough, a deep rumbling cough which made him gasp for breath and curl into a ball. James looked around quickly for Dora and was relieved to see her on her way with the needle that would give him temporary respite from pain.

Chapter Two
Zionville

Zionville was one of several small communities, tucked into the valley between Buckey's Knob and Snake Mountain, in the highlands of western North Carolina. Beyond Buckey's Knob and Snake Mountain to the north lay Tennessee. Zionville boasted nothing more than several farms, a general store and post office, a one-room school house and two churches, Methodist and Baptist.

Cove Creek ran through the valley. Its companion, a narrow dirt road (Route 421) called Valley Road, ran alongside, following the creek's twists and turns. Rutted and frozen in winter and potholed and muddy in spring, Valley Road was the lifeline that strung the communities of Zionville, Mabel, Mast, Cove Creek, and Sugar Grove together.

Zionville lay in the heart of the Bible Belt. Though its people were poor in worldly goods, they were rich in the bounty of the land, sharing both good fortune and hard times with each other. They planted their crops, raised their livestock, labored endlessly, morning to dusk, and believed steadfastly in the teachings of the Bible, assured that if they lived moral and Christian, lives their reward would come from the hands of God.

✉

Jennie turned from the sink, her hands dripping dishwater on the floor. "What was that, Mama? What did you say?"

Mama sat in her rocker, busy with the mending in her lap, consciously ignoring Jennie's angry tone. "I said, your Papa is coming home tomorrow. He wrote he'd try to get home sometime on the fourteenth of November and that's tomorrow."

Jennie was stunned. "How come you didn't say something 'fore this?" Mama stopped sewing and looked up into Jennie's angry eyes.

"Because I expected just this kind of reaction and so I put off tellin' you 'til the last minute. We ain't seen your Papa since July..."

"That's right, Mama, July. Ed left for the army and Papa didn't wait even one week..."

"I know, I know..."

Resentment had built up over the last months.

"You know as well as me, Ed left thinkin' Papa would maybe be shocked into behavin' like a man."

Mama looked about to say something, but Jennie didn't give her the chance. "Oh, he was shocked all right. Snuck off like a thief in the night."

"Jennie, it don't do no good to be bitter. Your Papa never did take to the farm, you know that, and for Ed to think by leaving Papa to take care of it all..."

Jennie slumped against the sink, dejected. "Mama, it isn't just that Papa doesn't work. He always manages to find money for drink and when he drinks..."

Mama ignored Jennie. "It will be good to have him home. Good fer him to get some decent food, sleep in a decent bed. God only knows how he's been livin' at the mines..."

Jennie tried to see inside her mother's head. *Why is it she chooses to ignore the kind of man Papa is?* Aloud she said. "If Papa missed your cookin' and sleepin' in his own bed, how come he didn't let you know where he was? You wouldn't know to this day if Luther Norris hadn't told you Papa was workin' alongside him in the mines."

"I don't like your tone of voice, young lady. Your Papa woulda' let me know in time. What's more, I 'spect you to keep a civil tongue in your head while he's home."

"Civil!" Jennie knew she shouldn't, but the unfairness of it fired her senses. "Civil to a man that hasn't done a full day's work in years, but finds the money to go out and get drunk."

"Jennie! That's a disrespectful thing to say about your Papa. He *does* work..."

"Have you seen any of the money? Ed's the only one ever brought any money into this house."

Mama's voice matched Jennie's in anger. "He said in his letter he would settle the bills we run up at the store ... that's the same thing. As for drinking, yes, your Papa has a weakness and the Lord says to show compassion for the weak. It gets lonely fer a man to be away from his family."

Jennie laughed. "So you're saying it's all right for a man to drink up what he earns 'cause he misses his family. I don't think even the Lord would understand that ... and the worst is not his drinking. Papa's temper..."

Mama was shocked. "Do not mock the Lord, Jennie. And this is your Papa's house. If he wants to come home, that's his right."

Jennie ignored the danger signals Mama was sending out. "A man who doesn't take care of his family has no rights as I see it..."

Mama's voice was hoarse with anger. "Jest you stop right there. It's not your place to say who will or will not come into this house."

The fire left Jennie, replaced by a bewildered sadness. She shook her head. "I don't understand. How can you stand up for him? He drove your son out of the house into a danger he didn't have to suffer. He's given all of us nothing but heartache and shame and..."

Mama raised her hand, palm outward, and shouted. "That's enough. I will not hear another word against your father."

Jennie walked down the front path and stopped at the gate. At sixteen, she was too old to swing on it anymore, but even so she climbed up and sat on top, her long legs almost reaching the ground. She missed talking to her brother, never more so now that Papa was coming home. They didn't exactly know where Edward was. In Europe for sure, but the army blacked out where that was in his letters, so all they could do was guess. She stared morosely at the house. It had always been more a prison than a home ... a place of whispers. They all felt it.

A rickety-railed porch ran along the front and wrapped around the house, saved from sagging by the log propping it up at the turn. On the porch, two ancient wood rockers and a swing kept their vigil, ready as always to welcome the weary. Paint everywhere was chipped away, down to the bare wood in places, and most of the shutters sagged. But since Papa left, the house had become a cocoon, wrapping the family warmly and safely together. They no longer kept a fearful watch at the window, expecting to see a figure lurching up the road. But they did have worries. The anguish of their brother, Ed, fighting a war in some distant place and the growing tab at Lije Proffitt's store. Mama's garden put food on the table, but she couldn't grow shoes or kerosene for the lamps, or material to sew their clothes.

Jennie sighed aloud, gathered her dress in a bunch so as not to tear it, carefully slid down from the gate and walked slowly back up the path. Tall and slim, she was almost a head taller than Mama, carrying herself with such confidence that most people thought she was putting on airs. There may have been a little truth to that. She had little patience for those lacking in drive and common sense, traits that came naturally to her. Even Ed, older than Jennie by three years often looked to her for advice.

She climbed the porch steps and dropped heavily into a rocker, shivering in the cold, damp air. A weak sun hung on the horizon, ready to sink below the mountain rim. The katydids had gone to wherever they go when winter approaches, and she missed their comforting drone. She pulled her wooly grey sweater more snugly around her and tucked her dress around her legs, and as much as she hated the itchy cotton stockings, they helped to ward off the chill.

Jennie brooded about her father. Dalton Wainwright was a bully ... drunk or sober. Big, broad-shouldered and strong, no one could stand up to him. The least infraction of his rules sent him into a black rage which the liquor only intensified. If they were lucky enough to see the storm coming his family scurried for cover like so many frightened rabbits ... if not they withstood the senseless beatings he meted out. Ed, at nineteen, hadn't yet developed the strength or courage to stand up to Papa, and so had as little defense against the man as six-year-old Hubie.

Sometimes Mama could distract Papa, but in the last few years his tantrums had worsened and her attempts to intervene only heightened his anger so Mama fled to the next room with her hymnal, singing as loud as she could, to drown out the mayhem.

To be fair, there had been some good times. Jennie remembered laughter mixed with discipline. Papa was always happy working the mules. He taught each of them how to handle the beasts, trusting Edward at the age of ten to work the mules at neighboring farms for a wage. But over the years as the drink took hold, the discipline turned violent and it became the pattern for him to take off his belt rather than to reason. It had been a long time since the family had laughed together.

The door opened and banged shut. Minnie strolled out to the porch swing and settled on it, moving it slowly back and forth with her feet.

"Heard you and Mama shoutin' at each other."

"Did you hear what we were shouting about?"

"Is it true? Is Papa coming home?"

Jennie nodded.

Minnie sighed. "I feel like running away."

Jennie reached over and patted her knee. "Maybe he won't stay. He might be coming home just for a visit."

Minnie frowned. "That's not what Mama wants. She *wants* him to come home to stay." She turned a puzzled gaze to Jennie. "Why would she want that, Jennie? Everyone is happier without Papa around."

"I don't honestly know, Min."

The swing groaned on its rusty chains as Jennie studied her sister. Min had a pretty heart-shaped face which showed to best advantage when her black curly hair was tied back, as it was now, away from her face. Hazel eyes, clouded now with worry at the prospect of Papa coming home, were framed by silky brows and long lashes. The plain cotton dress did little to hide her blossoming curves and Jen had to remind herself again that Min was only thirteen.

Minnie broke the silence. "It's all 'cause Ed left. Why did he have to go and join the army anyway? I wish ole Elijah Proffitt didn't have that ole crystal set in his store, then Ed wouldn't never a heard 'bout the war."

Jennie said. "If Ed hadn't joined the army, he would have found another reason to leave."

Minnie shook her head. "That ain't true, Jennie. I heard Ed say lots a' times he wants to live and die right here in Zionville. He loves the mountains."

"It's not Zionville he wanted to get away from, Min. It couldn't a been easy, him decidin' to go, knowing how much Mama and all of us depended on him. But you said it a minute ago, how you wish you could run away. I think Ed joined the army partly to run away from Papa. He thought maybe it would make Papa find work and be responsible."

Minnie nodded slowly, thinking it over. "So, Mama wants Papa to come home to ask him for money?"

"Well ... partly."

"Why else?"

"It's complicated, Min. I don't know the answer myself."

"Papa never did work much, did he?"

"Some. With the mules."

"That was a long time ago."

Jennie said, "Then Ed quit school. That was right around the time the mules died, remember?" Min nodded.

"Mama didn't want him to, but Ed hated school anyway and he loved working the farm, so it wasn't all a bad idea. Mr. Owen and some of the others, like Ben Combs and Tom Wooding, started paying him a hand's wages when they got busy. I helped, too, when Doctor Payne started finding work for me with his patients. I never thought of it as work. But I was lucky. I didn't have to leave school."

Minnie nodded soberly. "And so Papa didn't *have* to work cause you and Ed were bringing in money?"

"Maybe Papa didn't think of it that way, but that's what it amounted to."

"I heard Mama say Papa will pay the tab at the store. Think he will?"

"We'll have to wait and see."

The swing stopped creaking. "Jennie..."

"What?"

"I'm afraid of Papa."

The sun was gone. A cold wind picked up some fallen leaves from the buckeye tree and danced them across the yard.

Jennie shivered. Was it the chill wind or a premonition? "So am I, Min."

✉

Next morning the air was cold and heavy with the threat of rain. Great patches of mist hung like grey filmy curtains, dipping into the trees and blotting out the mountain tops. The dampness caused Jennie's short, brown hair to curl in little wisps about her face. It was a day to match her mood.

The hen pecked her way across the back yard. *Patience. I have to have patience. Eventually the stupid bird will end up close enough for me to pounce.* It didn't bother her knowing Clint would wring the chicken's neck and pluck it bare. They all loved Mama's chicken and dumplings after all, but Jen did begrudge giving up a good chicken so Papa could enjoy a homecoming feast.

The hen, still out of reach, pecked away. Jennie dug her hands in the pockets of her sweater and waited. The mist had turned into a light rain and Jennie could feel it soaking through her sweater. She lifted a lock of sodden hair away from her face and looked longingly at the house. Mama had a good fire going in the kitchen stove and the pungent smell of wood smoke filled the air. She turned back to the yard. *Where is that stupid bird now? Ah, there by the fence.*

Her prey drew closer, scratching and pecking at the damp ground. If the rain came down any harder, the hen would make its way back to the chicken house. The thought of trying to snatch one chicken from a flock of twenty angry, squawking, chickens in the confines of the chicken house renewed Jennie's determination to corner it here in the yard.

11

"Come on," she coaxed under her breath. As if the chicken knew its fate, it stopped and cocked its head.

Jennie heard shuffling behind her and turned to find Clint and Hubie sitting on the back porch steps watching her. She put her hands on her hips. "If you haven't anything better to do, Clint, you can fetch the chicken."

Clint stared solemnly back at her through a shock of lank, brown hair that hung over his forehead into his eyes. He was eleven, tall and thin, with bony knees poking through the holes in his overalls. He suddenly grinned. "Mama said fer *you* to get the hen, Jennie, and I don't never go 'gainst what Mama says."

Jennie turned to Hubie. "How about you?"

Hubie's overalls were as worn as his brother's. He was small for six, but wiry and quick. A crop of thick black curls covered his head like a cap. He shook his head gleefully, flashing a gap-toothed grin where front teeth would eventually be. "Like Clint says..."

Jennie cut him off with an angry wave of her hand. "Lordy, I know how to catch a chicken, I just thought if you didn't have anything better to do..."

She turned and found the chicken practically at her feet. Without thinking she leaped at it and ended up on her hands and knees in the mud, the chicken already flapping and scolding at the far end of the yard.

Clint strode past her and in a matter of minutes had the chicken cornered and in hand. He grinned at her on his way to the chopping block. "No time fer playin', Jen. Mama needs this here hen fer our dinner."

It was a cozy kitchen, as much sitting room as kitchen since the family spent most of their time there. To the left of the door was a black, cast-iron cook stove which also heated the room.

Mama stood at the stove, patiently stirring the contents of an iron pot. She was a woman young/old at forty with a figure still trim and youthful hidden beneath a long-sleeved, ankle-length dress and flowing white apron. Her long, grey-streaked brown hair was caught up in a neat but severe bun. Her face was lined and coarsened by endless hours in the sun.

Beside the stove was a long counter with a window above it, ending in a dry sink, the water being supplied by the bucketful from the spring behind the house. Jennie presently stood there, arms outspread, hands resting on the counter, watching the slashing rain make a muddy lake of the back yard.

Opposite the kitchen door, a battered old cupboard stretched the length of the wall, ending at the closet under the stairs. The cupboard spilled out dishes, pots and pans, towels, table clothes, canning, flour and corn meal from a warren of shelves, drawers and bins. Its surface was a catchall for sewing baskets, mending, school books, pencils and writing tablets.

A huge, overstuffed sofa and chair were drawn up to the stove beside Mama's rocker where they all gathered on the long, cold evenings, huddled up as winter winds found every crack and cranny in the old house.

A scarred and pitted round oak table, with eight straight-backed chairs arranged around it, stood in the center of the room. Beneath it, spread out in a great colorful circle, was Mama's hooked rag rug. They ate their meals at the table, gathered there to do homework, play games, and write letters. It was Mama's sewing table, too, where she transformed the washed and pressed flour sacking into underwear, shirts and dresses.

Clint and Hube sat at the table playing checkers with Helen leaning over Hube's shoulder squinting at the board. Miss Glenwood had sent word home from school that Helen needed glasses, but finding the money to buy them was another problem. Helen at nine was skinny as a rail and almost as tall as Clint. Her straight brown hair, parted in the middle, fell untidily to either side of her thin face.

"You can't do that, Hubie," Helen said. "You can only move crossways."

"Can too. That's the way I play checkers."

Clint sat back in disgust. "Hube, you know you can't jump straight across."

"Mama," Helen said, enjoying her advantage. "Hubie's cheatin'."

Hubie was indignant. "I ain't cheatin'."

Jennie turned from the window. "That's the rule, Hubie, you can only jump diagonal."

Helen smirked at Hube. "See, dummy, I was right."

Hube jumped up, overturning the checker board. "I ain't playin' no more." He swung around and glared at Helen. "And it ain't cheatin' when you don't know the rules."

Clint said. "You do so know the rules."

Jennie held up her hand. "Either you play the game fair, Hubie, or go find something else to do."

Hube grumbled but allowed Clint to reset the board. Jennie turned back to the window. "Where's Min got to, Mama?"

"Where else? Over to the Owens as usual. Can't imagine how Clara Owen 'lows that young'un to be underfoot all the time. Min spends more time in Clara's kitchen than she does here." Jennie said without turning, "You ever think Sherm Owen might be the one Min is visitin'?"

Mama replaced the top on the pot with a clunk. "Don't talk nonsense. They's jest little biddies." Mama turned her attention to the boys. "Let's clear away the game now, young'uns, and set the table. Your Papa should be home any time."

Hubie groaned. "We jest got the board set up again and now we got to put it away."

Mama said impatiently. "Come on, come on, now, Hubie, do as you're told."

Jennie watched her mother scurry about the kitchen, happy at the prospect of Papa coming home. Mama brought a white cloth to the table, barely giving the boys time to clear away the game before unfurling it, smoothing it down meticulously, all the while humming to herself. She looked up at Jennie and smiled. "Fetch the plates, girl. Helen, bring the silverware."

Jennie sighed. *What a lot of fuss over a man that probably won't notice anything but the food.*

Mama stood back. "Table looks nice, don't it? Papa will be pleased." The words were no more out of her mouth than there was stamping on the porch and they all turned as the door banged opened. Papa stood in the doorway.

Chapter Three
Papa Comes Home

James made it his daily duty to patrol the ward, checking in at each cot and ending up at the nurse's station to chat with Dora. At first Dora ordered him back to bed, but it wasn't long before she noticed the pleasure his visits generated and so his infraction of the rule was ignored. The small wiry nurse could handle patients twice her size, but she chose the compassionate treatment instead.

James and Pete continued to improve. The two of them kept the ward lively with their banter.

"Ya know, Pete, it's lucky the shrapnel hit you in the head. Any place else it could have done some real damage." James called out to Dora as she hurried by. "Isn't that true, love?"

Dora said over her shoulder, "I'm not getting into one of your nonsensical arguments."

Pete said. "Yeah? And if I was outta operation, who woulda looked out for ya then? I ain't heard of an Irishman yet could stay outta trouble."

James grinned. "*Me* trouble? Who is it gets himself entangled with the fair sex at every turn o' the road and then looks to the Irishman to rescue him?"

Pete feigned an innocent expression. "I don't never call that trouble, Irish, I call that practice."

Edward was not doing as well. Nighttime was the worst and James spent hours talking to him, trying to distract him from the pain.

"Aye, boyo, Ireland is truly a land smiled on by the Gods. In County Sligo, where I come from, Benbulben Mountain can be seen, flat on top as a pancake. In summertime the sheep make it up to the far reaches, showing below like white specks of cotton. As a tad, I remember wishin' with all me might to be one of the little four-legged buggers, sittin' away up there on top o' the world. And when I went to Canada I found the mountains there no less beautiful. Their high peaks covered in snow even in the summertime."

James sighed. "I've asked meself as many times as I have fingers, laddie, how it is I lost me sanity and ended up in all this muck and mire." He stopped and waited for a response from Edward. The soldier's pale face twisted in a weak smile.

"You know, Edward m'lad, you remind me a wee bit of me brother Danny. I asked him did he want to come along to Canada with me, but the lad, younger but smarter than me by a good bit, said home was where he wanted to be. I was nineteen when I left Ireland. That was, let's see, back in 1912, five years ago."

Edward began a deep rumbling cough. James watched him fighting for control and was about to call Dora when the boy turned to him again. James knew instinctively Edward wanted him to continue talking.

"The States is me ultimate goal when all this is over. Pete and me will be going back to Vancouver, Canada—Pete has family there—and then head across the border into the States. Say, I'm told, and maybe you can tell me if it is so, that all of Ireland can fit into the state of Texas with a good bit left over."

Edward smiled weakly without answering.

James went back in memory to dredge up stories of Ireland, and when words failed, would wrack his brain to remember the words to the Irish ditties he'd sung as a lad.

Edward coughed constantly, never taking his eyes from James, listening as though James' stories were important lessons. When the coughing and pain became unbearable, Dora was quickly at his side, administering the shot that gave him peace.

Dalton Wainwright (Papa) was two when his father, Calvin Wainwright, dropped dead of a heart attack while working a team of mules on their small farm in Mountain City, Tennessee. He was thirty-nine years old. The mules stood patiently by until Lurie, Calvin's wife, wondering why he didn't come in for the noonday meal, went out to the field to find him. Lurie, weak and ill from a series of miscarriages before Dalton was born lived six months before joining her husband in death. Neither Calvin nor Lurie found a foothold in Dalton's memory.

Nonny and Pap, Calvin's parents, in their mid-sixties at the time, gladly took on the responsibility of raising their only grandchild. They took him, along with the mules, back to their home in Vilas, North Carolina and through the years, found it easier to give in to their headstrong grandson's whims, naughty or otherwise, than to take time to teach him the basic rules of life much less the 'shalt nots' of the Bible. One thing they did teach Dalton, because he found it more like a game than work, was driving the two mules.

The boy discovered early that good looks and a ready smile eased his way in life and when, at fifteen, he decided he'd had enough school, there was nothing to dissuade him. Suddenly he was faced with earning a living in a world where charm counted not a whit. The boy was overwhelmed with self-doubts, well-hidden behind a bravado that fooled everyone, worst of all Dalton himself.

At eighteen, he made a monumental discovery. Liquor gave him all the confidence and self-assurance he needed. Then, one balmy night in June, Dalton met Lula Miller at a church social.

Lula, short and plain, was all but lost in the bevy of girls charmed by this handsome, magnetic young man. He joked and teased them all, unaware of the impact he had on Lula. For her it was love at first sight and she was fiercely determined to have this young man. The problem was since Dalton lived in Vilas, four miles from Lula in Sugar Grove, there was the problem of how she could pursue him until he was convinced he couldn't live without her.

Lula solved her problem nicely. As she knew most of the parishioners of the Vilas Methodist Church, it was easy to inveigle invitations. During the course of her comings and goings to Vilas, she managed to visit Nonny and Pap several times in company with the minister. It didn't take them long to discern who was the object of Lula's interest and when they found she was the daughter of the mill owner in Sugar Grove, they were overjoyed. They subtly conveyed to Dalton the advantage of being the son-in-law of a successful mill owner. Dalton, seeing the light, professed his undying love to Lula, and persuaded her to marry him.

Lula's parents, Clarissa and Mylart Miller, were thrown into a panic. Their words of caution (which Lula would normally have heeded without question) were met with impatience and stony stares. One month later Lula and Dalton were married.

Nonny and Pap were delighted, Lula was radiant, Dalton slightly dazed, and Clarissa and Mylart despairing, but hopeful they were mistaken in their initial judgement of their new son-in-law. They accepted him with a willingness to wait and see. Meanwhile, they offered the newlyweds the little white house in Zionville, which had stood vacant since Clarissa's widowed mother had passed away the year before, and the twenty acres on which it stood.

Dalton bided his time, certain that eventually Mylart would see his potential as a miller. The first year, with a lot of help, Lula and Dalton managed to get their fields plowed and a garden planted. That year Mylart came to regard his son-in-law as shiftless, with an insatiable thirst for liquor.

Pap died that first winter at the age of eighty-three, and in the spring, Nonny followed him, leaving Dalton a small inheritance. The invitation to join Mylart in the mill never materialized, and since the thought of spending his life working the farm depressed him, Dalton came up with a plan. Half his legacy would be spent on the purchase of two mules, the other half would go into a cache of moonshine. After the mules were trained, they would be put out for hire. From their earnings, some would go to Lula to run the house and the rest into Dalton's pocket to maintain his cache.

Since Dalton still enjoyed driving the mules, he would sometimes, if the mood struck him, hire himself out along with the mules, thereby collecting a day's pay for himself as well. The mules weren't always in demand, but Dalton was convinced he was doing his share. Lula was to run the house, see to plowing and planting (with the help of the mules unless they were elsewhere employed), cook, clean, and raise the children who arrived in due course ... Edward, first born, followed by Jennie, Minnie, Clint, Helen and Hubie.

Lula bore her hardships without complaint as Dalton, in her eyes, had never lost his charming ways, despite his love for "moonshine" which increased over the years. The mules provided a tenuous income, until they died within a year of each other at the ripe old age of sixteen and seventeen. By that time, they were no longer needed. Ed at fifteen, hired out for as much money as the mules. He was bringing in enough money for the family to squeak by.

Through the years Dalton's discontent grew. His public face remained one of good humor, but in the confines of home and family, his anger at not being chosen to run the mill forced instead to become a farmer, caused him to explode with anger for little or no reason. Predicting his stormy moods became a game, for which no one knew the rules, least of all the man himself.

Dalton kicked the door closed and dropped his leather satchel to the floor. "Confound it, Lu, get me a towel or somethin'. I feel like a damn drowned coon dog." His voice was coarse and gravelly. Rainwater dripped off his nose. He wore boots and a heavy wool jacket. His dark hair was plastered against his forehead.

Papa was still a handsome man, slightly stoop-shouldered with only a slight thickening around the middle. His features were even and his thick, black curly hair had no more than a smudge of grey around the temples. It was only up close that one noted the unhealthy flush to his face and the hollow pale blue eyes ... eyes as cold as a winter sky ... under hooded dark brows. Lula, all smiles, came alive. She hurried to his side and went up on her toes to kiss his cheek.

"Fetch a towel for your Papa, Helen. Here Dalton, let me have your wet things and we'll set them by the stove. Did you have an easy trip?"

"Easy 'nuff til it started comin' down like someone let the cork out." He sat on a chair by the table and pulled off his boots. Helen brought a towel and he began vigorously drying his hair and face.

Lula pulled one of the chairs up to the stove and draped his jacket over it. "There now. You jest get comfortable and I'll get dinner on the table. How did you get home?"

Dalton moved to the sofa by the stove. "Met up with Tom and Elsie Wooding in Boone. Did you know their daughter jest had a baby?"

"Yes. They been helpin' out for a day or two til' Jessie gets on her feet."

"Well, they wuz on their way home and I wuz lucky enough to spot 'em. They give me a lift in their rig. We left Boone 'bout ten or so. Halfway on the sky let loose."

The children stood silently by, wisely waiting until their Papa was ready to acknowledge them. He finally turned and said, "Well, now, you happy to see your Papa?"

Hube, grinning, dutifully kissed him on the cheek. Helen and Clint did the same, but Jennie stood without moving. *I'm not happy to see him. Why should I pretend I am?* Their eyes met and held and Jennie felt her knees go weak. *He can read my mind.* They stared at one another for a long moment, unsmiling, Papa's cold eyes boring into hers, before Jennie turned away.

The door flew open and Minnie came breathlessly into the kitchen. "Hello, Papa," she said, shrugging out of her sodden coat and hat hanging her wet things on the hook by the door, "Mr. Owen saw you gettin' outta the Wooding's rig and said he'd see you come mornin'."

Dalton grunted. "How's ole gimp anyways?" Jennie winced at Papa's cruel reference to Jeb Owen. The man worked harder with a

19

crippled leg than Papa ever did in full health. Minnie soberly bent and kissed him on the cheek.

"Same as always, I guess."

Lula said, "Now everyone's here, we can sit down and eat." They settled around the table and bowed their heads while Mama said grace. Jennie stole a look at her. When Papa first left, three months ago, Mama had seemed as relieved as the rest of them, but when no word came from him she turned moody and quiet and worry lines appeared around her eyes and mouth. Jennie attributed the change to concern about money. Then word came from Luther Norris that Papa was working in the mines and Mama began writing to him, begging him to come home. Now that he was here, Jennie was baffled to note, the lines seemed to be smoothed away, and Mama had a look of ... contentment? She dropped her eyes to her folded hands. *Dear God, let me understand.*

Mama's voice was soft and low. "Lord, we thank thee for bringing us together in good health, for the bounty of the garden which puts food on our table, and for your teachings which puts love into our hearts. We pray for Edward, our beloved son and brother away fighting in the war. Watch over him and send him safely home to us, just as you've brought our Papa home..." At this Jennie looked up at Papa. His eyes were closed and his hands piously folded before him. She could discern no change of expression. *Does he expect to stay, I wonder? If so we'll be no better off than we were three months ago...* "This we ask in the name of Jesus Christ. Amen." Mama looked up and said solemnly to her husband, "It's good to have you home, Dalt." Then she smiled. "Now, pass me your plate so's I can fill it. I know how partial you are to my chicken and dumplings."

Dalton handed down his plate. "That I am, Lu, that I am... so, what do you hear from the boy?"

Lula filled the plate and passed it back to him. He began to eat. "We ain't heard from Ed in two months. I jest got this awful feelin'"... Gravy dripped unnoticed to the white tablecloth as she spoke.

Jennie handed up her plate. "Ed is all right, Mama. You know he never was one to write much."

"The boy ain't never been away from home before. Wasn't never any need fer him to write." Lula spooned out the food. "I been studyin' on whether he ain't writin' cause he don't want to, or can't write cause he's too busy fightin'."

Dalton said, "Boy's old 'nuff to take care of hisself."

Lula sighed. "Pray to God he is."

All the plates were finally piled high with chicken and dumplings, fried apples, green beans and carrots and Mama's special pepper relish. Everyone began to eat.

"What's it like workin' in the mine, Papa?"

Mama scolded, "Hube, don't talk with your mouth full."

Papa repeated roughly, "What's it like in the mine? Well, Hube, imagine someone locking you in, say, the root cellar, where you can't stand up straight and where there ain't no light." He brought a huge spoonful of food to his mouth and chewed with vigor. "Add to that, mucky water sloshin' to your knees, and the only air to breathe filled with chokin' coal dust. That pretty well says it all."

Helen asked. "Without a light, how do you see what you're doin'?"

Papa heaped more dumplings on his plate. "They's jest enough light from one puny lamp so's you can see where to swing your pick." He set the platter down with a thud. "And you best keep the damn lamp burnin', else you won't see your hand in front of your face."

"Papa," Hube said in awe, "I think you are the most bravest man I know."

Dalton scowled. "It don't take bein' brave, Hube. Fact is, it's a mighty stupid way of earnin' a livin'."

Jennie choked on a mouthful. *Papa?... talking about earning a living?* She felt Mama's eyes boring into her. *Civil ... Mama wants me to be civil.*

Dalton finally scraped his plate clean, pushed it away from him and belched loudly. He got up and stretched. "I'm goin' out on the porch for a smoke."

Hube said, his mouth full, "Wait, Papa, dinner ain't finished. Mama made us a punkin pie."

"Too full of dumplings fer pie, son, I'll get me some later."

Lula hurriedly got up, fetched Dalton's jacket and handed it to him. "I can use a little air myself. I'll come out and set with you." She smiled at Hube's stricken look. "No reason you can't have your pie now, Hubie."

After the table was cleared and the dishes done, Jennie settled them all around the table with their books.

Hubie grumbled. "It's Saturday. Why do we have to do homework?"

"Because tomorrow is Sunday meeting and you won't have time to do homework. You have to be ready with your lessons come Monday morning, else Miss Glenwood will rap your knuckles."

"Why ain't ... aren't ... you doin' homework?"

Jennie put on her sweater and went to the door. "Because I've done it already."

The rain had stopped and a weak sun, low in the horizon, added little warmth to the damp air. Lula and Dalton rocked comfortably, Dalton smoking contentedly. Jennie went to the edge of the porch and sat down.

Mama stopped rocking. "Is that Doc Payne's buggy coming up the road, Jennie?" Jennie got up and went down a few steps for a better look.

"I believe it is, Mama."

In a few minutes the buggy, pulled by a great dappled grey horse, stopped at the Wainwright gate and Baxter Combs, young and agile, jumped down from the far side while Dr. Payne, taking his time, descended from the other side.

Doctor Jonathan Payne, spare and stooped, was probably 60 years old, but his deeply-lined face easily added another ten years. His manner was gruff and crusty, disguising a compassionate heart which found him always ready to leave the comfort of his fireplace when the need arose.

He was dressed in grey cotton trousers sagging at the seat, a wrinkled white shirt, and a threadbare brown suit jacket. A battered felt hat allowed just a fringe of grey hair to show beneath.

His usual unkempt appearance prompted the widows and maiden ladies of Zionville to feed and fuss over him, convinced all "the good doctor" needed was a wife. Doc, tactless in most instances, managed to keep the ladies at arm's length without ruffling feathers, while at the same time maintaining his bachelor status.

Doc tethered his giant horse, Penelope, to the fence, gave her an affectionate slap on the rump, and walked up the path with Baxter.

"Hey y'all," Doc greeted them. He patted Jennie's head as he climbed the steps past her and put his hand out to Dalton. "Good to see ya home agin', Dalt."

Dalton grasped his hand. "Good to see you too, Jont." Lula moved over to the swing. "Come along, and set a spell."

"Thank ya, Lu, don't mind if I do." He sat down heavily in the rocker. "Whew ... been a long day." He pushed the battered hat to the back of his head.

Baxter sat down beside Jennie. He was a bit taller than Jennie, very thin, with refined almost delicate features, deep-set hazel eyes and a shy grin. His black hair was thick and curly.

"Hey, Jennie." He gently pulled a small bundle of white fur from the inside of his shirt and laid it in her lap.

"Oh ... a puppy."

"We jest come from Aunt Pearl's. Her bitch, Daisy, had another litter and this'un is the runt."

"Look Mama, isn't he cute?"

Lula frowned. "You needn't think we're gonna keep that dog, Baxter. You can jest take it right back to Pearl."

Doc turned to Dalton. "You been a long time gone, Dalt. How are things goin' fer ya?"

"Pretty good ... pretty good. Thought it was 'bout time I check up on the wife and young'uns."

Jennie cringed inwardly, thinking of all the letters Mama had written, begging him to come home.

Doc nodded. "And what's the latest from Ed, Lu?"

"Not a lot. We jest pray from day to day he stays safe."

Doc said, "Prayin's bout all you kin do, I 'spect. I still don't know why the boy joined up. He coulda waited 'til he wuz called in the draft like Ev Proffitt is doin'. Matter fact, Lije'll throw a fit when that young'un is called up. Ev practically runs the store."

Lula cleared her throat. "Speaking of the store, Dalt, Lije 'lowed me to run up a tab. He said you could pay it whenever you got home."

Jennie just managed to suppress a grin when Papa mumbled something about seein' to it... *Well done, Mama. Papa wouldn't think of calling you down in front of Doctor Payne.*

Lula turned innocently to the doctor. "So, Jont, Baxter says you'uns are comin' from Pearl's. Is it her rheumatism again?"

Doc drew a hand over his face, rubbing his eyes as he did so. "No, it's Ada that's ailin'."

"Lands, that child sick again?"

"Yep. Poor little puny Ada. It's her breathin'. Well you know how she gets. Poor child has trouble fillin' her lungs. I left Pearl some dried pennyroyal to brew into a tea. 'Bout all's can be done for the poor young'un."

Jennie asked. "None of the others sick?"

"Nope, and the weather what it is, they's all inside cuttin' up fierce. It's pure bedlam over there."

Lula shook her head. "Five young'uns under the age of ten can make enough noise to raise the dead. Had six of my own but mine wuzn't close in age like the Norris children."

Dalton snorted. "Pearl takin' on them kids when Mary died was pure foolishness. A woman her age ... how old is she anyways, Seventy? Woman should be rockin' by the fire 'steada wipin' noses and changin' diapers."

Doc stretched his legs out and grunted. "Well, truth be, and you know it, Dalt, Pearl wouldn't have it no other way. She loves them young'uns like they wuz her own. If I felt Pearl was the worst for it, I'd step in, but everybody, kids included, seem better off for her being there. 'Sides, Pearl ain't got no kin in this whole world. It gives the woman a purpose."

Dalton snorted again. "Only thing I say is Luther should be sharin' the load. No denyin' the man works hard. I see 'em at the mines, but his place is home with his young'uns."

Jennie was aghast. How could he accuse Luther Norris of the very thing he was guilty of himself? She glared at Papa, silently willing him to look at her. He didn't and she dropped her eyes to her clenched hands. *Oh God! I wish I could find the courage to speak up to Papa.*

Doc was saying, "You remember, Dalt, how broke up Luther was after Mary died. He wouldn't a been much good to them kids if he stayed home."

Mama said, "But Dalton is right. When children are young as the Norris children, they need at least one parent to keep 'em straight."

"Could be you're right, but don't sell Pearl short. The woman handles them good enough... Not to change the subject, Lu, but what do you hear from Mylart? He still workin' hisself to death in the mill?"

"I don't think my Papa will ever stop working. The mill's what kept him goin' after Mama died, and you know yerself, Jont, people hereabouts would be lost without the mill."

"I ain't seen Mylart in a dog's age."

"I sent word to him Dalton was comin' home. He might be along for a visit."

Jennie noted the sour look on Papa's face when Mama spoke of Mylart Miller. Everyone, including Jont Payne, knew that there was no love lost between the two men.

Doc turned to Baxter. "Son, you want to tell these folks the good news?"

Baxter grinned shyly. "You tell 'em, Doc."

"Baxter here's gonna be the next doctor of Zionville."

Lula stopped the swing. "What do you mean, the next doctor?"

"Jest what I said. Over the years I put a little money by and since I got no one to spend it on, I decided to invest in Baxter. I talked it over with Ben and Frenda and suggested sendin' their son off to the academy in Boone come next September. Providin' he gets good grades, in two years we'll send him on to North Carolina Medical College in Charlotte."

Jennie's mouth dropped. She turned to face the lanky young man sprawled on the steps beside her.

"You ... you're going to medical school?" Baxter flushed and looked down at his hands. He avoided Jennie's intense gaze.

"Yup, I guess I'm gonna be a honest-t'-God doctor." Envy settled like a lump in Jennie's stomach. There was anger too, because Doc hadn't even considered her. She willed Baxter to look at her and when he did, she knew by his expression he was sharing her thoughts. Guilt for his good fortune was plain on his face. This angered her even more. Baxter had such soft and gentle ways, but this was no time for him to be sorry for her. It was a time to rejoice in a dream come true.

Baxter had shown an interest in being a doctor early on by doing odd jobs around Doc's office. Soon he was begging to go along on house calls and Doc found the extra pair of hands a help.

Baxter smiled shyly and Jennie surrendered to a flood of affection for him. Their friendship went back to the day they started school together. Neither remembered how the idea of their becoming doctors developed, but little by little the notion grew, helped along by Doc himself. Doc had encouraged Jennie to help with his patients. In time her experience and knowledge grew to the point where she was paid for her services, as much as twenty-five cents a day.

Jennie sighed and reached for Baxter's hand. She controlled her confused emotions and said sincerely, "Baxter, that's wonderful news."

Doc cleared his throat. "And that brings me to somethin' I been wantin' to talk to you and Dalt about, Lu. Now's a good time." He looked down at Jennie. "When I considered sendin' Baxter to medical school, I thought some about Jennie, too."

Jennie was appeased. *He did give me some thought after all.* She looked at the doctor expectantly.

Doc continued, "Jennie here would make one hell of a doctor, too."

Dalton laughed. "Jennie? A doctor? That's 'bout the craziest notion I ever heard."

Doc said, "No ... no it ain't, Dalt, and I should know. Them two young'uns been traipsin' after me for 'most eight years, askin' questions without hardly stoppin' to breathe. Been a help to me, too. Jennie, 'specially, has a way with the sick. So when I was thinkin' 'bout another doctor for Zionville, I thought of Baxter ... and Jennie."

Dalton said with disgust, "That's damn nonsense. Who ever heard of a woman bein' a doctor?"

Doc nodded. "And that's the reason I chose Baxter. No one would accept a woman as a doctor, in these parts anyways. But a nurse ... now that's something else. Jennie would make a wonderful nurse." Jennie's eyes flew from Doctor Payne to Papa.

Dalton said, his voice thick with sarcasm, "And are you gonna pay for Jennie's schoolin' too? Cause I sure as hell ain't."

Doc looked at Jennie and smiled sadly. "I can't afford to send 'em both to school, but I got to thinkin'. Sometimes people will leave money to a college or hospital sayin' the money be used to educate a child 'thout the means to make it on his own. It's called an endowment. I might jest look into that for Jennie."

Jennie felt a surge of excitement.

Lula said in a voice as unbelieving as Dalton's, "What do either Baxter or Jennie have to go to school for anyway? You never did, Doc, and look how people put their trust in you."

"I ain't denyin' that's true, Lu. I picked up my medical know-how from old Doc Shyler. Remember him, Lu?"

"Don't know that I do."

Doc continued, "He took me under his wing. Nobody I ever knew had as much sense of local remedies as Doc Shyler, or as much common sense. He taught me to think like a doctor. Had a dusty old set of medical books and he took me through them, explainin' as he went along like any teacher would. Then, a' course, he sent for the medical journals once they started being published. That's all that wuz needed back then. But times is changin'. They's new discoveries, new procedures. We're in the twentieth century now and backwoods medicine ain't enough anymore."

Dalton said. "Mebbe doctorin' is one thing, but Jennie don't need no more schoolin' to be a nurse. She does jest fine doing the jobs you get fer her."

Doc was quiet for a moment, staring out into the deepening dusk. "You might want to study on it 'fore y'say no, Dalt."

"Don't need to study on it. Jennie ain't goin' no place. She's needed right here at home." He looked at Baxter. "What does your Pa say 'bout all this?"

Baxter looked a little defensive. "Oh, Pa wants me to stay on the farm. Since I'm the last one t'home, Pa thought I would take over one day. He don't set much store by doctorin', if you'll pardon me fer sayin' so, Doctor Payne, but Ma, now she thinks it's a whopper of a idea."

Jennie squeezed Baxter's hand and grinned. "Baxter Combs, Doctor of Medicine."

The door banged open and Hubie stomped out on the porch. "Finished my homework..." He stopped short at the sight of the puppy sleeping peacefully in Jennie's lap. With eyes big and unbelieving, he flopped down beside her and reached for the puppy. "We got us a dog?"

Dalton scowled at the boy. "That cur ain't stayin' here." Hubie barely heard his father. He was nose to nose with the puppy, stroking him gently. "I ain't never seen such a beautiful dog. He's all white with a little pink belly. Look Mama, he's lickin' my face."

Dalton got up and stretched. "What say we go down to the store, Doc, and see who all is there?"

"Good idea." Doc got up stiffly from the rocker. "I'll say goodnight to you Lu, Jennie. Come along, Bax, I'll take you on home first."

Baxter looked at Lula. "I'll stay and visit with Jennie for a while if you don't mind."

Lula didn't answer. She watched soberly as the two men started down the steps. "Dalt..."

Dalton turned and stared coldly back at her. "What?"

Lula, flustered, looked down at her hands. "Nothing. Just ... don't be too late."

He continued down the steps. "Wouldn't think of it, Lu, my first night home."

As the buggy disappeared up the road, Jennie studied Mama's face, sure they had the same thoughts. Papa would join the others around the potbellied stove at Lije's store and before long someone would bring out the jug and then...

The sun was gone and night settled quickly over the valley, bringing with it a biting November wind. Mama, complaining she was chilled to the bone, got up from the swing and stretched her back.

"Come along, Hube." Hube, cradling the sleeping pup in his arms, turned and looked pleadingly at Lula. "Mama, *please* can we keep him ... *please*?"

Lula looked distractedly down at Hube. "Gracious, I forgot all about the dog." She looked at Baxter and said, not unkindly, "We got you to thank for this dilemma, young man. Hube, you heard what your Papa said."

Hube continued to plead with his eyes. Mama reached down and scratched the pup behind the ear. "We'll make up a bed for him on the back porch for tonight, but tomorrow he goes back to Pearl's." Hube opened his mouth.

"That's final," Mama said. She turned as she got to the door. "Don't you young'uns stay out too long in this chill lest you catch your deaths." The door banged shut behind her.

After a moment of silence, Baxter said. "You mad at me, Jen? Honest, I had no mind what Doc was planning. Three days ago, he jest up and told me. First thing I thought was you would be a better doctor than me."

Jennie sighed. "You know that's not true, Bax. You'll make a wonderful doctor. I guess I always knew it wasn't possible for me." After a pause she added, "Especially in the mountains. Here a woman raises a family, cooks and cleans and works in her garden. She might be accepted as a teacher or a nurse, but a doctor? Never."

"And Doc says there may be a chance of, what did he call it, a endowment?"

"But that's all it is, a chance. Nothing for sure. Even so, Papa wouldn't let me go."

"He'll change his mind, Jen. If he don't have to pay nuthin' how can he say no?"

"It's Papa's nature to say no to everything."

They sat quietly for a few moments, each into his own thoughts. Finally Jen broke the silence. "Tell me some of the things you and Doc have been doing?"

Baxter said with enthusiasm. "Well, Hode Sykes ... you know him, Jen, lives down to Sugar Grove?"

Jennie shook her head. "Don't think so."

"Well, anyways, his young'un, name's Grady, come poundin' up on horseback to Doc's front door day 'fore yesterday. Said his Pa's belly hurt fierce and would Doc come right away. Doc grabs his bag, stops by my place and I jump in with the buggy barely slowin' down and off we go, following Grady. On the way Doc starts talkin' 'bout maybe it being appendicitis." Jennie sat forward in excitement, her attention complete.

"Doc explained the whole operation to me right down to the last stitch as we skittled along. So ... we finally get to Sugar Grove and sure 'nuff, Sykes wuz doubled over, groanin' and moanin' and sweatin'."

Jennie, eyes big, said, "Was it appendicitis?"

Baxter kept a straight face as long as he could, then grinned and said, "Naw, it were jest a bellyache."

Jennie leaned over and rapped his shoulder hard. "Oh you, I thought I was going to hear about some fancy doctoring."

He laughed. "I wuz disappointed too, but I guess old man Sykes wasn't. Doc jest told Mrs. Sykes to boil up some wild raspberry, red oak bark, and geranium leaves into a syrup and give it to him. We never heard no more so guess he's all right by now."

"Your Pa really against your being a doctor, Baxter?"

"He never was all the times I talked about it, but now I have a chance to be a real doctor and all of a sudden he objects."

"It's cause he never thought it would happen. Will it stop you?"

"That's what Doc asked me. I hate to leave Pa when he feels like he does, but...

"He's just like Papa. They feel we're running out on our responsibilities by getting an education, when in fact ... oh bother, Bax, I'm getting cold." Jennie stood up and stretched. "Best we say goodnight."

Baxter stood up beside her and reached for her hand. "You got to promise when I become a doctor, you'll be my nurse."

"And I'll stand by your side and mop your brow when you finally operate on poor old Hode Sykes."

Baxter laughed. "We'll get them ole appendix one way or 'nother. See ya in church tomorrow. He went down the steps, turned and waved. The gate creaked and clanged shut. Jennie stood unmoving, enjoying the solitude of the cold, quiet night. Her dreams seemed somehow within reach, and on the other hand, never further away. She turned to go in. Tonight was bath night.

✉

"Clint," Mama called, "Let's get the tub out. Time for baths."

Hubie groaned. "How come I hafta take a bath? I ain't even dirty."

Mama ruffled his hair. "You're dirty as sin, young'un. You ain't had a bath since last Saturday."

Earlier in the day, the boys had filled several buckets from the spring and lined them up by the stove to take the chill off the water. When the last bucketful was emptied into the tin tub, Mama added hot water from the gently whistling kettle on the back of the stove.

Jennie, in the meantime, drew several kitchen chairs up to the tub and draped them with towels for privacy. "You go first, Min. I was first last week."

Mama said, "Don't use too much soap, Min, that Ivory soap costs five cents a bar."

Chapter Four
Hubie's Escape

"There was a time, Pete, Dora and me thought you weren't gonna wake up. We were about to throw you an Irish wake." James turned to Dora and winked. "Isn't that true, love?"

Dora plumped up Edward's pillow. "If you say so, James. Of course, none of us have ever been to an Irish wake. Maybe you'll tell us about it."

Pete raised himself on his elbow. "I can't wait."

"Och, yes, well, an Irish wake is a celebration, and may God in his wrath strike me dead if this isn't true Edward m'lad... when a body gives up the ghost, we stand the corpse in the corner and put a glass of ale in his hand. Then the pipers start to play and everyone does the Irish jig."

Dora smiled uncertainly. "You don't really mean..."

James grinned. "Aye, and sometimes we get the corpse to join in."

Peter fell back on his pillow. "And since there is so much alcohol in the corpse you can pop him right in the ground."

"How did you know, laddie? Saves the poor widow woman the cost of preserving him."

It was Sunday meeting day. The bed felt warm and cozy and Jennie snuggled even further into the bedclothes. Minnie made a snuffling noise and Jennie turned, thinking she was awake, but Min turned on her side and the snuffling stopped. Jen rolled over on her back and stared up at the ceiling.

She'd meant to stay awake last night and listen for Papa to come home, but sleep came on her soon as she'd crawled into bed. She was sure the pattern hadn't changed. There wasn't a man in the valley didn't like Papa, so when he showed up, the jug showed up as well in celebration. Lije Proffitt always had moonshine at the store. Papa was very genial when he drank in public, but he behaved much differently once he closed the door of his own house.

Jennie threw the covers off and her nagging thoughts as well. Going to the window she rested her hands on the sill, shivering in the morning chill. Off to the west the sky was leaden grey and she wondered idly what the almanac had to say; probably snow.

She thought of how much Ed loved the snow. Winters past he would get out the toboggan their Grandfather had made for them, stored now in the rafters of the cow shed, and carefully clean and wax the bottom so it would be fast and smooth over the snow. They would all pile on and careen down the hillsides laughing and screaming, sometimes turning over, sometimes crashing. Mama never forgave them for crashing into her favorite apple tree, leaving the tree badly damaged. Jennie felt the small scar from that disaster. Doc had had to take three stitches in her chin. *Is there snow on the battlefields of Europe, I wonder? And how do you keep warm with only a tent to sleep in?*

Sighing, she turned back to her bedroom. It was a small room (probably not much larger than Ed's tent) with one window, and room only for the bed she shared with Minnie, a marble-topped bureau and a small bed for Helen in the corner. After Ed left for the army, Helen begged Mama to allow her to sleep in Ed's room. Mama thought Jen should have it, being the oldest, but Ed was Helen's hero. If it gave her comfort to sleep in his room, then so be it.

Jennie went quietly to the bureau, pulled open her drawer, and rummaged around until she found a clean pair of cotton stockings, a pair of muslin drawers, and a short-sleeved vest. Pulling her flannel nightgown over her head, she dressed quickly.

She chose a simple cotton print from the dresses hanging behind the door, slipped it over her head and wriggled it down. Easy enough to change into her Sunday meeting dress after the chores were done. After a few fast strokes with a hairbrush, she slipped from the bedroom, in her stocking feet, into the narrow hallway. There was no sound from Mama and Papa's bedroom down the hall, nor from Ed's, where Helen slept. The boys' room, across the hall, was empty, Clint no doubt doing the milking. Heaven only knew where Hube was. She crept down the narrow staircase.

At the bottom, opposite the stairs, was the door to the front porch and to the left, the door to the parlor used only on special occasions. She turned right into the kitchen and walked quickly to the stove at the far end. It had been banked for the night and now she adjusted the damper and added wood from the bin beside the stove. In minutes the fire began to crackle. She put on her apron and her warm wool coat and stepped out onto the back porch. Slipping into her yard shoes by the back door, she hurried across the yard to the privy, thankful not to have to wait in line. When she came out, Hube was sitting on the back steps, the pup on his lap.

"Hubie, you know what will happen if Papa sees that dog." Hubie soberly stroked the puppy.

Jennie had a thought. "I know. Why don't you take him over to Clara Owen and ask her to take care of him for a while. Maybe we can talk Papa into letting you keep him."

Hubie brightened. "Think so, Jen? You think Papa will change his mind?"

Jennie was sure he wouldn't, but she didn't want to deal with the problem right now. "He just might."

Hubie got up and started down the steps, holding the dog tenderly to him. "You'll like it over to the Owens, Soldier. They got kittens and baby chicks you can play with." He put the pup on the ground.

"You named him?"

"Yep. Named him after Ed."

"That's right nice, Hube." She watched him walk around the side of the house, his shoulders hunched, the pup frisking along at his heels. *What would it hurt to let a little boy have a dog?*

She called after him. "Meet me at the spring, Hube, and you can help me fetch the water." He waved without turning. Jennie picked up the bucket from the side porch and headed for the spring behind the pasture. As she neared the cow shed, she could hear Clint talking to Lizzie, his words punctuated by the sound of the milk hitting the pail.

Jennie poked her head in the door. The two cows stood side by side, Clint milking Lizzie, big with calf, and Libby patiently standing by waiting her turn.

"Mornin', Clint."

"Mornin', Jen," he answered without turning or changing his tone of voice.

"Lizzie behavin' herself?"

"She's extra techous this mornin', poor girl, so I'm milkin' her first."

As if to prove the point, Lizzie swung her muddy tail and caught Clint across the mouth. He sputtered and spit. "Lordy, Lizzie, if you ain't the ornriest cow I ever knowed." Lizzie reared her head, stamped a hoof, and gave a long low bellow.

Clint grinned at Jennie as he drew a sleeve across his mouth. "That's her way a' sayin' she's sorry."

Jennie shook her head, smiling. "I think you were right first off, Clint, she's just ornery." Jennie turned from the shed, ran past the chicken house and along the fence line enclosing the pasture. She came to the creek at the back of their property and, slowing only slightly, sprinted across the footlog bridge and landed on a flat rock, as big as a table top, on the other side of the creek.

Beyond the rock was their spring house built over the spring that bubbled from the side of the mountain.

Jennie flopped down on the rock, breathing heavily, her breath coming out like smoke, and waited for Hube. She leaned back on her hands and looked up at the sky. There was not a trace of blue. Off in the distance Grandfather Mountain was lost in the grey hanging clouds and she wondered if the old man was concerned that he might soon be blanketed in snow.

The Owen property backed up to the creek, as theirs did. After a few minutes Hube came along the creek, jumping from rock to rock, his face sober as he paused long enough after each jump to choose just the right rock for his next move. She marveled at how agile and sure-footed he was. He finally landed beside her.

"Mrs. Owen say she'll watch Soldier?"

"Yeah, but Puss ain't too friendly."

"Puss is a new mama, she's only worried about her kittens. Soon as Soldier figures that out they'll get along ... and we don't say ain't, we say isn't."

Jennie got to her feet. "Come on, let's wash up so we'll be ready for breakfast. Don't get your coat sleeves wet."

She walked to the trough that protruded from the spring house, putting her hands under the icy water that gushed out and emptied into the creek.

"It's too cold, Jennie. 'Sides, I don't need washin'. Last night was bath night, 'member?"

"You've been playing with the dog, Hubie, you have to wash your hands and face. You have to brush your teeth, too." Hubie sighed, cupped his hands under the water and groaned loudly, making sputtering noises as he splashed water on his face. Jennie fumbled in her coat pocket, brought out two birch twigs and handed one to Hubie. Together they bent over the water and vigorously brushed their teeth. When they finished, Jennie held out her apron for Hube to dry his face and hands, then dried her own.

"That damn water is cold."

"Hubie."

Hube grinned. "Sorry, Jen, that slipped out."

She frowned at him. "The commandment says thou shalt not curse."

"They ain't ... isn't ... no such commandment."

"It's one of mine. Now, you fill the bucket, I'll get the eggs."

She pulled open the heavy wooden door of the spring house, letting it bang shut behind her. One small window let in just enough light to see by. A trough channeled the spring water through the small house to the creek outside.

Jennie lifted a crock of butter and a basket of eggs from the cold running water and fitted them carefully into the large pockets of her apron. The milk jug she carried in her arms.

Outside, Hube had already filled the bucket with spring water and was struggling to carry it across the bridge.

"Let me help, Hube."

"I got it, Jennie. I'm pretty strong you know."

"Yes. I can see that."

Together they walked slowly back along the path, Hubie grunting under the weight of the bucket.

Mama was at the stove and the aroma of country ham browning in the iron skillet filled the kitchen. Hubie set the bucket beside the sink. "I think snow's comin'."

"That should make you happy."

Jennie emptied her apron pockets on the table. "I think we best set the winter box out on the porch. Any day now, the spring house is apt to be snowed in."

Mama nodded without turning. "I'll get Clint to do that this afternoon."

Jennie took off her coat and went to the stove to warm her hands. "Where's Papa?"

Mama didn't answer right away. Finally she said, "He's still sleeping."

"Then he did come home last night."

No answer.

"Is he going to Sunday meeting?"

Mama said without turning, "I have no idea and you ask too many questions. Get the young'uns to the table so's we can get breakfast over with and get ready for church."

Sunday was always a long, busy day. Sunday school, morning church meeting, home to get dinner on the table, a few hours' rest and then back to church for evening service. Mama taught Sunday school and unless they were at death's door, no one missed church, morning or evening.

When they returned from morning service, Papa was sitting in the rocker by the stove, staring morosely into space. The girls, careful not to meet his gaze, hurriedly put aprons on over their Sunday dresses and started dinner.

Mama said, "It's a shame you didn't go to church, Dalt. Everyone wuz asking fer you." Jennie stole a look at Papa to see his reaction.

Dalton snorted. "Buncha damned busybodies."

Lula laughed nervously. "No they ain't. They wuz jest sending their regards is all. Think you could go to evening service with us? I told everyone mebbe you would."

Oh, Mama...

Dalton stopped rocking. "You got no business makin' plans fer me, woman."

Lula flushed. "It's been a long time since you been to church, I jest thought..."

Dalton pushed himself out of the rocker and grabbed his jacket from the hook. He shrugged into it as he went out the door. "Don't wait dinner fer me."

✉

Despite what Papa said, Mama waited dinner for him. When it was obvious he wasn't coming home, they sat down to a quiet meal. Jennie ached to say 'I told you so', but Mama was so obviously distressed, she didn't have the heart.

After the meal was over, Mama settled in her rocker to read her Bible while Jen and Min cleared away the dinner dishes.

Earlier, the boys had wrestled the heavy, hinged wooden box from storage under the stairs and placed it on the back porch. In cold weather, it substituted for the spring house, and Clint, pulling a cart (with Helen grumbling behind him), had gone out to the spring house to bring back whatever supplies were stored there. Mama asked, "Where's Hube?"

Jennie said. "He's playin' with Soldier."

"Who?"

"He named the pup Soldier."

Mama frowned. "I forgot about the dog. If your Papa comes home and finds that pup still here, no tellin'"...

Jennie interrupted. "Mrs. Owen already said she'd watch the dog for awhile in case Papa changed his mind, but Hube is so crazy about the pup, he can't leave him be. I'll tell him to take the dog back to the Owen place."

Mama stopped listening. She seemed to be engrossed in her Bible, but Jennie was sure she didn't even see the pages. *Is she worried about Papa? Sad? Why isn't she angry? Gone three months and first chance he gets...*

In the months Papa had been gone, they had all gotten out of the habit of watching for him, which was unfortunate, because at that moment, he surprised them by stumbling in the front door.

Mama closed her Bible, quietly got up from the rocker and went to Dalton. "Let me help you with your coat."

He pushed her aside. "Don't need no damn help. Get outta coat when ...damn ... ready." Jennie could smell the liquor from across the room. He staggered over to Mama's rocker and fell into it. Min dropped her head, concentrating very hard on the dishes but Jennie's disgust was so great she couldn't help but glare at him. He caught her look and she stared back for a moment before dropping her eyes, annoyed that it was so easy to fall back into the old pattern of cowering in his presence.

Before long, his head fell back and he began to snore. Mama looked at their worried faces and whispered. "He'll be all right once he's had a nap."

But Papa didn't have his nap. Hubie burst into the kitchen with the puppy in his arms. "Mama, you won't believe what this little critter..." He stopped short at the sight of Papa.

Lula tried to shush him, but it was too late. Papa was awake. He took one look at the puppy in Hubie's arms and lurched to his feet, sending the rocker flying. Before any of them could move, he had Hubie by the scruff of the neck and began shaking him so hard the frightened puppy fell from his arms. With his heavy boot Papa kicked the puppy across the room. It yelped and scurried into a corner where it cowered, whimpering softly. Hubie struggled, but Papa held him fast.

"Didn't I say get rid a' that cur? Didn't I? Didn't I?" Hubie stopped struggling and cringed, realizing at last that he couldn't get away. Mama and Minnie disappeared, but Jennie was rooted to the spot, compelled to stay, a hot burning anger in her chest.

Papa whipped off his belt, holding Hube down with one hand. The frightened child, sobbing quietly, threw his arms over his head, waiting for the blows to fall. In that instant Jennie screamed, "Stop!"

Papa, looked up, surprised. He released Hubie. For a moment the boy was frozen in place, but when he realized Papa no longer had a grip on him, he half crawled, half ran for the door, scooping the frightened puppy up in his arms on the way. Jennie faced Papa, his eyes wild and unfocused, the belt raised above his head. She moved quickly so the table was between them, scarcely able to breathe, her heart pounded so.

Suddenly Papa brought the belt down with a crash, striking the table. She watched in horror as his arm went up again and again, each time bringing the belt crashing down, cursing wildly with each blow as if he still had his defenseless son under the strap.

Jennie backed away. The door was ajar and she kicked it open, raced around the porch, down the steps into the yard, out the gate and down the road, heedless of the cold. She stopped, out of breath, and put her hands to her face.

There was no sound on the quiet roadside but her ragged sobbing. Finally she stopped and took a deep, shuddering breath.

It was the first time any of them had stood up to Papa, if only to shout one word. Anyone who would take a strap to an innocent child was a coward, and all you had to do with a coward was to face him down. How had she missed that fact all these years?

She became aware of the cold, wrapped her arms around herself and slowly headed back to the house, wondering if Papa would still be there, suddenly hoping that he would. She began to run, not as much from the cold as from the exhilaration that coursed through her. She wanted to face Papa, unaware the adrenaline firing her blood masked the danger of a slight sixteen year old girl facing down a raging, drunken man.

She reached the gate, threw it open, making it bounce off the fence, ran up the porch steps and in the front door. Her heart pounding, she ran to the kitchen, but Papa was gone. She stood motionless in the doorway, then walked slowly to the table and ran her hand over the new scars on its surface.

The next morning, without a word, Papa left, striding angrily down the road, his satchel swinging wildly in his hand. He had said nothing to anyone, including Mama, and now she stood on the porch, watching him disappear from view. Jennie couldn't tell from her expression what her thoughts were, but the rest of them breathed a sigh of relief.

In the days that followed, Jennie tried to talk to Mama, to tell her what happened the afternoon Papa held the strap over Hube, but Mama repeatedly changed the subject. It was finally clear Mama didn't want to hear it. Papaw once said dreams die hard. It was clear that Mama was holding on to her dreams with all her might, even after all the long sad years. Mama's dreams would die *very* hard.

Chapter Five
Bad News

A flap at the far end of the tent was pulled aside and sunlight streamed in, offsetting the accompanying chill. James, turning his head, saw that Edward was tightly curled up and for the moment, sleeping. On his opposite side, Pete snored away blissfully until a poke from James made him roll over.

Doctor Foxborough ducked through the tent flap. Tall, gaunt and bespectacled, he was dressed in a field jacket over army regulation trousers and heavy field boots. The only hint to his profession was the stethoscope around his neck. His drooping shoulders and the sparse hair gave a first impression of old age, although he was no more than forty. His accent was clipped and precise.

With Dora following closely, he made his way down the aisle, stopping at each cot and giving instructions. At Edward's cot he asked. "Is he sedated?"

Dora answered. "Yes. He can't go much more than four hours without a shot."

The doctor took off his spectacles, rubbed his eyes, then returned the glasses to the bridge of his nose. He leaned over the quiet figure, mumbling as he listened intently, "Bloody hell..." Finally he straightened, staring for a minute at Edward, then went to the foot of the cot to update his chart.

James whispered. "The lad isn't doing so good, is he?"

"No. Not good. Looks like an infection has set in."

"Aye, and what...?"

"There is only so much we can do for him here. We're only a field hospital after all. We'll probably send him to a proper hospital where they have better facilities for treatment. So, James, let's take a look at that shoulder."

James said as Dora gently undid his bandages, "You're a Britisher, but I'm trying to guess from where."

Foxborough smiled. Dora stood aside and the doctor stepped in. "Hmmmmm. Looks good." He probed gently and James winced.

James said, "I'd say you're from the coast, Devon maybe."

The doctor straightened. "Can you lift your arm?"

James managed to raise his arm several inches.

The doctor nodded, pleased. "You're lucky. The shrapnel went deep, almost severed the muscle, but it is healing nicely. I think the stitches can come out." He pushed his spectacles up, "And you're right I'm from Devon ... and _you're_ from the north of Ireland."

James grinned. "Sligo. We're both right."

The doctor turned to Pete and gently nudged him awake. "So Peter, let's take a look at that head wound."

Peter grunted, carefully rolled over and allowed Dora to unwind the cap of bandages. The doctor gently probed, "Headaches?"

Pete answered, "Only Irish."

Foxborough laughed, "All right, Dora, looks good enough for the stitches to come out here also. Now, Peter, over on your stomach. I want to look at your other wound."

James asked, "How does his back look?"

The doctor, concentrating, said offhandedly, "It's a bit further down than his back."

James said, "His ... Oh Christ, you mean he got it in the ass?"

Peter raised his head indignantly. "Irish, I swear, if you give me a hard time about this, so help me God, I'll...I'll..."

James held up his hand, his face a perfect mask. "No, no, laddie, fortune has smiled on you. You may be up for a medal. I think it's called the "Purple Arse.""

✉

"Jennie?" Hube poked his head inside her bedroom. "You think mebbe they ain't no school today?"

"There will definitely be school today, Hube. There's no more'n an inch of snow on the ground."

Hube's head disappeared and Jennie heard a muffled "damn".

"Hubie!"

"Sorry, Jen."

Jennie shook her head and turned to Min, stretching lazily in the bed beside her. "Come on, Min, that means you too." Jennie dressed quickly and hurried downstairs into the warmth of the kitchen. Mama sat in her rocker, Bible open in her lap.

Jennie said, "Mornin' Mama," as she shrugged into her coat and hurried out the door to the privy. She could hear the cows in the cow shed, Lizzie making contented snuffling noises as Clint milked her. As she came out of the privy, Hube and Helen were in a pushing match to see who would be next in.

"I was here first, Hubie. You let go'a me."

"Was not. I was here first."

Jennie separated them and gave Helen a shove. "You go first and hurry up. Hube, you'll just have to wait your turn."

Jennie quickly ran up the porch steps and into the kitchen to escape the bickering and was surprised to find Mama still in the rocker. She was soberly reading, apparently unconcerned about breakfast.

"Mama? You feel all right?"

"No. I'm poorly this mornin', Jen."

Jennie sat down on the sofa facing Mama, worried. Mama rarely felt poorly. At that moment Helen and Hube noisily invaded the kitchen. "Mama, Hubie didn't wait for the privy. He peed in the yard."

Hubie, all innocence, said, "You wouldn't a wanted me to pee my pants, Mama, would ya?"

Lula scolded. "I can't abide your nonsense this morning. Jest the two of you go gather your lessons fer school." Hubie sent a mischievous grin Jennie's way and clattered up the stairs after Helen.

"You want me to stay home with you today?"

Mama sighed deeply and got up from the rocker. "No need fer that, chile, jest see the young'uns get off to school. I'm gonna lie down, see I can shake off this sick headache."

Jennie watched Mama plod heavily up the stairs and decided to ask Doctor Payne what he could do for Mama. It was obvious she was more depressed than unwell.

Jennie busied herself making a pot of grits and filling the lunch pails. Clint came in and set the pail of warm milk on the sink. "Where's Mama?"

"Back in bed. She's feelin' poorly."

"It's 'cause Papa left." Jennie looked up quickly, surprised at Clint's understanding. She bent over the lunch pails as she spoke, afraid to show too much anger. No sense letting her feelings color the way Clint felt. Better he form his own opinions. "Seems Papa would rather be anywhere but his own home, Clint, and Mama's finding it hard to accept that."

Clint took off his coat and hung it up, his back to Jennie. He mumbled softly. "It's 'cause Papa is selfish ... and a coward too. We all know that." He turned and walked from the kitchen without looking at her. Jennie shook her head sadly. *Hard facts to learn about your father,* she thought.

Using the end of her apron as a pot holder, she began to fill the bowls set out on the table with grits, calling, "Time for breakfast, Clint. Call the others."

✉

Jennie and her brothers and sisters said good-bye to Miss Glenwood and set out on the two mile walk home from school. At the same time, Prosper Truall's wagon rattled along Valley Road from the opposite direction, his horse Fanny encouraged with an occasional flick of the reins on her rump, to a faster pace than usual. The wagon was headed for the Wainwright farm.

Prosper was the Methodist minister of the Zionville church, as well as the postal carrier. Three days a week he traveled to Boone to pick up the mail. This day his large moon face was grim under the warm wool cap. He had an unwelcome task to perform. It was his duty to deliver the telegram, and what could it be but a message of doom?

Edward was away in the war and this was an official government communication. He would need all the skills of his ministry to soften the brutal words. The big man flicked the reins again, his great girth straining at the seams of the black oilskins he wore. He sniffed the air. Snow was on the way.

The wagon held two passengers; Doctor Payne and Mylart Miller. In anticipation of the telegram's grim news, Prosper had made a special trip on the way through Sugar Grove to pick up Lula's father. They had decided it would also be a good idea for Doctor Payne to join them.

Papaw Miller sat straight as a post, barely swaying with the movement of the wagon. He was clean-shaven with an abundance of neatly combed, snow-white hair, and he was bareheaded. A large nose and grim mouth were set in a weather-tanned face and above, piercing blue eyes looked out from under scraggy white brows. He wore a worn grey wool jacket, buttoned up to the neck, over brown cotton trousers. His eyes were focused on Fanny, as if by sheer will he could make the horse go faster. The three men were sober and silent as Fanny, winded by the unusual pace, pulled up to the Wainwright gate. Mylart led them up the path and opened the door.

Lula turned from the stove and smiled when she saw it was Papaw, but her smile faded as the doctor and Prosper, dutifully wiping their feet on the rug at the doorstep, followed him into her kitchen. Papaw gently led Lula to her rocker before Prosper handed her the telegram.

43

It was as they all suspected. *It is the sad duty of the Government of the United States to inform Dalton and Lula Wainwright that their son, Edward Wainwright, has been wounded in action.*

While the news was devastating, it was a joy and comfort to have Papaw in their midst. Through the years, knowing the limitations of his son-in-law, Papaw, and Mamaw too when she was alive, had endowed each of their grandchildren with the security of feeling special and loved. Mama, needing the love and support as much as any of her children, leaned on Papaw as well. Though never discussed, it was obvious Dalton deeply resented the loving hold the old couple had over his wife and children.

That Dalton lacked ambition and drank too much was a known fact. What Papaw didn't know, but suspected, was the increasing violence in his son-in-law's behavior. Lula, who wouldn't acknowledge any shortcomings in her husband, had somehow instilled a code of silence on the subject in her children.

In the years since Mamaw died, Papaw hinted to his daughter that it might be best for her and the children to move into the home place in Sugar Grove with him. Lula wouldn't hear of it. Nor would Papaw consider moving to Zionville. The old man insisted he couldn't leave the mill, although the real reason was that he would never tolerate Dalton's behavior.

Clint, Hube and Helen were settled around the oak table, doing lessons. Minnie was visiting the Owen family and Jennie, mending in her lap, sat beside Papaw on the sofa, his long legs and unshod feet stretched out to the stove. Mama, in her rocker concentrated on the patch she was sewing on Hube's overalls. Papaw broke the silence. "It ain't jest the boy you're worried about, Lu, is it?"

Jennie looked sideways at Mama. Mama always said if ever there was something she didn't want Papaw to know, she daren't face him because he could look into her eyes and right into her mind. Mama had her head bowed. Jennie was sure Mama's main concern was for Edward, but knowing Mama, she was worried about Papa too.

"Lord, Papa, I got enough worries to supply all of Zionville."

"If one of yer worries is 'bout the tab at the store, I took care of it."

Lula looked up, frowning. "You didn't have to do that, Papa. I would've taken care of it."

Mylart nodded. "When Dalton sent you the money?"

Lula set her mouth in a straight line and ignored her father's sarcasm. "Yes, as a matter of fact." Mama dropped her head again. "I'm expectin' Dalton to send me some money any day now."

Papaw didn't pursue it. "As far as Ed is concerned, I can't believe Lije and me ain't had no luck with the Red Cross. They been tryin', but 'course there ain't any telephone lines 'cross the ocean available except to the military."

Helen pushed away from the table and came to stand beside Papaw. "Could a letter get through, Papaw?"

"Tried that too, child. No answers. Guess we'll know when we know." There was a look of utter misery on the child's face. Papaw asked, "You finished your lessons, Helen?"

"Almost."

The old man patted the sofa next to him. "Come sit by your ole Papaw for a minute or two."

Helen sat down between Papaw and Jennie. He put his arm around the slender shoulders and pulled her close. "In all your born days, young'un, have you ever knowed your Papaw to be wrong?"

Helen looked up at him, half anxious, half smiling. "No."

"Then you got to believe me now, if you never believe me again. Ed is all right. The telegram said he was wounded, not dead. He's in a hospital somewhere being taken care of and it's only a matter of time 'til we hear."

Jennie saw the big tear slide slowly down Helen's cheek. Papaw pulled out his red kerchief and gently wiped it away. "Worse thing you kin do is give up the faith. Ed needs our prayers, but most of all he needs for us to not give up on him."

Helen took the kerchief and blew her nose. Jennie looked quickly over at Hubie, afraid he was going to jeer at his sister's tears, but the boy was listening to Papaw just as closely as Helen was.

"I'll try not to be sad, Papaw."

"That's my girl. Now you finish up your homework and jest maybe I can find some peppermint sticks in my satchel."

"For me too, Papaw?"

"For everyone, Hubie."

Jennie sat beside Papaw on the sofa, feet curled up under her, a book in her lap. Papaw drew on his old crusted pipe, and watched, amused, as Hubie and the pup rolled on the floor at his feet. After a few minutes the pup, exhausted, crawled onto Hubie's lap and slept. Hube gently stroked him. "Ed ain't never gonna meet this smart little feller." Jennie looked up from her book.

Papaw took the pipe out of his mouth. "Why do you say that?"

Hubie looked up at Papaw, his eyes shiny with unshed tears. "Cause he's layin' hurt somewheres over ... over 'cross the ocean, and won't never come back and I don't know why."

Papaw leaned forward with his elbows on his knees, his hands loosely holding the pipe. Hube continued to stroke Soldier, the tears finally welling over and running down his cheeks.

Jennie made a move and Papaw gave a slight shake of his head. "Son, I guess I can't say exactly why myself, but I know Ed and it was more'n jest wantin' to see some excitement made him join up. You know the 'Pledge of Allegiance' Hubie?"

Hube looked up, nodded. "We say it in school every morning, like this." Hube put his hand over his heart. "I pledge allegiance to the flag of the United States of America and to the republic for which it stands. One nation, indivisible, with liberty and justice for all."

Papaw nodded. "That's good, Hube, that's good. Ed knew the pledge too and when the country got itself in trouble, he heard the call for help. I guess Miss Glenwood musta told you when you pledge your allegiance to somethin' it means you will protect it with your life. And sometimes you get hurt doin' that. Ain't that right?" He waited for a nod from Hube.

"Ed gave more'n jest words out of his mouth, he gave somethin' of hisself and that makes us proud, don't it?" He waited for another nod. "And now the whole country can be proud of him."

Hube's voice was low and trembly. "But is he comin' home?"

"You bet he is, and he's gonna have a medal pinned to his uniform, too."

"A medal, Papaw? Honest?"

"Yes Hube, an honest ta God, damn medal."

Jennie cringed, but stifled a smile as well.

"Jen," Papaw said, "Where are the boys at? Seems their Mama thinks they need a haircut."

Jennie grabbed her coat from the peg by the door. "I'll find 'em."
She returned shortly, herding Clint, grumbling loudly, into the kitchen.
"Found one, Papaw. It's gonna take some doin' to find the other one."

Papaw said, "Sit down, son."

The boy, sullen and angry, sat on a kitchen chair while Jennie draped
a towel over his shoulders. "This is a waste of my time. I got things to
do."

"It's wintertime, Clint," Jennie said. "There's not much for you to
do outside." Jennie grinned suddenly. "Or maybe you're talking about
schoolwork? That's it. You can't wait to get to your school books."

Clint glared at her and dropped his head. Jennie was suddenly sorry.
It wasn't like Clint to be so touchy. "Clint, I was only fooling. What's
the matter?"

Papaw caught her eye and Jennie recognized the message.

Papaw started with the scissors and comb. "I think we got us an
angry young bull here. Who you angry at, son?"

"Nobody."

"Mebbe you don't know it yerself, but I'd guess you wuz mad as
hell at yer brother Ed."

Jennie was startled. What was her Papaw saying?

Clint's voice was muffled. "He had no right goin' off like that,
gettin' hisself hurt and all."

Papaw nodded, and for a few minutes there was no sound but the
clipping of the scissors. "Could be you're right 'bout that. Makes no
sense courtin' disaster. That what you think?"

"I need Ed home here, more'n they need him over there." Papaw
kept busy with his hands and said nothing.

Clint's voice was strained. "I need him here, Papaw. I need him so
much and he jest went off. We wuz gonna work the farm together, him
and me. He had great ideas 'bout fixin' things and now..."

"Ed's gonna be back," Papaw said. "Didn't say in the telegram
that he wuz bad wounded, jest that he wuz wounded. This war nonsense
is jest temporary. Ed loves the farm and he told me when he left, he
wouldn't be goin' if he didn't know you would handle things while he
was gone. Didn't he tell you that?"

"No."

"Well, that's what he told me. Even mentioned Lib and Lizzie.
Said you wuz only one could handle them ornery cows."

"They ain't really ornery. You jest have to know how to talk to them."

"See? That's what Ed meant. I don't think he meant fer me to tell you, but he said he wuz proud of you and knew you could handle things good till he got back to help you."

"He said that, Papaw?"

"Right as rain, Clint. Now hold still so's I don't make a poor job of this hair cuttin' business."

Jennie went up on tiptoes and kissed the old man's cheek.

✉

"Papaw, this is the smartest damn ... darn dog you ever did see."

"I can see he is, Hube, I can see he is. And since he's smart like you say, then the best thing you can do fer him is to teach him some manners."

"Papaw, dogs don't gotta have manners. They's jest dogs."

"No, that's not true, Hube. Jest like you go to school to learn yer lessons, dogs got to learn too, and you have to be the teacher."

"Like what do I teach him?"

"Well, first off, not to torment yer Mama's chickens."

Jennie turned from the sink. "Has that dog been runnin' the chickens, Hube?"

Hubie gave his grandfather a look of betrayal. "Not much, jest a little."

"If he doesn't stop, Hube, the chickens will stop layin' and Mama will tan your hide," Jennie said. "Probably make you get rid of Soldier, too."

Papaw reached down and patted Hube's head. "Tomorrow mornin', Hube, me'n you will teach Soldier here some manners."

✉

Jennie and Papaw sat side by side in the porch swing. It was cold on the porch, but the kitchen was stuffy and Papaw wanted to smoke his pipe.

Jennie pulled her coat closer and stuffed her hands into her pockets. "Seems nothing good is happening to us, Papaw." The old man tamped the tobacco firmly into the bowl of his pipe, clenched it between his teeth and lit it. Jennie could only see his outline and the glowing red of the tobacco as he drew on the pipe.

"We know Ed is wounded and not dead. That's something."

"But we don't know how bad off he is and the Red Cross hasn't been able to find out for us."

48

"I know in my bones Edward's all right. Boy's as strong as a ox."

"I know, I know. But then there's Mama. All she can talk about is letting Papa know so he can come home and give us comfort." Jennie gave a scornful laugh. "Papa comforting us, can you picture it?"

Papaw drew on his pipe letting the smoke seep slowly from his mouth. "Edward is his son. Man has a right to know."

"Of course he does, but for Mama to expect him to sit by and hold her hand is ridiculous. The only comfort Papa knows is what he finds in a jug and that don't help anybody but him."

Jennie stopped just short of telling Papaw how really bad Papa got when he drank, deciding there was no sense burdening an old man.

Papaw turned to look at her. "That all?"

"It isn't fair you should have to take care of the tabs we run up at the store. I've asked Doctor Payne if he can get more work for me and he says he'll try. I can only help out on weekends right now. When school is out I'll be able to take on more, but that's four months away..."

They sat in silence, the swing moving back and forth. "You're out of school for good come April, right, Jen?"

"Yes."

"And you want to be a nurse?"

Jennie gave a short laugh. "Isn't much chance I can do that, Papaw... Did you know Doctor Payne is going to put Baxter through medical school?"

"I heard. That's a mighty fine thing fer Doc to do."

"First off I was kinda hurt Doc didn't think of me, but then Baxter deserves a chance as much as I do. Anyway, Doc said he thought I might get some help from an endowment, that's when..."

"I know what an endowment is, Jen, but you know, there's a lot of competition involved in being chosen."

Jennie was quiet for a long while. "So you're saying there isn't much chance..."

"Didn't say it couldn't happen, and we'll sure look into it, but I have another idea." Jennie waited patiently while Papaw took another draw on his pipe.

"It will cost a bit for you to get an education, money I ain't got. So first thing we got to overcome is the cost." Jennie couldn't believe what she was hearing.

"Now, I wuz thinkin', there's that strip of land 'tween this place and the Owen place and Jeb Owen has been after me to sell it to him. I ain't been interested 'fore this, but if he still wants it, we might bargain some."

Jennie nodded and waited.

"We don't know how much a nursing education will cost, but the money from the land might jest cover it."

"Papaw, you mean...?"

"Yep. You're gonna be a nurse."

Jennie was breathless. "Oh Papaw, how wonderful of you... I can't believe..."

Papaw said, "You understand it won't be right away. Jeb won't be able to hand over any money 'til he sells off some of his crop and cattle. It might take a while."

"Papaw I've thought about it for so long without ever thinking it could happen. I guess I can wait for however long it takes."

"There's another little point to make, Jen. It would mean you'd have to live away from home, think you could handle that?"
Jennie nodded excitedly. "I think so. I could come home often to visit."

"Life beyond the mountains in the big cities ain't easy, even for them born to it. They's people would take advantage of a mountain girl like you, and you not even know it 'cause you're that trustin'. It ain't in you to be deceitful. " He waved his pipe in the air. "All kinds a' charlatans out there." He stopped to draw on his pipe.

Jennie was careful not to sound too impatient. "I really can take care of myself, Papaw, I'll be seventeen in three months."

"Well, we'll see what develops."

"You'll never be sorry, Papaw. If I become a nurse I'll be able to work in a big hospital, somewhere, say, in Johnson City or Winston-Salem or Charlotte. I'll earn a decent salary and then I'll be able to pay you back."

Jennie drew back and stared long at Papaw. "You didn't just come up with this plan this moment, did you?"

"I been studyin' on it some."

"And you remembered how I always wanted to be a nurse."

"Ed and Clint jest always took for granted they'd be farmers while all Min seems to long for is a husband and babies. Helen and Hube ain't formed enough to say what they want to be yet, but all you ever talked about was doctorin' or nursin'. So, if it's at all possible..."

Jennie impulsively threw her arms around Papaw. "You are the best Papaw in the world. And here I've been saying nothing good's been happening to us."

Papaw disentangled himself. "Hold on, now, hold on. Don't let's set the cart before the hoss. Let's us jest keep this 'tween ourselves for now. First we got to get this matter of your brother sorted out and I tell you true, Jen, we're gonna hear any day now he's comin' along fine."

Chapter Six
Exchanging Letters

"So, boyo, you're off then."

Edward nodded soberly. He sat hunched over on his cot with his packed duffel bag beside him. He mouthed the words, "Thank you, James."

"Nothing to thank me for, Edward m'lad. We're gonna miss you, Pete and me ... Dora too."

Edward wrote something on his pad and handed it to James. James read it then looked at Edward. "You want me to write to your family?"

Edward nodded.

"Yes, I can do that, only if you promise, when you get to where you're going, you will write to them too. I'm going to tell them in the letter they will soon be hearing from you."

Edward looked down at his hands and shrugged.

James slid off his bed and stood in front of Edward. "Look at me, laddie." When Edward turned his face up, James found it hard to speak. The boy's face was grey with pain, his hair lank, falling over a sweaty forehead. His eyes were wet and he struggled to keep the tears from spilling over.

James sat beside him and put an arm around his shoulders, speaking softly. "Edward m'lad, I know you're hurtin' and life seems grim, but you can't give up. You're a fine, strappin' lad with a lot of fight left in you." The tears slid down Edward's cheeks and he swiped angrily at them.

"Who'll run that farm if you don't go back? Who'll keep the wolf away from the door?... And away from your sisters, too, I might add."

Edward gave him a weak smile.

"You can beat this, Edward. Now give me the address to write to and I'll get a letter off to your Mum."

Edward opened his duffel and rummaged around inside. He came up with a handful of pictures and handed them to James while he wrote his address on the pad. James looked idly at the pictures.

"This your family?"

Edward nodded. As James leafed through the pictures, Ed wrote, *Minnie, thirteen*. James raised his eyebrows. "Very pretty." He went to the next picture. Edward wrote *Hubie six runt*. "I guess that means he's the youngest." Edward nodded.

James stopped at the next picture, holding his breath as Edward wrote, *Jennie, sixteen.*

Later, James couldn't recall any of the other pictures. "Edward, would you mind my writing to Jennie?"

Edward smiled. James said, "We'll have to thank Jennie for getting you to smile, boyo."

Edward wrote, *Want picture?*

James grinned. "You bet."

✉

James sat cross-legged on his cot staring at the picture. He felt a tightness in his chest and the lump in his throat made his jaws ache. The girl was standing on a sunny hillside, surrounded by a field of flowers. A light breeze blew her curly hair to one side and billowed her skirt so that she had to hold it down with one hand. The other hand was raised in a wave to someone unseen. Her smile was broad, showing small, even teeth.

She was so familiar. *How can the face and figure of a girl I've never met set me heart to bouncin' so?* He ran his fingers over the snapshot. "But I know you, Jennie," he whispered, closing his eyes.

It was as if they had grown up together. Didn't Jennie lisp when she was five because her two front teeth were missing and no one could understand her but James? Didn't he protect her from the bully boys, walk her home from school and carry her books? And *surely* he remembered them running in the heather and laying in the sun when they got tired, telling each other secrets. Certainly it must be James she was waving to in the picture.

He put the picture aside and picked up his pencil. He would write the letter he promised Edward, and at the same time, ask if Jennie would write to him...

Dear Mrs. Wainwright,

Let me introduce myself. My name is Pvt. James B. Culhane. Your son, Edward, and I have shared the same hospital ward and I'm writing at his request since the lad says you know he has no hand for it. I took some shrapnel to my shoulder and arm, but fortunately not my writing arm.

Pete strolled over and perched on the edge of the cot. "Who ya writin' to?"

"I promised Edward I'd write to his Mum."

"He get off all right?"

"Aye. They bundled him up and took him off in the lorry. I'm guessin' he won't be coming back to the fighting. They'll be sending him home."

Pete nodded. "Think he'll get better?"

James shrugged. "Dora says with proper treatment he should improve, but..."

"I wouldn't change places with him even it meant going home."

"Aye, I wouldn't either."

Pete looked grim. "Doctor Foxborough talk with you?"

James nodded. "Looks like we'll be on our way soon, too."

"I'm gonna miss the clean sheets, and the food, and..."

"We wouldn't be goin' back, laddie, if we weren't able to carry a gun."

Pete was sarcastic. "Yer sayin' we should be grateful we're in good shape so's we can go back to fightin', and maybe pick up more shrapnel and..."

"I didn't say it made sense, Pete, but sooner we get on wi' it, the sooner it's over with. How's yer head?"

Pete nodded. "All right. Headaches are gone."

"And yer..."

Pete bristled. "Fine, I'm feelin' fine, all right? Ya see I'm sittin' down."

James grinned. "Don't go gettin' yer bowels in an uproar. I was just askin'."

Pete got up and started off. "You can sure put a guy in a hell of a mood."

James watched Pete stalk off, pleased to see he didn't limp. He went back to his letter...

I'm sure when you were notified the lad was wounded you were sore worried, as any Mum would be. This morning Edward was sent off to a proper hospital where he will get the special treatment he needs. I wish I could tell you more but it would only be censored. Before he left, he said to tell you he will be fine and not to worry, that he loves his family (I understand there are quite a few of you) and he will write as soon as he is able.

Edward showed me pictures of all of you. I wondered if you would allow Jennie to write to me. I'd love to hear about the mountains Edward loves so much.

By the date on the calendar, I see we will soon be into a new year. Be the good Lord willing, 1918 will see an end to this madness.

Sincerely,
Pvt. James B. Culhane

When the letter arrived at the Wainwright home, Hubie did a wild jig around the kitchen, Soldier barking at his heels, while Papaw sat on the sofa, one arm around Mama, the other around Helen, allowing them to weep on his shoulder. Clint gulped wildly, so as not to cry. Jennie and Minnie scurried about the kitchen preparing a meal of celebration.

Minnie asked, "You gonna write to James?"

Jennie grinned. "You bet."

Dear James,

I can't tell you the relief we felt when your letter arrived. We weren't able to get any information after the telegram came about Edward being wounded even though Elijah Proffitt, (he runs the general store) and Papaw (that's our grandfather, Mylart Miller) tried to get the Red Cross to find out for us. We didn't know how serious it was, whether he would live or not. Then your letter came. It is good to know he is in a proper hospital where he will get the treatment he needs.

Mama and Papaw and all of us, Clint, Hube, Minnie, Helen and me thank you from the bottom of our hearts, for writing to us. Papaw knew all along that Edward would be all right, but I'll have to admit, the rest of us were sore worried. We are hoping to hear from Edward soon.

I will be more than happy to exchange letters with you, James. Mama says it isn't proper for a girl to write to a stranger, but none of us think of you as a stranger. Papaw says I should pretend Edward introduced us.

Papaw went back to his mill in Sugar Grove. We all begged him to stay with us, but he said visitors are like fish, they all smell bad after a few days. He said since we know Edward is safe, it was time for him to go home and tend to business. We are going to miss him. I'm sorry about your shoulder. I hope it feels good soon... of course then you have to go back to the fighting and that isn't so good. I wish more than anything I could be there and help in the hospital. I'll close for now, James, and wait to hear from you again.

Sincerely,
Jennie Wainwright

Dear Jennie,

I'm glad I wrote to let all of you know about Edward. If I'd known how worried you were, I would have written sooner. Since he is not a hand at writing, I'll have to hear how he is faring through your letters. He's a fine lad, homesick for his mountains and from the little he could tell me, I would be homesick too. So you don't feel as though you are writing to a perfect stranger, let me tell you a bit about myself.

It's been my dream to go to the States from when I was a wee lad back in Tubercurry. That's a small town in the county of Sligo, on the northern coast of Ireland. I grew up on a farm as well, so we have something in common.

I went to Trinity College in Dublin, all the while dreaming of going to the States. After two years, I could wait no longer and said to myself, time to go. It being easier for the Irish to gain entry into Canada, I emigrated there, with the intention of one day crossing the border into the States.

In Canada, what with my book learning, I was hired on in the office of the Atlantic/Pacific Railroad. That's where I met Peter Sampson, who was a fireman on the line. He has been my good friend ever since and when Canada entered the war, Pete and me enlisted in the army together. While it was not exactly the way my dream was supposed to go, I did cross the border into the States as a Canadian soldier, and left New York on a troop ship. Can't say I saw much of the States...

"That's the Virginia coastline, Pete. We're picking up more ships. Can you count them?"

James and Pete joined the soldiers that crowded the rails, watching the busy harbor.

Pete put his hand up to shield his eyes against the glare of sun on water. "Looks to me like four more troop ships and one, two, no three more subchasers. That makes, let's see, eleven troop transports, twenty-two battleship cruisers, and seven torpedo boats in all."

"Good Christ," James said, "ships as far as y'can see. Well, the sayin' is, there's safety in numbers. There's a thousand men on this ship. If you figure a thousand men on each of the other transports, that makes eleven thousand men. Enough to boggle the mind."

Pete grunted, "Let's hope it's enough to boggle the Boche."

They turned from the panorama as a bell sounded.

James said. "There's the call to chow. Think you can handle it this time, bucko?"

"Don't think so. Just the smell sends me t'the rail."

"And that means y'want to sleep on deck again?"

"You can go below, Irish, but last night I just managed to get myself into the damn hammock when my stomach started churning and I had to get out in a hurry. I caught my foot in the hammock and landed on the guy below me and what did I do? I heaved all over him, myself and a few others t'boot. Might just as well sleep up here in my bedroll where I'm handy to the rail."

"Aye, I'm sure the fish will be happy."

Pete gave him a withering look...

It was a blessed thing to be on land again. Even so the land kept pitching and rolling 'til we got our land legs. We didn't stay in England but one day and then crossed the channel. It was a pleasure to meet the folk of the land. The girls came out of the houses and walked along with us arm in arm and all we could do was smile. We didn't understand a word they said...

"Parlez-vous francais?"

Pete grinned. "I don't parley nothing, senorita, but I sure wish I did."

James laughed. "This is France, Pete. They aren't senoritas, they're mademoiselles... means miss. Just keep smilin', they'll understand that."

"If that's all it takes, I'll smile 'til my face cracks. Say, Irish, I think this one likes me. I'm gonna hide her in my duffel."

"Best make sure she doesn't have a brother..."

Pete and I even managed to land in the hospital at the same time. Pete took a blow to the head and I've been telling him how lucky he is it was his head it being hard as a rock.

By the time you get this letter, Pete and me will have rejoined our company since we are healed well enough to carry a rifle and pack again. We'll miss the comfort of clean beds and regular meals, but sooner we get this job done, the sooner we can all get on with our lives.

I'm going to miss Edward and I'll pray he gets well in a hurry. Write to me again, Jennie. Your letters will find me wherever I am.

Regards,
James

James walked toward Dora, his arms outstretched. "So, lass, 'tis goodbye then." He enclosed her in a bear hug.

"James. You're on your way. The ward won't be the same without you."

"Aye, you'll have to keep the lads in good spirits without my help. Now, I don't want you shedding any tears. It saddens me to leave the lassies grieving."

Dora suppressed a smile. "Grieving? I'm looking forward to the peace and quiet."

James pecked her on the cheek. "Thank you, Dora love. You're a lass wi' a good, kind heart. If ever I see a bedpan again, I'll think of you."

She laughed. "That's a flattering thought... James, take care of yourself... and Peter, too."

"Aye, I'll do that."

She watched him walk away. He stopped at the tent flap, turned, waved and ducked out.

James sat on his bedroll before the campfire and cursed the cold that made his shoulder stiff and aching. He pulled the blanket closer and huddled nearer the campfire. After almost a month in the hospital, it was hard adapting to living on the move again. Pale moonlight filtered through high clouds, the harsh light doing nothing to soften the mean, frozen landscape.

All about him were subdued sounds of the sleeping camp—groans, coughing, someone calling out in his sleep, and the snapping embers of dying campfires. He should be asleep like his mates, but sleep wouldn't come. He looked down at the letter in his hands and drifted off to a different place. A place far from the cruel ruin of war—Zionville. He reached inside his tunic and drew out Jennie's picture.

Each time he looked into the laughing eyes he was overcome by the same feeling, that she was sister, lover, and friend all in one. The awareness caused his heart to ache so strongly it was almost physical, and it was some time before he recognized the ache as the numbing loss he'd felt all through his younger years. It was a loss he had learned to bury as he grew older. It had been a long time since he'd felt its anguish.

He threw the last of the wood on the fire. It was not the best of light and his fingers were numb with cold. He opened the letter to read it again.

Dear James,

It was like getting a Christmas present, hearing from you again. Our Christmas was a meager one, but we are all so happy knowing Edward is getting well, that we none of us cared.

We got word from a nurse in a hospital in Paris, Le Hospital de Sacre Coeur, that Edward was admitted and is being treated. We were a little disappointed that Ed himself didn't write, but we will just have to be patient.

Now I will tell you a little about us. Zionville isn't much of a town, not even a town, just some farms up and down Valley Road. There's the Methodist church we go to and a Baptist church, a school house, and Elijah Proffitt's general store. Mr. Proffitt has a crystal set and he tries to get the news but the set doesn't work too good, us being in the mountains. He sends for newspapers from the big cities, too, and when I can, I go to the store to read what is happening. But the papers don't tell you much except what they want you to know.

We studied about the British Isles in school. Tubercurry is a pretty name (not so plain like Zionville). When you write again, I would love to hear more about your town and about Canada too. You have done so much, and the furthest I been from home is Boone, about fifteen miles from Zionville.

I turn seventeen in March and will be done with school in April. Papaw and I talked about maybe me going to nursing school, but there are a lot of "ifs" attached to it. I know if anyone can help me it will be Papaw. He is very smart. He runs the grist mill in Sugar Grove which is about five miles south of Zionville.

It puzzles me how you could leave college before you finished your schooling when book learning is all I can think about. By the way, Miss Glenwood says you have a fine handwriting. She passed your letter (I hope you don't mind) around our class so they could see how proper handwriting should look.

I don't know if I was supposed to laugh about Pete being seasick. Sounds awful. No one hereabouts has ever been on a boat, so we don't know what it feels like. In summer we bathe in Cove Creek, behind our house, and that's the closest we get to water.

I'm glad you have a friend like Pete. It must mean a lot to have someone you trust close to you. I wish you could have stayed close to Ed too. Our minister Prosper Truall, says we should pray for the boys in the war and so we do, at every meal, at bedtime, and most all day Sunday, more especially for Edward and now for you and Peter too. Try to take care of yourselves.

Yours truly,
Jennie

James folded the letter into the envelope, too weary to answer it now. He stared for another minute at the picture, then slipped both inside his tunic.

Time now for sleep. Reveille would come all too soon and then they'd be on the move again to God knew where. A gust of wind swirled around the campfire causing the last of the embers to glow feebly one last time before dying. Tiredly James pulled his bedroll apart and crept inside, pulling the cover over his head. The moon slid behind a cloud, throwing the land below into darkness.

Chapter Seven
Aunt Pearl Needs Help

"Jennie," Doc said, "both Pearl and Ada are feelin' poorly. Pearl's rheumatism's flared up again and she can't hardly get out of bed."

"You say Ada too?"

"This weather ain't the best fer her lungs, you know, and it's more'n Pearl knows how, to keep her quiet. Now with the weekend comin' up, Junior and Betsey will be home from school along with the two youngest and they'll all be runnin' 'round like a herd 'a untamed colts."

"I'll be glad to look in on them, Doc," Jennie said.

The cold, misty February morning found Jennie, wrapped in her warm, wool coat and dark blue knitted hat pulled well down on her forehead, trudging down the road to the Norris cabin. She struggled under the weight of a large basket containing a jug of milk, two loaves of Mama's bread, a crock of butter, and two jars of apple butter. The *Ladies Home Journal* magazine Miss Glenwood had allowed her to borrow was tucked under her arm. As she carefully maneuvered the frozen, rutted road, her thoughts turned to the Norris family and Aunt Pearl.

Pearl Gawley stood 5'1", weighed not much more than 100 pounds and, except for her occasional bouts with rheumatism, had all the spunk of a banty rooster. She was a maiden lady, churchgoing and God-fearing, and when Mary Norris died in childbirth, Pearl was one of the first on the scene. She took over the care of the newborn Abel and when the children's father, unexpectedly ran off to Virginia to work in the mines, there seemed no other solution but for Pearl to remain in the Norris household and care for the five children.

Luther came home sporadically to do any necessary repairs on the cabin, see to the tab Pearl had run up at the general store and settle accounts with Doctor Payne and Jennie. After a few days, his duty done, Luther was off again to the mines.

It was hard for the neighbors to accept what seemed to be Luther's uncaring attitude towards his children, although they pointed out that Luther was the most responsible person in Zionville. Why, even before he married Mary he had their cabin built and a well dug, and the first year after Ada was born, the barn was up. Why now would he turn irresponsible and leave his children when they needed him most?

But those who knew Luther well knew the loss of Mary took the man's will to live; going off to the mines was his way of dealing with it. So his friends were willing to allow him what time he needed to straighten his life out, even if it meant leaving his children in Pearl's care. In the meantime, everyone agreed that while Luther was unlucky in losing Mary, he was lucky in finding Pearl.

Aside from Pearl's obvious skill in handling the children (and no one knew where that skill came from since she'd never had children of her own) was her talent for storytelling. The stories were based on fact, but Pearl dressed them up to where they became a wonderful mix of fact and fiction. Jennie remembered the last time Pearl visited Mama.

"Lula," Pearl said, "You know how Buelis Green can kick up a fuss, be she a mind to?"

Mama nodded and smiled. "Lands, yes! Buelis is like a fire-cracker, and Harley knows jest how to set her off."

Buelis and Harley Green owned one of the farms along Valley Road and while they toiled endlessly to clear their rock-strewn pasture, the rocks seemed as numerous as the day they inherited the farm from Harley's dad ten years before. Buelis and Harley had no children and were devoted to each other, but squabbled endlessly, their bickering a great source of amusement to all who knew them.

Aunt Pearl laughed and slapped her knee. "Buelis a firecracker. That's her all right. Well, seems Buelis was complainin' that Harley never paid her no mind. Can't say I blame the man—sometimes Buelis goes on and don't seem to get nowhere. Anyways, 'Harley,' she says, 'I could hold my breath till I die and I swear you wouldn't take no notice'.

"Well, ole Harley takes his pipe outta his mouth and says real sober like, 'but a body would sure 'preciate the quiet, Buelis'."

Pearl chuckled and Lula grinned expectantly. Pearl continued. "That really set Buelis off, and she jumps up shouting, 'I can make it real quiet for you, Harley, real quiet. I can jest go drown myself,' and since Harley didn't do no more than grunt, she takes off in a great huff headin' for the creek."

Lula laughed and Pearl said, "Wait, Lu, they's more. Harley goes back to his reading and smoking and after a while decides to see what Buelis is up to. He comes up to the creek and there's Buelis sitting in the water up to her middle. 'Buelis', he says, quiet like as ever, 'if you're serious 'bout this drownin' business, you got the wrong end up."

The mist was lifting and Jennie quickened her pace, eager to check on the family. As she rounded the turn in the road, Luther's cabin came into view. It was a large cabin, set back about 40 feet off the road with the land cleared in front and Pearl's garden along one side. Cove Creek could be heard gurgling along somewhere at the rear of the property, lost in the underbrush. On the other side was a grey weathered barn about 30 feet from the cabin. After Mary died, Luther sold off the cows, and now the barn stood vacant. As Jennie approached, a small white dog ran from the barn, barking and wagging not just her tail, but her whole backside.

Jennie stooped to pet her. "Hello, Daisy." The dog rolled over on her back and Jennie dutifully scratched her stomach. "I met your offspring. He's a cute little feller... looks just like you."

She turned from the dog and climbed the steps, pushed open the door and stepped inside. The Norris children were huddled together on the sofa, dressed haphazardly... Betsey and Iva Lee in cotton dresses, no stockings on their skinny legs, Junior in soiled coveralls without a shirt, and Abel in a sagging, wet diaper and nothing else.

Betsey jumped to her feet with a little squeal and rushed to wrap her thin arms around Jennie's waist.

Like the Wainwright house, the main room was both kitchen and sitting room. It was a large room, shrunken in size due to the overabundance of furniture. When Pearl realized the Norris cabin would be her permanent home, she reluctantly gave up her home place. Most everyone agreed (but wouldn't say in Pearl's presence) that it was just in time. With both her sisters gone, Pearl lived alone, with no one to do for her, in a house coming down around her ears. But while the house itself was in disrepair, the furnishings were not. Pearl liked to boast her Papa and his Papa before him were the best carpenters in Watauga County. So Luther and the children moved Pearl and her belongings to their cabin, cramming everything in, down to the last stool.

To the left of the entrance were two doors that opened into the bedrooms. The five children slept in two big beds in the far bedroom and Pearl slept in the other in a handsome four-poster bed.

The iron cookstove was tucked into the far corner opposite the entrance with Pearl's enormous maple rocker and matching footstool close by. Beside the stove was a dry sink with a cabinet beneath which held dishes and cooking utensils. A tall cupboard rose beside the sink, allowing for a work space with shelves above crammed with Pearl's canning and bins below filled with flour and cornmeal.

In the far corner, a long pine table, highly polished, with attached benches on either side was pushed into the corner.

Centered on the right wall between the two windows was a large sofa (Luther's bed when he was home). Flanking the sofa were two matching chairs, one in front of each window, partially blocking what little light filtered in from the misty morning. Scattered about the room were all manner of small tables, chairs, and rugs. And the surprising overall effect of this cluttered, bulging-at-the-seams room was one of homeyness and comfort.

The children all began to talk at once. Pearl's bedroom door was open and Jennie could see Pearl propped up in bed dozing. The other bedroom door was closed and Jennie assumed Ada was still asleep. Jennie put a finger to her lips. "Shh, quiet, you'll wake Aunt Pearl and Ada."

Betsey whispered, "I'm kindly glad you're here, Jennie. I wuz jest studyin' on what I was gonna feed these young'uns. They's not much to eat." Jennie looked down into enormous brown eyes in a thin little face. *An eight year old thinking of her brothers and sisters as the 'young'uns'.* Betsey was not pretty, but had a natural sweetness. Jennie smoothed the uncombed, mousy hair back from the child's brow.

"Well now, we'll just have to do something about that. I've got some good things in this basket. Will you put it on the table, Betsey and let me get my coat off? Junior, is there any wood in the bin? It's cold in here."

Without answering, Junior went to the wood bin and peered in. He held up two fingers. "They's two more logs left." He opened the door of the fire box and one at a time, threw the logs on the fire.

Jennie grinned at him. "Thank you, Junior. Later you and Betsey can bring in some more wood. In the meantime let me check on Ada and Aunt Pearl, and then I'll fix y'all some hot grits. How's that?"

Junior grumbled, "Wisht you would hurry up. I'm 'bout ta die I'm so hungry."

Iva Lee looked mournful and Jennie patted her on the head. "I guess you all are. I promise I'll hurry. Meantime, Betsey, will you change Abel's diaper?"

Jennie tiptoed through the open door and stood by Pearl's bed. At first glance, the old lady looked no more than a child. Her body took up but a third of the bed and her face, in repose, was smooth and free of lines. Her wispy white hair, usually in a neat bun, was spread out in a youthful halo on the pillow. Jennie, unsure about awakening her, was about to leave when Pearl opened her eyes. "Here's my angel," she said and held out her arms.

Jennie perched on the side of the bed and leaned over for a hug. "Is it your old achin' bones, Aunt Pearl?"

"Yep, the old rheumatiz' again. Doc says nothin' much to do but rest."

Jennie noted the swollen knobby hands. "I'll boil up some poke roots and make a poultice. See if that won't help some."

Pearl nodded and winced as she tried to shift her weight in the bed. "I 'preciate your comin' to see to my brood, Jennie. They's wild 'thout a hand to keep them heshed. 'Specially that Junior."

"Doc said they were running around like untamed colts."

"All 'cept Ada. When the weather turns damp and cold like it is now, the child can't hardly catch her breath. It jest takes ever' ounce of fight outta her, poor mite."

Jennie rose from the bed. "I'll look in on her now and come back in a bit with some breakfast for you."

Pearl smiled. "Sounds good, Jennie. Rheumatiz' is hard on the bones, but it don't keep a body from gettin' hungry."

Ada lifted her head from the pillow as Jennie opened the door. The room was even more chilled than the kitchen and Ada had the covers pulled up to her chin. When she saw Jennie, she quickly sat up and held out her arms.

The child was ten, but seemed much younger. Her slim body was lost in an oversized white muslin nightgown. An abundance of red-gold curls, now a mass of tangles, hung below her shoulders. Skin, deathly white, showed small blue veins at the temples and large, blue-green eyes under long curling lashes stared out soberly. A small rosebud mouth, parched and chapped, opened in a grin as Jennie bent to return her hug.

"Well, you don't look sick to me, little one," Jennie teased. "Are you pretending so everyone will make a fuss of you?"

"I ... don't want to ... stay in bed, Jennie ... but Doctor Payne says I got to." The words were punctuated by painful gasps.

Jennie picked up the thin little hand and smoothed the fingers. "You just do exactly like Doc says and you'll soon be playing with Betsey and the others. Do you think you can eat something for me?"

Ada nodded. "I'll try, but I ain't drinkin' anymore a' that ole' pennyroyal tea."

Jennie laughed. "Well that's what Doc prescribed, but let's see what else we can come up with." She wrapped Ada in a blanket and carried her out to the kitchen.

The kitchen was warming up nicely and Jennie began making breakfast. She stirred the grits into boiling water, sliced Mama's bread and opened the apple butter, then watched as the children, Ada included, barely waited for the grits to cool before gobbling them down. A whole loaf of bread and most of a jar of apple butter disappeared as well.

Jennie brought breakfast to Aunt Pearl, who managed to sit up and eat with relish. After the dishes were cleared away, Pearl directed Jennie to a cupboard, where she found some warm shirts for Junior and Abel and stockings for the girls. Aunt Pearl made room for Ada and Iva Lee to crawl in bed with her, answering the questions that arose as she flipped through the *Ladies Home Journal*.

Betsey and Junior dressed and went outdoors to bring in wood while Abel, cranky and fussy, finally allowed Jennie to rock him until he fell asleep for a nap. The rest of the day was busy for Jennie. She cleaned the cabin and gathered clothes for washing, refereed fights between the children and cared for her two patients.

⊠

Aunt Pearl tried hard, but she was a terrible patient. Wrapped in her old flannel robe, she wobbled into the kitchen and settled into her rocker. "Land sakes, Jennie, I'm bout to lose my senses laying in there on that bed."

"Well, the bed certainly looks comfortable enough."

"I ever tell you the story 'bout that bed?" Pearl didn't wait for an answer. "My Papa's Papa made the bed—did the carvin' and all, and my Grandma made the coverlet.

"When Mama followed Papa to the great beyond," Pearl began, "the bed, feather mattress, and coverlet along with everything else wuz left to me and my sisters, Ruby and Opal, and since none of us ever married and we all lived under one roof, they wuz no squabblin' over who wuz to get what. Only problem wuz, who wuz gonna get to sleep in the bed." Pearl chuckled. "Ruby said since she suffered with a bad back, she was sure Mama meant for her to have the bed. Opal pooh-poohed that notion, sayin' she was a fitful sleeper and it only made sense she should have it since she was awake the most to enjoy it. Now I had to think me a story that would allow me to claim the bed, and darned if I could think of a thing. Well, I studied on it some, and this is what I come up with.

"I says, all my life I been sleepin' in a short bed and that's why I never growed proper. I says now with the big bed, maybe I'd grow me a few more inches so's to be as tall as the two of you."

Jennie laughed. "Did that get you the bed?"

"Well it stopped us from squabblin' and we all had a good laugh. In the end we decided to take turns, but always giving up the bed to anyone who got sick. 'Course now the girls are gone and I get to sleep in the bed all the time, and you know it jest ain't as comfortable as I remember it when I only got to sleep in it every third night."

"That's quite a story. Is it true?"

Pearl grinned. "Mostly."

"Shall I make biscuits and gravy for supper?"

"Sounds good. They's some canned beans and things in the cupboard over yonder." Pearl rocked contentedly. "This ole rocker." Pearl sighed. "Gonna fall apart some day. Only hope I'm not in it when it do. My sisters and me use to fight over who wuz gonna sit in it."

Jennie rummaged beneath the sink and brought out Pearl's iron fry pan. "Seems you and your sisters did a lot of fighting over furniture."

Pearl laughed. "Come to think on it, guess we did. 'Bout the only thing we ever did fight over."

"Everyone remembers you and your sisters, Aunt Pearl. The three of you did a powerful lot of good around here. Wasn't anybody could be sick without one or the other of you come to help."

"That's a fact, now ain't it. We kinda had a reputation to live up to. Mama always called us her "jewels "...you know, us being named Pearl, Ruby and Opal. We had to shine bright and help where we could. Kinda foolish when you think on it, but it was a way of keepin' us young'uns on the right path." Jennie smiled at the old woman.

"I think your Mama had the right idea."

The room fell quiet except for the creaking of Pearl's rocker and the sound of the sausage sizzling in the fry pan. "I surely miss them," Pearl said, "I'm the only one left. Would miss 'em more if I wasn't so all fired busy with these young'uns every day of my life. Ada, 'specially. I worry 'bout that young'un."

Jennie turned from the stove with a wooden spoon in her hand. "Just what does Doc say can be done for Ada, Aunt Pearl? The pennyroyal tea doesn't seem to help all that much."

"It helps some. Doc says it's asthma. Nothing much he can do but he says she'll more'n likely outgrow it."

Jennie turned back to the sizzling sausage, breaking it up with the spoon. "That's something to hope for... You ever sorry you took on this brood of Luther's?"

Pearl stopped rocking. "Sorry? Jennie, I love 'em like they wuz my own. 'Course I never intended to move in, but couldn't seem to get away. Luther was so pitiful, he didn't know up from down those first days and the children wuz all broke up too. Then, a newborn baby needin' care."

"Remember, Aunt Pearl, those first days after Mary died? Doc asked me to stay and help. You were so scared you'd drop Abel."

Pearl laughed. "That's a fact, Jennie, I feared I wuz gonna drop the poor little'un on his head."

"You're doing fine now."

"With the Almighty givin' me a boost ever' so often and you coming to lend a hand, I guess we ain't doin' too bad... Child, you hear from Ed yet?"

"Not from Ed himself, but the hospital—Miss Glenwood says it's pronounced Le Hospital de Sacre Coeur—anyway, they notified us that Edward is there and receiving treatment."

"And your Papa. You hear from him?"

Jennie kneaded the dough with fervor. "Mama wrote to him when we heard Ed was wounded, but Papa never even wrote back. The man doesn't care one way or the other about any of us."

"Lands sakes, Jennie, you keep punching the dough that way, our biscuits are gonna be hard as rocks."

Chapter Eight
Good News About Edward

Lord, lassie, you don't know what a great boost it was to my spirits to be hearing my name in mail call.

I'm in your prayers, you say, but if I was to choose between letters and prayers, I'd say a letter does more to lift the spirits of a lad, however, a bit of prayer now and again can't hurt. I'm relieved you heard from Edward, if not directly, at least that he arrived safely in Paris. It is foolish of me to tell you not to worry as you will anyway, but try to keep faith that he will get better. At least he is out of the fighting. That is something to be thankful for.

Now as for you wanting to be a nurse. It's a grand dream, Jennie. While in hospital, I admired the nurses and their ability to handle the sorrowful job they set themselves. They worked around the clock and were so tired they could barely stand up. You must ask Edward someday about Dora. She took care of us and there was not a one of us who wouldn't marry the lass if we could.

As for you being here where we are, it's a harsh world outside your mountains. I know that being on a farm you eat well from the garden. Believe me, the lads and I dream about food pretty much all the time, and your spring water ... like nectar. We get meager rations of food, mostly dried, and as for the water...

"Come on, laddie, let's get naked and wash off this grit and grime."

"You mean you're gonna dunk in the river? God Almighty, Irish, it must be damn near freezing."

"Sun's out, Pete, and there's no ice on the river. When will we get another chance like this?"

Pete watched unbelieving as James shed his uniform, grabbed soap and towel and made a dash for the water. All up and down the river bank, naked bodies flew through the air and landed in explosions of water, howling at the first shock of cold water.

Pete reluctantly joined in.

After their bodies were scrubbed clean, shirts and socks and underwear were dumped into the water, and an entire company of soldiers lined the banks doing their wash.

Pete sat clutching a blanket around him, morosely staring at the clothes festooning bushes and low hanging tree limbs up and down the river's edge. "Looks like Saturday morning back home." Pete's mouth drooped and his shoulders sagged.

James turned to look at the laundry fluttering in the brisk breeze, then back at Pete. "And what is it about our duds blowing in the breeze that minds y' of a Saturday morning. Ya look like yer about to blubber."

Pete looked up with a scowl. "Damn it, Irish, I ain't about to blubber. It's just seein' the wash like that reminds me of Mom. No crime in missin' yer Mom, is there?"

James relented. "Sorry, boyo, can't say as I know what that's like."

A gust of wind blew off the river and Pete went into a spasm of shivers. "God, I got goose bumps big as ostrich eggs."

James grinned. "When I said let's wash our clothes, Pete, I didn't think you'd throw *everything* in the water."

"All right, all right, so I didn't think. You my mother or somethin'?"

"You're gonna look a little strange going through the chow line naked as a jay bird." Pete gave him a withering look. James turned away to hide his grin.

Pete went back to reminiscing. "Mom and my sister Gloria did the wash every Saturday morning. It had to be Saturday 'cause Mom and Gloria both worked. Gloria hated doin' wash, but it kinda looked like fun to me, winding the clothes through the wringer and all. Then they would take the clothes and hang 'em on the line."

"I thought it was the sight of our clothes stretched out on the ground and hanging from the trees that reminded you..."

"No, no, we had a proper clothesline and clothespins."

James shook his head. "Sometimes, Pete, you are a bloody puzzle."

"What?"

"Never mind. I'm gonna write me letter."

"You write more letters than Shakespeare."

"Shakespeare wrote plays."

"Same thing."

James shook his head again and started to write...

You are surprised I could leave college before I earned my letters, but I tell you Jen, my urge to come to the States was so strong I could not wait another year, another month, not even another day. Canada was a necessary detour, as is the war, but be the Good Lord willing, one day I will see the States. All of this is not to say I haven't a deep love for my birthplace. The town of Tubercurry is a fair spot with a park at its center, called "the square", where the merchants have their shops. Streets go off the square (like the spokes of a wheel) and are lined with houses that are all connected. The people step out of their front doors right onto the walkways.

I lived on a farm on the outskirts of town with my Da and my brother Danny. Our Mum died when Danny was born, but Aunt Mag, that's my Da's sister, came in to do the cooking and washing. It was a sad life without a Mum. Da was not one to coddle, nor was Aunt Mag. Da hadn't the patience to teach us much more than the business of running the farm, which we learned at an early age. But we managed, Danny and me. At the week's end we brought our wares to town along with the other farmers and sold them in the square.

We did have fun. Summer days my friend Jimmy Anderson and me would get on our bicycles and ride down to the river bank and fish. More often than not I'd have Danny on my handlebars. Danny is five years younger than me and he followed me around like a mouse follows cheese. The pity is he didn't want to follow me to the States. Then Sunday it was church. We attended the Church of Ireland and my Da was unyielding about attending services. Many a Sunday morning I would nod off and feel his elbow in my ribs.

When you write again, Jennie, tell me more of your family and your life in the mountains of North Carolina. Your letters will follow me wherever I am.

I will write no more for now.

Your soldier friend,
James

P.S. You mentioned my handwriting. Our school masters were strict. A rap on the knuckles was enough to ensure we wrote proper.

71

Jennie finished reading the letter to Baxter. They sat side by side, perched precariously on the gate. It was something they had done every day after school for as long as either of them could remember, sitting on the gate ... talking. Jennie was all smiles as she folded the letter and slipped it back into the envelope. "So. What do you think? Sounds interesting, doesn't he?"

"Sounds like maybe *too* interesting."

"What do you mean?"

"You don't want to encourage someone you never met to write like they wuz your closest friend in the whole world."

"Oh phooey, Bax, you sound like Mama. What possible harm can there be writing to a poor soldier in a war thousands of miles away? Besides, Edward knows James. He wouldn't have allowed James to write to me if James was some sort of boogy man."

"Jest the same, Jen, don't you go givin' him no encouragement."

"You're just an old worry wart," and she gave him a playful shove. Baxter began to lose his balance, made a grab for Jennie, who lost her balance as well, and the two of them toppled off the gate, landing in a heap in the muddy yard. After the first shock, they sorted themselves out, sat back and laughed.

"Think maybe we're gettin' too old fer this, Jen?"

Jennie leaned back on her hands and stretched her long legs out. "Old has nothing to do with it, you pulled me off."

"You made me lose my balance."

"Did not."

"Did too."

"All right, I give... Say Jen, I got some news fer you. Ma got a letter from her cousin Serina in Canton, Ohio. Her daughter, Gayle, wants to come out fer a visit. That makes Gayle my cousin too, don't it?"

"I don't know. Never heard you talk about her. What's she like?"

"Ain't never met her myself. She's eighteen and her Ma says she's restless. Whatever that means. Anyway, Ma says to Serina to send her on out."

"That's great, Bax, I can't wait to meet her. It will be fun to hear about life in the city. Goodness knows, we could use a little excitement around here."

Minnie came through the gate and stopped short. "What in the world are the two of you doing sitting on the ground?"

✉

"Along with them eggs, they's 'bout two pounds of butter in this basket, Jen, but don't jest say to Lije they's two pounds, make sure he weighs it."

"Yes, Mama, I always do."

Minnie stood at the door. "Come on, Jen, let's go."

"And the list," Mama went on, "you remember what I want you to get in exchange?"

Jennie sighed. "Yes, Mama, I've got the list right here in my pocket, see... matches, baking powder, salt..."

"All right, and mind the eggs..."

"Yes, Mama, I'll make sure not to break the eggs."

Mama called after them. "And don't dawdle. It's 'most suppertime and it'll be gettin' dark soon."

Minnie pulled Jennie out the back door, around to the front steps and out to the road.

"I swear Mama doesn't give me credit for having brains."

Minnie nodded. "She thinks we're still little'uns."

Jennie looked sidewise at Minnie. "In your case it's true, but I'm seventeen."

"Only just, Jennie, and I'll be fourteen in August. That ain't little."

"Guess that's right, you're 'most a grown woman."

"That riles me, Jennie. I know fourteen ain't growed up yet, but I ain't a little'un either."

Jennie grabbed Min's hand. "I was only teasin', Min, don't go gettin' mad."

The afternoon sun was warm for March and felt good on their backs. "Jennie, us talkin' about being growed up, can I ask you somethin'?" She didn't wait for Jennie to answer. "I was jest wonderin'... how do you know when you're in love?"

Jennie looked at Min and raised her eyebrows.

"You read a lot, even Doc's medical books. What I'm askin' is, what are you supposed to feel when you're around a boy you like, and well, you know... I mean sometimes I like him to be around and then sometimes I just want him to go away. Lordy, Jennie, I don't know what I mean."

"There's nothing in Doc's medical books that would give me a clue how to answer that."

"Don't make fun, Jennie, I need you to tell me."

Jennie stopped grinning and tried to act serious. "Let me guess. It's Sherm Owen, isn't it?"

Minnie concentrated on the road and nodded.

"When did you decide you liked Sherm Owen as a beau? He's been like one of your brothers and now, all of a sudden, he's someone you may be in love with?"

Minnie looked at Jennie, her eyes shiny and dreamy. Jen felt a hint of alarm. "He's changed. He don't seem so much like a brother no more."

"How about Sherm? Does he feel the same way?"

"He ain't never said, but I think so. I just want to know.." Minnie fell silent, confusion written on her face.

"How to manage your emotions?"

"That's it, Jennie. How do I keep from gettin' all choked up when Sherm's around? Sometimes I even get feelin' dizzy and sick at my stomach."

Jennie gave it some thought before answering. "I don't know what to tell you, Min, except maybe you're growing up. Your emotions will be easier to handle the older you get. Until then, if Sherm makes you feel so... uncomfortable... just try not to see him... alone, that is. See him at church parties and walk home from school with others, not just Sherm. Maybe don't go over to the Owens as often as you do."

From the confusion still on Min's face, Jennie knew her advice would blow away on the wind. She squeezed Min's hand and smiled at her. "Not easy growing up, is it?"

Min smiled weakly. "You won't tell Mama, will you?"

Now that the harsh winter was all but gone, the men had moved from in front of the potbellied stove to the porch that ran the entire front of the store where, without so much as a pause in the conversation, they continued their discussions of the war, cattle, crops and the state of their health.

As the girls approached they could see Jeb Owen, Harley Green, Otis Fenley and Tom Wooding sprawled out comfortably on the rickety rocking chairs, old kegs and boxes that made up the porch furniture.

Jeb and Clara Owen were the Wainwright's neighbors. Their farm was by far the biggest and most successful in Zionville. Jeb and his sons, Sherman and Clay, spent most of their time improving their stock and keeping the buildings and fences in good repair. Jennie didn't know what they would do without the Owen family. Lula turned to Jeb whenever a crisis arose and he was always willing to help. He was about fifty-five, a handsome man, (but for tobacco-stained teeth) medium height, with a strong stocky build, flawed unfortunately by a limp. Story was he jumped from a tree as a youngster and broke his leg. His Pa had to set it while his Ma held him down. It never healed properly and it angered Jennie when Papa referred to him as "Ole Gimp".

Otis and Tom owned farms side by side further up Valley Road and were almost as dedicated to farming as Jeb. They were the best of friends but physically were direct opposites. Otis was short and slightly built with a long face that seemed to stretch out his features and large horsy teeth that filled his mouth to overflowing. He was never seen without a cap. Jennie heard Mama say once she wondered if Otis had hair.

Tom was large in height and girth, though solid and muscular, with a large nose and mouth and equally huge hands and feet. He was enormously strong. Story was he could lift a bull clean off the ground without breathing hard, but Jennie tended to think that a bit of a story. Tom's son Jacob, was courting Otis's daughter, Emmaline.

Of all the townspeople, Jennie loved Harley the best. He was the only one Jennie knew that read more than just the almanac. Whenever he got hold of a book, he made sure Jennie got to read it too. With his glasses pushed to the top of his head, his slight stature and mild-mannered, dry, sense of humor, he looked more the scholar than farmer. In truth he hated farming, but like so many in the valley, he was tied to the land. His joshing (more often than not directed at his wife Buelis) was usually delivered with a pipe clenched in his jaw, lit or unlit.

Jennie and Min climbed the stairs. The men were busy passing the time of day as well as the moonshine jug and Jennie could feel her face flush. Most of the men in the valley could handle liquor and be content with a social drink or two but there were others, like Papa, who seemed to need it almost as much as breath itself. Because of that it revolted Jennie to see even the innocent passing of the jug.

Jeb greeted them. "How're the Wainwright young'uns today?"

They paused on the steps. Minnie returned his smile. "Jest fine, Mr. Owen, jest fine."

Harley took the pipe out of his mouth. "Jeb here says you got some word about Ed? That so?"

Jennie nodded. "He's safely in Paris in a hospital, but we don't know anything about his condition."

Jeb said. "Edward may be skinny, but he's strong as an ox. I can attest to that. He'll be fine, Jen."

"Thanks, Mr. Owen, that's what we think too."

As Jennie opened the door, Harley said "If you see Buelis in there somewhere, Jennie, tell her I'd like to get home fer supper some time today."

"Lord love us," Otis said. His face was flushed and Jennie wondered if he hadn't a nip or two more than the others. "I thought that woman drowned herself."

Harley said, the pipe back in his mouth, "No such luck."

Jennie and Minnie left them laughing and stepped into the store. A cowbell attached to the door handle announced their entry.

The store was small, roughly 30 x 50 feet with a 15 foot ceiling. There were four windows, two on each side. At its center was a black potbellied stove, cold now but a popular gathering place in the winter when it gave out great waves of heat.

To the left of the entrance was a long counter. Behind it reaching from floor to ceiling were shelves stacked with all manner of items; coffee pots, buckets, kerosene lamps, perfumed soap, rosebud salve, matches, combs, lamp oil, castor oil, sulphur, white sugar, coffee beans (both green and roasted), salt, pepper and baking powder.

On the corner of the counter nearest the door was a cash register, a space for tallying purchased items, and a scale.

Beyond the counter were barrels of nails, chains and ropes and wagon wheels, grinding stones, hand saws, axes and hammers, and in the corner, a large spigoted barrel of kerosene.

Along the back of the store were racks of shoes, shelves with bolts of calico, gingham, flannel, sheeting, and all manner of sewing necessities; buttons, scissors, thread, elastic, and colored ribbon.

To the right of the entrance was the post office. It was no more than a long counter with a large scale at the far end and a strongbox for stamps. Prosper Truall dumped the mail here every other day where it was sorted and fed into cubbyholes that lined the wall behind the counter, one for each family in Zionville.

Lije's desk was tucked into a corner behind the counter on which he kept pen and ink and his ledgers, but more importantly, his crystal receiving set.

Elijah and Effie Proffitt owned the store. The two of them looked so much alike, especially with their long white muslin aprons on, they could almost pass for brother and sister. They were the same height, same dark coloring, and both wore glasses. As well as looking alike, they thought alike. One started a sentence and the other finished it.

The oldest of their eight children was Everett. Everett had wanted to enlist in the army when Ed Wainwright did, but his father said it would be time enough to go when he was called. Sarah was next in line and the same age as Jennie. Sarah and Ev were as competent at running the store as their parents. The rest of the Proffitts ranged in age down from Randall, fifteen, to Sissy, three. Jennie greeted her friend. "Hey, Sarah."

Sarah looked up and smiled. She was short and round and had a chubby face. Her skin was delicately pink and flawless, one of the benefits of working indoors out of the sun's glare. Since she saw just about everyone in Zionville on a regular basis, she knew all the latest gossip.

"Hey, y'all. Bout time you'uns come in fer a visit." She wore a white apron with big pockets and a blue scarf on her head that pulled the hair away from her face.

Sarah took the butter and eggs from Jennie and placed the butter on the scale. "Two pounds, three ounces butter and three dozen eggs. I'll leave them here for Papa to put in the spring house."

Minnie said, "We come in to hear what's happening in Zionville these days."

Sarah leaned over the counter and whispered. "I heard our good preacher Prosper Truall is tryin' to cut in on Jacob Wooding."

"You mean with Emmaline?"

"Of course with Emmaline. Who else?"

Minnie was properly impressed. "No!"

Jennie said. "Jacob and Em aren't formally engaged. Mr. Truall can call on her without it being improper."

"Improper or not, Jacob is mad 'nuff to chew nails."

Minnie said. "That man is slow movin' as a turtle. Can't picture him gettin' mad at anything."

"Me neither," Sarah said, "but then Emmaline ain't much better. Can you imagine Prosper Truall and Jacob Wooding having words over Emmaline Fenley?" They all agreed it was unlikely.

Sarah asked Jennie. "Baxter tell you his cousin is comin' fer a visit?"

"Yes, but that's all I know, except her mother says she's restless and needs a change. Neither Baxter nor I could figure out what that means... restless."

Sarah took on a mischievous expression. "I was in the store when Mrs. Combs was talkin' to Mama and I jest sorta listened in."

"That's called eavesdropping, Sarah."

"Lordy, Jen, nobody'ud know anything if a body didn't snoop a little once in a while."

Minnie said impatiently. "Go on, Sarah, go on."

"Anyways, Mrs. Combs said Gayle, that's the cousin, was keepin' company with unsavory characters."

Minnie gasped. "Now that's what I call gossip."

Sarah was anxious to continue. "That ain't all. Seems like there's an older man or somethin'."

"An older man!" Minnie said. "Go on Sarah, go on."

"I didn't hear no more. Mama saw I was listenin' and give me a look that curled my toes. They's jest now startin' to uncurl."

Clara Owen walked up behind them. "What's startin to uncurl?"

They all turned at once. Minnie whispered, "We were jest talkin' 'bout Baxter's cousin that's comin' fer a visit."

Clara nodded. "Gayle, yes. The girl's gonna need friends, Minnie, I hope you and Jen and Sarah will be kind to her."

Clara Owen was beautiful. Unlike most of the ladies of Zionville, she allowed her hair to fall in soft brown waves to her shoulders rather than pull it into a severe bun. Her eyes were as green as spring grass, wide spaced and framed with long dark lashes. Her figure was generous and she had a gentle quiet nature. Today she wore a pink print dress, her best color, with a wide, rose-colored collar that matched her bonnet.

Gossips wondered why a pretty young woman like Clara would choose to marry a rough man like Jeb Owen, a good deal her senior. But it was a good marriage. Lula once remarked that when Jeb looked at Clara, it was like he was looking at a queen and Clara in turn thought of Jeb as the best man on the face of the earth. Whenever Jennie saw them together she thought of Mama's remark and it always warmed her.

Clara and Minnie were especially fond of each other, and as a result, Minnie spent most of her free time at the Owen household. Clara encouraged the visits, saying it was nice to have another woman in the house, but Jennie now knew the other reason—Sherman Owen.

Jennie noticed the bolt of calico under Clara's arm. "You gonna make yourself a dress, Mrs. Owen?"

Clara looked down at the calico. "Thought I would. I'm tired of sewing fer the boys and Jeb. I feel like I want to sew somethin' pretty fer a change." She turned to Minnie. "You like this pattern, Min? It's pretty, isn't it? Little white daisies on a blue background."

Minnie nodded and the longing was plain on her face. "Yes, it's real pretty."

Clara hesitated for just a moment. "You know, Min, I think I'll just buy this whole bolt. You and me'll make us a dress. How will that be?"

Jennie grinned. For once Min was speechless.

Mr. Proffitt bustled up behind Sarah. "Let me take care of that for you, Mrs. Owen."

Sarah winked at Jennie and let her father take charge. As the girls moved away from the counter, Sarah whispered. "Papa falls all over himself to help Clara Owen, except when Mama is here. Come on, let's sit down fer a bit and visit. My feet are sore. I been standing since early mornin'.

Min said. "Let me have the list, Jennie, I'll shop. You visit with Sarah."

Jennie and Sarah walked to a bench beside the cold potbellied stove and sat down.

Sarah said, "Don't know if it's true, but I heard Dr. Payne is gonna send Baxter to medical school."

Jennie nodded. "Yes. It's true."

Sarah pulled the scarf from her head and ran her hands through her hair. "I kinda thought Baxter'd be a teacher. Remember how Miss Glenwood always put him in charge of the young'uns? He could always make them mind." She laughed. "I always thought it was 'cause he scared 'em. He's so tall and skinny, sorta like a skeleton."

"That's unkind, Sarah. Baxter wouldn't hurt a fly. The kids minded him because they like him. Besides, his arms aren't long, it's just his shirt sleeves are always too short."

Sarah laughed out loud and gave Jennie a shove. "Oh Jennie, that's funny."

Jennie turned serious. "Baxter deserves a chance, Sarah. To be a doctor is all he's ever wanted and 'til now he never had a hope it would happen."

"And you, Jen, all you ever talk about is bein' a nurse. It's funny. My Papa could afford to send me to school to be a nurse, but all I want is to get married and have my own place." She gave Jennie a sad smile. "Ain't much of a dream, is it?"

"Of course it is, Sarah, and if I were smart I'd settle for the same thing. It's just... darn, if Baxter's dream can come true, maybe mine will too."

"It will, Jen, it will." Sarah looked cautiously over her shoulder, then reached into her apron pocket and pulled out a paper packet.

"What's that?"

Sarah carefully unwrapped the packet. "It's snuff. I stole some from Ev's room. I been wanting to try it for a long time."

Jennie grinned nervously. "You're not aiming to try it right now, are you?"

Sarah looked around again. "Papa's busy and there ain't no one around, so here goes." She quickly pinched a small amount between her fingers and before Jennie could stop her, slipped it between her gum and lip. Almost immediately her eyes began to water.

Jennie giggled. "Well... how is it?"

"Don't know yet, but my lip is getting numb. Here, you wanna try some?"

Jennie pushed her hand away. "No thank you, Sarah, not for me."

Just then, Lije came up behind them. "Sorry girls, for interrupting, but I need you up front now, Sarah."

Sarah gave Jennie a stricken look and, averting her face from her father, walked ahead of him to the cash register. Jennie trailed behind them trying to keep a straight face.

Min was waiting for her at the counter. "I got everything Mama wanted, Jen, we best get home. What you grinning at?"

Jennie gestured towards Sarah who was standing before her father nodding at his instructions. When he turned away from Sarah they caught a glimpse of her face. It was ash grey.

Jennie whispered, "What happened to the snuff?"

Sarah croaked, "I swallowed it."

✉

The next afternoon Clara walked as quickly as she could down Valley Road, trying to avoid the puddles that had collected from last night's rain. Her coat collar was turned up against the chilly March wind whistling down the mountainside.

She'd gone to the store to get her mail and asked for the Wainwright mail as well, thinking to save them a trip, and when Effie Proffitt solemnly handed her an official-looking letter for Lula from France, she all but fainted. She surmised it could only be tragic news.

She hesitated at the Wainwright gate. Maybe she should go get Jeb and let him give it to Lula. She'd all but decided on this plan when Jennie came to the door and called out to her.

"What are you doin' standin' out there in the chill, Mrs. Owen? Come inside."

Clara had no choice. She gritted her teeth, climbed the Wainwright steps and followed Jennie into the kitchen.

Lula smiled warmly at her as she turned from the stove. "Clara, a visit, how nice."

"I can't stay long, Lu, I just... that is I been to the store for the mail and..."

Lula's face fell. She reached for the arm of the rocker and sat down heavily. "And you got a letter for me, that it, Clara?"

"Oh Lu, I wish I didn't, but yes. It looks official." She fumbled in her pocket and pulled out the envelope.

Jennie reached for it. "You want me to open it Mama?"

Mama looked grey. "Yes, Jen, you open it."

Clara, still nervous, removed her coat and sat down on the sofa. Mama remained silent.

Jennie leaned against the table and read to herself for a minute and then looked up and smiled. "It's good news, Mama. The doctor says that since Ed has greatly improved, he will be sent to the Walter Reed General Hospital in Washington, D.C."

81

Mama slumped back in the rocker. Clara got up from the sofa and went to her and took her hands. "Oh Lu, how wonderful. Your boy's coming home."

Jennie said, "At least he'll be in the States and not some foreign country where we can't get to see him."

Lula wailed, "He might just as well be in a foreign country, Jen, how are we gonna get to Washington, D.C.?"

Chapter Nine
Pete's Escapade

The procession stretched out ten miles long, the road a surging mass of trucks and humanity, all slogging along in a cold persistent drizzle. On one half of the road, James' division headed towards the front, the men staggering from exhaustion as well as their loaded backpacks, dispirited by the unrelenting push forward.

On the other side of the road, a line of soldiers in rags, unrecognizable as uniforms, headed back, wounded, unshaven and dirty and broken in health. As the columns passed each other, James caught the eye of a French soldier, who smiled at him, drew his hand across his throat in the universal gesture of death, and called "to ze Boche!" James saluted him.

As dusk approached, they came to a halt on the outskirts of a small French village. Word was passed down the line they would make camp there. The soldiers dropped their packs, secured the area and gratefully pulled out dry rations. They ate in silence, too spent for conversation.

By the time taps sounded, the men, encrusted with the grime and dust of the road, footsore and aching in every muscle, were already snoring in their bedrolls... all but James. He lay awake, thanking God they'd come to a halt, knowing that in the morning he could write to Jennie. Perhaps even the mail would catch up with them. Jennie was his link between the harsh world he lived in and the innocent world of Zionville. He allowed his eyes to close and immediately sleep engulfed him.

It was April. The air still held a chilly bite, but gone was the penetrating cold of winter. Spring rains had Valley Road awash in mud and caused Cove Creek, already swollen from mountain runoffs, to come close to overflowing its banks. The air was fragrant with the scent of early wildflowers and pastures were starting to show green.

Hube ran down the muddy road, black curls bouncing, blissfully ignoring the spray of mud that splattered in all directions. His tattered overalls were wet and muddy to the knees and he ran with one hand over his pocket to protect the letter inside.

His companion, Soldier, crusted in mud, ran from one side of the road to the other, inspecting every bush and fence post. Hube called over his shoulder, "Come on, dog, betcha can't catch me," and the pup came running, as heedless of the muddy potholes as Hubie. The two of them raced along the split rail fence that enclosed the Wainwright property.

Hube climbed the rickety gate, the dog barking at his heels, and pushed the ground with one foot to get the gate swinging. After a few minutes he jumped from the gate letting it bang shut behind him, barely allowing Soldier to squeeze through, and continued up the dirt walk past the buckeye tree. Mama's chickens ran in squawking confusion in all directions.

"Come on, Soldier, leave Mama's chickens 'lone. 'Member what Papaw learnt ya!" He leaped up the front steps and followed the porch around to the back door, grabbing the swing in passing and setting it moving violently back and forth. He shouted at the top of his voice as he ran.

"Jennie, a letter... a letter from James." Jennie, flushed from the heat of the oven, came to the open kitchen door mopping her face with the hem of her apron.

"Lands, Hube, I'm not deaf." She grabbed him by the scruff of the neck as he made to push past her into the kitchen. "Don't you step a foot on Mama's kitchen floor with those muddy shoes or she'll blister your backside." She looked sternly at the dog. "And that means you too."

Hube swung around grinning. "I wasn't comin' in, Jennie, honest. But lookit here." He dug the letter from his pocket with great ceremony and handed it to her. "A letter from James."

Jennie smiled as she took the letter and turned back to the kitchen.

Hube sat down abruptly on the back steps and began to pull off the muddy shoes without bothering to untie them. "Mama n'all is still workin' in the garden. She says maybe the Sears catalog is in and would I go see, but Mr. Proffitt says they ain't come in yet. You wuz lucky I went 'cause there wuz yer letter right in our ole cubbyhole."

He jumped through the door and plopped himself on a chair by the kitchen table, a pleased expression covering his face. "Ain't ya gonna read it?"

Jennie grinned at him. "Ain't, Hubie?"

"I ain't in school. I don't hafta watch how I talk."

Jennie frowned at him.

Hubie sighed. "All right... aren't ya gonna read your letter?"

"Not just now. I'll save it for later tonight when I have more time." She tucked the letter in her apron pocket knowing full well as soon as Hubie was out of sight she would read it. She reached over and ruffled his hair. "But I thank you kindly for delivering it."

She turned back to the stove and opened the oven door, standing back for a moment to let the first rush of heat out. With a corner of her apron, she drew out a huge pan of corn bread and placed it on a rack on the kitchen table.

Eyes closed, Hubie leaned over the corn bread, inhaling noisily. "Can I have a piece, Jennie?"

"Lordy, Hube, you just stuffed yourself at dinner. You can't possibly be hungry."

"I know I ain't... aren't hungry, Jen, but my stomach thinks I am."

"Well, you can just tell your stomach this cornbread is for supper."

Hube let his eyes fall to Jennie's pocket. "I wanna know what James has ta say."

"Tell you what, Hube, if James talks about anything at all interesting, I'll read y'all the letter tonight at supper. How's that?"

Hube, disappointed, said, "I guess so."

Jennie looked out the back window. "Clint still out by Lizzie?"

"Yeah. She ain't dropped her calf yet."

"Poor girl. Tell you what, Hube, why don't you take a piece of cornbread out to Clint. He's so anxious about Lizzie he didn't come in for dinner. He must be starved."

"I will if you give me a piece too."

"You little schemer. All right, you can have a piece too. Then you better hustle back to Mama. She must be waiting to hear about the catalog."

Hube slid from the chair and went out the kitchen door, dropping to the porch and struggling into his shoes, Soldier making the whole operation more difficult by licking his face. Jennie carefully carved two pieces of the corn bread from the pan and gingerly handed them to Hube. "Careful, they're hot."

Hube stuffed the one piece into his mouth. He said between gasps, "Lordy, that's hot." Jennie shook her head. He leaped off the porch, holding Clint's piece of cornbread high in his hand and headed for the cow shed.

Jennie called after him. "You better wipe the crumbs off your chin, Hube, or Mama will know you've been samplin' the corn bread."

"That's all right, Jen, Soldier already licked 'em off."

After he was gone she shook her head at the great clumps of mud left on the porch.

She sat down at the table and with great anticipation, drew the letter from her pocket...

Dear Jennie,

Now that we have halted our mad rush for some rest, I have the time to write to you. Word is we will stay here, on the outskirts of a quaint little village, for a time. The thinking must be that there is no sense in killing us with marching before we have a chance at the Boche.

And now, lass, I guess I must say happy birthday to you. It is seventeen years you are, right? Having no idea at all what the date is, I'm assuming your birthday has come and gone (you said it was sometime in March).And your Papaw; has he said more about helping you to become a nurse? Seems we both have a dream... yours to be a nurse and me to see the States, and who's to say, Jen, maybe one day we'll both find our dream.

The village we are near has a public square at its center. The middle of the square has a well with a fountain where the local women come to do their wash. They visit and jabber at great length as they work, and there is a good deal of laughter despite their hardships. Today me and my mates took our wash to the well and knelt beside the women, which caused a great deal of tittering and giggling. We didn't mind. We tittered and giggled right along with them...

"Jim, look at that beautiful girl on the other side of the fountain... no, don't look now. She'll know we're talking about her. She's about the prettiest thing I ever saw."

"Every girl you've seen of late, bucko, has been the prettiest. Too bad you don't know the language."

"I know some, Jim. You just watch me and learn something."

Pete strolled leisurely around the far side of the fountain and approached the girl. She was struggling with an overloaded wheelbarrow of wet clothes. Jim sauntered closer so he could hear the conversation.

Pete smiled broadly. "Parlez-vous English?"

The girl looked up and smiled, shrugging her shoulders. "Je ne parle pas anglais, Monsieur."

The girl was indeed pretty, James thought. Her skin was honey brown and she had a great wealth of black curly hair that framed her face and fell halfway down her back. She wore some sort of pinafore with laces at the bodice, and her large bosom seemed about to burst out. Her expression was pleasant but serious.

Pete was not in the least daunted. He nodded and pointed to himself and said, "Pete" then pointed to her and waited.

She smiled and said "Germaine."

Pete turned to James and mouthed the words. "See? What did I tell ya?" He turned back to Germaine and took over the wheelbarrow. "Here, let me get that for you."

The last James saw of them, they were strolling down the street, Pete effortlessly pushing the load of clothes and at the same time conducting what looked to be an animated conversation. It was late when Pete came back to the camp and James roused himself enough to ask, "How did it go?"

"I guess it musta been 'bout the worst date I ever had in my whole life."

James laughed. "I thought language wasn't a problem."

"That wasn't it. Honest to God, she had relatives comin' outta the woodwork. Little sisters and brothers, mother, a couple of aunts and I swear to God, Irish, even a grandfather. They all stayed around to visit. Then the grandfather brings out this bottle and I think, hey, I'm gonna get some of that good French wine I been hearin' 'bout. Well, Christ, it tasted just like vinegar, but they was all watchin', so I had to drink it... smilin' all the while."

"So you didn't get to spend any time alone with Germaine?"

"Alone?... I tried to take her for a walk, but everyone tagged along. Looked like a damn parade marchin' around the square." James tried to keep a straight face.

"That ain't the worst of it. After we all ended up back at her house, I got the feeling it was the end of our date and when I stood up to go, damned if they didn't all stand in line and every one of them kissed me on both cheeks, her grandfather included. He had a big wet moustache that reeked of garlic. I almost gagged."

James couldn't help but laugh. "Didn't you at least get to kiss Germaine goodnight?"

"Yeah, and it ain't funny. I got to kiss her... on both cheeks." James pulled the blanket over his head.

> *Your talk of Aunt Pearl puts me in mind of my Da's sister, Aunt Maggie. She was no-nonsense, was Aunt Mag. A mere twig of a woman with the strength of an ox. But Pearl and Mag are different in a way that matters most. Mag saw it her duty to take care of her brother's motherless sons, but nothing that said she must love them as well. Pearl, on the other hand loves the children in her care without any responsibility towards them at all.*

> *To be fair, Aunt Mag had three boys of her own. She just didn't have enough love in her to take on two more. Ah well, it's a long time ago, Jen, and if I ever resented it as a child, I've long since put it to rest.*

> *The mail has not yet caught up with us. I am praying it will before we are on the march again.*

> *My love to you, girl,*
> *James*

Jennie went quickly to the cupboard, opened a drawer and withdrew her writing box. She should be out helping the others in the garden, but the kitchen was tidy, her work done, and the house quiet... a perfect time to answer James' letter.

Dear James,

> *Wonderful news! Ed is to be sent home. Well, not exactly home, but to the States at least. He is to be transferred to the Walter Reed General Hospital in Washington, D.C., which sounds as far away as Paris, but we are thankful that he will be on American soil at least.*

> *We still have no idea what his injuries are and since Ed hasn't written us in his own hand, Mama is thinking the worst.*

I tell Mama they wouldn't be sending him home if he wasn't better. We wonder how hard it will be to get to see him.

Yes, my birthday has come and gone. I've also finished school. I loved school and I especially love Miss Glenwood. I've always tried to copy her manners and the way she talks. Miss Glenwood says proper manners and proper speech are not hard to learn and that it is admirable to have pride in oneself, but Mama says I must not become too prideful since pride is one of the deadly sins.

Miss Glenwood says I must continue learning and the Lord knows I would like to. Mr. Owen still plans on buying the land from Papaw, but it may be a while before he can come up with the money. It is hard to be patient. There is the problem, too, of Papa. He is against my going off to nursing school. He says since Ed is gone, Mama needs me at home, and I understand this. But he doesn't seem to understand how my being a nurse would benefit everyone. Or, maybe he does understand and is just being spiteful. I'm sure that is more the reason. Papa is a hard man to understand...

Jennie stopped writing and stared through the open doorway. The mountains were still winter brown, hiding the promise of spring. She leaned her chin in her hand, debating whether to tell James about the real Papa. She wanted James to know he wasn't alone in having a Papa that was far from perfect.

She thought of the little boy who grew up without a loving mother, confused by a cold, demanding father and loveless aunt, and a little girl, frightened by a brutal, unfeeling Papa. Both were damaged in some way. Heartache took many forms.

Chapter Ten
Jennie Visits Papaw

They arrived by train in the middle of the night. It was black as pitch with a steady rain beating down.

"Move." The sergeant walked through the cars, poking shoulders as he passed.

James shook himself awake. In the dim light of the railway car soldiers were stumbling to their feet, gathering gear and staggering to the exits.

"Lord, God Almighty," Pete grumbled, "where the hell are we?"

James shielded his eyes and squinted out the window. "Can't tell. It's pourin' rain." He turned to Pete. "Not that I'd know anyway. Come on, time to rise and shine."

"God damn it, Irish, you piss me off with that tone of voice when I feel like shit."

"I feel like shit too, but grousing doesn't help."

James struggled under the weight of his pack and started off down the aisle with Pete muttering under his breath. "I swear to God, if I ever get out of this damn army..."

"That's the spirit, laddie, think o' the day we'll be gettin' out."

"I said if *ever* I get out, not when."

By 5:00 A.M. with supplies and artillery loaded on the wagons, they moved the mules out. Mud sucked at their feet as they staggered along in the downpour, entangling themselves in half hidden barbed wire, and stumbling into the rain filled trenches left by the retreating Boche. They struggled on through the day along shell-pocked roads, through one razed village after another. The rain turned to a heavy mist.

Dusk found them close to the front, the dull thud of cannon shot and whine of shells frighteningly close. No lights were allowed. They unhitched the mules, unloaded supplies and camouflaged the big guns, all the while on guard for silent raids. They worked steadily through the night and with dawn approaching, they were allowed to rest and build campfires.

James crawled back to their campsite with an armload of firewood. "It's damp, but we can get a fire goin' wi' it."

Pete looked about to say something, but James stared him down and he changed his mind. Instead he brought out his matches and with some choice words and several tries, the flame took hold. They brought out their food to warm over the fire.

"Warm or cold this stuff tastes like cardboard."

James deliberately chose his words. "Chewin' is good for the teeth."

Pete spat the food out of his mouth. "Shit... what the hell is it with you?"

"Pete, you're no better or worse off than the rest of us. If we get down, we won't get up again, so what I'm sayin' is make the best of it."

"There ain't no *best*." James decided to give up and turned to his bedroll, leaving Pete to grumble into the fire. He was too weary to argue. The guns racketed unmercifully, and he wondered idly if when the din was no longer part of every waking moment, would his ears adjust to quiet?

They were ordered to catch what sleep they could. When it turned dark, they would haul the big guns to the front to reinforce the artillery already there. If the Boche stood their ground, it would be over the top again for him and his mates and memories of creeping through no-man's-land on his belly made his stomach churn. His bedroll was as wet as the clothes he wore and after several attempts at finding a comfortable position, he gave up and closed his eyes. He conjured up thoughts of Jennie on a hilltop with the wind blowing her hair.

"It's right kindly of you, Mr. Owen, to carry me along with you to Sugar Grove. We haven't seen Papaw much this past winter and we all worry 'bout him livin' alone like he does."

"No trouble, Jennie. Plenty room in the wagon and Bro don't mind. He's a right sociable ole hoss. Speaking o' your Papaw living alone, I allus wondered why he don't move in with y'all. Must be lonely livin' in that big ole house these past three years since your Mamaw is gone."

"Papaw wouldn't leave Sugar Grove. The mill holds him there."

Jeb nodded. "Guess that's reason 'nuff." Jennie glanced at the man in the wagon next to her. An old battered straw hat covered his head and he wore bib overalls with neat patches at the knees. His red flannel shirt was stained with sweat, the sleeves rolled up to his elbows. Jeb rooted around in a pocket and came up with a plug of tobacco, bit off a piece and settled it in his cheek. "Your Papaw 'spectin' you, is he?"

"No, but if he isn't home I can set on his porch and wait on him. He's never far from his home place."

"If he don't come back, young'un, you jest come lookin' fer me at the store. I plan to spend the night with my sister and she can put us both up if it comes to that."

Jennie nodded. "I'll do that."

"I rightly admire your Papaw, Jennie. He's a mighty fine gentleman. Yep, a big man's Mylart Miller. More ways n' one." Jeb looked sideways at Jennie and grinned. "How big a man is he anyways, 6'7", 6'8"?"

Jennie grinned too. "There abouts, I guess. They say he's so tall he drags his feet when he's on horseback."

Cove Creek bubbled along to the left of the road, at times disappearing into the underbrush only to rejoin them around the next turn. The mountains stretched up on either side, dotted with redbud trees and dogwood in bloom. The mixed smells of apple blossom and lilac filled the air.

Jeb pulled a soiled kerchief from a hip pocket, took off his hat and mopped his brow. "Whew... it's unseasonable warm, ain't it? Only May and it feels more like July."

Jennie agreed. She'd long since taken off her grey sweater and folded it beside her. When she got to Papaw's, the cotton stockings would come off too.

"Talked to your Papaw 'bout that strip o' land lies 'tween your place and mine, Jen. Mylart says he's willin' to sell it to me if I still want it." Jeb turned to face Jennie. "Said he wanted the money so's you could go to nursin' school. That a fact?"

Jennie smiled and nodded. "You understand it's only a loan, Mr. Owen. When I've gotten my education and start bringing home some money, I'll repay Papaw."

"I'm sure you will, Jen. I plan on givin' Mylart a more'n fair price for the land since it's goin' fer sech a good cause."

Jennie felt tears sting the back of her eyes. Her own Papa couldn't see the worth of her getting an education and here was Jeb Owen, a neighbor, willing to help. Of course Jeb and Clara Owen were more than neighbors, more than friends even. They were more like kin. She knew Jeb Owen would be embarrassed by an excess of gratitude, none the less, Jennie reached over and planted a kiss on his weatherworn cheek. "I guess you know pretty much how important this is to me, Mr. Owen and I thank you kindly for understanding."

"Jest make us proud, Jen, is all."

"I'll surely try."

There weren't too many people in the country with money. A person considered well off was one who owned land passed down from one generation to the next. Jeb Owen was a good example. He was the youngest of five children in his family and the only boy. By the time his father passed on, all four girls were married with homes of their own, which left Jeb to inherit the homeplace and the fifty acre farm. With diligence Jeb had increased his herd to 25 cows, was the proud owner of a prize bull, Herman, (that he hired out for stud), plus two horses, Sis and Bro.

It was much the same for Mylart. When his Papa, Walter Miller died, the estate was divided between Mylart and his two brothers, Samuel and Dean. Since neither of the brothers were interested in the mill or the homeplace, they were happy enough to let them go to Mylart as his fair share of the estate.

Mylart was ambitious and hard working and over the years, with careful planning, had accrued several tracts of choice land while maintaining and improving the old mill. Now he was considered a wealthy man, but cash poor like most everybody in the valley. As was the custom, a portion of every bushel of grain Papaw ground was his payment. He could sell his grain for cash or use it in trade at Grundy's store for essentials. Payment in cash was rare. All his holdings would be Lula's one day. It was a sore spot with Papaw that his two sons, Garrett and Mylart, Jr., at the ages of eighteen and nineteen, decided to go west to find their fortune. And now, as Papaw got older, the problem arose as to who would run the mill.

Jennie looked back into the wagon bed. "What all you got to trade this time?"

"Let's see, I got an old plow back there needs some work, couple of kerosene lamps 'thout shades, two, three picks and a shovel needin' new handles and a few other pieces."

"Mama said you'd almost rather trade than farm."

Jeb chuckled. "Almost. Tradin' and bargainin's one of the pure joys left in life."

Jennie picked up the napkin she had tucked beside her and opened it up in her lap. "Would you like a jelly sandwich?"

"Don't mind if I do, Jen." He leaned over the side, spit out his wad of tobacco and wiped his mouth on his shirtsleeve.

They passed the Baptist church and a half mile further on, the Methodist church. The creek had disappeared behind the churches, but now it appeared again out of the brush.

They munched on thick slices of Lula's bread with grape jelly while Bro kept a steady, plodding pace. Jeb didn't hurry him. The road twisted and turned, passing small weathered cabins half smothered in wisteria and banked by bushes of blooming lilacs. "How-do's" were called out from the porches as they passed, the women churning butter or cradling sleeping babies in their laps as they rocked gently back and forth.

It was close to two in the afternoon and the sun had lost most of its heat when the road, and creek, veered right. The wagon rumbled into Sugar Grove. They passed a red farmhouse on the right and waved to a hefty woman and three boys working in the garden. Further along was a one-room school house, deserted now for the summer, white paint faded and peeling. Next was the livery stable and noisy blacksmith shop and beyond that a neat white clapboard church that stood back from the road on a small rise.

Across the road was the general store run by Jacob Grundy and his wife Rosella. A group was gathered in rockers on the porch, same as the general store in Zionville. The men waved as they passed.

Next to the store was a fenced-in pasture rising to an imposing two story, fieldstone house. It was Papaw's home place. Cove Creek, which had lost itself in the wooded area behind the town, now coursed down the rise where ten or more cows grazed languidly along its banks. The creek would continue on its way to eventually empty into Watauga River in Tennessee while Valley Road took the opposite direction into Boone.

Bro cautiously pulled the wagon over the sturdy log bridge, which spanned the creek, and up the road to the house. "Whoa, hoss."

The wide porch across the front of the house held two comfortable wicker rockers with faded cushions, a small table and a swing. The swing had been Mamaw Rissa's favorite spot and Jennie pictured her sitting in it, snapping beans from her apron and throwing them into the white agate pot set beside her. Jennie missed Mamaw, badly.

"Ain't no sign of your Papaw, Jennie."

Jennie jumped down. "He may be back at the mill. Do you want to come set on the porch a spell?"

"No, think I'll get on back to the store."

"All right, I'll be waiting here at the fence tomorrow morning at 9:00 for you to pick me up. That be all right?"

"Well, sure 'nuff. Mind what I said—if your Papaw don't show up, you find me at the store."

"I will... and thank you."

Jeb slapped Bro gently on the rump, turned the wagon around, and traveled back along the way they'd come, towards the general store.

Jennie walked up the path, pausing as Papaw's prize rooster strutted across her path, his glossy red and green feathers glinting in the sun. The old rooster was followed by several bedraggled white hens and Jennie waited patiently for them to pass. Jennie greeted the rooster, "hello, Henry."

She climbed the porch steps and called as she reached the screen door, "Papaw."

After she'd waited a moment, and there was no answer, she stepped into the cool living room. The room smelled musty, evidence of closed windows and doors over the winter months.

Jennie noted the neat appearance; the overstuffed sofa still covered with Mamaw's knitted quilt, the chairs and foot stools drawn up to the fireplace, and Mamaw's knickknacks still cluttering shelves and tables. Over it all there was a feeling of emptiness, of a house unlived in.

She hurried through the room and into the kitchen, again seeing nothing out of place, walked quickly to the open back door and peered out. The sight of the freshly plowed garden showed the first sign of ongoing life at Papaw's home place and Jennie sighed with relief.

Her eyes traveled beyond the garden to where the land rose gently. Papaw's springhouse was built into the side of the rise where the brook ran through it, and 50 feet or so beyond the spring house was the mill. It was a grand old structure, aged and weatherworn but in good repair. Beside it the giant water wheel idly turned in the late afternoon sun.

Jennie was worried that Papaw was getting too old to run the mill. The responsibility of the mill should be passed to younger shoulders. Trouble was, who would that be? They'd long given up the idea of Garrett or Mylart, Jr. coming back to take over and Papa was discounted for obvious reasons. For a while Papaw's hopes had lain with Edward, but Edward's interest was farming. The solution would be to sell the mill, but it was a solution no one dared mention.

Jennie found no sign of Papaw. After calling several times to be sure, she retraced her steps to the porch.

The cushioned rocker felt wonderful. She dropped her bundle of clothes and thought how riding over a rocky mountain road was hard on the bottom. She rolled her stockings down and took them off, wriggling her toes with pleasure.

The swing, gently swaying in the afternoon breeze, caught her attention and she thought again about Mamaw Rissa. Her death had taken them all by surprise—a lingering cold that turned into pneumonia. Papaw, the one everyone leaned on, suddenly became the helpless one and they all despaired of him ever being the same again. Mama and the neighbors did what they could and finally, after a year, Papaw began to take interest again in life and in his mill.

Mamaw had been tall and spare and to the day she died, her hair was as black as when Papaw married her. Papaw used to tease, saying she used stove black on her hair and Mamaw would pretend to be angry. She was always busy—mending, baking, hooking rugs— and while her hands were busy she told stories. Mostly about Papaw.

Stories about Mylart Miller were legend in the mountains. For one thing, his height was amazing. Wasn't anyone came near being as tall or strong as Mylart Miller.

Mamaw's favorite story was the time Papaw almost got killed. Jennie closed her eyes and could almost hear Mamaw's voice.

..."Well now, you know your Papaw holds on to a penny 'til it fair squeaks, but once he 'most got hisself kilt chasin' after a bargain. One day he was out back at the mill and two shifty lookin' boys come along on hosses, sayin' they had some good land in Tennessee cheap, mebbe Maylart would be interested in, and would he go with 'em and see. Your Papaw says sure, and come in the house to get his poke of cash money which he hid in his boot, saddled up old Queen and the three of 'em took off.

"They took him down the mountain and 'long through the woods and when Mylart asked how much land they was fer sale and jest 'bout where it wuz, they put him off, and that's when your Papaw begun to get 'spicious. Well, dark settled in and they decided to camp fer the night and go on in the mornin'.

"Mylart tethered Queen close by and settled hisself by the fire and pretended to go to sleep. Sure nuff, them fellers started talkin' in whispers and Mylart stretched his ears and heared em' say as how they uz gonna wait to be sure he uz sleepin' and then kill em' and take his money."

"Well, your Papaw sure didn't wait fer 'em to make their move. He leaped to his feet and uz on Queen so fast them boys didn't know what uz happening. One of 'em pulled out a rifle and took a shot at him as he uz flyin' past, but it missed him. Well, it scairt poor ole Queen so bad she jest kept a runnin' and finally when Mylart uz able to rein 'er in, he sees that shot had took half of Queen's ear clean off."

Jennie remembered Queen with a ragged ear. Whenever she asked Papaw if it was a true story, he'd just grin and point to Queen and say, "Ask my ole hoss here, she'll tell ya true." Queen lived to be 25 years old, and when she died Papaw mourned her like a member of the family.

Jennie got up and shuffled restlessly along the porch. As she stood at the rail, looking up the road, there was Papaw, coming from the direction of the blacksmith shop. He wore bib overalls, a long-sleeved white shirt, and a battered felt hat.

He didn't notice Jennie standing at the rail, and she waited silently. It wasn't until he had turned up the walkway that he saw her. After a moment of surprise, his face broke into a grin.

"Well, I swarn, if it ain't my favorite grandchile, Jennie."

Jennie came to the top of the porch steps and waited for him to reach her. He bent his head and she stood on tip toes to kiss his leathery cheek.

"Hello, Papaw." She tried to contain her pleasure. Papaw hated to be fussed over.

Papaw drew back and looked anxiously at her. "Everything all right ta home, Jen? It ain't Ed, is it?"

"Everyone's good, Papaw and yes, it is about Ed... good news."

"Well now, that's fine. Come and set so's we can visit and I can rest my ole bones at the same time."

He lowered himself stiffly into one of the rockers, reached up and removed his battered old hat, threw it on the table and ran his fingers through the mane of white hair. "Now. Tell me 'bout Ed."

Jennie sat in the other rocker. "Well, first we got a letter from a nurse at the ...Le Hospital de Sacre Coeur. It means the Hospital of the

Sacred Heart, in Paris. The nurse wrote that Edward had been admitted and was being treated. Nothing more than that, but at least now we knew he was in a proper hospital. Then last week we got another letter. This time from a doctor. He didn't say what Edward's injury was, but assured us Edward had greatly improved since being admitted.. so much so that they were transferring him to the Walter Reed General Hospital in Washington, D.C. The bad news is we haven't yet gotten a letter in Ed's own hand and that worries Mama."

Papaw had been watching Jennie intently as she spoke and now he relaxed and smiled. "Well now, that's fine... jest fine. Washington, D.C., eh?"

"I think Mama would like to visit him when he gets to the States, just to see for herself he's all right, but for her to go all the way to Washington, D.C.. that's a far piece, isn't it Papaw?"

Papaw nodded thoughtfully. "It might be managed. We'll have to see."

"When do you think they'll send him home?"

"In time, Jen. Like always, we got to be patient."

"It's hard to be patient."

"Comes with age, young'un."

They rocked for a while in comfortable silence. "So, Papaw, how have you been this winter?"

"Had a bout or two of rheumatiz." He looked down at his hands and flexed them. "But it's eased up with the warm weather. You ride over with Jeb?"

"Yes... said he'd carry me back with him tomorrow."

Papaw rummaged in his pockets until he found his spectacles and put them on, then rummaged some more and came up with a small square of wood and a penknife. He began to whittle.

For an hour they visited. Papaw asked in turn about Clint, Min, Helen and Hube and Jennie related stories about Mama and the neighbors. "Also, Papaw, Lizzie finally dropped her calf, a beautiful heifer. Clint has been begging Mama for us to keep him."

"Still gonna sell him to Jeb Owen?"

"Mama says, like always, that was the bargain. Mr. Owen's bull services our cows and when they drop their calves, Mama sells them to Mr. Owen. But Clint don't look on it that way. He considers the calves ours."

"Clint's gotta learn farmin's a business." Without looking up, Papaw asked, "What do you hear from the Irishman?"

"I just love his letters, Papaw. I brought them all along with me and you can read them later. He's set on coming to the States after the war. We might just get to meet him one day."

"And your Papa, Jennie, what do you hear from him?"

"Not a word, Papaw. Mama writes to him, but we don't even know if he gets the letters."

"And no money I 'spect." Jennie shook her head.

"Pearl and Ada haven't been well and Doc had me helping out there, so I was able to give Mama a little money, but not enough to pay the tab at the store. Mr. Proffitt has been so good about that."

Papaw concentrated on his whittling. "I'm gonna give you a little somethin' before you leave, Jen, to take care of Lije's bill. No need to tell your Mama."

Jennie felt ashamed and angry. "I'm going to be able to take care of the bill at the store one day myself."

Papaw smiled at her. "I know you are, Jen. Jeb tell you me and him made a deal on the land? When I told him what the money was for, we agreed on a price of $500. It ain't worth that much, but he insisted."

"It's embarrassing that Mr. Owen thinks more about me than my own Mama and Papa."

Papaw nodded. "I can see how you might feel that way, Jen, but don't be too hard on your Mama. She's afraid to let go. I know she wants what's best fer you. It's just a matter of convincin' her to make the right decision and given time she will, regardless of what your Papa says."

Jennie felt encouraged. "You really think so?"

"I know so."

✉

They crouched in the trenches. James knew the routine. Suddenly the barrage stopped and the silence was deadly. They awaited the klaxon's loud shriek... and waited... and waited.

God, what torture. *Sound the damn klaxon and be done with it!* Still the silence prevailed. One by one the soldiers cautiously stood and stared out over the deserted wasteland. The Germans had retreated.

Chapter Eleven
A New Arrival

The troops had no sleep the night of May 30th, travelled by lorry all day and far into the night of the 31st. They began marching by 4:30 the next morning, crossing the Marne River and moving towards Chateau-Thierry to strengthen the line against the enemy north east of the city. They passed through small deserted villages, marched along roads pockmarked with shells and littered with overturned trucks and tanks, arriving at the front by mid-afternoon. They had eaten almost nothing in all that time, but since they were heading towards a fight the thought of food held little appeal.

The front line had been held by the French for six straight days, the men fighting without rest or nourishment, and when the fresh troops arrived, the French began retreating back through the line leaving it to the Americans and Canadians to defend.

On June 4th, the Germans made a determined assault, but the line held. All through the month there was heavy fighting, but at the end of June the Germans had been routed... at a cost of 8,000 casualties.

Jennie Dear,

I am weary, girl. I don't know when I have gone so long without sleep or food. But I don't want to fill your head with my miseries. Pete and I are bearing up well, despite the discomforts of soldiering, so do not fret. The one thing that saddens me is the lack of mail.

We've marched through devastation too hard to describe, through villages that once were lived in by people just like you and me. There are shell holes and debris everywhere. It's enough to break your heart knowing these villages were inhabited by people now wandering homeless...

"Pete, over here." James was standing in the doorway of a bombed out house.

"What did you find?"

"Come have a look. It's a bit of good luck." James turned back inside and Pete followed him in. It was a canteen. Dust and rubble was everywhere, but some of the shelves were still intact and loaded with supplies.

"Damn, Irish... soap, towels and here's some canned stuff."

James was rooting around opening drawers and cabinets. "Whoa... look at this." He held up a pair of field glasses. "This is a beauty." He hung it around his neck and continued to rummage.

"Irish." James looked up. Pete had his finger to his lips. He pointed to a door ajar with steps leading down on the other side. They walked cautiously to the door, opened it wider and listened. Guttural noises came from the cellar below. They looked at each other and nodded.

Pete put his mouth to James' ear. "Do you think it's...?"

James shook his head. "Not this far behind the line. Let's find out exactly who, or what, it is." Very slowly they crept down the steps, James in the lead, rifles at the ready. A dim light shone through two, tiny, grimy windows on the far wall and they squinted to see.

Suddenly James broke into laughter. "Saints preserve us, Pete, look what we got here." Two American soldiers were sprawled on the floor, asleep and snoring, each clutching an empty bottle of champagne.

One of the soldiers roused and sat up. "Where am I?"

James laughed. "The official name is *Lucy-le-Bocage*, but let's just say you're in heaven."

The soldier held up his bottle. "If we're in heaven, thish muss be nectar. Help yourself." He pointed to a case of champagne open at his feet. James and Pete looked at each other, made themselves comfortable, and joined the party. By this time the other soldier was awake and started to sing.

"If the ocean was whishkey and I was a duck
I'd dive to the bottom and never come up..."

That bit of fun lasted but a short time, lass, and we soon joined our mates. It is hard to write on the move, Jen, so I will write no more for the present. In this mad world, it is a comfort to know that somewhere there lives a young and beautiful lass who for some unlikely reason takes the time to write to a very grateful soldier. Be the Lord willin', your letters will catch up with me soon.

My love to you, girl.

James

The phlox grew high by the side of the Wainwright porch. Lula's rose bushes, in full bloom, stretched across the front of the house, alive with an army of buzzing bees.

In the vegetable garden, corn rose thigh-high and lettuce, cabbage, beets and peas grew steadily toward harvest time. Leafy stalks of sugar cane stood tall and motionless.

The sun was hot and everything and everyone wilted in the breezeless heat of the afternoon. It was June 29th, Hube's 7th birthday.

The porch was crowded. Pearl and the children had walked up the road to help eat the birthday cake and now that it was consumed, Hube and Junior had disappeared, anxious to try the new bow and arrow Papaw had made for Hube. Helen, Betsey and Iva Lee contented themselves playing with their dolls under the buckeye tree and Jennie and Minnie sat on the porch steps, sewing on their new dresses, Ada between them.

"Your dress is gonna be pretty, Jennie," Ada said.

"Oh," Minnie teased. "Mine ain't gonna be pretty too?"

Ada grinned. "'Course yours too, Min. I like the little white daisies."

Lula sat in a rocker picking through a pile of mending at her feet and Pearl in the other rocker cradled Abel, fast asleep in her lap, his head gently lolling as she rocked rhythmically.

Papaw sat next to her, tilted back precariously in a straight chair, smoke from his pipe settling in a cloud over his head, immense boot-shod feet resting on the porch rail. Beyond him, Clint sprawled comfortably in the porch swing.

"It's a hot day, but a pretty one, ain't it?" Pearl sighed. "June's always been my favorite month." She shifted the sleeping child in her lap to a better position.

Jennie said without looking up from her sewing, "June's 'most over, Aunt Pearl. Next Saturday is the Fourth of July picnic."

Minnie said. "Sherm and Clay and a lot of the boys has been cutting the hay in the field by the church, making it nice so's people can walk on it. And you should see, Aunt Pearl, the big pile o' scrap wood and brush they got for the bonfire."

"That so. Hard to think the year's half gone already. You plannin' on stayin for the picnic, Mylart?"

"Don't know as I will, Pearl. Can't stay away from the mill too long."

"That's a pity." Pearl said, "It's a good time to see how folks is doin' and all. Luther's gonna try to get home. How about Dalton, Lu? Is he comin' home maybe?"

Lula kept her eyes on her mending. "Don't know."

Pearl said. "Oh, I forgot to mention, Lu. Frenda Combs' cousin come in from Boone with Prosper day 'fore yesterday."

Mama lifted her eyes and smiled, pleased, Jennie noted, that the subject of Papa was dropped. "Heard she wuz comin'. You meet her yet?"

Papaw said through the pipe clenched between his teeth, "you ain't met her, now's yer chance, ladies. Looks like Baxter comin' down the road with a young lady I ain't never seen before."

Jennie and Minnie both stood up as Baxter and his cousin came through the gate.

"Hey y'all. Want you to meet my cousin Gayle Morgan, from Ohio."

Jennie was speechless.

The girl that clutched Baxter's arm was beautiful. Her perfect smile was accented by a dimple in each cheek. Her eyes were the palest green Jennie had ever seen with lashes that swept up almost to her eyebrows. The hair that fell in curls to the middle of her back was an unusual and lovely shade of red.

Her figure was perfectly proportioned. She wore a filmy, white, long-sleeved blouse with a neckline that plunged just far enough to show the top of her bosom, and a straight brown skirt buttoned down one side that stopped at mid-calf. Jennie didn't recognize the material. Her shapely legs were sheathed in silk stockings. She wore brown high heels with a strap across the instep fastened with a pearl button.

Jennie could do no more than stare.

Gayle seemed quite comfortable with the sensation she was causing. She looked from Jennie to Minnie, then addressed Jennie.

"This must be Jennie. Baxter's told me so much about you."

"Hope it weren't all bad." Jennie gulped, and inwardly groaned. *Hope it weren't all bad. Stupid. It isn't even good English.*

Gayle smiled. "Of course it wasn't." She turned to Baxter and tightened her arm in his. "Baxter wouldn't lie, would you honey?" The red started at Baxter's collar and crept slowly upward.

"Ah, uh, no I guess not, I mean, no, course not... I wouldn't lie." He grinned feebly at Jennie.

Lula said, "Come on up on the porch, child, and set a spell. Clint, run in and get a chair from the parlor for the young lady."

Gayle withdrew her arm from Baxter's. "Oh, please don't bother, Mrs. Wainwright, I'll just sit here by the girls." Ada moved over and the four of them sat down in a row on the steps, Gayle carefully arranging her skirt. "Who's this little darling?"

Ada hung her head and Jennie finally found her tongue. "Oh, I'm sorry, Gayle, where are my manners? This is Ada Norris and this is my sister, Minnie, my mother, Aunt Pearl Gawley with Abel in her lap, my grandfather, Mylart Miller, and that's my brother Clint over there on the swing."

Gayle gushed, "I'm so happy to meet all of you. My cousin Frenda said I'm going to love Zionville... I do already."

In the awkward silence, Gayle turned to the three girls who had left their dolls under the buckeye tree and stood staring up at her. "And these are...?"

Jennie couldn't help grinning. The girls looked about as dumbstruck as if they'd stumbled across the Virgin Mary sitting on the top step of the porch. "My sister, Helen, and Iva Lee, and Betsey Norris."

There was an uncomfortable silence.

Pearl broke the spell. "It's nice to have you here, young'un, and jest in time for our picnic next Saturday."

"A picnic. Don't think I've ever been to one." She looked down at Baxter standing awkwardly at the bottom of the steps. "You'll have to show little me what to do, Baxter honey."

Baxter shifted to his other foot. "Show you what to do, well I guess...I don't know. Ain't nothing much to a picnic. Ya eat a lot is all."

Minnie said, surprised, "Lordy, you ain't never been to a picnic? Just what do you do for fun in Canton?"

"Oh, we have lots of house parties and dancing—then of course there's the theatre."

Minnie sighed. "Golly..."

Jennie noted the soft lilting way she talked. "You might end up being bored then, Gayle. Life's a lot more simple around here."

Gayle looked down again at Baxter. "Baxter promised I wouldn't get bored, didn't you, Baxter, honey?"

Baxter gulped. "Yeah, well, I thought they's things..." His voice cracked and he stopped in embarrassment.

Gayle laughed. "Isn't he just precious? Just like a little boy."

If anything, Baxter turned a deeper red and it was at this point, Jennie thought later, that her opinion of Gayle would never rise above her bootstraps.

Jennie smiled sweetly. "I'm surprised, Gayle. (She fought not to add "honey"). Seems like you'd know *exactly* what to do."

If Gayle caught the sarcasm, she ignored it. "Canton is much too sophisticated for picnics. I tell you, I find the country pretty much of a shock after the city."

Min said, a little touchy, "Well, you ain't really seen much of Zionville yet."

Jennie didn't wait for Gayle to respond. "Do you go to school?"

"God, no. I've had enough school. Couldn't wait to get out. I've been working for the Public Service in Canton, but I just recently quit... to find something better. But first I thought I'd take a little vacation. Do you? Go to school?"

"No, but that's a long story. What is the Public Service and what did you do?"

Gayle took a lock of her hair and played with it. "It's a utility company... sells electricity and gas. I did lots of things. I filed, and wrote up reports, just... well lots of things."

Gayle's fingernails were long and tapered and polished with a clear polish. Jennie looked down casually at her own hands and was horrified to see her nails were broken and uneven... how? Oh yes, the garden. She sat on her hands. "And do you take shorthand? Miss Glenwood said there is a way to take down dictated words quickly by using marks instead of letters. It's called Pitman shorthand."

Gayle stared at her dumbly and Jennie had the feeling she'd caught Gayle off guard.

"Pitman shorthand? Oh... oh yes. Well actually no, I don't take shorthand. You have to go to a special school to learn it. It's incredibly difficult. I just might do that, though—one day."

Jennie caught a glimpse of Minnie. Her mouth actually hung open, and when she looked at Baxter he looked just as entranced.

Jennie said. "I can't imagine why you left. Sounds like a perfect job."

Gayle turned her sea green eyes on Jennie. "I thought I told you. I plan on finding something better, something more in tune with my, uh, talents." Gayle fluttered her eyelashes. "I believe one should strive always to better oneself, don't you?"

Jennie stuttered. "Yes of course, but well, sure... I guess."

How does she do that? Make me feel like a two-year-old... must be that trick she does with the eyelashes.

Baxter found his voice. "Sorry we can't stay longer. We jest come by so's I could interduce Gayle to y'all. Mama said supper was almost ready when we left."

Mama said. "Why don't you stay and have supper with us? We have plenty."

Baxter looked at Gayle and hitched from one foot to the other. "I guess we could, that is if you'uns want to, Gayle."

Gayle laughed again. "You'uns. I just love the way you all talk." She stood up and turned to Lula. "I think not, Mrs. Wainwright. Cousin Frenda is expecting us. But thank you for the invitation."

Gayle got up gracefully, holding out her hand to Baxter like a queen descending the throne. She turned at the bottom. "It was nice meeting all of you. Jennie, we'll be seeing a lot of each other, I hope."

Jennie nodded. "Oh, I'm sure."

As they walked up the road, arm in arm, Gayle leaned in close to Baxter and said something that made him laugh. It was the first time Jennie could remember that he didn't turn and wave at her.

Papaw broke the silence. "From the look a things, she all but has that young man roped and tied."

"Oh I don't think so Papaw. Baxter has too much sense than to be... to be..."

Papaw chuckled. "What's the matter, Jen, can't find the right word?"

Mama said, "Certainly is a pretty young thing."

"Did you see her clothes?" Minnie said, "I ain't never seen clothes like that 'cept in the Sears catalog."

"And her shoes," Pearl added. "It's a wonder the chile didn't break a leg comin' down the road in them high heels, what with the condition Valley Road is in."

Clint sighed and they all turned to look at him. "I think she's beautiful." At that moment, Hubie and Junior came tearing around the corner of the house, Junior wet up to his knees.

"You been in that creek, young man?" Pearl called out.

Junior ignored Pearl and kept running, Hubie close behind. They disappeared around the other side of the house.

"That young'un don't never listen to a word I say."

Papaw chuckled. "Like all young'uns, Pearl, he ain't got any ears."

"It ain't Junior's bad, Mylart, jest he don't think 'fore he acts. When I try to punish him, he runs off and I can't ketch him."

"When you get to our age, Pearl, only thing you *can* catch pretty good is a cold."

"That's a fact, but I hate to leave it to Luther to punish the boy. All he wants to do is love his young'uns when he comes home, not scold 'em."

Lula asked. "How's Luther doin'?"

Pearl stopped rocking. "Wish that man could find hisself a good woman's what I wish. It's been two years since Mary passed on and it's high time he started livin' agin."

Lula stopped sewing. "You know you're right, Pearl. Now who do we know would be good for Luther?"

Papaw eased his chair forward and knocked his pipe out over the porch rail. "Luther'll find his way all in good time."

"Little help from us wouldn't hurt, Papa."

"Sometimes, Lu," Papaw scraped the blackened pipe bowl with his pocket knife, "that's called interference."

Ada piped up, "A good one for Papa to marry would be Miss Glenwood."

They all turned at the same time to stare at Ada.

Lula stifled her laughter. "Little pitchers with big ears."

Libby began lowing by the meadow gate and Clint immediately got up. Papaw chuckled. "Clint and them cows minds me of a young mother with a bawlin' newborn." Papaw brought his feet down from the railing so Clint could pass.

As Clint passed Ada, he said, "Come on, Ada. I'll show you Lizzie's new calf." Ada immediately got up and followed him off the porch.

Lula shook her head. "Clint works 'bout as hard as a full-growed man."

Papaw snapped his knife closed and returned it to his pocket. He began repacking his pipe. "Responsibility never hurt no one, Lu."

"I suppose, and the boy's doin' what he loves. Him and Ed are a pair. Farmin' means everything to the both of them. Funny, Dalton don't care one bit fer it. Must be they take after you, Papa."

Papaw struck a match on his boot and put it to his pipe. When he had it drawing nicely he swung his boots back up to the porch rail. "Speakin' of Ed, you heard anything more?"

"No, Papa, not a word. I spect to hear any day now he's in the hospital in Washington, D.C. Then maybe that young'un 'll take it on hisself to write a line or two. That's all I want, just a line or two to see for myself he's comin' on."

Minnie sighed. "I'm tired of sitting. Guess I'll jest take a little walk down the road."

Jennie said, "And maybe bump into Sherm Owen as he just happens to be going for a walk too?"

Minnie bristled, "I ain't said I was goin' walkin' with Sherm Owen, Jennie."

Papaw laughed, "Well, my little Minnie's growed up and thinkin' 'bout boys, is she?" Minnie turned fire red and started down the porch steps.

"It's most supper time, Min," Jennie said. "If you have extra time, why don't you give Mama some help with the mending?"

"Jennie, I get tired of you bein' Miss Bossy."

"Don't argue, girls." Mama looked at Min and smiled. "I guess you kin go walkin' if you've a mind to, Min. Just be back by suppertime."

Minnie looked back and gave Jennie a triumphant smile as she went through the gate.

Pearl said. "You still writin' to the Irish boy, Jennie?"

"Yes, we've been corresponding, but the mail is pretty slow."

Pearl said with a straight face, "You ever hear what they say 'bout Irishmen, Jennie? They's either drinkers, lovers or poets. Which do you suppose your Irishman is?"

Jennie said with some exasperation, "He's not my Irishman, Aunt Pearl, but, if he were I'd surely hope he's not a drinker." Jennie looked pointedly at her mother. "I never could abide a drinking man." Pearl tried to keep a serious expression and Mylart cleared his throat.

Mama glared at Jennie. "Well, that leaves a poet or a lover, child, and I don't guess neither one would be much at makin' a livin'."

The awkward moment was interrupted by a horse-drawn buckboard that rattled up to the gate from the direction of the general store.

Prosper Truall rolled his great girth out of the buckboard and tethered Fanny to the fence. He wore clean levis and a white shirt open at the neck, with the sleeves rolled up to his elbows. He removed his broad-brimmed straw hat as he walked up the path and his bare scalp, wet with perspiration, shone like a beacon in the afternoon sunlight.

When Prosper was a young boy he carried a Bible around, the way most children carried a toy, and was known to jump up on a bench or chair when the opportunity arose to preach. In his spare time, he helped his father deliver the mail.

After he finished school, it was a toss-up as to whether he would continue in the postal service or enter divinity school, and divinity school won. When Preacher Woolson of the Zionville Methodist Church died, a series of guest preachers were invited to the pulpit to allow the congregation to choose a replacement. One of the preachers that showed up was Prosper and the parishioners were so overjoyed to see him, they decided on the spot that he should stay. Not only did he stay to preach, but when his father could no longer stand the rigors of delivering the mail, Prosper went to work for the postal service as well.

"Afternoon, folks."

"Well, Prosper, come sit with us," Lula said.

He drew a kerchief from his back pocket and wiped his face.

"Been doin' some church visitin' today. Seeing all you good folks settin' here I figured I'd stop, see if there was any more news about Ed." He reached over and shook hands with Papaw. "How're you, Mylart?" He lowered himself to sit beside Jennie on the top step.

"Doin' fine, Prosper, doin' fine. Last we heard about Ed is he will be comin' home to the States. We understand his condition is improving."

"Still don't know what the problem is?"

"Humpf, government don't tell you nuthin'. Just know that whatever it is, Ed is improving."

Prosper nodded. "That's good news... good news. I guess there are a lot of boys not so lucky."

Papaw nodded. "Yep. That's a sad fact."

"So how are things at the mill?"

"Busy," Papaw answered, "but I get a mite lonely for the young'uns, so I put aside a day or two and come visit."

"Papa knows he could come live with us if he had a mind to."

"We talked about that, Lu. People depend on the mill."

"You ain't gettin' any younger, Papa."

"True, true... maybe when Ed comes back we'll make some changes."

Lula said. "Seems I heard something about a revival meeting at the Baptist church, Prosper."

"Yes, planned for the first week in August. Dr. Pierce is making a sweep through the mountains, and he's got the Baptist church of Zionville on his calendar."

Aunt Pearl looked at Lula with a grin. "Have you passed that news on to Buelis and Harley Green, Preacher? If ever a body enjoyed a revival, it's Buelis Green. She's particularly fond of Dr. Pierce."

"I'd say we are all partial to Dr. Pierce, he is a right forceful man. I'll make sure the Greens know the date."

Pearl asked. "Preacher, you still boardin' with Frenda and Ben Combs?"

The Preacher nodded. "It helps them out and it's convenient for me too, seein' as how it's just down the road from the church."

"Reason I asked wuz, I wondered what they thought 'bout Baxter apprenticin' with Doc Payne?"

"I think Ben is disappointed. He says Baxter is so het up about doctorin' he doesn't have time for his chores."

Pearl laughed. "Well, it looks to me he's gonna have even less time for his chores, now he's got to entertain his cousin."

Prosper smiled. "Oh you met Gayle, did you? Frenda's pretty happy to have another woman in the house, although I understand the girl isn't much interested in farm work."

Jennie said, "She doesn't even know what a picnic is."

"Well, she'll find out Saturday, won't she?" Prosper said.

The boys came tearing around the corner of the house again and fell on the grass under the buckeye tree, Ada trailing behind. Abel stirred and sat up rubbing his eyes. Pearl stroked the blond curls. "You had enough sleep, pet?" She set him gently on his feet. "Guess it's time we headed home."

"Won't take but a minute fer me to get some supper on the table," said Lula. "Why don't y'all stay? You too, Preacher."

"Lands, Lu, I don't guess you got 'nuff food in this world to feed all these young'uns of mine. They's fulla birthday cake anyway." Pearl pushed herself from the rocker and called. "Come along children, time to go home."

Prosper stood up and put his hat on. "I thank you kindly for the invite, Mrs. Wainwright, but I best get goin'." He turned to Pearl. "Would you and yer young'uns like a ride home in the buckboard?"

"Why, we'd kindly like that, Prosper. Looks to me like they'd be right happy to ride 'steada walk. Sure it won't trouble you none?"

"Not at all." Prosper turned back to Lula and took her hand. "I'll make special mention of Ed in my sermon next Sunday."

Lula smiled, "We'd 'preciate that."

Ada, standing by Jennie, pleaded, "Do I have to go, Aunt Pearl, can't I stay with Jennie?"

Jennie let her arm fall across Ada's shoulders. "Let her stay for supper, Aunt Pearl, I'll see she gets home before dark."

"All right. You mind Jennie now, child. Come along Junior, I said come along right this minute."

With the children riding in the buckboard bed and Aunt Pearl comfortably seated beside Prosper, they headed off down the road. Prosper called over his shoulder, "See y'all Saturday."

Lula gave a final wave from the porch rail before turning to go into the house. "You keep on with your sewing, Jen, I'll get our supper started."

"Just one minute, Lu," Papaw said, "sit down. I got somethin' to talk to you about." He carefully placed his boots once more on the porch rail. Jennie knew what the conversation would be about. Lula settled herself back in the rocker and looked from Jennie to Papaw.

Papaw said. "I'm gonna get some money from the sale of that land over yonder and I aim to give that money to Jennie so's she can get her nursin' education. What do you think about it?"

Lula looked from Papaw to Jennie and back again. "Well... I don't know, Papa. Last we talked about that was when Dalton was home and he seemed to think..."

Papaw interrupted. "I don't rightly care what Dalton thinks, Lu, I'm asking what you think."

"Well, I 'spect when Dalton comes home we'll talk about it. I can't rightly go ahead and give my blessin' to a plan he don't know nuthin' about."

Jennie's attention went back and forth between the two of them. She ached to put in a word, but decided to wait.

Papaw slowly withdrew his boots from the porch rail and looked squarely at Lula. "Since Dalton don't seem to give a hoot ner holler about anything else goes on around here, I don't think you got to worry about *what* he thinks."

"Oh no, Papa. I couldn't do that. It wouldn't be proper. Dalton is, after all, the man of this house."

Papaw was silent for a long time while Lula fidgeted. Finally he said. "The man of the house. That what you think Dalton is, the man of the house? He ain't a man, never has been and never will be and what you're doin' is leavin' it all up to him to decide your daughter's future. I hope you can live with that."

Chapter Twelve
The Church Picnic

Jennie Girl,

The mail has finally caught up with us and your letters are more treasured than gold.

Great news about Edward. Being on American soil is going to help him get better, you'll see. As far as the doctors giving you no clue about his injuries, they are not allowed to divulge such information, for whatever reason I don't know, but now he is in the States, they will be able to tell you. He is a lucky lad to be home and to have so many people concerned about him. I'll be anxious to know how he is doing.

We are presently in a small deserted village. It must be a poor village as the houses are no more than huts made of stone with thatched roofs. I could almost be in Ireland. Guilty as it made us feel, we accepted the luxury of being billeted in one of these houses and for the first time since leaving Canada, I am sleeping with a roof over my head. The folk that lived here fled, leaving all manner of furnishings, clothing, bed covers, even a table with the moldy remains of a meal. Sad enough to leave all your possessions behind without having them mucked about by strangers. Playing the role of intruder fills me with shame, though I'm thankful for it all the same.

So here I sit at a table with the flickering light of a candle at my elbow writing a letter as though I were comfortably settled in my own house. A strange way to fight a war. There is much to tell you, Jennie, but no way it would go uncensored. It will have to keep. One day I will fill your fair head with grand stories.

Jen, dear, I've read over and over the part of your letter you wrote about your father. When I think of the heartache he has caused you and your family down through the years, my Irish blood boils within me. I saw so much of the drink in Ireland and the ugly temper that accompanied it. The women and children suffered for it. I can understand your Mum's dilemma completely. Draw strength from the knowledge that

*your father won't always have a hold over you. One day you
will be able to walk away, as I did, and he will be no more than
a sad memory...*

Pete sat down at the table with James, watching him frown in
concentration over the letter. "You writin' to Jennie?"

James looked up with his thoughts on the letter he was writing.
"Let me ask you, Pete, what kind of father did you have?"

"Father? What the hell has that got to do with a letter to Jennie?"

James leaned back in the chair. He pressed the top of the pencil to
his chin and stared into the darkness beyond the candlelight. "What
indeed, Pete. Here I've been tellin' Jen what a sad life I had as a tad.
What a harsh, unfeeling Da I have and all the time... ach, well, Pete, let
me finish me letter."

"How do you find so much to write to someone you don't know?"

James looked defensive and Pete held up his hand. "I ain't findin'
fault, Irish, I'm just curious. I can't think of anything to write to my
own mother, much less a stranger."

James stared down at the half-written letter. "Aye, but that's just it,
ya see, Pete. Almost from the beginning, Jennie was no stranger. She's
a friend I've known forever. When I open one of her letters, it's like
she's here beside me, talking. I can feel her, understand her. God, Pete,
I think I'm in love wi' the lass."

Pete was quiet for a moment. "You think you love her? You ain't
never seen her, or touched her or..."

"I know, I know, Pete. God knows that's important, but isn't part
of love wantin' to share what you think and believe in? That part I can
do in me letter. I could write all night and still find things I have to tell
her." He stopped frustrated. "I can't explain it."

After a long pause Pete said morosely, "You asked me what kind of
a father I had. My Dad died when I was twelve. I loved him so much
and for years after he died I was one angry kid. Couldn't understand
how he could have just up and left me like he did. Even now sometimes...
God, I gave my Mom a bad time. I got into all kinds of trouble..."

Pete's voice faded out and he sat morosely staring into the dark.
James sat quietly beside him, careful not to break into Pete's reverie,
knowing it was important for Pete to say these things.

Finally Pete looked at James and shook his head. "Damn, Irish, I haven't thought about my Dad in years and now when I do I find I'm still as confused as ever about his dying."

"Time, laddie, for us both to forgive our fathers. It wasn't your Dad's choice to die, and my Da has no idea to this very day how his actions hurt Danny and me all these years. It's time for us both to put it all to rest."

Pete said. "Wish to God I could do that, Jim, but every time I get close to someone, I back off... thinkin' maybe they'll leave too. I envy you. It must be great to get close to someone, even in letters. Me, I'll never be able to do that."

"Ye canna say that, laddie, ye don't know..."

"Yeah I do. I talk a good story, Jim, but when it comes right down to it..."

James could find nothing to say. Pete got up and slowly walked off. After a moment James turned again to the unfinished letter before him, Pete's words running through his mind. It was true. Jennie was more than just a girl he wrote to. Jennie was the one that mattered and it was time he told her so.

The urgency to write it all down made his hand shake and he had to compose himself before he again picked up the pencil to write...

In saner times, lass, I would wait until we met face to face and give you time to know me in person, but God forbid, if something should happen to me in this damnable war, then I would have missed the opportunity. And I want to say this. Bear with me.

I've always known, deep down, there was something more than a Mum missing in my life, but I never knew exactly what until now. When I first saw your picture, something stirred within me and as we began to exchange letters, I slowly realized all I ever needed was a gentle person to take the time to listen.

It's hard to explain. Even in the hell that surrounds me, I am happier than I have ever been. Jen, do you believe in destiny? It is said each man's destiny is written the day he is born. I am certain it is mine to hold you in my arms, look into your eyes and tell you in person what I feel in my heart. Tell me if you feel it too, and I will help destiny along by coming

to Zionville when this war is done. Please don't think me daft.
I'll say no more. I will dream of you tonight.

Love,
James

The day dawned clear. There was no mist to burn off and though the air was crisp and cool, the almanac promised a hot and rainless fourth of July.

Mama cautioned, "Leave enough room in the basket for the cake."

Jennie said, "Land sakes, Mama, are we going to feed everyone, or is all this food just for us Wainwrights?"

"Well, I spect there'll be some at the picnic won't have much, so I put in a little extra." Mama wrapped the apple cake in a clean white towel and carefully fitted it into the basket. "Guess that's 'bout all. You girls can take the basket out to the road so's Jeb can load it on his wagon. Min, see to the others while I tidy myself up a bit." Lula hurried up the stairs.

Minnie called after her, "Clint and Hube already left. Clint said he wanted to get to the field early and get us a good table. Come on, Jen, you take one handle and I'll take the other."

"Careful," Jennie said, "it's heavy." They maneuvered the large basket out the front door and down the steps.

"We're just in time," Jennie exclaimed, "here come the Owens'. Look, they put straw hats on Sis and Bro." The girls struggled up to the gate.

"The horses dressed up for the picnic, Mrs. Owen?" Minnie called, "They look right stylish."

"And don't think they don't know it," Clara Owen said. She wore a new dress, the blue print with white daisies.

Jennie said. "Sis and Bro aren't the only ones stylish, Mrs. Owen, your dress turned out pretty."

"Thank ya kindly," Clara smiled, "Pity we didn't get your dress done in time, Min, we coulda gone as look-alikes."

Minnie laughed. "Just as well. I plan on enterin' the pie eatin' contest and no one wears a new dress to eat pie."

Jeb, meantime, had loaded the picnic basket on the wagon.

"Where're the boys?"

Jennie said, "Went on ahead. Clint says he's gonna get us a good table."

Lula tied her poke bonnet on as she came down the steps, Helen running ahead.

Clara gave Lula a hand up beside her and motioned to Helen. "Come sit on my lap, child, make more room for Jennie and Minnie back there."

"She ain't too heavy for you, Clara?"

"Not a bit, Lu." Clara smoothed Helen's hair away from her face. After a moment of straining, the horses got their foothold and started off.

"Sherm and Clay went on ahead too," Clara said, "I don't guess I'll be seeing much of them today 'cept of course to eat. They'll be busy chasin' after the girls more'n likely."

"Sherm, specially," Jeb added. "The dang young'un walks 'round the house love struck most the time. Don't hear half what I say."

"Sherm sweet on someone? Who is it?" Lula asked. Jennie gave Min's arm a squeeze and giggled, and Minnie glared at her to be quiet.

Clara shook her head, "Don't know that it's anyone in particular. Jest his age, I guess."

The road was alive with people headed to the picnic ground. Wagons overflowed with men, women and picnic baskets and throngs of children ran in and about waving small American flags. The air was filled with laughter and shouting.

The wagon pulled off Valley Road onto Cemetery Road, rumbled along a short distance and stopped at the church. Cemetery Road continued adjacent to the field, and at the far end crossed a narrow bridge that spanned Cove Creek and continued up the hill on the far side to the cemetery at the top.

Jeb lined his wagon up with the other wagons alongside the church and everyone piled out.

"Helen," Mama said, "see you can find Clint and Hube and send 'em back to help with the baskets." Helen ran off.

Jeb unhitched the horses and gave them each a gentle slap on the rump to set them galloping off into a small fenced in area of the field to join the other horses, mules and oxen.

Clint and Hube came running towards them, followed by Soldier romping along with them.

"Got us a real good spot, Mama," Clint called. "Helen is sitting on the table mindin' it. Come on, follow me." He and Hube picked up one of the baskets between them and headed off across the field with Lula and Clara following. Minnie caught up with the boys and helped Hube who was struggling to keep up with Clint. Jeb hefted the other basket off the wagon bed and he and Jennie followed the others, carrying it between them.

The picnic field was clipped and trimmed back and set up with roughhewn wooden tables under the big maples that encircled the field. Early arrivals had their tables covered with colored cloths or with sheets clean and bleached from the sun. While the men busied themselves setting up games and horseshoe sites, the ladies, enjoying a day without chores, stood around laughing and talking. The children added their shrieks and laughter to the general bedlam.

Clara spread a checkered cloth on their table and smoothed it down. "Lu, there's Luther with Aunt Pearl. I didn't know he was 'spected home."

"Pearl told me he was gonna try."

Luther looked over at that moment, waved and smiled, and came towards them, Abel perched on his shoulders. He was not a tall man but broad-shouldered with thick muscular arms and for all his sturdy build he carried little extra weight. He had thick red hair and sported a remarkable full beard and moustache, neatly trimmed and combed.

"Mighty good to see y'all," he said as he and Jeb shook hands.

"Good to see you, Luther," Jeb said. "You come home for some of Pearl's biscuits and gravy?"

"Can't deny, Pearl's biscuits call me home every so often."

Lula said, "You could stand to add a few pounds. Looks to me like you ain't been eatin' too good. I know when Dalt comes home I can't hardly fill him up. Matter a fact, I thought Dalton would be coming home too. Did you see him? Did he maybe say anything to you?"

Luther shifted Abel more comfortably on his shoulders. "Don't see much of Dalton at the mines, Lu. He works a different shift than me, but I'll look him up when I get back and see he's all right."

Lula forced a laugh. "Oh, I 'spect he's all right, maybe jest too tired to make the trip."

"That's true enough. I spend most my free time catchin' up on sleep."

Jennie said. "We were all remarking how good Ada looks, Mr. Norris. Doctor Payne's just as pleased as can be."

"My Ada's a fighter. She don't let nuthin' get her down."

Abel grabbed a handful of his father's hair and pulled. Luther winced. "Whoa...I best peel this young'un off my shoulders for he pulls my hair clean outta my head." He stretched up his arms and lifted the squirming child from his shoulders, setting him on his feet. Abel took off at a run. Luther called over his shoulder as he ran after the child, "See y'all later."

"That's a mighty good man. Too bad there ain't someone..." Clara commented.

Lula turned to Clara with a broad smile on her face. "Just the other day, Pearl and I was sayin'...

Jeb broke in. "Ladies, stop right there. Let the man run his own life. Sides, Pearl does jest fine with the children."

Clara sighed. "I wasn't jest thinkin' of the children, Jeb, I was thinkin of Luther too. It would be such a good thing for him. He needs some tender handlin'."

A whistle sounded.

Jennie said, "Sounds like the Preacher is about to start the children's games. Come on, Min, let's go watch."

Min turned to Lula, "You need us here, Mama?"

"No, you go ahead. Just keep an eye on Hube and Helen, see they don't get tramped on. Those older boys get rough sometimes. We'll be over soon's we get settled here."

Jennie and Minnie joined the crowds on the sidelines of the field and soon picked out Hube, Helen and Clint, all ready to take part in the games. The Preacher blew his whistle again, trying to get everyone's attention.

"All right, children, let's quiet down so I can explain the first race. This will be the sack race for boys and girls eight to twelve. Everyone in that age group go down to where Mr. Green is standing and he'll give each one a sack. Climb in the sack and when you all have it tied on securely, line up. Mr. Green will blow a whistle and you'll hop up the field and cross this line here. There's a prize for the first and second ones across." A cheer went up and the youngsters all made a rush for the far end of the field.

Jennie felt someone take her arm and turned to find Sarah grinning at her, holding a chubby little girl by the hand.

"Hey, Sarah, how many of the Proffitts are in this race?"

"Lord knows, Jennie. Josh is only seven, but he thinks he's eight, so he's off and runnin' 'long with Grover and Susie. Got all I kin do to keep Sissy here from tryin' to join 'em."

Jennie leaned down and patted the little blond girl on the head. "You'll be old enough next July picnic, Sissy."

"Don't get her hopes up, Jen, she's only jest three."

Jennie said, "You see Baxter anywhere?"

"Yup. He's here with Gayle somewheres. Ev says she's the prettiest thing ever hit Zionville and he ain't far wrong. She was in the store with Mrs. Combs yesterday and I wuz introduced."

"What did you think of her?"

"She seems nice. Can't tell much from just "hello"."

Sarah's attention went back to the free-for-all in the middle of the field. "Look Jen, Ada's going to try too, and there's Betsey. I don't think it will be fair, there are too many older boys."

Sarah went up on tiptoes to see better. "Grover's the one you gotta watch out for. He's mean as a snake."

Jennie giggled. "What an awful way to describe your own brother."

Sarah pulled Sissy up on her hip and grinned back at Jennie.

"Well, that's what he is."

Lula and Clara joined the girls along with others ready to root for their own. When the whistle sounded, a roar went up and everyone began to shout. Some of the racers fell immediately and struggled to gain their footing while others took off like rabbits, only to tumble further on down the field.

The crowds along the way shouted their support. Halfway through the race everyone could see that Clint Wainwright had the lead, followed closely by little Betsey Norris.

Jennie jumped up and down, "I don't know who to root for."

Sarah, with Sissy sitting on her shoulders, asked, "Where's Josh? Oh God, Jennie, he ain't even left the starting line."

Min shouted above the noise, "Clint's in the lead, come on Clint."

"And here comes Betsey..."

Clint fell over the finish line to a great cheer from the crowd with Betsey close behind.

Sarah took off to the starting line to disentangle Josh from his sack, Sissy jouncing on her shoulders. "See y'all later."

In a few minutes Clint strode proudly through the milling crowd, grinning broadly, holding up a shiny pocket knife.

Jennie took the knife and turned it over in her hands. "That's a mighty fine prize. What did Betsey win?"

"I dunno. I didn't wait to see."

Helen limped up, pouting. "Somebody tripped me or I woulda won. Guess what Betsey's prize was... a pretty hairbrush and know what dopey Betsey did? She gave it to Ada. Said Ada had ought to have the brush 'cause she has the prettiest hair." Helen shook her head in disbelief.

The sack race was followed by the three-legged race and the egg in the teaspoon race, but there were no more winners in either the Wainwright or Norris families.

"Hey, Jennie," Baxter strolled up with Gayle on his arm.

"Hey... been lookin' for you."

Jennie felt a little of the awe she'd felt when she first met Gayle. The girl was dressed in a white blouse with puffed sleeves and over it a pinafore made of polished green cotton, the color matching her eyes exactly. Her hair was gathered on top of her head, in a fountain of curls, with a green ribbon holding it all in place. Jennie's hand went self-consciously to smooth her own hair back.

"Baxter and me just judged the pie eating contest. Goodness, I never saw so many pies disappear so fast."

"That's a fact, Jen. I swear when them kids heard the whistle, they went face first into the pies."

Jennie laughed. "Sure you weren't sampling the pies, Bax? You got cherry juice on your chin."

Gayle turned him around. "I'm not surprised. Here, let me get that, honey." She pulled a white hanky from her bosom, wet it on her tongue, and gently wiped his chin. "There now." She tilted her head to one side and smiled at him. "That's better." She turned back to Jennie and turned the smile on again.

I think I'm gonna throw up, thought Jennie.

Baxter said. "Guess who won. Grady Sykes from Sugar Grove. Remember Grady, Jen? His Pa's the one cheated me outta the appendicitis operation."

Gayle was mystified. "What? What were you cheated out of?"

Baxter said, "Jen'll tell you all about Hode Sykes. I told the Preacher I'd round up people for the egg toss contest. See y'all later." He waved at them as he hurried off.

Gayle looked at Jennie expectantly. Jennie said. "Oh, it was just one night Baxter and Dr. Payne were called to Sugar Grove to help Hode Sykes who was having a problem. Doc thought it might be appendicitis, but it turned out to be indigestion. Ever since, Baxter jokes about Sykes having cheated him out of an appendicitis operation."

Jennie started to stroll towards the egg toss site and Gayle followed along. Gayle said. "I was *thrilled* to hear Baxter's going to be a doctor."

"It will take a lot of hard work, but it's what he's wanted all his life."

"Hard work, of course, but I know Baxter can do it. He'll make a wonderful doctor."

Jennie glanced sideways at her. *Just how do you know that? You only just met him.*

Gayle continued, "I understand there is a real need for doctors all around the country. Why he could go just about anywhere and make *oodles* of money."

Jennie stopped, causing Gayle to stop too. "But Baxter already knows where he's going to practice medicine. Right here in Zionville."

Gayle took the white hanky from her bosom again and gently patted the perspiration from her forehead. "Well, that's what he says now... but who knows?"

Jennie said impatiently, "Doctor Payne is paying for his education and that was one of the provisions, that he would come back to Zionville to practice medicine. Baxter would never go back on his word. "

Gayle used the white hanky to fan herself. "Don't you know that old saying, Jennie, promises are made to be broken?... Oh don't look so stricken, I'm only teasing."

"Sorry, but some things just aren't funny. If you know Baxter at all, and of course you don't since you just met him, you'd know he would never break a promise, especially to Doctor Payne."

They continued walking. Gayle said, "My, my, you do get huffy on the subject don't you. But I am curious. Why would anyone waste years of medical training in a backwoods community like Zionville? Forgive me for saying so, Jennie, but a practice in the big city would be so much more of a... of a challenge for him. Don't you agree?"

Jennie stopped again and faced Gayle, her mouth open. Gayle dropped her head to one side and smiled, all innocence. "Well, don't you?"

Jennie tried hard not to show her annoyance. "He'll get all the challenge he can handle right here in Zionville."

"Not near as much as he would get in, say, Canton."

Jennie refused to argue with her and they continued to the egg toss site. Prosper was explaining to everyone what the egg toss contest was. "Couples line up here, facing each other, and toss an egg between them. Last couple with an unbroken egg wins."

Gayle, with the ever-present smile, said, "Sounds easy. Are we going to enter, Baxter?"

Baxter turned to her in surprise. "You think you can do it?"

Gayle gave Jennie a smug look. "Of course. What can be hard about tossing an egg?"

"Easy as eatin' pie," Jennie said.

Baxter took Gayle by the arm. "Well, if you're sure. Come on."

Jennie watched them line up with the others. She thought idly that last year she was Baxter's partner. There were about fifteen couples, among them Emmaline and Jacob, Minnie and Sherm, Sarah and her brother Randall. At the last minute Prosper pushed Aunt Pearl and Buelis from the sidelines into the group. Buelis laughed. "Lordy, I know how to cook an egg, don't know much about tossin' one."

Buelis Green was an attractive woman of forty, big and solid with thick chestnut hair which she wore plaited and wrapped around her head. Little wisps of hair escaped, forming a fringe around her face, softening sharp features. She was well-liked, but most everyone agreed it was hard to take her constant prattle. Her taste in clothes ran to the bizarre.

Prosper passed out the eggs. "Now y'all just toss the egg to each other, and after each toss, you go back a step. The couple left with the unbroken egg is the winner. Ready?"

The contest began and the eggs began to fly. Baxter called out. "Ready, Gayle? Here it comes."

Gayle held out her hands and the egg passed right through them to splatter in a mess of egg shells and egg yolk down the front of her pinafore. "Oh dear... Oh, Baxter. Look what you've done!"

Jennie kept a straight face. *Even in a backwoods community like Zionville, we know how to catch an egg.*

✉

Food appeared on the tables; platters of cold fried chicken, bean salad and slaw, biscuits and pots of jam, cakes and jugs of cider and grape juice that had been cooling in the icy creek water.

The shouting was reduced to contented murmurs as everyone settled down to eat. After the meal, the little ones were coaxed onto blankets for a nap and the older ones played ball or splashed around in the creek. The men congregated for the tug of war and the ladies sought each other out to catch up on the latest gossip.

Lula and Clara strolled over to sit with Pearl, who dozed placidly in her rocking chair. Jennie sat on a blanket at her feet, Ada asleep in her lap, Iva Lee and Abel stretched out for naps at her feet.

"Well look at you, Pearl, all the comforts a' home," Lula said.

Pearl opened her eyes and greeted them. "Yes, Luther said I wouldn't last the day out sittin' on a puny bench so he packed up my rocker. Come, set a spell."

Lula motioned to Ada. "The child all right?"

Jennie gently stroked Ada's hair. "Aunt Pearl convinced all three they would go home before the bonfire tonight if they didn't take a rest."

Buelis and Frenda Combs strolled up. "Mind we join y'all?"

The ladies greeted each other and Lula and Clara made room for them on the benches. "Feels good in the shade," Buelis said. "Don't know how the menfolk can stay out in that sun."

"Spendin' all their energy on pullin' a rope," Lula added.

Pearl said. "Well, they's all young'uns at heart. Tellin' time is tomorrow when they come up with sore muscles and backaches."

"Did y'all hear about the egg toss?" grinned Buelis. "Me and Pearl won, can you beat it?"

Lula said with a straight face, "What? The egg?"

Buelis looked confused and Lula laughed. "That's called a pun, Buelis. You know, beat it?... the egg?"

The joke dawned on Buelis and she laughed loud enough to rouse Abel. They all watched in silence as he sat up for a second or two and then flopped down again. Buelis put her hand over her mouth. "Sorry," she said.

"Gayle missed the egg Baxter threw," Jennie said, "and made Baxter take her home. Said he threw the egg too hard."

"I heard," Lula said. "All over her pretty pinafore." She turned to Frenda. "How is she enjoying her visit?"

"Humph. Girl's uppity as sin. Don't know why it is, but city folk seem ta look down on country folk. You ever notice that?" Frenda Combs was tall and thin with sharp features, a long nose and small mouth. Her iron grey hair was pulled back in the same bun most of the women wore. She seemed a stern woman, but Baxter got along with her well.

"Don't like to complain, her being s'far from her Mama, but the young'un don't do much. Don't seem to have much energy 'cept fer sittin' on the porch, and mebbe walkin' to the store."

Clara nodded. "Effie Proffitt says she comes in the store most every day."

Frenda continued, "I kindly wish the girl would help me in the garden, but she says she don't know a thing about it."

Buelis fanned herself with her bonnet. "Is she homesick mebbe?"

"Don't seem to be. Baxter and her have their heads together all the time. Hafta keep remindin' Gayle that Baxter has chores. He can't set on the porch swing and visit all day."

Jennie felt a twinge of jealousy. *Hmmm. Doesn't find the time to visit me anymore.*

Pearl said to Lula. "Speakin' a visitin', how come Dalton ain't here today?"

Lula said, offhandedly, "Couldn't get home." The women looked at each other but said nothing.

"Say, Buelis," Clara said, "seems I heard something about Jacob Wooding proposing to Emmaline Fenley. Is that right?"

Buelis grinned, "Well, let me tell you." Buelis leaned into the group. "You know Emma and Jacob have been seein' each other regular for most two years now, but Jacob never seemed in a hurry to put the question to her."

Pearl nodded. "Even Cora, her own Mama, says she wished they'd make up their minds one way or 'nother."

"Well," Buelis continued, "seems Prosper's been stoppin' by the Fenley house to visit and it slowly dawned on Cora that he was stoppin' by to visit Emmaline, not her and Otis."

Buelis paused to enjoy the moment. "Anyway, one night last week, Cora says, Emmaline uz sittin' out on the porch when Prosper comes by and joins her on the swing. Cora kept peekin' out at them and notices Prosper has his arm stretched out along the back of the swing around Emmaline and they uz jest talkin', quiet like."

Buelis paused again. Lula was exasperated. "For goodness sakes, Buelis, go on."

"Well, after a time, here comes Jacob up the walk. Now, Cora says, she wuz 'bout glued to the window. Jacob stops short seein' Prosper with his arm around Emmaline. He takes the steps two at a time and grabs Prosper by the front of his shirt and hauls him right off the swing, which wuz quite a job since Prosper must outweigh Jacob by 'bout a hundred pounds."

Clara gasped, "Lord a mercy."

Pearl stopped rocking. "Then what?"

"Cora couldn't hear exactly what was said, but it was somethin' like... I don't care if you are the Preacher, you keep your hands off Emmaline and your ass off this porch."

The ladies were shocked and Buelis was enjoying herself.

"Cora says Prosper, always the gentleman, says 'if the lady wants me to go, I will, but you aren't telling me what to do.' Then Otis gets all nervous like and goes out on the porch to smooth things over and he says Prosper apologized for causing any disturbance and goes home."

Clara said, disappointed, "That's it?"

Buelis grinned. "No, the best part is it weren't maybe half an hour, Emma and Jacob come in all smiles like to tell them they uz engaged."

"Well," Lula said, "guess Emmaline can thank Prosper fer stirrin' the pot."

Buelis laughed and slapped her huge thigh. "I say anyone wuz to be thankful it'd be Prosper. He coulda ended up with Emmaline."

✉

Jennie lay on her stomach on the grass, her eyes closed. She thought of James' letter. *He pays me the best, most personal kind of compliment and then says 'don't think me daft'. Are we in love?* Suddenly thoughts of her conversation with Min popped into her mind. *I can't explain what love is to myself, how can I possibly explain it to Min?*

She rolled on her back, keeping her eyes closed, thinking of her answer to James' letter...

How do I know what love is, James? I know I love the way
you write, funny and interesting. I know I worry about you
being in danger all the time and the cruel conditions you live
in. I am warmed by your tender ways with others, Ed in
particular. I am excited and breathless when I hold one of your
letters in my hand before opening it... so does all this add up
to love? If so then surely, I must be in love. And so to answer
your question, yes, you must come to Zionville after the war...

"Whatcha smilin' at, Jennie?"

Jennie opened her eyes. "Hey, Baxter." She sat up and rearranged her dress. "Just smilin', is all. Did Gayle come back with you?"

"No. Says she had 'nuff picnic for one day. Says her dress is ruined and she blames me. Wouldn't even listen when I tried to apologize."

"She'll get over it. Come on, sit down by me. You want anything to eat?"

"Lord, no. I'm stuffed."

"So," Jennie said, "How come you're not in the horseshoe contest?"

"I been eliminated already."

"Not much for horseshoes, huh?" Jennie broke off a blade of grass and began to nibble on it. "How's it going with Doc?"

Baxter's face lit up. "We read somethin' in one of his journals 'bout how they don't use splints anymore. The latest way to protect a broken limb is a plaster cast. You soak a lot of bandage in wet plaster and wind it round and round the limb and when it dries it's hard as stone."

"Nobody round here's ever had one."

"I know, and you see how poor the limbs heal with just the splints. You tell a body to stay off a broken leg and it ain't possible for them to do that, but if the limb is in a plaster cast, they can still move round pretty good. Doc says he's gonna look into it."

Baxter was intense and serious. He'd been that way since they'd both started first grade. Because he was undersized and his brothers' hand-down clothes fit so poorly, he made a great target for teasing. It was about the time the two children were in fourth grade that Jennie saw something in Baxter the other boys lacked, a sweetness and caring and the ability to forgive the cruelest jokes... even laughing at himself sometimes.

They'd begun to walk home from school together; there was always something to talk about, especially when they began tagging after Doctor Payne.

Baxter caught her staring and flushed. "Guess I get carried away sometimes, don't I?"

His hair was in his eyes and she reached out and smoothed it back from his forehead. "Don't make your life all work, Baxter. A body needs to relax once in awhile."

"That's what Doc says. But you know, Jen, I don't think of medicine as work. I can't tell you what a good feeling I get when someone stops hurting because of something I did... or I guess I should say something Doc did since he tells me what to do. But I'm learning."

A comfortable silence fell between them.

"Papaw talked to Jeb Owen about selling him that property between our farms, Bax. Looks like there will be enough money for me to go to nursing school."

Baxter looked surprised. "Jen, that's great." When she didn't respond he said, "it is, isn't it?"

"Well it certainly answers the biggest problem, but there is another problem... Papa. You remember what he said that night on the porch... and Mama won't give her blessings unless Papa thinks I should go."

"So what are you gonna do?"

"I'm going to start sending away to nursing schools for information. For Mama's sake, I'd like to have Papa's permission, but with or without it, I'm going to school."

Baxter nodded. "Good. You need help, Jen, you let me know."

Jennie smiled, "I will." After a moment she asked, not looking at him. "You ever thought maybe you'd rather practice medicine somewhere else; maybe like in Charlotte... or Canton?"

Baxter looked shocked. "Jen, you know me and Doc always talk about when I come back here to practice. You know that. How come you ask such a thing?"

"I was just wondering. You could probably make a lot more money in Charlotte." She looked up and waited.

"Don't you think I thought all about that? But money ain't the reason... Golly, Jen, I don't know why you're talking this way. We always... besides, I owe Doc Payne so much. Everything in fact. If it wasn't for Doc..."

Jennie started to laugh. "Baxter, don't carry on so. I was just asking."

"Funny, you asking that. Gayle asked the same thing."

"Oh? And you told her just what you told me?"

"Of course."

"And she didn't tell you you could make *oodles* of money elsewhere, that you need challenges in your life?"

"You and Gayle been talkin' about me, Jen?"

"As a matter of fact, yes. And it sounds to me like she's trying to put a bug in your ear about maybe going to Charlotte to practice medicine."

"How could she do that? I already promised Doc I would come back to Zionville."

"Just remember that." Jennie looked at him solemnly.

Baxter's face was serious. "You don't like her much, do you?"

"I don't know her well enough to like or dislike her, Bax. Neither do you."

"Oh I think I know her pretty good, Jen. We been sittin' up talkin' most every night and it ain't all about me bein' a doctor. She confided in me, and I don't want you to repeat this to anyone, Jen, that her bein' so pretty is sort of a curse. She get's a lot of unwanted attention, from men, and her bein' so innocent and all, she don't know how to handle it."

Jennie wanted badly to laugh. But she didn't dare. Baxter was serious and she knew better than to make him feel foolish. Of all the self-absorbed nonsense! "Well, she is pretty, Bax, I'll say that, but as far as not being able to handle some man getting familiar..."

"But that's you, Jen. You could handle it fine, I know you could. But Gayle's so little and dainty and scared of men. 'Sides, she's here all alone away from her family and friends. I wish you would kinda look out for her, that is when I'm not around."

Jennie bit her tongue. Now was not the time to say anything about the letters Sarah said Gayle was getting. Baxter was too captivated by Gayle to listen to reason, but given time, she was sure Gayle would cook her own goose. Meantime... "All right, Bax. I'll keep an eye on her."

Baxter was noticeably relieved. "Great, Jen. I knew I could count on you... Gayle too."

"No more talking, Baxter, let's go find Min and Sherm."

Afternoon wore on and evening set in, with katydids and crickets welcoming the dusk. Children made a contest of seeing who could catch the most fireflies. Exhausted mothers coaxed tired and fretful babies onto their laps. A great bonfire was built in the center of the field and the people gathered around, sitting comfortably in groups. A guitar began strumming, feet began tapping and Frenda Combs got up to conduct the singing.

"I wish I had a big fine horse
And corn to feed him on
And Shady Grove to stay at home
And feed him while I'm gone."

Ben called out, "Now let's jest hear from the ladies."

"Shady Grove my little love
Shady Grove I say
Shady Grove my little love
I'm bound to go away."

Jeb Owen took up the chorus.

"Went to see my Shady Grove
She was standing in the door
Her shoes and stockin's in her hand
And her little bare feet on the floor."

"Now let's hear how loud the menfolk kin sing."

"Shady Grove my little love
Shady Grove I say
Shady Grove my little love
I'm bound to go away."

Buelis got to her feet.

"A kiss from pretty little Shady Grove
Is sweet as brandy wine
And ain't no girl in this old world
That's prettier than mine."

"Everybody sing: Shady Grove my little love..."

The young folk could contain themselves no longer. They jumped to their feet and danced around the campfire with much stamping of feet and 'yahooing'.

One song led to another and then another. The dusk deepened into a velvet dark and sparks from the bonfire lifted bright as the fireflies into the night sky. Finally the exhausted dancers settled down and the tones of a dulcimer drifted over the tired picnickers. A young boy stood and started to sing and the dulcimer took up the melody. The young voice rose sad and clear on the night air.

"Hug me close dear mother closer
Put your arms around me tight
For I'm cold and tired dear mother
And I feel so strange tonight."

Several other voices joined in, singing harmony.

"All day long while you were working
As I lay upon my bed
I was trying to be patient
And think of what you said

How our King, oh blessed Jesus
How He loves His lambs to keep
And I wish He'd come and take me
In His arms that I might sleep.

Just before the lamps were lighted
Just before the children came
While the room was still and quiet
I heard someone call my name.

131

All at once a window opened
On a field of lambs and sheep
Some were at the brook a-drinking
Some were lying fast asleep.

In a moment I was looking
On a world so bright and fair
Which was filled with little children
And they seemed so happy there.

And the mother pressed her darling
close to her own dear burning breast
To the heart so near broken
Lay the child so near at rest.

At the solemn hour of midnight
In the dark and lonesome deep
Lying on her mother's bosom
Little Bessie fell asleep

Come up here little Bessie
Here and live with me
Where little children never suffer
In the long eternity..."

The last notes slowly faded and were finally lost on the night breeze. Jennie sat unmoving, unable to shake the words. Her eyes searched the crowds and settled on Luther Norris. He sat cross legged on the ground with Ada in his lap. His head was bent over hers and he was weeping. Jennie felt a shiver run down her spine.

Jeb's wagon stopped at the Wainwright gate and the tired Wainwright family trooped up the walk, Clint carrying the empty picnic basket. As they got to the porch steps a figure moved out of the shadows.
It was Papa.

Chapter Thirteen
Gayle's Plan

It was late afternoon and Jennie sat wearily on the porch swing. Today had been a canning day (forty-eight jars of beans!) and her feet were sore from standing. Mama was still at the Owens' with Helen and Min, and goodness only knew where the boys were.

And Papa? It was a blessing he didn't spend much time around the house. But one thing rankled her. He'd been home almost a month and in all that time Mama had not approached him with Papaw's plan to get her the money for school. So it was up to her to do the job herself. The thought of facing Papa wasn't pleasant, but there was no way around it. So... the very next opportunity she would ask... no, tell... Papa of her plans. Mama would *have* to accept it.

There was one thing they were all thankful for, however. When Soldier, who knew only that Papa was a member of the household (good or bad), bounded up to greet him, they all held their breath. Papa merely looked down at the dog, gave Mama a scathing look, and walked away. Soldier, still wagging his tail and insisting on a greeting, would have followed Papa but for Hubie who distracted him into a game of 'you can't catch me'.

Jennie decided to go to the spring and wash off the grime of the day. Might as well get a pail of water while she was there. She rounded the corner of the house, picked up a bucket and headed for the spring.

The cows were grazing in the pasture and the calf was nuzzling Lizzie to nurse. The calf would be joining Jeb's herd in another few weeks and Clint would continue to argue, to the last minute, that they could handle another cow. Clint felt like Mama was selling one of his children.

She ran along the fence, swinging the bucket in a wide arc and stopped short within a few feet of the log bridge. Min and Sherm sat close together on the rock, talking and giggling. Jennie crossed the bridge and stood over them. "Minnie? What are you doing out here? I thought you were with Mama and Helen visiting Mrs. Owen."

Minnie looked up innocently. "Hey, Jennie. Sherm and me wuz talkin'." In the silence that followed a locust sounded its long mournful song, starting softly and rising then falling away into silence.

Jennie put the bucket down and sat beside them. "I don't think this is a good idea..."

"I know, Jennie, I know, but Sherm said he had something for me and..."

"I jest wanted to give Min a present fer her birthday. See? It's a locket." Minnie reached up to her neck and cradled the locket in her hand so Jennie could see it.

"Yes, it's very pretty, Sherm, but you could just as well have come to the house to give it to her. Couldn't you?"

He cleared his throat. "Yeah, I guess, but I didn't want no one seein' me give a girl a present, is all."

"And where did you tell Mama you were gonna be, Min?"

Minnie shrugged. "Mama didn't ask, so I didn't tell her."

"Well," Jennie stood up, trying not to show her exasperation, "It's most supper time. Come on. Help me fill the bucket, Min, and we'll go back together."

Sherm and Minnie stood up and faced each other. Minnie said, "I purely thank ya, Sherm. I'll never take the locket off, not even when I take a bath."

They left Sherm standing on the rock. Minnie turned and waved at him. Halfway back to the house Jennie said, "Didn't you ask me how you should handle your feelings about Sherm, Min? And what did I tell you? I told you it would be best if you didn't see him alone. So how come I find you and him alone, way out by the creek?"

"You heard him, Jennie, he was embarrassed 'less someone see him give a girl a present is all." She looked down at the locket. "Sure is pretty, ain't it?"

Jennie shook her head and they walked the last few feet to the back porch in silence.

⊠

Papa seemed to be several different men. Moody and silent when he was cold sober, he spoke only when he had to. When he had a little liquor in him, he was talkative, sometimes funny, maybe a little quarrelsome. But when he was drunk he was mean and nasty and looked for reasons to be angry. When the girls entered the kitchen, they found Papa alone, sitting in Mama's rocker. They noticed he had been drinking, but he looked up and smiled. His jug sat beside the rocker.

He's smiling, Jennie thought. Maybe this would be the time to talk to Papa. He just might listen if she presented it right. She sat down on the sofa opposite him, her stomach in knots.

Papa reached for his jug and took a long drink from it, then balanced it on his knee. "Where's yer mother?"

Jennie said. "Over to the Owens, I think."

"Min," Papa called. "Go over, get yer mother. This is my last night home. Time there was dinner on the table."

He's leaving tomorrow. I've got to say something now.

"All right, Papa." The door closed behind Minnie.

Jennie fought with herself, wondering if she should put the conversation off. Finally she said, "Papa, did you know Papaw is thinking of selling that piece of land between our place and the Owen place to Jeb Owen?"

Papa took another short drink and balanced the jug on his knee again. He wasn't smiling any more. His eyes were slits... red and watery. He stared at Jennie. *Maybe this isn't a good time after all.*

"What'd he wanna do that fer?" His words were slurring.

I misjudged. He's drunker than I thought. She plunged on.

"Well, Mr. Owen offered him a good price and Papaw said he'd think about it." Papa continued to stare at her. *Oh God... Oh God...*

"And jus.. jus what do Mylart need money fer?"

Lula bustled in the door, followed by Min and Helen and the boys. "I wuz jest comin' up the walk as Min wuz comin' to get me, Dalt. I'll get supper on the table right now, Come on girls, give me a hand."

Stifling a sigh of relief, Jennie rose quickly from the sofa and made a big production of looking for her apron.

Jennie sat on the gate, trying to keep her balance. Supper had been a quiet affair. Even Hubie kept his attention focused on his plate and when the meal was over, Papa fell on the sofa and within minutes was snoring loudly. There was no way Jennie was going to be able to talk to him tonight (not in the condition he was in) so she would have to confront him in the morning no matter what. There wouldn't be another opportunity.

It really didn't matter to her one way or the other what Papa said, she was going to school anyway, but for Mama's sake Papa had to be told.

She looked up and was surprised to see Gayle walking down the road towards her. Baxter was nowhere to be seen.

"Hey, Gayle. You out walking all alone? Where is Bax?"

Gayle wore her green pinafore. Jennie noticed there were no stains on it, but Gayle didn't look quite as well groomed as usual.

"Hello, Jennie." She looked around as if to be sure they were alone. "Baxter has chores. Do you have some time to talk to me? It's important."

Jennie slid down from the gate. "Sure. You want to go up on the porch and sit?"

Gayle said, "No ... no, I don't think so. Let's just walk a ways down the road."

They turned and started walking. After a few moments of silence Jennie said, "Something wrong? You look so serious."

Gayle took a deep breath. "Well, it's just... look, Jennie, I can't talk to anyone else. I'm hoping you will help me."

Jennie nodded, encouraging Gayle to go on.

"Well, back in Canton, there is this man I worked with, actually I worked for him, he was my boss. He's been writing me letters and saying he's going to come to Zionville to get me."

Jennie halted. Gayle stopped too. They faced each other. Jennie said. "To get you... does he mean it in a threatening way, or...?"

"No, no, he means he wants to carry me off."

Jennie tried to read Gayle's expression. "Carry you off like... like a knight on a white horse?"

Gayle smiled. "Something like that. He claims he's in love with me and can't live without me. It's the reason I came to Zionville, to get away from him."

"Have you told Baxter and his folks? We can get the sheriff from the next county to..."

"No, no. I don't want anyone to know. Particularly Baxter and his parents."

"Why not? It would seem logical to me to turn to them first."

"Well, I don't want to get them involved. They've been so kind. I don't want to repay them with a lot of trouble..."

"I don't understand, Gayle, what is it you expect me to do?"

Gayle nervously ran a hand through her hair. "Well, here's what I thought. Maybe you and I can go into Boone one day, like you know, shopping, and then I'll take the train..."

"To where? Back to Canton?"

Gayle hesitated a split second. "Yes. I think I can handle Josh... that is, I can handle things better from home."

They started walking again. Something wasn't right. This didn't tie in with what Baxter said. He said she was shy and frightened of men because of their unwanted attention. But would any man be so persistent without any encouragement at all? "What was the sense in coming to Zionville in the first place?"

"I just thought he would give up, but it seems... it seems like my going away has just fueled the fire."

Jennie slowly nodded. "And you -- you don't return his feelings?"

Gayle said without a pause, "I loathe him."

Jennie thought her expression didn't quite go with the strong words. "Well, you'll have to give me some time to think about this, Gayle, it means we'll have to lie."

Gayle took Jennie's hand. "I know I'm asking a lot, Jennie, but it's so important. I'm so frightened. Don't take too long."

Jennie nodded weakly.

"And not a word to anyone, promise?"

"Yes... yes, I promise."

$$\boxtimes$$

Jennie didn't sleep well that night. What in the world was she going to do? She'd promised she wouldn't say anything to anyone, and that meant she couldn't even talk it over with Baxter. Gayle particularly didn't want Baxter to know. And why not? According to Frenda Combs, Gayle and Baxter spent every evening with their heads together so why not ask Baxter to help her? If she did what Gayle suggested, it meant lying to a lot of people, and lying was something Jennie never did. She wasn't even sure she believed the story. Something just didn't ring true.

And then there was the conversation she planned to have with Papa in the morning. Jennie tossed and turned.

Minnie lifted her head. "What's the matter with you tonight, Jennie. You're bouncin' around so much I can't get to sleep."

"Sorry, Min. Must be somethin' I ate."

$$\boxtimes$$

Papa came down the stairs carrying his satchel. He wore clean pants and a white shirt with the sleeves rolled up. His curly black hair was neatly combed and he looked, surprisingly, well rested.

"Hube, you wait on the porch and tell me when Prosper's wagon is comin' down the road and I'll give you a penny."

Hubie pushed away from the table, almost knocking the chair over, and scurried out the door. Jennie turned from the sink at Papa's voice. *It's now or never.*

Lula came from the stove with a steaming bowl of grits and a large pan of cornbread. "You'll need somethin' warm in your stomach, Dalton, there's a bit of a chill in the air." She brought a pot of coffee to the table and filled his cup. Dalton dropped his satchel by the door and came back to sit at the table.

Jennie said, hesitantly, "Papa?"

Dalton poured milk over his grits and turned to Jennie with raised eyebrows. Jennie took this to mean she had his attention.

"Papa, we talked about this in the past..."

Lula interrupted. "Not now, Jennie, your Papa is almost out the door. This ain't the time." Mama was wringing her hands and Jennie felt sorry for her, but it had to be said sooner or later.

Who knew when Papa would be home again?

Jennie took Mama's hand and squeezed it. She turned back to Papa and continued. "We talked about my going to nursing school in the past and you didn't see how we would be able to afford it, but Papaw has sold that strip of land between our place and the Owen's place to Jeb Owen, and he said I could use that money for schooling."

Papa ate his grits in silence, never raising his eyes to Jennie. Jennie thought this was a good sign. "So, if you were worried about where the money would come from..."

The only sound in the room was Papa's spoon against the bowl. Jennie looked at Mama and Mama shrugged. They both watched in uncomfortable silence until he was finished. He scraped the bowl clean and wiped his mouth on the back of his hand, leaned back in his chair—balancing on the two back legs—and stared up at Jennie. He continued to stare for another moment or two. Jennie tried hard to meet his gaze without wavering. *He's playing a game.*

Finally he said, "What makes you think it's about money?"

Jennie was confused. "Well, I thought..."

"Truth is, girl, it ain't 'bout money at all. What it is about is, I don't particular like you makin' all these big decisions without my say so." He brought the front legs of the chair down with a clunk, reached for a slice of cornbread, took a huge bite, chewed and swallowed. "And I don't particular like you goin' behind my back and gettin' your Papaw to finance this big idea of yours."

He brought the coffee cup up to his lips and blew on the coffee before taking a sip, watching Jennie over the rim. "You see, girl, a man what is a man, is in control of his household." He turned and very pointedly looked at Lula, with a strange smile on his face. Lula opened her mouth and Dalton raised his hand for silence. He turned back to Jennie.

"No, it ain't money I'm concerned with." He put the last bite of cornbread into his mouth and again chewed and swallowed, before continuing. "It's more like I'm concerned with you showin' the proper respect for authority."

Jennie remained silent. *Where is this conversation going?*

He went on. "And what exactly does authority mean? It means putting all the facts in front of your Papa and letting him decide the right and wrong of it. Now in this case, your going off to school ain't right. I've decided it ain't right for one child to get everything while her brothers and sisters get nothing."

"What...?"

Papa held up his hand again for silence. He got up and carefully pushed the chair back under the table and stood over Jennie, so close she had to look up at him. "It also means not interferin' when your Papa is dealin' out discipline."

At the word discipline Jennie nodded her head in understanding. *Ahh! So that's what this is all about.* Now she was angry. How could the man be so small-minded? The adrenaline began to flow. She took a small step back so she could look more easily into his eyes, and said in as calm a voice as she could muster.

"Let me understand, Papa. You mean you would begrudge me an education that would benefit everyone in this family, because I stepped in and prevented you from unjustly beating a boy one-third your size to a bloody pulp. Is that what this is about?"

Papa smiled broadly and shook his head. "Jennie, Jennie, Jennie. You use the word prevent. See that's what I'm talkin' about. You're the child—I'm the Papa. It's my place to make the decisions about everything, whether it be going to school, or seein' the children mind their Papa."

Jennie was seething. She stumbled over her words. "And do you think... what makes you think... ohh, I really don't care what you think. Papaw has the money for me and I *am* going to school."

Hubie stuck his head in the door. "Mr. Truall's wagon is comin' down the road."

Dalton shook his head as if it was a waste of time to try to get through to a dull child. He turned his back on Jennie and picked up his satchel. "We'll see, girl, we'll see." He turned and beamed a warm smile at them before he went out the door. "Thank you Lu, that was a mighty fine breakfast."

Chapter Fourteen
The Camp Meeting

The Canadians, Australians, and New Zealanders (known as shock troops because of their aggression and initiative) were ordered to join the British Fourth Army under the command of General Sir Henry Rawlinson. Their objective was an attack east of Amiens to drive the enemy away from the vital Paris-Amiens-Calais railway.

Days before the attack, Allied air fighters engaged German reconnaissance planes to draw attention from the ground movement. False radio traffic (which pinpointed the Canadians in their old position) was sent out. Every aspect of the upcoming attack was wrapped in secrecy.

At 4:20 A.M., the morning of August 8, 1918, mist thickened along the front. The bombardment began. Behind the curtain of fire and steel, the troops moved forward over the German position. Amid the shifting mist and smoke, the enemy collapsed.

"For God's sake, Irish, come down off that cloud. You're gonna get yerself killed."

"Yer right, Bucko." James did a little jig before flopping down beside Pete in the trench. "Won't do to get too confident, but we have the Germans on the run. They've all but given up and there's victory in the air... don't you smell it?" James wrinkled his nose. "Well I smell something... maybe it isn't victory. What the hell is that smell?"

Pete looked defensive. "Don't smell that bad. It's my socks. I'm washin' them here in my helmet..."

My Dearest Jen,

I feel we are moving closer to the end. I can't say much, and perhaps even this will be censored, but the thought I may meet you one day soon, has my spirits soaring.

We've been on the move, so there's been no mail for some time. I'm waiting patiently to hear your thoughts on my last letter. I hope I didn't shock you, lass, and I think I almost know what you are thinking. A lad away in the war, grasping at any kind word and twisting it into what he wants it to mean. I'll admit, it may be in part true. Your letters do take me to a better place, but it's more, Jen. All my mates carry pictures. Your picture alone stirs up feelings I've never had before and if you agree, lassie, I'll come to Zionville to find out what those feelings are.

I'll meet you tonight in my dreams.

Love, James

The sun sank out of sight leaving only its rays to reach up from below the rim of Snake Mountain and streak across the sky, shading the undersides of the clouds a mix of rose and purple. Already the heat of day was beginning to dissolve into the cool of evening.

The dusty road was crowded with wagons creaking along at a slow pace, overflowing with ladies sitting primly in their Sunday-best prints with babies in their laps, young girls smoothing out nonexistent wrinkles in ruffled pinafores and men in go-to-meetin' shirts and trousers.

As well as the wagons, there were people on foot. Young ones were herded along in front of their Mamas and Papas where they could be managed while little ones, unable to walk, rode comfortably on the shoulders of the young and strong. Noisy boys dressed in knickers and bow ties ran around the wagons, scuffing up clouds of dust with their newly shined shoes.

The evening was alive with people laughing and waving and calling back and forth in a mood of celebration. All hurried along the road to the field adjacent to the Baptist church where an impressive blue and white striped tent waited in the twilight to receive them. It was "camp meeting" time.

Jennie and Minnie walked side by side, Jennie tall and slender in her new blue print dress and Minnie in her new daisy print with a matching ribbon in her hair. Lula walked behind. With one hand she checked the bun at the nape of her neck to ensure that it was still in place and then glanced down to see that all the buttons down the front of her long black skirt were still intact. Her shirtwaist was white starched cotton with long sleeves and a small round collar that fastened under her chin.

She held Hube's hand firmly. He was dressed in Clint's outgrown dark blue serge knickers and white shirt, both clean and mended. His hair, so carefully slicked down with water before leaving the house, was now curling around his shoulders. He was still sulking. He had argued in favor of his overalls, but his Mama held firm. Helen, in direct contrast, skipped along by Lula's side, happy to wear Minnie's hand-me-down pink dress. The added ruffle made it brand new. She whirled around every other step admiring the way it swung out. Minnie had tied one of her own ribbons in Helen's long straight hair.

Hube was complaining. "Mama, if my friends see you holdin' my hand, they's gonna josh me fierce. Ain't it enuff I'm wearin' these here ole knickers?"

Lula dropped his hand. "Well then, jest you mind and stay close... there's Buelis and Harley."

Jennie followed Mama's gaze. "Oh no," she said under her breath and nudged Minnie with her elbow to look.

Minnie gasped. "Mama, I can't believe a body would go out in public looking like that." Buelis wore a dress of orange plaid material topped off by a jacket of startling blue.

Mama grinned. "You can sure see Buelis comin' aways off what with them outlandish clothes she wears. She don't give a never mind what anyone says. Guess you have to give her credit for that."

Minnie continued to stare. "I give Mr. Green credit fer jest walkin' by her side."

"Don't be disrespectful, child," Mama said, suppressing a smile. At that moment Buelis spied the Wainwrights and headed towards them, calling and waving as she came.

"Evenin' y'all." She fell into step with Lula and began talking immediately.

Jennie grinned at Harley, who seemed content to walk behind, the smoke from his pipe curling up around his head and disappearing in the light evening air. He winked at Jennie.

Buelis was gushing, "I was saying the other day to Harley, wonder when Dr. Pierce would be comin' round to preach again and don't you know Reverend Truall stops by to tell us 'bout the camp meeting... ain't that right, Harley?" Not waiting for his answer, she continued, "A rousing camp meetin' makes me feel so good. It carries me along for days after." She paused to take a breath. "It don't make no difference we ain't Baptists it's the word of God no matter who says it. Ain't that right?"

Minnie whispered, "I'm surprised she stops to breathe."

Buelis continued, "Why, there's Pearl and her young'uns. Wasn't it good to see Luther with his children at the picnic? It's a shame he wuzn't able to stay fer the meetin', but Pearl says he ain't paid 'less he puts in the time at the mines."

She rattled on, "Harley and me thought maybe we'd see Dalton this evenin', Lu."

"Dalton left two days ago," Mama looked busily around. "Now where did that Hubie get to? I told him to stay right here by me and now he's off and gone."

Jennie looked over her shoulder at Mama and sensed her exasperation with Buelis. Mama never discussed Papa's actions with anyone if she could help it. Problem was, Buelis asked so many questions. But it looked like this time Mama had been successful in distracting her.

Buelis took Lula firmly by the arm and steered her along. "Little'uns that age don't seem to stay put, now do they? Come on, Lu. He can't get into a whole lot of trouble at a camp meetin'. We'll find him inside." Without Hube to fuss over, Lula reached down, grabbed Helen's hand and dragged her along.

The tent was not large, perhaps 30 x 50 feet. Guide ropes ran from the sides of the tent outward to spikes hammered into the ground. Inside the tent sturdy posts, spaced ten feet apart, ran the length of the tent down its center and stretched the tent upward to a height of 20 feet. A center aisle ran front to back.

The entrance flaps were thrown open and light from kerosene lanterns attached to each post spilled out into the darkening night. The ground inside the tent was covered with a carpet of sawdust.

Hard benches were set up in rows on either side of the center aisle. At the far end, opposite the entrance, was a wooden platform two feet off the ground that held a rough hewn pulpit.

The front of the platform was festooned with a banner that said "There's Power in the Blood". Behind the platform, two flags were attached to the back of the tent, one the red and white flag of the church, the other an American flag.

To the right of the platform, a little birdlike woman sat at a black-lacquered upright piano, her hands poking at the keys and her thin legs jerking up and down on the pedals. She appeared to be singing, but no sound could be heard above the din of the crowd.

Jennie leaned close to Mama's ear. "Mama, Min and I are going to look for Sarah."

Lula nodded and followed Buelis and Harley down the aisle.

The two girls scanned the milling crowd. Jennie spied Clint with a group of boys and was relieved to see Hube with him. She caught Hube's eye and they exchanged waves.

Minnie said, "I see Sarah, Jen, over there. Yoohoo, Sarah."

They waited for their friend to squeeze her way through to their side. She was breathless when she reached them.

"Whew... looks like this tent might explode. Let's find some seats so's I can faint in comfort."

Minnie said, "I see Deelie, Jennie. She's wavin' fer me to come over. I'll see y'all after the meetin'."

Jennie watched Minnie push her way through the crowds to Deelie and noticed Sherm Owen scurrying to make a place for her. Meantime, Sarah had spotted two seats and called over her shoulder to Jennie.

"Come on before they're taken." They scrambled over and seated themselves. "That was lucky, most of the seats are gone already." Sarah sighed with relief. She looked behind her, then to either side.

"You looking for someone, Sarah?"

"I jest don't want anyone to hear this. I got somethin' to tell you. I'm jest as glad Minnie ain't here, cause I don't want to seem like I'm gossipin' ner nuthin', but I thought you ought to know. Don't know if there's anything wrong, but I thought..."

"For heaven's sake, Sarah, what is it?"

"Well, it's about Gayle Morgan. The days Prosper Truall drops off the mail, she comes in the store. She always buys somethin', magazines, candy, always somethin', and then, almost like an afterthought she goes to the post office, mails a letter and asks if there's any mail for her and darned if there isn't somethin' for her every time. So, me bein' nosy like I am, I started checking the mail before she comes in. The letters are always from Canton and..."

"Well, that's about what you'd expect, isn't it, Sarah? She does come from Canton after all. All her friends are there and..."

"Yeah, but Jen, the mail is always from the same name. Mr. Josh Cummings, and I checked the letters she mails out and that's who she writes to, Josh Cummings. And when she gets her letters, she puts them in her pocket like she doesn't want anyone to know she's gettin' mail. She acts guilty almost."

So, Jennie thought, *I was right. There is something strange about Gayle's story.* When Gayle told her about the man who was supposedly bothering her, she let the name Josh slip out and according to Sarah, she was getting mail from him and sending him mail as well. *Doesn't sound like she's afraid of him. Why lie about it? And Baxter wants to protect poor little frightened Gayle.*

Sarah flapped a hand in front of Jen's face. "Jennie... Jennie, where are you?"

"Oh, sorry, Sarah, I was just thinking about what you said. I'm sure there's a simple explanation."

"Speakin' of the devil, Jen, there's Gayle and Baxter in the back with Baxter's Ma and Pa."

As Jennie turned, Baxter caught her eye. He leaned down and said something to Gayle and the two of them left their seats and made their way down the crowded aisle. Baxter had his arm protectively around Gayle's shoulders. *I'm caught in the middle of something. Miss Gayle Morgan has some explaining to do.*

Jennie noticed how good Baxter looked. His trousers and shirt were spotless and his hair combed neatly back. He looked so happy. She felt a little hurt that he had so completely deserted her, and for a person who was, at best, a liar.

Gayle wore the brown skirt with the side buttons, but this time she wore a short, fitted matching jacket as well, with a pale yellow blouse beneath. A frilly collar showed at her neck. Her cheeks were smooth and flushed and there was a light color on her lips. Heads turned as she passed. It occurred to Jennie that Gayle had purposely tried to look pathetic three nights ago when she'd asked for help.

Sarah whispered as they approached, "Lordy. The girl dresses like she's the Queen of England."

Gayle gushed, "Isn't this exciting? I've never been to a tent meeting before."

"Actually, Gayle," Sarah said, "it's called a camp meeting, but it being held in a tent I guess you could call it a tent meeting, too. Did Baxter warn you about Dr. Pierce? He gets pretty carried away sometimes."

Gayle turned worried eyes to Baxter. "What does Sarah mean, carried away?"

Baxter grinned. "Nuthin' really." He pulled her close to him. "He jest gets loud and sometimes throws himself off the platform."

Jennie added, "It's called religious zeal."

Gayle smiled uncertainly. "My goodness. That does sound ambitious."

Sarah said. "He has a voice can be heard clear over to Boone. You s'pose he's a real doctor?"

Baxter laughed. "He calls hisself one but he ain't. I asked Doc Payne about that and Doc says he can call hisself anything he wants, jest so long as he don't try to set no broken bones."

A hush fell as the preacher entered through a flap in the side of the tent.

Baxter turned Gayle around. "Come on, Gayle, we best get back to our seats." Gayle looked back over her shoulder at Jennie and their eyes met. She mouthed the words—*I have to see you.*

Jennie thought, *And I have to see you.*

Dr. Pierce was 5'7" in his boots, very thin but agile enough to manage the 2 ft. step up to the platform with an inconspicuous jump. He wore a black frock coat, shiny with age but carefully mended and pressed. His white shirt and stiffly starched collar were immaculate, and his flowing black tie added an uncommon touch. He stepped up to the pulpit, mounted the stool placed there to give him added height, and with a dramatic gesture swept a hand through his abundant salt and pepper hair.

He carefully placed his worn Bible on the pulpit, took out a sparkling white handkerchief from his pocket and unfurled it with a flourish, reaching in his pocket at the same time to retrieve his spectacles. He cleaned the glasses meticulously, placed them on his nose and returned the handkerchief to his pocket. He was an imposing presence.

Jennie, along with everyone else, sat spellbound watching the performance.

In the silence the tent billowed with a sudden gust of wind making a snapping noise, stirring the sawdust on the ground. Dr. Pierce stared unblinking out over the congregation. When he was sure every eye was on him, he raised his arms, palms down, and said with fervor, "Raise your hand if you love Jesus." His voice was strong and resonant and carried easily to the far corners of the tent.

The congregation responded, calling out "Amen" as they raised their hands.

"We'll begin by singing the hymn 'There's Power in the Blood". The preacher looked towards the piano and said, "Sister Mary Lee, if you will."

There was a rustling as the congregation rose. Sister Mary Lee banged out the opening bars of the hymn and the jubilant voices bellowed out in chorus. Above all rose Doctor Pierce's magnificent tenor voice.

"Would you be free from the burden of sin?
There's Pow'r in the blood, pow'r in the blood;
Would you o'er evil a victory win?
There's wonderful pow'r in the blood.
There is pow'r, pow'r, wonder workin pow'r
In the blood of the Lamb.
There is pow'r, pow'r wonder working pow'r
In the precious blood of the Lamb."

The hymn ended lustily. Doctor Pierce stretched out his arms and said, "That was mighty good singing. Let's give ourselves a handclap."

Everyone laughed and started clapping their hands.

"Now let's clap for Jesus," the preacher shouted.

The tent exploded with people clapping and shouting "Amen".

Sarah leaned over to Jennie, "I know he ain't much in size, but standin' up there at the pulpit with his arms raised like that he looks 'bout 10 feet tall, don't he?"

Jennie smiled and nodded. "He certainly does."

The preacher called for silence.

"As we sing the next hymn 'When the Roll is Called Up Yonder', Brothers Eustace and Odes will pass the plates. Brothers and sisters, the Lord will shine His holy face upon you and your generous gifts will be repaid tenfold."

Jennie thought, *I wonder where he thinks the generous gifts will come from. Mama only brought a few pennies from the jar, and she's no different than any of the others.*

Sister Mary Lee once more pounded out the introduction and again the voices rose with vigor.

As the last strains of the hymn died down, Brother Eustace collected both the plates and the humming and rustling gradually subsided as everyone settled down.

Dr. Pierce leaned forward on the pulpit, folding his hands over his Bible and stared out at the waiting crowd. He stared first right, then left and finally straight ahead.

"We've all been to Sunday School," he began, speaking softly. "Don't know bout y'all but my Mama had me in church before I could walk. I was listenin' to the word of God before I could write my ABC's and soon's I could talk, I learned to recite the Ten Commandments.

"I guess maybe I wasn't too different than you, my good friends." He gestured grandly, encompassing the entire congregation.

The crowd responded. "Amen, Preacher, Amen."

"Yes, I had to recite the Ten Commandments every day of my life. I can close my eyes," and he closed his eyes and raised up his face, "and see myself, a puny little young'un, standin' in front of his Mama, sayin' Thou shalt not kill, Thou shalt not steal," ...His voice began to thunder... "and the very first commandment, Thou shalt love the Lord thy God with all thy heart and with all thy soul and with all thy mind..."

"You tell us Preacher," someone shouted.

"...and the second commandment... Thou shalt love thy neighbor as thyself... Do you remember that one? Thou shalt love thy neighbor as thyself."

He stopped and pounded the pulpit with his fist glaring out at the rapt congregation. "And what do we see, my good people, what do we see every day, day in and day out? We see our brothers and sisters abusin' themselves with drink, abusin the perfect bodies God gave us all, breaking His commandment, Thou shalt love thyself."

"Amen, Amen."

"Breaking the second commandment leads to the breaking down of all the commandments... coveting thy neighbor's cattle, coveting thy neighbor's wife, taking the Lord's name in vain and praying to the graven image of the God 'LIQUOR'".

Buelis Green rose from her seat, raised her arms high and shouted "I'm a sinner, Lord, I'm a sinner."

Harley pulled her back down beside him.

Sarah nudged Jennie and giggled.

Jennie whispered. "Sarah, be still."

The preacher responded. "Yes, sister, we're all sinners. There's too much sinnin'"... Dr. Pierce shouted and beat his chest... "and not enough prayin' and givin' over to Jesus Christ."

"Oh God, Oh God, tell us preacher."

"We got to get back to religion. We got to get back to the commandments. "Love thy God as thyself... see yourself in God's image... no more prayin' to the God LIQUOR. And who is the God LIQUOR? He's the devil... D-E-V-I-L."

"Amen, Amen."

The preacher began again, softly, "Brothers and sisters," "tonight,"... here his voice rose... "we're gonna make the devil mad."

"Tell it, preacher, tell it."

The little man pleaded in a whisper for God's flock to follow the path of righteousness... give up their waywardness. He came down off the stool and around to the front of the platform. He got down on his knees and implored them, with tears in his eyes, not to forsake the Lord.

Jennie watched, fascinated. *No wonder the people run to hear him. He's an actor as well as a preacher.*

"When it comes time to die, it doesn't matter how many hours you read the word of God. He doesn't care about the time you spend reading. It's the time you spend livin' like he wants you to. We have to fall back in love with God. We have to fall back in love with ourselves. Let's ring the bell for God."

"Yes! Yes!" shouted the congregation. "Amen. Tell 'em preacher, tell 'em."

Jennie looked around at the faces of the congregation and wondered how many thought of themselves as sinners. No wonder Papa didn't want to come to a camp meeting. He would have thought Dr. Pierce was preaching directly at him, but instead of being ashamed, it would have angered him.

She thought of James and wondered if they had camp meetings in Ireland. Somehow she couldn't picture him raising his arms and declaring himself a sinner, but then again she didn't know. There was so much they didn't know about each other. *When he comes to Zionville...*

"You're in the fire, brothers and sisters."

Jennie came back to the camp meeting with a start.

The preacher was standing before the pulpit with his arms outstretched and in the next moment he leaped into the air.

"You're in the fire... in the fire," he shouted and did a somersault in the aisle. The congregation gasped in unison. He sprang nimbly to his feet, his black coat covered with sawdust.. "You're all in the fires of hell." He leaped back on the platform and began to pace back and forth.

The crowd stood as one and raised their arms and shouted "tell us preacher...tell us..."

The little man was worked into a frenzy. His brow dripped with sweat and saliva flew from his mouth.

"Oh, God, we have sinned." He held his arms up and threw his head back and closed his eyes. "Our sins lay heavy on us. Jesus, Jesus, intercede for us. We want to repent. We want You to enfold us in Your loving arms, to shield us from our evil ways."

"Hallelujah brother..."

"Thank the dear loving Lord..."

A man pushed his way through the crowd and fell prostrate in the aisle, oblivious of the crowds. His body twitched, his hands clenched, and he panted in loud animal sounds. He was lost in the throes of religious fervor.

Doctor Pierce, as carried away as any of them, continued to call out. "Jesus knows who you are. Who will come to Him? Who will repent and confess his sins? Don't make Him beg. Make Him proud instead." There was much sobbing and shrieking and beating of chests.

"Come forward... come forward and pray to God to forgive you," he shouted. "Ask him to reach in the fire and pull you out."

"Amen, brother, Amen..."

Baxter was drawn into the surge toward the platform and knelt with the rest in the aisle. One man leaped to his feet and shouted, "My sins lay heavy on my soul... I'm unworthy to sit in the sight of God." He fell to his knees and cried out, "Jesus I repent my great sinning ways. Help me rid myself of sin."

Another man, rapture lighting his face, stood and raised his hands. "You can be saved, brother. Look at me. Two years ago I'd a been dead drunk somewheres, thinkin bout where I could find more liquor. I was in the fire. I was praying to the God LIQUOR."

151

"Tell us, brother." The congregation came as one to their feet, swaying and clapping. Encouraged, he went on. "I was drunk all the time... couldn't work, couldn't think straight, couldn't do nuthin' but drink."

"Amen...amen..."

"Then I come to the Lord and He straightened me out... Yessir, He pulled me from the fires of Hell."

Sarah nudged Jennie, "look who's goin' up to be saved..."

Jennie saw the orange plaid dress kneel before the pulpit and watched as the big woman began to sway back and forth oblivious of the crowd, her face alight from within. Jennie looked at Sarah sternly and whispered in her ear... "Now don't you laugh. Buelis is sincere and I think we should respect that."

Sarah covered her mouth with her hand. "You're right, Jennie, I won't laugh, that is unless she starts singing like last time."

All at once Buelis burst out in song... "Oh how I love Jesus, Oh how I love Jesus..."

Sarah bent over, convulsed with silent laughter. Jennie poked her with her elbow.

Buelis, loud and off key, continued singing, her voice heard over the prayers, "because He first loved me..."

Sarah raised her head. "Oh Lordy, Lordy," she gasped. "Where's Harley?"

Just then Harley, with a resigned look on his face and his unlit pipe clenched firmly in his mouth, pushed his way through the kneeling congregation to his wife's side. Buelis sobbed loudly. "I'm here, Lord, waitin to be saved from the fires of hell."

The preacher reached out his hand from the platform and placed it on Buelis' head. "Yes, sister, yes... the Lord Jesus Christ hears you and forgives you."

Sarah climbed up on her seat. Jennie looked at her in dismay, "Sarah, come down from there."

Sarah, still giggling, said, "I gotta see what's happening."

Buelis began to sway, threatening to topple over. As Harley reached for her she abruptly changed direction and the two of them collided with a loud thud. They ended up in a heap, Buelis sprawled atop Harley. The sinner who was pulled from the fires of Hell hurried to help, his foot landing on Harley's pipe, causing him to loose his footing and

152

sprawl on top of Buelis. Sarah, in a fervor of her own, shook with laughter and Jennie, horrified, tried to pull her from her perch.

Somehow the struggling bodies in the sawdust managed to sort themselves out and Harley, his tie askew, limping, and without his pipe, got Buelis to her feet and turned around. She drooped against him, completely oblivious of all the excitement. They staggered up the aisle, Harley bent almost double under her weight. Buelis, the light of paradise on her face, began to sing again, "Oh, how I love Jesus..."

As they passed up the aisle, Sarah, holding her sides, collapsed on the bench.

Jennie looked hurriedly around, hoping Sarah's outburst would be mistaken for rapture instead of mirth. She bent over the giggling form, scolding in a whisper, barely able to keep a straight face.

"Now stop it, people are starting to stare at us."

Sarah, beyond the ability to stop, looked up at Jennie with tears coursing down her face. "I can't... I can't help it."

Jennie pulled her to her feet. "Lean on me."

They started up the aisle towards the tent entrance, stepping over people as they went. Jennie, biting her lip to keep from laughing, bent over Sarah and whispered in her ear, "If you feel like singing, go ahead."

Sarah went into fresh spasms of glee.

They stumbled over Baxter who was kneeling in the aisle and when he looked up and saw Sarah bent over in Jennie's arms he jumped up in alarm. Mistaking the muffled convulsions for crying, he cleared a path for them and when they were finally out of the tent, Sarah slipped to the ground holding her sides. Baxter turned to Jennie with a questioning look.

Jennie shrugged. "You know our Sarah."

Chapter Fifteen
Malassy Bilin'

August 21, 1918 - British Third Army launched an attack north of Somme.

August 23 - Fourth Army joined with the Third, widening the front to thirty-five miles.

August 26 - First Army launched an attack on the River Scarpe. The German line staggered under the onslaughts.

August 29 - Bapaume on the Somme front fell to the New Zealand Division.

August 31 - Australian Corp took the powerful German bastion near Peronne, while French Third Army took Noyon. The German front groaned under the increasing blows.

September 12 - U.S. First Army under Pershing took 15,000 prisoners and 460 guns with 7,000 casualties, east of Verdun.

September 18 - Australians joined British Third and Fourth Armies.

September 26 - U.S. First Army, under Colonel George Marshall, deployed to Argonne sector, joined French Fourth Army and struggled four days through Argonne Forest against German defense. Took 18,000 prisoners.

September 27th - Under cover of dawn, the hurricane bombers bombarded the terrain below, leaving even more devastation than had already existed. The morning was misted and humid as the First Army Canadian Corp moved forward.

They were advancing on the most formidable German defense zone, twenty-five miles behind the front, the Hindenberg Line.

It was ten miles deep and a maze of belts of barbed wire. Their objective was the Canal du Nord. The canal was dry, but presented a broad obstacle sunk between high embankments. After two days the Canadians gained a lodgment twelve miles wide and six deep in the German defenses.

The German Army was close to collapse.

October 15th - 1,700 died in Berlin from influenza.

"Jennie, I think you've been avoiding me. You promised you'd help me and..." Gayle stood before Jennie, frowning and serious, the sea green eyes staring angrily at her from under the improbable lashes, the red gold hair in disarray from the wind.

They faced each other by the shoe rack in Lije's store. Jennie had expected a confrontation sooner or later and had thought long and hard about what she would say.

"I'm sorry if you've been anxious, Gayle, but I've had to do a lot of thinking. First of all, what you want me to do, lying in particular, is against the Bible's teachings and..."

Gayle was exasperated. "Oh nonsense, Jennie, a little white lie can't hurt anyone." The girl was no longer the sweet, appealing person she had presented herself to be, and Jennie marveled at what an actress she was.

Jennie said, "Let's find some place private, Gayle, I have some questions that need answers."

"There isn't any place private in this whole stupid... stupid Zionville. We might just as well stay right here. Now, what is it you want to say?"

"All right, Gayle. First, I don't think you have been quite honest with me. You told me this man, Josh, was sending you threatening letters, that he is in love with you and threatens to come to Zionville and cause some trouble. But it seems you have been writing just as many letters to him. That sounds like you've been encouraging him." Jennie stopped and waited for Gayle to answer.

Gayle was expressionless, her face a cold mask. "Just where did you get that information?"

Jennie was exasperated. "Come on, Gayle, you said yourself there is no privacy in Zionville. Sarah sorts the mail here in the store. She saw the letters from Josh and just as many letters from you to him. Why not be honest with me? What is going on?"

Gayle drew her hand through her hair, an affectation Jennie had come to recognize, paced a few steps, stopped and returned to face Jennie. "All right. Here's the truth. Josh is a married man. We worked together and, well... we fell in love. That simple. The complicated part is, his wife found out about us and demanded Josh put a stop to it."

Gayle began to pace again and Jennie felt a twinge of pity for her. If she was still acting, Jennie couldn't tell.

"It was awful. I wanted us to run away together, but Josh said it was impossible, with the responsibility of a wife and two children..."

Jennie felt a little sick.

"...My mother didn't know what was going on, only that I was unhappy and losing weight and she thought my coming to visit Cousin Frenda would be good for me. So I came to Zionville. In the beginning, with Baxter so attentive and Cousin Frenda and Uncle Ben so concerned, I thought I would be able to forget Josh, but I couldn't get him out of my mind. In time we began to write to each other and..."

Jennie interrupted. "Who wrote first?"

Gayle, absorbed in her story, was almost unaware of Jennie. She stopped pacing. "What?"

"I said who wrote the first letter?"

Gale resumed pacing, ignoring the question. "I decided we needed to discuss our problem..."

"You wrote to him first, didn't you? He might have been trying to straighten out his life..."

"Don't you understand? He has no right to just push me aside. That's what I wrote and told him. And he agreed to meet me in Johnson City... to discuss our future."

Jennie didn't want to believe. "In other words, you wrote to Josh and put pressure on him."

Gayle was indignant. She straightened the jacket of her brown suit and swept the hair back from her face. "That is a despicable thing to accuse me of. Josh is in love with me. He just needed a little time to think things through and now he wants to meet me in Johnson City. That's where I was going, not back to Canton."

Jennie was sad, appalled and angry at the same time. "Let me see if I understand. When you left Canton, Josh had decided to stay with his family and work things out, but you started writing to him, telling him he was really in love with you... and if he didn't see things your way, you would come back to Canton and make life miserable for him... am I right?"

Gayle stared coldly at Jennie for a long moment and then a smile lifted the corners of her mouth. "I must say, I always thought country folk were so pure and simple they couldn't possibly figure out anything more complex than a grocery list. Well, don't worry, Miss Prim, I'll get to Johnson City on my own. I'll leave a note saying I was unhappy and restless and decided to run away. No one will believe the preposterous story about me and a married man running off together." She smiled maliciously, "You *do* remember promising not to say a word to anyone, don't you Jennie? I have your word on that, in case you've forgotten."

Jennie ignored the gloating tone. "There is Sarah, you know. She saw all the letters going back and forth between the two of you."

"Sarah? Sarah is a little gossip and everyone knows it. She wouldn't be believed." Gayle straightened her jacket, drew a hand through her hair once more and turned to go. "Since you are the only one who really knows why I'm going, I can be honest and say thank you for the most boring time of my life. I couldn't be happier leaving."

"That makes two of us, Gayle. Just one more thing. Why did you let Baxter believe you cared for him?"

Gayle smiled. "Poor, sweet Baxter. Sweet, but a child. He was a diversion. I had to do something to occupy my mind or I would have gone mad in this Godforsaken place."

✉

October 15, 1918

Dear Mrs. Wainwright,

I am sure you are concerned about your son, Edward. I apologize for the long delay in writing you, but for a period of time, I was afraid I would have to write a letter with quite a different content, and my thought was to give you no information until such time as we could be more explicit as to the outcome of his condition.

Edward came to us a very sick boy, having ingested a considerable dose of chlorine gas. I am happy to report that after a touch and go beginning, he has steadily improved, to the extent that we can now discuss his release. He fought courageously, both on the battlefield and in dealing with his injuries.

While the young man has been in no condition to write until now, I am sure you will hear from him personally in the near future. Until such time, he asks me to convey his love and concern for you all. He is a brave young man and I feel privileged in having known him.

Sincerely,
Thadeous T. Granger, M.D,
Walter Reed General Hospital

Lula clasped the letter to her chest, not knowing whether her heart was beating wildly in anger, relief, or perhaps pride at the doctor's words. Oh, how she longed to see her son.

157

⊠

"Good day for the malassy bilin'," Lula said. "The frost is early this year. Last year it didn't come frost 'til early November. Reach down that picnic basket from the cupboard fer me, Jen."

Jennie was lost in thought. It was hard to get excited about the molasses boiling when her thoughts were so mixed up about Gayle and the effect her disappearance had on Baxter. He was sure it was somehow his fault and Jennie was just as certain she couldn't tell him the truth. To tell him Gayle had just been amusing herself with him would be too cruel.

The girl's disappearance had caused a great uproar. The story was, she'd gone for a walk one afternoon and never returned, leaving most of her clothes and a note explaining her unhappy state of mind. Serina, Gayle's mother, absolved Frenda and Ben of any blame, saying Gayle had always been headstrong and would come to her senses in time. It seems Gayle had given her parents no end of trouble in the past, and since Serina herself was disinclined to send out a search party, the furor settled down.

But now Jennie was left with trying to assure Baxter that Gayle's disappearance wasn't in some way his fault. She listened by the hour, trying to convince him that Gayle was a troubled young woman and there was nothing he could have done to make a difference. He wasn't yet convinced.

"Jennie... you hear me? I said, fetch the picnic basket."

"Sorry, Mama."

Hube pushed away from the table, grabbed his cap and sweater from the peg and flung open the kitchen door. "I gotta get over and help Mr. Owen." Soldier scrabbled at his heels.

"Wait for me, Hubie," Helen shouted, cramming the remains of a biscuit in her mouth.

Lula said, "Now jest hold on, you can both wait and carry this basket over to Clara."

Hubie kicked the door shut and flopped back into his chair. "Then I guess I got time fer another biscuit."

Minnie began clearing away the breakfast dishes. "One day, Hubie, you're gonna be so fat, instead a walkin' we're gonna have to roll you round."

Helen giggled. "Roly-poly Hubie."

Hube glared at Helen and turned to Lula. "Mama...!"

Lula quieted him with a wave of her hand. "Jen, while yer at the cupboard bring over two jars of my cucumber pickles. Let's see... fried chicken, two loaves of the bread I baked yesterday, the pickles, 2 jars of beans and a half dozen fried apples pies." Lula thought for a moment... "Guess that's enough."

Clint reached for the last biscuit. "We gotta get the rest of our cane down. I got it 'most cut yesterday, but not all. Hube has to help with the rest."

Mama said, "Land sakes, that's right. Luther asking you to cut his cane put us back some. Clint needs you to help, Hubie, so soon's I get this basket packed, you and Helen run it over to the Owens. Helen can stay and help Clara and you get back to the cane patch and help Clint."

She turned back to the basket, carefully packing the jars in the bottom, fitting in the loaves of bread and pies and laying the platter of fried chicken, wrapped in a white towel, over it all. "That ought to help feed the lot come dinner time."

Hube hefted the basket off the table and struggled toward the door.

"It too heavy, Hubie?" Lula asked.

"Naw, it ain't heavy."

Helen grabbed one handle of the basket and Hube didn't refuse her help. The door banged shut behind them.

"I watched the Owens set up the kettles and the press yesterday, Mama," Minnie said. "Who all are comin' to the bilin'? I know Aunt Pearl will be there... who else?"

Lula said, "Bein' as Jeb has the only decent press hereabouts, no tellin' how many will show up."

Minnie said, "Sherm has their cane cut and stripped. Said he and Clay would be over to help Clint get the rest of ours down this morning."

Clint pushed away from the table, wiping his mouth on his sleeve. "I don't need no help 'cept Hube. We can manage ta cut our own cane 'thout Sherm and Clay."

Minnie stopped in place with a platter in her hands. "Now that's just plain bullheaded, Clint. With help, you can finish the cane in half the time it'ud take you and Hubie."

"Min's right, Clint," Mama said. "Took you and Hube two days to get Luther Norris's cane cut and that was a good job o' work, now you need a little help gettin' ours down. 'Tween you and Hube and the Owen boys we'll be ready with our cane 'long with the rest. Don't look a gift horse in the mouth."

Clint put on his sweater without a word and went out the door. Jennie stood at the kitchen window. The dazzling rays of the sun sparkled on the frosted ground turning the yard into a diamond-studded wonderland. "Sure is pretty out there." She watched Clint come out of the shed, scythe over his shoulder, and head for the cane patch. "I wish Clint would stop fretting, he hardly smiles anymore."

"I know." Mama sighed, "Luther paid good money fer gettin' his cane down. Gave Clint a feelin' of responsibility. Now he thinks he's head of the household, which don't give him time to smile... Come along girls, let's finish up here so's we can lend a hand too."

When Mama and the girls arrived at the cane, Sherm and Clint were energetically swinging their scythes, hacking down the eight foot stalks and throwing them to Hube and Clay for stripping. Clay Owen was the same age as Clint and a picture image of his brother Sherm, handsome and well built. Clint looked pale and thin in comparison. Bro stood by patiently waiting for them to load the stalks on the wagon. The scent of wood smoke drifted on the nippy autumn air.

Sherm stopped and leaned on his scythe. His eyes fixed on Minnie. "Good day for the bilin." Minnie returned his smile, then dropped her eyes.

Lordy, thought Jen, they make no bones about how they feel and Mama don't even notice. She stole a glance at her mother standing with hands on hips surveying the cane.

"I see it's 'most cut," Mama said. "The girls and I will take over the strippin'. Clint, you and Sherm get the rest of the cane down and Hube and Clay can load the wagon."

They worked in silence. When it was finally cut and loaded Lula and Jen climbed up beside Clay, who held Bro's reins. Clint and Hube perched precariously atop the stalks in the wagon bed.

"Y'all go on ahead," Sherm called. "Me and Min'll walk over." Jen thought to herself, *that Sherm is a schemer.*

Bro pulled the heavy load away from the patch, Soldier running along side barking and snapping at his feet.

Hube shouted, "Soldier, you mind you don't get stomped by 'ole Bro here. He won't stand fer no foolishness."

The horse pulled out onto Valley Road, treading cautiously over the roadway, slippery with a mixture of melting frost and fallen leaves. He lumbered slowly down the road and turned in at the Owen gate, up the drive and into the yard where it seemed all of Zionville had gathered for the molasses boiling. Jeb was waiting for the wagon and directed Clay. "Pull in over yonder, son."

The wagon came to a halt near a mountain of cane where Otis Fenley, his horselike face sober in concentration, was chopping the stalks into small pieces to be fed into the press. Hube jumped to the ground and handed down his mother and sister. Clint stayed atop the cane and began unloading the stalks to Jeb who added their cane to the pile.

Close to the pile of cane was the large press and Sis, harnessed to the sweep, slowly circled around keeping the rollers in motion.

At the center of the yard two black iron kettles were positioned over a grate with a fire burning brightly beneath each of them. Steam, mixed with the aroma of cooking cane juice, rose from the kettles, drawing swarms of bees.

Across the yard big Tom Wooding, swinging his axe high in enormous knuckled hands, chopped wood for the fires, stopping now and again to send a stream of tobacco juice over his shoulder. Harley, pipe in mouth, ferried the wheelbarrow loaded with firewood across to the kettles.

At the press Buelis, prattling nonstop, and Elsie Wooding, frowning to hear what Buelis was saying, fed the cane through the press, sending a steady stream of bright green juice into buckets on the far side. As the buckets filled, they were emptied into the kettles.

Cora Fenley and Aunt Pearl stirred the boiling cane. From time to time the ladies used their bulky flat paddles to skim off the green foam that formed on the mixture as it boiled, then dunked the sticky paddles into buckets of water by their side for rinsing.

"Junior," Aunt Pearl called, "Get Hubie to help you dump these buckets in the creek and bring back some fresh water." Hubie's ears perked up at his name. He dashed to Pearl's side and grabbed one of the buckets, sticky water sloshing over the sides, and raced after Junior to the creek.

161

Pearl shook her head. "Them boys is like two peas in a pod. Everything is a game."

Clara Owen weaved in and out, circling the yard with a steaming pot of coffee filling empty mugs. She called, "Get yourself a mug, Lu, and have some coffee."

"I will in a minute, Clara," Lula said and joined Buelis and Elsie at the press. They smiled in greeting as she approached.

Lula raised her voice over the hubbub. "They's gonna be plenty of malassy when we's finished today."

Elsie nodded and Buelis answered, "It'll take us most the day to bile it all."

Sherm and Min strolled into the yard. Jeb called out. "Where you been, boy, we gotta get Lu's cane unloaded."

Jennie walked across the yard and took the paddle from Cora. "I'll take over for a while, Mrs. Fenley."

"Well, thank ya kindly, chile," Cora said. She lifted her apron to her face and mopped the perspiration from her brow, swatting at bees as she walked away. The children raced through the yard.

Pearl said. "Look at that Ada... ain't she a wonder?"

Jennie followed her gaze. Ada, dressed in coveralls like the rest, shouted "Hey, Jennie," the small face flushed and wreathed in smiles, the auburn curls bobbing as she ran.

Jennie said, "She looks as healthy as I've ever seen her."

"Be the good Lord willin' she stays that way through the winter," Pearl called after them. "Betsey, you mind Abel don't get in any mischief."

Jennie felt a small rush of annoyance. Seemed Betsey was forever in Ada's shadow, watching over the younger ones and never getting credit for the help she was to Pearl. But it didn't seem Betsey noticed. They watched as the children disappeared around the corner of the house.

"I swarn," Aunt Pearl said, "here come Ben and Frenda with more cane." The Combs wagon rolled into the yard with Baxter at the reins. He lifted a hand in greeting to Jennie.

Ben Combs, gaunt and thin as his wife, eased himself stiffly from the wagon and turned to give Frenda a hand down. He called out, "Mornin' y'all."

The heat and monotony of stirring the cane dulled Jennie's senses. She swatted mindlessly at the bees. The noisy yard faded and she thought of James... *Wonder what he'd say if he could see me sweating over a giant pot of boiling cane? Do they raise sugar cane in Ireland, I wonder? I must ask him.*

For the hundredth time she pictured him walking down the road towards her. He was smiling, and as he got closer he opened his arms...

"Jennie... Jennie," Aunt Pearl called, "you dreamin', chile? You be careful of that bilin' pot."

The sun was overhead. Clint and Clay took over the press, while Jeb and Harley took charge of the boiling kettles, freeing the women to gather in Clara's kitchen to prepare the noon meal. They would gather at the long wood table, set up under the maple tree that wasn't yet completely bare of leaves.

"Jennie," Mama said, "take this platter to the table and find Min for me. She should be here to help us. Can't seem to keep track of that child."

Jennie carried the platter to the table and looked around, remembering Min and Sherm by the woodpile, heads together in conversation. Now they were nowhere to be seen.

Buelis made a place on the table for the platter. "Your Mama can surely fix a plate of fried chicken, Jennie. My, that looks good, don't that look good, Harley?"

Jennie suppressed a smile. Harley was across the yard but Buelis didn't seem to notice. "My chicken jest never seems as good as your Mama's. Now biscuits, that's something else. I can swear by my biscuits."

Elsie came out on the porch carrying two pitchers of grape juice.

"Here, Elsie," Buelis called, "let me take one of them pitchers so's you don't trip. I 'member trippin once with a pitcher of grape juice. Good gracious, I wuz all over purple. What a mess it did make! Liked to have killed myself."

Jennie took advantage of the interruption to slip away to look for Min. Turning, she collided with Baxter.

"Whoa, Jennie, where you goin' in such a hurry?"

She gave a nod towards Buelis and raised her eyes.

"Oh," Baxter smiled, understanding. "Let's walk a bit over yonder." He took her arm and steered her away from all the activity.

163

They strolled in silence for a few minutes. Finally Jennie asked. "You disappointed not to start at the Academy this fall?"

"Yeah, I guess. I thought by puttin' it off a month or two, Pa might come around, get use to the idea of me bein' a doctor, but he ain't budging a bit. Even Ma can't change his mind... Maybe I ain't ready to go yet, either, Jen. I ain't exactly had my mind on the Academy lately."

"Baxter, you can't let Gayle color the whole rest of your life. I know you were fond of her and I'm sure she was just as fond of you, but she chose to leave, which means she wasn't ready to settle down. You aren't either. You've got *so* much to do."

"I know everything you say is true, and I didn't really believe Gayle when she said she would be willin' to be a doctor's wife in Zionville. I ain't quite that dumb, but I still feel kinda responsible. We were so close I shoulda seen somethin'."

Jennie sighed inwardly. If Baxter only knew how tired she was of the subject of Gayle! Especially since she had to continuously come to Gayle's defense instead of blurting out the truth. "Well, no one forced Gayle to run away. She did it of her own free will. Let's just hope she's all right wherever she is..."

Jennie purposely changed the subject. "What's Doc doin' lately? I thought he might join us today."

"He's been pretty busy. Some cases of influenza has showed up. Funny, it ain't nuthin' like the influenza we had past years. Folks been much sicker and the remedies that use to work don't seem to work no more."

"Is Doc worried that maybe...?"

"He won't talk about it, but ya can't help but worry that we might get hit bad, like in Europe. Anyway, Doc says fer me to take a break and give a hand to the bilin'."

Jen looked back across the yard. "Have you seen Min anywhere? Mama's looking for her and since I don't see Sherm either, I've got a feeling the two of them have slipped off somewhere."

"Min and Sherm? I thought it was Min and Grover Proffitt."

Jennie laughed. "No, after giving it a great deal of thought, Min's decided she's in love with Sherm Owen and I best find her before Mama starts looking. Wonder where they are?"

Jennie looked towards the barn and noticed the door ajar. "I wonder." She looked at Baxter, put a finger to her lips and together they quietly slipped into the gloomy barn. They were hit with the strong barn smell and Jennie wrinkled her nose.

Hearing giggling, Jennie walked across the hay-strewn dirt floor, stopped at the horse stall and peeked around. Sherm had Min pressed against the side of the stall, kissing her.

Jennie said sharply, "Minnie... Sherm..." They jumped apart and swung around to face Jennie.

Sherm was red-faced. "Ah, we wuz jest talking."

"Just talking... Sherm, that wasn't just talking."

"All right, Jennie, so we wuz kissin'."

Minnie found her voice. "Jennie, why is it you're always trailin' after me? I'm old enough to look after myself."

Jennie said. "I don't think fourteen is old enough for what you and Sherm are doing."

"Not old enough?" Minnie argued. "Jennie, some people get married at fourteen."

Jennie said, mockingly. "Certainly not you and Sherm."

"No, Jennie, me and Sherm ain't studyin' on gettin' married, but we sure like to kiss." She looked at Sherm and giggled. Sherm started to laugh and Baxter joined in.

Jennie, hardly able to keep from laughing herself, said, "well, Mama's looking for you and I don't think you want her to find you in the barn kissing Sherman Owen."

"One thing, though, Sherm." Baxter said. "You wouldn't want people to talk about Min and that's what would happen if they see the two of you sneakin' outta the barn."

Sherm looked surprised. "What could they say 'bout Min? She ain't done nuthin'."

"But you can't go off hiding in a barn and expect people won't notice and talk. They'd be sure the two a you wasn't in here inspectin' the livestock."

Sherm nodded, understanding. "Yer right, but God, it's terrible hard..."

Minnie blushed. "We wuzn't doin' nuthin' but kissin'."

Jennie said, "We know that, Min, but... oh, come on. We best get back to the yard before someone else comes looking for you two."

The cow bell clanged, calling everyone to the table. Jeb unharnessed Sis, slapping her rump as she ran through the pasture gate to join Bro.

Everyone took turns at the pump to wash the sticky cane syrup from their hands and faces and then all gathered at the table to eat.

There was chicken and ham, plates of sausage patties, hot sweet yams, bowls of green beans, biscuits fresh from the oven and stacks of fresh bread, sliced thick. There were pots of apple butter and grape jam, apple pies and cakes.

Baxter climbed over the bench and sat beside Jennie. Talk ceased while Jeb said the blessing and began again as the food was passed around. Tom leaned across the table to Lula, his jowls bobbing up and down as he chewed. "What's the latest news from Ed, Lu?"

"Well, now, I got some good news. I got a letter from Edward's doctor at Walter Reed General Hospital in Washington, D.C. That's where they sent the boy from Paris. Don't know jest when, but looks like Edward will be released soon."

Tom nodded, still chewing. "What wuz his injuries?"

"Chlorine gas. The doctor says he swallered chlorine gas."

There was silence around the table. Finally Otis said. "Good God Almighty. You say he's well enough to come home, Lu?"

Lula nodded. "Doctor says so, but if it ain't soon, I'll jest take a trip to Washington and see for myself."

"That's a mighty long way, Lu." Otis said frowning. "All the way to Washington, D.C. I don't know..."

Lula dismissed his misgivings with a wave of her hand. "Don't know as it will come to that, Otis, but I'm willin' to make the trip, I'm that worried."

Clara reached across the table and took Lula's hand. "Don't blame you, Lu, I'd feel the same way."

Harley said. "The war news looks good. According to Wilson we got them Germans on the run. Jest might see an end to it soon."

"God willin'," someone said.

Cora Fenley, her plain face lively and smiling, said, "Me and Otis got some news to share with y'all." She pushed her eyeglasses more comfortably in place and waited, savoring the attention. "Emmaline and Jacob are makin' plans to get married come next spring."

Everyone began talking at once.

Lula said, "That's good news, Cora, for you too, Elsie."

Buelis spoke up loud and clear. "'Bout time, I says. Them two been keeping company fer, how long's it been now, Cora? Three years?"

Cora looked embarrassed. "Well, seems like forever. Some folk knows right off when marryin' is right fer them and then it takes others a while to decide. I jest say when it comes to marryin', best make sure it's what they both want."

Jennie's eyes were drawn to Min and Sherm. They were sitting across from one another, smiling and nodding in agreement with Cora.

Elsie put her hand to her mouth and giggled. She was a tiny woman, almost fragile, and when she stood beside her husband, the top of her head came well below his shoulder. "I jest hope it don't take them that long to decide on young'uns. Our daughter, Jessie gave Tom and me a beautiful granddaughter and now we're lookin' fer a grandson."

In the middle of the afternoon they came to the end of the cane pile. The last piece slid through the rollers and the last bucketful was added to the bubbling syrup in the kettles.

"That does it," Jeb called. "This is 'bout the best we ever done! Two kettles full." He unhitched Bro from the rigging and walked him to the barn calling over his shoulder, "Sherm, fetch Sis and bring her along. These ole hosses earned their oats today."

The women sprawled on the benches, ready to relax. Clara came around with the coffee pot and refilled mugs while the men pulled the press and rigging apart and hauled it to the barn to be stored. The kettles were left to bubble, the fires beneath them kept just hot enough to keep the molasses at a slow boil.

Slowly the juice that started out a bright green in the morning turned a rich brown in color. Each of the ladies would take home a share and cook it further to make it thick and dark. The sun was low in the sky.

Jeb called out. "Let's get the kettles off the fire boys, so's the womenfolk can scoop out that malassy."

Each kettle was equipped with four iron loops, two on either side. Jeb pushed a sturdy pole through each set of loops on the first kettle and with Harley, Otis, Tom and himself in position at each end of a pole, said loudly, "put your shoulders to it... on the count of three... one, two, three," and the kettle was smoothly lifted and set on the ground. They repeated the operation with the other kettle.

The ladies set buckets of water from the creek on the embers so there would be hot water to wash the kettles down after the molasses was dipped out. Lanterns were lit as the sun disappeared behind the rim of Rich Mountain. Embers from the fires flickered softly adding their meager light to the lanterns.

The children, tired but having gotten their second wind, raced around the yard. Pearl suddenly clapped her hands and got their attention. "You young'uns come over here. Right here by me. Time y'all settled down."

She took Abel onto her lap and the others reluctantly gathered around.

"Yep, guess it were comin' on nighttime jest like now when ole man Grey first seen the boat. It be a story my mama told me... a story her mama told her and her mama 'fore her. Must be true. All them good ladies 'ud rather die of the shakes 'for they'd lie 'bout anything." Pearl fell silent, slowly shaking her head and smiling. She had a faraway look in her eye.

They all waited. Finally when it appeared Pearl was satisfied to wait them out, Clay said, "You gonna tell us the story or what, Aunt Pearl?"

"Y'all want to hear the story?"

The children all shouted "yes" and huddled in closer, as much to warm themselves against the chill that settled over the yard with the disappearing sun as to hear the story.

"Well," Pearl started, "they wuz a man, name o' Grey, owned a pretty big mill by the edge of a great pond that wuz deep and dark as sin. Far side of the pond was all covered in briars and tall cypress trees. One night Miller Grey wuz standin' by the water's edge when outta them dark bushes a boat comes inta view with jest one rider."

Iva Lee whispered. "Were it a man or a lady?"

"Hesh, child, and I'll tell ya. It were a beautiful lady and old man Grey could see she wuz in distress."

Iva Lee said, "What does that mean?"

Junior gave her a shove. "Means she wuz all worried, dummy."

"Now I ain't gonna go on if you'uns won't be still and listen," Aunt Pearl scolded. "Miller Grey bein' a good Christian man, asks the lady does she need lodging and she says yes. Well sir, he takes her in and after a day or two the old man was smitten... that means he fell in love with the lady... and asks her to marry him."

"Aw, Aunt Pearl, is this a dumb love story or somethin'?"

"Now jest wait, Hubie, it gets better. The miller and the beautiful lady get married and after 'bout a month, strange things start happenin' in the mill. Sacks of meal split open with the innards spilt out, nails mixed up with the corn so's to break the grinding wheels. All kinds o' mischief wuz happenin'.

"Well, the miller, jest 'bout crazy what with all the goins on decides he's gonna get to the bottom of it all. So one dark night he hides in the mill and as luck would have it, a bad storm comes up... so bad it shakes the mill 'til it most falls apart. Then the thunder and lightnin' starts up and when it wuz at its worst, he hears a poundin' at the door."

Iva Lee got up and climbed onto Pearl's lap along with Abel and Pearl hugged them both close.

"Now ole man Grey don't know what's out there so he grabs an axe lyin' near by and waits while the knockin' at the door gets louder."

Pearl stopped and looked around at the dirt smudged faces. "Mebbe you young'uns want me to stop?"

Iva Lee looked up into Pearl's face. "I guess you could if you want to."

Junior got to his knees. "We'uns all want to hear the rest, don't we." He looked around at the nodding heads.

"Well, all right then. Suddenly the mill door flies open and a horde of cats rushes at him from out of the storm. One springs at his throat... he swings his axe cutting its front paw. The cat screams in pain and flies out of the mill, all the rest of the cats follerin'."

Iva Lee whispered, "I don't think I like Miller Grey."

"Hesh up, Iva Lee," Junior snapped.

Pearl continued. "Guess you kin 'magine the old man wuz rattled. He ran to the house where he finds his wife in the bed, her hand dangling from her wrist. She rears up in bed ahissin' and scratchin' and springs past him. After he gathers his wits 'bout him, he follows her to the pond."

Iva Lee uncurled and sat up straight. "Is that the end of the story, Aunt Pearl?"

Junior said disgustedly. "No it ain't, Iva Lee, will you jest hesh your mouth?"

Pearl pulled Iva Lee close and went on. "The miller disappeared that night and weren't seen alive again. Long 'bout a week later, a fisherman finds his body floatin' near the far shore, his fist clenched on somethin'... and when they pried his hand open guess what they found?"

"I know," Junior shouted, "a axe."

"No, some grain from the mill."

"He caught up with his wife and pulled some hair clean outta her head."

"No, no... it were a fish."

"Well, now," Aunt Pearl said, "I'll tell ya what wuz in his tight closed hand... the lopped off paw of a cat."

Clay snorted. "That story ain't true. Yer sayin' his wife turned into a cat. Ye're joshin' us, Aunt Pearl."

Pearl smiled shaking her head. "I told ya', my Mama tole me and her Mama tole her. I'll leave it to y'all ta decide."

A harvest moon rose in the dark sky with clouds drifting across its face. With the help of the lanterns, the yard glowed brightly.

Clara got up and stretched. "Guess them kettles is cool 'nuf fer us to scoop out the malassy, don't you think ladies?"

Pearl lifted first Iva Lee off her lap and then Abel. "We best get on with it, now the sun's gone, a chill is settin' in."

The women gathered around the kettles with jars and cans of all shapes and sizes and began to ladle out their family share of the molasses. Pearl scolded Junior, who impatiently pushed in beside her.

"Now you jest set over there, Junior. Time to sop the kettles is when we is finished here."

Finally the kettles were emptied. "There," Pearl said, "that's the end of it. Now where are the young'uns with their sticks? They can sop the kettles now."

With a shout the children moved in, Junior first with the rest following, their sticks honed and ready to scrape the last of the molasses from the kettles. Lula and Pearl held up the little ones so they could get their share, and with much laughing and lip smacking, the kettles were scraped clean.

Pearl turned to Lula, laughing. "Last year, Junior was so 'fraid he wasn't gonna get enuf, he fell head first into the kettle. Had to wash ever blessed thing on his body, 'cludin' his shoes."

Cora and Buelis dumped hot water from the buckets into each kettle and with some of Clara's lye soap added, the ladies soon had the kettles scrubbed clean.

The long day was over. The moon was full and the stars glittered in the cold October sky. Lanterns glowed dimly in the darkened yard as each family tiredly gathered their belongings, their children and their molasses.

"Good night y'all" everyone called. The wagons creaked one by one out of the Owen yard. "Good night..."

Chapter Sixteen
Good News

Hi Mama and all,

Guess you was wonderin' if you would ever hear from me again. Doctor didn't want me to write until I was feeling good. He says it won't be long before I can go home. I was hoping it would be for Christmas, but now it don't look like it. I sure like getting your letters. Please keep writing. I'll write again soon.

Love, Edward

Jennie struggled up the steps into the general store, a clumsy kerosene can in one hand and a box to go in the mail for Edward in the other. A raw wind swept in with her and she hurriedly kicked the door shut. She set the can by the door and unbuttoned her gray sweater, welcoming the mixed aroma of spices and shoe leather, kerosene and coffee beans. With windows and doors barred against the cold, heat from the black potbellied stove crackling at the heart of the store intensified the pungent smells.

Now that the beef was sold off and gardens plowed under, the store became a haven where the men and womenfolk gathered on long cold afternoons exchanging ideas, recipes and gossip. Jennie waved to Harley and Jeb sprawled in chairs around the stove, their booted feet up to the heat. Jeb called out, "Anything more about Ed, Jennie?"

"Got a letter from him, finally. A short one, of course. He says he is doing better and hopes to be home soon. Not for Christmas, though. We're sending him a Christmas box."

Jeb nodded and Jennie went to the post office counter. Otis and Tom were in conversation, speaking softly, beside Lije's desk behind the counter, while Lije, with his headset on, tried to pick up some news on the crystal set. He was frowning in concentration. Sarah was sorting mail and looked up as Jennie approached, reaching for the box and placing it on the scale. "Must be cold out, Jen, your face is red as a beet."

Jennie put her hands up to her face. "Wind's pretty strong out there. Your Pa have you working today? I thought it was Ev's day in the store on Friday."

Lije looked over, frowning, and said, "Quiet please, girls."

Sarah put her hand to her mouth and shrugged her shoulders. She continued in a much subdued voice. "Usually is, but Pa sent him inta Boone today to pick up somethin' special. Sides, I'd rather be here than home tendin' to them kids. Postage is fifty cents, Jen. Want me to put it on your tab?"

Jennie nodded. "If you don't mind, Sarah."

Sarah came out from behind the counter. "Let's move away from here so's we can talk. What all you sendin' Ed?"

The girls strolled to the counter by the front of the store. "Mama put in an apple cake. Don't know what condition it will be in when he gets it, but Mama says even if it's just crumbs he'll like it. A couple jars of apple butter and one of grape jam. Miss Glenwood sent Helen home with a pad and a pencil for us to send and Clint put in an almanac. Lets see, what else... I knitted socks and Helen and Hube made cards at school. Nothing much, really, just things so he'll know we're thinking of him."

"That's real nice, Jen."

Buelis turned from the bolts of material at the back of the store and called out, "Jennie, you tell yer Mama I'll stop by fer a visit one day soon 'fore it gets too cold to stomp 'round outdoors."

"I'll do that, Mrs. Green." Buelis wore a knitted wool cape of every color in the rainbow. It covered her great girth from shoulders to knees and ended in an uneven fringe of bright red wool. She gave Jennie a dazzling smile before turning back to the material. Sarah beamed at Jennie and her mischievous grin prompted Jennie to whisper. "Now don't you get started on Mrs. Green."

"Can't help it, Jen, that woman jest tickles me til I can't help but bust up laughin'. She looks like she's dressed for a costume party." They both turned to look at Buelis again.

Jennie said, "Do you know anyone happier than Buelis Green?"

Sarah nodded. "Y'ere right, Jen, and if it bothered her what folks thought, she wouldn't dress like that. You have to admit, though, that cape takes the prize."

Jennie smiled. "It sure does."

"So, Jen, anything else we can do fer ya today?"

"It's Helen's birthday tomorrow, she'll be ten. Mama made her a new dress. Well it isn't really new, it's one of Min's old ones Mama cut down, but it's pretty. Mama wants me to pick out some new buttons for it."

"Your Mama sews good, Jen, so do you and Min. Me, I'm all thumbs when it comes to sewing."

"Lordy, Sarah, if we didn't all sew we'd go naked."

Sarah giggled. "Guess we're lucky our Mama can order from the Sears catalog else *we'd* all go naked."

"We need some kerosene too. Can your Papa get it for me?"

Sarah looked over at her father. "Lordy, Jen, can you wait fer a spell? When Papa get's goin' on his crystal set, it's worth your life to interrupt him."

Jennie looked over at Lije. His face was blank with concentration. Otis sat on the edge of the desk with the same expression, leaning his head close to the set. Tom stood back, arms across his chest, nodding his head, waiting patiently to hear what was going on.

"You hear anything lately from James?"

"Yes, as a matter of fact..."

Jennie My Dear,

I've just finished reading three letters from you. They came at last mail call and truth, Jen, they transported my tired bones to a better place. I've been waiting for a particular letter and it was one of the three.

I asked you if you want me to come to Zionville after the war and you said yes. I didn't know how disappointed I would have been had you said no, until I read your written words. You describe your feelings better than if you were an Irish poet, lass. Something good will come of our meeting. I promise you. I can feel it...

"Ya got a shit-eatin' grin on your face, Irish. Musta been a pretty good letter. You answerin' it already?"

James, still smiling, looked at Pete sitting cross-legged on his bed roll. It was his first reaction to be annoyed at the interruption, but Pete was almost as involved with letters from Jennie as he was and he couldn't be angry.

"Jen wants me to come to Zionville after the war."

Pete drew back in mock surprise. "Really? I coulda told ya that. Shoulda asked me."...

By now I expect you've heard from Edward. Will it be possible for anyone in the family to visit him? The lad will be needing comforting and I can think of nothing better than a visit from his Mum... or my darling Jennie. How is his health? I'm hoping the news is good. I would like to write to the lad, so in your next letter give me his address.

I was interested in your description of what you call a camp meeting, sounds inspiring and at the same time fun. There was no fun involved in our church going, and I say where's the harm in people enjoying themselves while hearing the word of God? And you being Methodist and accepted at a Baptist camp meeting... in Ireland religions don't mix. The Protestants and Catholics keep their distance from one another, and that's on a good day...

James looked up from his letter. "You ever hear of a camp meeting, Pete?"

"Camp meeting?" Pete stopped to scratch his head. "Well... this is a camp and we're meeting all kinds..."

"No, no. Jen explained to me what a camp meeting is. The Baptists hold them every so often. Has to do with religion."

Pete nodded, waiting for James to explain. "Seems they, the Baptists, gather in a large tent and the preacher stands before them and beseeches them to come forward and be saved."

James stopped and Pete continued to stare. "Saved from what?"

"From hellfire and damnation."

Pete nodded slowly. "You think maybe them preachers is talking bout the war? God knows war is hellfire for sure. If that's what they mean, damn, Irish, just tell me where to go. I'll be first in line."

✉

There was a shout from Lije at the crystal set. He tore off the head set and shouted with excitement. "The good Lord has answered our prayers. The war is over."

For a moment everything stood still and Jennie could hear her heart thumping in the silence. Then everyone started talking at once. Jennie turned to Sarah, grasped her hands and held on tightly for a moment. Without saying a word, Jennie whirled around and was out the door, buttons and kerosene forgotten. She flew over the frozen rutted road, turned in at her gate, rounded the house and clattered up the back steps.

174

"Mama... Mama..." Jennie burst into the kitchen.

Lula started in surprise. "Lands, child what's the matter?"

"The war, Mama, the war... it's all over."

They put their arms around each other and wept.

November 12, 1918
Dear Jen,

This will be a short but happy note. The war is over, lass, and praise God I've come through with all my senses. The guns fell silent at 11:00 a.m. yesterday, November 11. Like magic, the boom of the cannons ceased and no-man's-land came alive with Yanks setting American flags in every shell hole. One lad said he is going to take his rifle home, plant it in the ground and watch it rust. Fair sentiments of us all.

A bugler began to play the Star Spangled Banner and you could hear soldiers up and down the line singing at the top of their lungs. My heart swelled and fair burst. As night fell, the front lines were ablaze with rockets and flares, all in celebration. Girls from the Red Cross and Salvation Army passed among us with fudge and doughnuts and coffee and beautiful as they were and as starved as we were for company of the fair sex, all I wanted was sleep.

I'll not write more, as things are moving fast, but will write again when I can. God knows when that will be. As you can imagine there is a lot of confusion, so much that I fear this letter may not get through. The best of it all, Jennie, is I'll be meeting you one day soon.

Love,
James

It was two days before Christmas. They had all hoped Edward would be released from the hospital in time for Christmas but the latest report from the doctor, while still optimistic, did not say when he could come home. Edward's letters, as few and far between as ever, were brief, but cheerful. The Christmas box had been received and appreciated. Papaw was coming for the holidays and despite the fact Papa was coming as well, Jennie was contented.

Mama, Jen and Min were busy in the kitchen baking pies while Clint, Helen and Hube were out scouring the hillside for their Christmas tree.

The kitchen was a combination of smells. Cinnamon from the apple and pumpkin pies cooling on the table mixed with the aroma of cooking cabbage from the black iron pot on the back of the stove. Added to that was the forest smell of pine cones and boughs overflowing the basket in the corner.

"Mama," Jen said, "I guess we have enough pies to last through next year."

"Well, you know how fond your Papa and Papaw are 'bout my pies."

"Six pies ain't a lot," Minnie said, "you know how the menfolk eat... like they ain't ever gonna eat pie again."

Lula laughed. "That's a fact, and then, a course they's Hube."

The back door swept open and the children piled in, their cheeks rosy with cold. Clint dragged a huge pine tree behind him. "Lands sakes, don't let all the heat out, young'uns," Lula scolded, "hurry and close the door."

Clint shoved the door closed with his foot and stood the tree on it's end. The top brushed the ceiling. "Ain't she a beaut?"

Lula looked skeptical. "It's too big, Clint. Time you get the stand on, it won't fit in the parlor."

Clint leaned the tree against the wall and shrugged out of his coat. "It ain't too big."

Hube pulled off his coat and threw it carelessly towards the peg by the door, where it caught and held. "Don't worry, Mama, me and Clint will make it fit."

Helen shivered and held her hands to the stove. "We went all over the hill. They wuz some puny ones we coulda cut down, but then we saw this'un and knew right off it wuz the right one."

Hube spied the pies and leaned over the table, sniffing loudly. "Can I have a little bitty piece of this'un? You won't even know it's gone."

Min slapped his hand. "The pies are for when Papa and Papaw are here, not before."

The boys half-lifted, half-dragged the tree between them through the kitchen with Helen dancing in front, leading the way into the parlor. "We're gonna trim the Christmas tree. I want to put my paper chain on it, the one I made in school with colored paper. Miss Glenwood said it was the longest and best chain she ever did see."

"And we'll pop some corn tonight and string it," Min added.

Helen said, "And my chain's gonna be the longest, just like last year."

Hubie looked at her with disgust. "Wasn't longest."

"Was too." She turned to Mama, "It *was* the longest, Mama, wasn't it?"

Lula shook her head. "Let's not argue, children, this year you'll both make the longest. Girls, go get the decorations from the closet in the back bedroom. Hube, you haul in some firewood so's we can keep the fire goin' in the parlor."

Supper was a boisterous meal, with everyone in high spirits.

"Mama, this is my favorite supper."

"Hubie, every supper is your favorite."

"But potatoes and cabbage is my best favorite."

After the kitchen was put to rights, they gathered in the parlor and spread out before the fireplace. The only light in the room was from the crackling fire. Clint threw on some pine boughs and the woodsy fragrance filled the room.

"Mama," Hubie begged, "Can we please let Soldier come in the parlor? Please? Please?"

Lula sighed. "Don't know when I seen such a pitiful face. I'll say yes only if you promise to keep him off the settee."

Hube scrambled out of the parlor and returned followed by Soldier, who was wagging his tail furiously. He made the rounds, greeting everyone, and stopped to sniff the tree.

"No," Hube shouted and fell on the dog. "This ain't like outdoors, Soldier, you can't pee on this tree."

The boys set the tree in the rough wooden stand and Clint, standing precariously on a chair, trimmed a little from the top. Jennie stood back. "Turn it a bit to the right, Clint, no, the other way. That's it. That's perfect."

"Clint said, "See? They's plenty room on top fer the angel."

Lula carefully unwrapped the Christmas angel and handed it to Clint who secured it to the topmost branch. While the girls hung the rest of the decorations on the tree, they all listened, though they knew the story well, of Mama's Christmas angel.

"There weren't much money that first Christmas your Papa and I was married, but we had plenty to eat and the house was warm and cozy. Your Papa went out in the woods and got us a big tree. Come Christmas morning there was this box on the table there and Dalton says 'go on, Lu, open it up' and when I did there was the prettiest angel, all white and gold. Your Papa had ordered it from the Sears catalog and he kept it hidden from me 'til Christmas morning."

Jennie found it difficult to credit Papa with a sentimental streak, but the story must be true. Mama wouldn't lie. All the same, she would like to hear another version of "the Christmas angel".

Mama brought out the ancient corn popper and ran her hands lovingly over the perforations in the metal box. "Your Papaw made this, back when I was jest a little'un. Papa said he made it for me. Course he didn't, it was for all of us, but it did come to me in the end, didn't it?" She opened the top of the box, dumped in a cup of corn kernels and fastened the lid on. Clint screwed on the long wooden handle.

They took turns holding the popper over the fire, waiting for the first kernel to pop and when it did a cheer went up. The smell of popped corn mingled with the aroma of pine boughs and soon the agate bowl set in their midst was overflowing. The contest began to see who could make the longest popcorn chain.

Helen complained, "Hubie, you keep eating the popcorn, there won't be enough for the tree."

"It don't matter," Min said, "we can always make more."

"Let's sing some Christmas carols," Lula said, "to get us in the proper spirit."

Helen started in a clear high voice. "Silent night, holy night"... and they all joined in.

The firelight glowed warmly on their faces and cast dancing lights on the walls. One carol after another was sung and the popcorn chains grew while the logs in the fireplace crackled and snapped. The corn was all popped and the logs burned down. They climbed the stairs to bed. The house grew still.

⊠

Christmas Eve day was overcast. According to Clint, who quoted the almanac, today would be cloudy but tomorrow, Christmas, would be sunny and cold.

The tree was resplendent with long looping strings of popcorn and Helen's colorful paper chain. Slightly tattered decorations made in school

178

from every past Christmas hung beside the colorful balls from Sears Roebuck that Lula had surprised them with last year. The small Christ Child in the manger Papaw had whittled three years back hung on one of the sturdier lower branches.

In the afternoon, Hube, keeping watch on the front porch, shouted, "Here comes Papaw's wagon. He's got Papa with him. They's just passing the store. Me n' Clint's gonna meet em." The door banged shut.

Lula and the girls exchanged their aprons for sweaters and hurried down the walk, as the wagon, with Hube and Clint running behind, rolled to a stop by the gate.

"Well, now," Papaw called, "ain't this a sight? The prettiest girls in all of Zionville waitin' to greet us."

He climbed down carefully from the wagon and stretched his back. Jennie went up on tiptoes to kiss him. "Your rheumatism again, Papaw?"

"Jest a tetch, Jennie, jest a tetch."

Dalton jumped down the other side, reached in the wagon bed and retrieved his leather satchel as Lula came up to greet him.

"Train inta Johnson City wuz packed, so wuz the train inta Boone. Had ta hike to Sugar Grove and yer Pa put me up fer the night."

Minnie and Lula walked on either side of Papa, followed by Helen and Hube struggling up the walk behind them, sharing the weight of Papaw's satchel.

Hube said over his shoulder, "What all ya got in this here ole satchel, Papaw, it weighs most as much as me."

Jennie came up behind him and ruffled his hair. "It can't weigh much then, you're such a pip-squeak."

Hube looked indignant. "That ain't true, Jennie, I'm pretty big, ya know."

"I know you are, Hube, I was just teasing."

Clint spied Mylart's rifle on the floor of the wagon and picked it up." You gonna do some huntin' while yer here Papaw?"

Mylart reached for the gun. "Thought mebbe I would, son. They's a sack of wheat flour and a sack of corn meal here. What say you drive the wagon round back and unload it. You can take care of ole 'Lazarus' while yer at it."

Clint smiled happily, climbed up on the wagon seat and flicked Lazarus lightly with the reins. The wagon moved deftly into the wagon road beside the house.

The table was spread with a clean white cloth and set with Mamaw's china dishes which Lula took out only on special occasions. The food was plentiful; beans and sausage, boiled ham and cabbage and slices of hot fresh-baked bread.

Papaw said the blessing and ended with "and Lord, we thank thee for watching over Ed."

After the meal was cleared away, they gathered in the parlor. Papaw eased his great frame into the armchair and set his satchel by his side. Helen climbed into his lap. "Gotta good fire goin' there Clint." Papaw praised his grandson.

Lula sat down beside Dalton on the settee and reached for his hand. "Feels good to sit down."

Clint and Hube and the girls sat on the floor before the fire.

"Well, now," Papaw said, "I think there might just be some things in my bag here fer all you young'uns."

Helen jumped from his lap. "What, Papaw, what do you have in your bag?"

"Why don't we jest see." He reached in the bag and pulled out two packages, handing one to Hube and one to Helen. They tore off the plain brown wrappings.

Hube jumped up and down with excitement. "A whistle, Papaw."

It was intricately carved and polished as smooth as glass. He put it to his lips, blowing a shrill blast and they all cringed. "Papaw, how did you know this is just what I wanted?"

Lula looked at her father with mock exasperation. "Just what we *all* wanted, Papa."

Helen held up a little carved wooden cradle. She said solemnly, "Now Dolly has her own bed. She don't hafta sleep with me."

Papaw smiled. "Jest what I had in mind when I made it." He drew the rest of the gifts out of the bag. There were ribbons for Min and a book for Jen.

Jennie squealed with pleasure. *"Pride and Prejudice.* Thank you, Papaw. Miss Glenwood told me about this author, Jane Austen. I love it. Thank you."

"And thank you for my ribbons too, Papaw, my old ones are getting raggedy," Min thanked her grandfather.

Papaw turned to Clint. "And that leaves Clint." He reached around to his rifle leaning against the back of his chair. "Think you can handle my old rifle, son?"

Clint's face flushed with pleasure. "You're gonna give me your rifle, Papaw?"

"I think you're old 'nuff." He turned to Dalton. "What do you say, Dalton?"

"You ain't aimin' to hunt no more, Mylart?"

Papaw said, "Naw, the ole rheumatism holds me back some. Clint might as well have the use of my old twenty-two."

Dalton said. "You take care that rifle boy, it's a lot more gun than that little BB gun you got now."

"Lordy, this is the best present I ever got." He looked at Papaw, his eyes shining. "Thanks, Papaw. Next year I'll get us a turkey for the table."

Papaw nodded. "Mebbe we can take it out tomorrow and see you can handle it."

The fire burned low. Dalton rose with exaggerated effort. "I can't get comfortable on this settee, Lu, guess I'll turn in."

Just then, Soldier, his fat belly low to the floor, crept silently into the room. Dalton spotted the dog first and with one step scooped the dog up with his booted foot and swung him towards the door. Soldier landed with a yipe, scrambled to his feet and ran, tail between his legs, out of the room.

Hubie shouted, "*Noooo!*" He jumped up and ran after the dog, giving his father a dark look over his shoulder.

Dalton shouted after them, "I don't like the smell of dog in the house. You keep that damn cur outside where he belongs."

"Soldier ain't trouble, Dalt," Lula said, "he's a good dog."

Dalton turned to Lula. "Like I said, I don't like the smell a dog in the house." Without another word he stamped from the room and up the stairs.

Lula broke the awkward silence. "Guess it's time we all went to bed. Come Clint, girls. You comin', Papa?"

"No, think I'll have a pipe 'fore I turn in."

As Jennie leaned over to kiss Papaw goodnight, he said, "Stay a minute, Jen, I want to talk to you."

Jennie sat down at Papaw's feet. "Nothin' wrong, is there, Papaw?"

Papaw took his time filling his pipe and lighting it. Jennie knew enough to be patient. Finally he settled back and said, "Jeb Owen come into Grundy's over to Sugar Grove a while back to do some tradin'. Said he sold some beef this fall."

Papaw drew on his pipe and Jennie sat patiently, knowing where the conversation was going and letting Papaw do the telling in his own time. She could barely sit still. "Yep, Jeb says he got a good price fer his beef and give me the five hundred dollars fer that strip of land he wants."

Jennie couldn't wait for him to finish. She said grinning from ear to ear, "That my education money, Papaw?"

"It's what we agreed on, ain't it?"

✉

True to the almanac's prediction, Christmas day dawned sunny and cold. Hube leaned back in his chair at the breakfast table. "I'm so full up I hurt."

Minnie scolded, "If you didn't make such a little pig of yourself with the molasses and biscuits, you wouldn't be hurtin'."

Helen giggled, "Hubie the pig, oink oink."

"I ain't no pig, you are...."

Papa rapped his hand on the table and gave Hube and Helen a black look. "That's enough."

The children stopped immediately.

Lula, quick to avert any unpleasantness, said, "Today is the birth of our Lord. I think it fittin' we all go to church and give thanks." She looked hopefully at Dalton.

"Not me," Dalton pushed his plate aside. "Think I'll jest stretch out in the parlor and take me a nap."

Jennie saw the disappointment in her mother's face.

Lula tried again. "Folks ask 'bout you all the time, Dalt, it would be a good chance to see everyone."

"I said no. Ain't a church goin' man, you know that, Lu."

Jennie bit her tongue. *The one thing Mama asks and he can't find it in his worthless bones to do it.* She moved to the sink and busied herself with the dishes, afraid if he saw her face he would read her thoughts.

Defeated, Lula pushed her chair back from the table. "Well, the rest of us will go. Come along, young'uns, let's set the kitchen to rights and then we'll get dressed."

✉

The Wainwrights took up one whole pew. Jennie heard scuffling and stole a look over her shoulder. The Owen family was settling in behind them, Sherm Owen making sure he sat behind Minnie. Jennie noticed her sister didn't even pretend to be annoyed when Sherm tugged her hair. Lula turned and whispered "Merry Christmas to y'all" and Papaw reached back and shook hands with Jeb.

The Proffitts sat in a line at the rear of the church, close to the door in case any of the younger children became too noisy and had to be taken out. Sarah waved and smiled at Jennie. Emmaline Fenley sat primly with her parents and the Wooding family, Jacob Wooding leaning over every so often to whisper into her ear. Emmaline was smiling sweetly.

Miss Glenwood was there in a royal blue cape and matching hat with a feather. Jennie noticed with a sudden shock that Lucy Glenwood was sitting with Luther Norris and Aunt Pearl. Was it a coincidence? The memory of Ada on their porch saying she thought her father and Miss Glenwood would make a nice couple came rushing to mind. Jennie caught Ada's eye and they exchanged grins. Jennie wondered if Ada was remembering the same thing.

Harley and Buelis sat in the choir loft, Harley for once without his pipe; Buelis with her colorful garb suitably covered by a choir robe.

Reverend Truall ascended the pulpit and the congregation settled down.

After the service, the Reverend stood at the church door and greeted his congregation.

Jennie waited patiently by the wagon. It was cold and she did a little dance to keep warm, pulling the collar of her brown winter coat closer around her neck. Mama, inclined to gossip with her friends after church, was talking to Cora and Otis Fenley. Where were the others? She spied Helen showing her friend Jo Anne her new cradle and though she couldn't see Hube, she heard the whistle sounding off somewhere. Papaw, his arm draped over Clint's shoulders, was in deep conversation with Jeb Owen. It was good Clint had Papaw to look up to... and Min... where was Min? There she was, batting her lashes at Sherm while he playfully tugged at her curls.

Baxter came toward her smiling, a package tucked beneath his arm. "Been lookin fer you Jen, didn't see you in church. I was feared mebbe you didn't come today." His Sunday suit was neatly patched, but threadbare, and he hunched his shoulders against the cold. A clean white shirt showed beneath the jacket.

"Hey Baxter." She returned his smile.

He held out the package. "Merry Christmas."

"What's this, a present for me?"

"Open it. I hope you like it."

"You shouldn't have done this." She tore open the package. It was an old frayed book, titled *Thoughts on Nursing.*

"Baxter, wherever did you find this? It's by Florence Nightingale."

Baxter looked pleased with himself. "I asked Miss Glenwood did she know where I could find something on nursing and she said she would find something for me. Sure nuff, she did. It ain't new. The binding was comin' apart and I fixed it some. Doc looked it over and he says it's a good book, out of date, but a good book."

Jennie leafed through the pages. "I'm just so surprised, Baxter, this is a wonderful present. Thank you so much." She impulsively reached up and kissed him on the cheek.

"I thought you'd like it, Jen. 'Bout nursin' and all."

"I'll keep it as a reference book... now I'm going to school."

"For sure, Jen?" His face broke into a smile. "Your Papaw gave you the money for school."

"Yes. He told me so last night. Now all I have to do is tell Papa."

Baxter sighed. "Yeah. I still ain't sure *my* Pa is gonna come around 'bout lettin' me go to the Academy." Baxter reached for her hand. "Anyway, Jen, we got Doc and your Papaw on our side."

Jennie suddenly felt good about the day, the future, and herself. "They're two powerful allies, Bax."

Minnie and Helen walked toward them and Baxter self-consciously dropped her hand.

"Why don't you come over to the house this afternoon, Bax," suggested Jennie. "You can come for dinner if you like."

"Thanks, Jen, I'd like to come over, not for dinner though, Ma's expectin' me to be home, all the family... you know." Minnie and Helen walked toward them. Baxter waved at them as he turned to go. "I'll see you later then Jen." She watched his lanky figure walk quickly up the road.

"What you got there?" Minnie pointed to the book.

"Baxter gave me this book on nursing." She held it up for her sister to see.

Minnie was unimpressed. "It ain't even new."

184

"No, it isn't new," Jennie said, "but it's one of the nicest presents I've ever gotten."

✉

"Lula, this roast chicken would melt in your mouth. Hand me over the sweet potatoes, Clint."

"Next year we'll hunt us a turkey, right Papaw?"

Mylart smiled at Clint. "Right as rain, young'un."

"Pass the biscuits, Jen, and the butter."

"I want some more gravy."

"What do you say, Hube?"

"Please."

"You've had your share of the sweet potatoes, Helen, let Papa finish them."

"Mama, I'm so full."

"That's an old story, Hube. Did you save room for pie?"

"Them pies look a picture."

"What'll it be, apple or pumpkin, Papaw?"

"I'll take a piece of each, thank you."

"That coffee I smell, Lu?"

"Pass the cream."

"Well, Lula," Papaw said, "Guess that was 'bout the best meal I ever et."

"Papa, you always say that."

Min moaned. "I can't believe it. It takes so long to get the meal together and in no time at all we're all layin' back with our bellies 'bout to bust and the table full of dirty dishes."

✉

The fire in the parlor spit and crackled. Clint and Papaw sat with their heads bent over the checker board while Dalton dozed on the settee. Hube and Helen played quietly for a change on the floor, their game of 'fox and goose' spread out before them. Lula and Min were in the kitchen, Jen could here their voices. She tried to concentrate on the nursing book in her lap.

Lula called from the kitchen. "Jen, Baxter's here."

She quickly marked her place and put the book aside and rose as Baxter came into the parlor.

Papaw looked up from the checker board. "Merry Christmas, son."

They all called out, "Merry Christmas, Baxter."

"Merry Christmas to y'all too. Hey Jennie."

Jen noticed he wore levis and a flannel shirt and his warm jacket.

"Feel like going for a walk? It ain't too cold out."

"All right, let me get my coat."

The late afternoon sun was close to setting, directing it's weak rays across the frozen meadows. Baxter took her arm and they walked in comfortable silence.

"Jen, I got somethin' I gotta say."

Jennie's smile faded when she saw his serious face. "Baxter, what is it?"

"I was awful confused this summer what with Gayle and all. Now she's gone and I can think clear, I can see she wasn't the kind of girl I want at all. I don't know how I coulda been so fooled."

Jennie sighed with relief and grinned happily at him. She'd waited three months to hear Baxter say this. "She sure was pretty, though."

"She was pretty, Jennie, but only on the outside. I still don't know how she coulda jest gone off like that, makin' Ma and Pa and her own mother and father worry like she did. Ma says Aunt Serina still ain't heard from her."

Baxter stopped and turned Jennie to face him. "I actually thought I was in love with her." He let his arms drop and began to pace back and forth in front of her. "I don't know how I'm gonna make you believe me, Jen, after the fool I made of myself over Gayle, but it's you I love, not her." He stopped pacing and looked earnestly into her face.

Jennie was stunned. "Baxter..."

He spoke in a rush. "I guess I always loved you. I think it goes back to when we wuz kids. The other kids 'ud make fun of me and you use to stick up for me, remember? Then all those years we spent with Doc, you and me. We shared so much. I think knowin' Gayle is what woke me up to what I shoulda realized all along. I love you, Jennie."

He saw the shock on her face. "It's for honest true, Jen." He repeated softly, "I love you."

He put his arms around her and she buried her face in his jacket. She felt the rough texture against her cheek. Tears welled in her eyes. *He can't be in love with me, he's my best friend.* Her thoughts flew to James. How can I think I'm in love with a man I've never met, and not love someone I've known all my life? She drew away and looked up into his face. He was waiting for her to say something.

"I don't know what to say." She saw the disappointment in his eyes.

"I thought I can't go on like always, now I know how I feel, and not let you know."

She put her hand on his arm. "We've been such good friends for so long. Golly, Bax, nothing happens to me but I don't think right away, I got to tell Bax."

"You think maybe that's love?"

"I don't know. Well, maybe it is. I just don't know."

"Jennie, you got to promise..."

"No Baxter, I can't promise anything."

"I mean just promise to think about it."

She nodded, serious. "I guess I could promise that..."

Before she realized it, he pulled her into his arms and kissed her, softly. She felt a little dizzy and breathless.

Jennie sat by the fireplace, a book open in her lap. After trying to read the same passage for the third time she snapped the book close. No sense trying to read. There was too much to think about. Baxter's declaration had her mind in turmoil. It would solve a lot of problems if I loved Baxter, she thought. Why don't I? Or do I? I know him inside and out and he's such a good friend and fun to be with. Maybe *that's* what love is.

She got up from the settee and began to pace... and the money for her education. She could, of course, not mention it to Papa at all and just enter school. Once she started, what could he do? Come after her? Not likely. But that would leave Mama to face Papa alone and that wouldn't be fair. No she'd have to tell him.

She stopped pacing. Now would be the time. Min and Helen are over at the Owens, Papaw took the boys out to test the rifle, and the last she saw Papa, he was napping on the couch by the kitchen stove. She heard Mama coming down the stairs and went to meet her.

"Come into the kitchen, Mama, I have to talk to you and to Papa, too."

Lula looked startled. "What about?"

"Papaw settled with Jeb Owen about the property. He has the money for me."

Mama looked uneasy. "But I thought..."

"I hope you didn't think Papa had me scared into changing my mind."

"I ... I really don't know what I thought. And you want to tell Papa? Now?"

Jennie nodded. "No time like the present."

In the kitchen, Jennie shook Papa gently by the shoulder. He came awake with a start. "I want to talk to you, Papa." Mama sat down in her rocker, automatically folding her hands in prayer. Jennie pulled a chair around so she was facing them both.

Dalton grumbled. "What's so all-fired important you have to wake me up?"

Lula looked worriedly first at Dalton and then at Jennie. "Maybe this ain't a good time, Jennie."

"It will only take a minute, Mama," Jennie said.

Dalton sat up and looked at the two of them with a sullen expression. "Well... get on with it."

"I'll come right to the point, Papa," Jennie said. "Then you can go back to your nap. When you were home in July I told you Jeb Owen intended to buy that strip of land from Papaw and that Papaw was going to give me that money for my education..." she stumbled a little, remembering Papa's threat that she would never go to school. She took a deep breath and continued. "Well, Papaw got the money from Mr. Owen, so..."

Papa stared at Jennie, a little groggy. "Huh?"

"I said..."

"I heard what you said."

Jennie started to get up, hoping the discussion was ended. "Well, that's all I've got to say, then."

Dalton said sharply, "Sit down. It ain't all I got to say."

Jennie sighed and sat down again.

"I thought I already made it clear you ain't goin' nowhere. You selfish little snot. You're plannin' to leave your mother and everyone else and go traipsin' off to school like you ain't got no responsibility?"

Jennie's mouth fell open. Papa had just described himself. She laughed at the irony and said sweetly, "But Papa, isn't that just exactly what you do?" Dalton's face darkened. Jennie hurried on. "You go off to the mines and don't so much as look over your shoulder when you're leaving. Do you worry that Mama doesn't have the money for the tab at Proffitts'? Are you here when one of your children gets sick in the middle of the night and needs Dr. Payne?"

Dalton sputtered. "It ain't your place to question what I do or don't do. You think you're so high and mighty and you know what you are? An ignorant farm girl ... nothing more than a poor little ignorant farm girl. Mylart's a fool, throwin' his money away."

Jennie smiled, proud of her self-control. "You're right, Papa, absolutely right. I am just an ignorant farm girl. That's why I want an education, so I won't end up being just a farm girl. No, Papa. Papaw won't waste his money. I'm gonna make him proud."

Jennie got up and carefully replaced the kitchen chair where it belonged. "That's all I have to say, Papa. Now you can go back to your nap."

Chapter Seventeen
Influenza Strikes

Doctor Payne confronted the rising incidence of a particularly vicious strain of influenza with a deep sense of dread, the papers on the counter at Lije's store confirming his deepest fear. While the United States still rejoiced the war's end, it now faced a war of another kind.

The troops returning from the battlefields of Europe brought with them the deadly virus, first infecting the big cities and gradually spreading to the more isolated areas.

The outbreak struck Boone, coming in by train from Johnson City. Within a week, cases were being reported in all the outlying districts.

✉

January 18, 1919 began with a snowstorm. The first flurries transformed the barren fields into a white wonderland, but as the day wore on, the gentle flakes turned needlelike, whipped through the air by winds gusting in ever-mounting fury, forcing the daily gathering around the stove in Lije's store to be abandoned.

Mama's rocker was pulled up close to the stove, a blanket covering her legs. She dozed in the dim light of the late afternoon, mending untouched in her lap. Minnie and Helen sat at the table doing school work and Hube ran from window to window, Soldier at his heels, giving a steady report on the storm.

Helen said, "Hubie, you be quiet! I can't concentrate." Jennie, on the sofa, looked up from the shirt she was sewing buttons on and smiled at Hube and his dog. She remembered how angry Papa had been at Christmas because Hubie had allowed Soldier in the house. What would he say now if he knew Soldier slept at the foot of Hubie's bed?

Lula sighed and Jennie looked over at her. "You look a mite peaked, Mama, you feeling all right?"

"This cold is making my bones ache. I'll be all right soon's the storm lets up."

Hube left the window. "Mama, I think I'll go outdoors. I can see the storm better from out there."

"Now I never heard such nonsense in all my born days. The wind would carry you to kingdom come."

"Well, I could tie myself to ole Soldier here and 'tween the two of us we wouldn't be blowed away."

"You just stop your frettin' and be happy you have a warm stove to put your bottom up to. When it stops storming is time enough for snow playin'. Ain't you got some school work to do too?"

"Naw, I done it all." He turned and abruptly fell on Soldier, and the two of them began tumbling around the kitchen.

Jennie said. "Maybe sending him and Soldier outside isn't such a bad idea, 'least then we could enjoy some peace and quiet."

Clint could be heard on the porch stamping the snow from his feet. The door opened and he hurried in, followed by a billow of wind and snow. "I throwed some ole blankets over Lib and Lizzie," he said as he kicked off his galoshes, "poor ladies are 'bout froze to death." He went to the stove, drawing off his mittens and held his hands to the warmth. "No sign of the storm lettin' up yet." He shrugged out of his coat and wool hat and hung them on a peg. "Come on, Hube, get the checkerboard and I'll play ya." Jennie smiled at Clint with gratitude.

Mama was asleep again in the rocker. Jennie gently removed the mending from her lap and put away her sewing basket.

Throughout the house, timbers groaned and creaked. The bitter blast found its way into every chink and crack, bringing with it small mounds of snow that settled on windowsills and crept beneath doorways.

Mama left her rocker and took to her bed complaining of a headache and achy bones. When she didn't reappear by suppertime, Jennie went up to her bedroom. Lula was in her flannel nightdress snuggled deep under the covers.

"Mama?" Jennie shivered in the cold bedroom. The only sound was the beating of the snow against the windowpane.

Jennie tried again, "Mama, you want some supper?"

Lula didn't respond. Jennie bent over and felt her forehead and stood up abruptly. Mama had a raging fever.

Everyone scurried about. Helen made a bed on the sofa by the stove while Min and Jen, with Mama leaning on them, made their way down the stairs and into the kitchen. They tucked covers around her.

Mama roused briefly. "What ... where ... That you Dalt?"

Minnie whispered, "Jennie, you don't think it's..."

Jennie fought the fear that bubbled up in her throat. "I don't know, Min, it could be."

"Oh God, what are we gonna to do? With this storm we'll never get word to Doc, there's jest no way."

"I think I could get through to Doc right now," Clint said.

Jennie shook her head. "Maybe so, Clint, but you'd still have to get back and it's nearly dark. No, we'll just tend to Mama here by the stove where she'll be warm and see what tomorrow brings."

Helen began to cry and Hube stood quiet and wide-eyed. Jennie herded them all to the table. "Listen now. Mama is sick. She's taken care of us enough times and now it's our turn to care for her. No squabbling and everyone does their chores. All right?"

The swirling snow and dark skies brought night on early and at five o'clock the lamps were lit. They nibbled on cold ham and leftover biscuits and tried to ignore the howling storm.

Mama swung from raging fever to frightening chills that made her body shake uncontrollably. All they could do was press cool cloths to her forehead when the fever rose and rub her hands and feet when the chills took her.

The storm continued to shake and rattle the old house as the evening wore on. At bedtime no one wanted to leave Mama. Jennie said, "I'll stay down here. The rest of you go on up to bed."

Minnie argued, "I can't go to bed and leave you and Mama down here all alone."

Jennie took her aside. "Min, between you and Clint you have to comfort Helen and Hube. They're scared. Clint can see to Hube and you can bring Helen into our bed." She put her arm around Min. "I think it's what Mama would want you to do."

Min bent over Mama. "Guess you're right, it's just..."

Clint brought in more firewood from the porch and stacked it in the woodbin. "You need us, you holler, Jen."

Jen nodded. Helen hesitated and tears began to slide down her cheeks. Minnie pulled her close and whispered, "You can sleep with me tonight." They followed Clint and Hube up the stairs.

Jennie knelt beside Lula. She took her mother's parched hand and held it to her cheek. The thought of being in charge frightened her.

Around midnight the wind that roared like a lion down the mountainsides, driving the snow before it, magically turned gentle as a lamb and now the snow fell whisper soft in the valley.

By morning light they were relieved to see the storm had played itself out but dismayed at the mountainous snow banks left in its wake. It was windy and bitter cold and the skies remained overcast and grey. Mama was no better.

Clint pushed his breakfast plate aside. "I'm gonna get Doctor Payne."

No one disputed his decision. He pulled on his galoshes and shrugged into his warm woolen coat while Jennie drew his red wool hat down over his ears and wound his scarf snugly around his neck.

They stood in a row at the front window as he made his way down the walk through knee-high drifts to the gate, struggled to open it, and then out into the road, which looked like a white desert. He turned and waved and for a long time they watched the red hat bob up and down until it was gone from sight. Wind swirled the snow around and his tracks were gone.

Sherm showed up on their kitchen doorstep with a shovel in his hand. His grin disappeared when he saw Min's face. "What is it, Min?"

"It's Mama. Come in so's I can close the door." Sherm stood by the back door, the snow melting in a puddle around his feet.

"Mama's sick and we think it's influenza. Clint went to get Doc. We're waitin' on them now."

The young boy looked helpless. "What kin I do, Min?"

"Maybe you could clear the walk around to the back door ...and Sherm, could you clear a path to the privy?"

The morning wore on. Lula began to cough, frightening them with the deep strangling sound. Chores kept them mercifully busy. The cows were milked, the chickens fed, wood overflowed the wood bin, and a bucket of water from the spring sat in the sink.

Sherm showed up at the door again, carrying a covered dish, and handed it to Jennie. "Some stewed chicken Mama made fer ya Jen. Mama wants to know anything we kin do?"

Jennie said grimly, "Just pray is all."

It was just before noon that Hubie, keeping watch at the front window cried out, "Here they come."

Penelope, floundering through the snow banks on Valley Road stopped at the gate, steam rising from her flanks. Doc and Clint slid off and led the horse down the cleared pathway around to the back door. Doc untied his medical bag from the saddle and left Clint in charge of Pen. Minnie helped him off with his coat and Hubie dropped to the floor and pulled off his galoshes.

Jennie said, "We're so glad you're here, Doctor Payne."

The old man blew on his hands and rubbed them together.

"I wuz gettin ready to go down to Sugar Grove anyway, Jen. Otis Fenley's Ma and Pa are right bad."

Clint came in the kitchen door, his face red with cold. "Lib and Lizzy are sharing their blankets with Pen, Doc."

"I kindly thank ya, Clint. Now, let's have a look at your Mama."

They moved with him to the sofa and watched in silence as he opened his medical bag, took out a thermometer and placed it between Lula's parched lips. He listened to her chest for a long time with his stethoscope. When he took the thermometer from her mouth and held it up to the light, Jennie asked, "Is it very high?"

"'Fraid so. Chest sounds bad..."

No one said a word. Doc snugged the covers around Lula and steered Jennie away from the sofa. The rest quietly followed.

Doc produced a small bottle from his bag. "I'll give you some aspirin to help with the fever and once the fever drops, you can try a poultice to help bring up the mucus. Mind you burn the rags. You can brew you some cherry bark tea, see if she'll sip it."

Jennie nodded wordlessly.

Doctor Payne continued, "If you kin get her to sit up every hour or so and rub her back, that'll help with the congestion. Try and get some broth into her too, but don't fight her if she won't take it. Fever should break in a day or two but it's the congestion in her lungs that's the worry. There's not a whole lot we can do but wait."

Jennie stared at him, the concern plain on her face. Doc put an arm around her. "Lula is a strong woman and a fighter. She's gonna be fine." Doc turned to take his coat from the peg.

"Doc," Jennie said, "Mrs. Owen made some stewed chicken. It's heating on the stove and there's biscuits and hot coffee. Come eat something before you go out in the cold again."

"Don't mind if I do, Jen. Somethin' warm 'ud be good." They solemnly gathered round the table and made a pretense of eating. Doc said. "I been in Sugar Grove all last week, workin' with Doc Tester down there. Stopped and checked on your Papaw."

Jennie missed a heartbeat.

Doctor Payne read her face and held up his hand. "Mylart's fine. He asked bout y'all."

"I'm glad he doesn't know about Mama," Jennie said, "He might just try to get here."

Clint pushed away from the table. "Guess I better do some snow clearin'. You wanna help, Hube?" The boys somberly put on their coats and slipped into their galoshes and left the kitchen, quietly closing the door behind them. Helen helped Min clear the table.

Dr. Payne leaned over and took Jennie's hand. "Mylart told me about selling that land to Jeb and what he plans to do with the money. Can't say how good it makes me feel, Jen, to know you're gonna get a chance, same as Baxter."

Jennie smiled at him. "Thanks, Doctor Payne. It looks like both Bax and me are going to get some firsthand experience. Have many come down sick in Zionville?"

"A few, so far, and a lot in Sugar Grove, too. Doc Tester had his hands full there, so I rode down to help out, but when Prosper come through with the mail and said they wuz startin' to get sick here in Zionville, I thought I best come back. Prosper give me a list a names of those he knows about and the list is growin'. Only problem is nothin' much I can do. This influenza, nothing like I ever seen before.

"But this too shall pass, young'un. This too shall pass." He gave Jennie's hand a final squeeze, picked up his coffee cup and took a last sip. "Best be on my way to Sugar Grove."

Doc struggled into his galoshes and Jennie helped him into his coat, trying desperately to think of a reason for him to stay.

He saw the look in her eyes. "You can handle it, Jen."

She gave him a weak smile. "I know I can, Doc, but Mama isn't just another patient, she's Mama."

He wrapped his wool scarf around his head, hat and all and said in parting, "Your Mama would say it's in God's hands."

She watched him disappear down the road, clinging to Pen's back, the horse lifting each foot high through the snow.

Helen stood by her side. "Jennie," she whispered, "I'm scared. Everybody's gone. Papa to the coal mines and Ed in the hospital and now Mama so fierce sick."

Jennie put her arms around the skinny little body and stroked the long straight hair. "I know, Helen, we're all worried. But Mama wouldn't ever leave us. She knows we all love her and need her."

Night came. Clint filled the woodbin, checked the fire in the stove and followed Min, Helen and Hube up to bed. Jennie settled herself in Mama's rocker, pulling the patchwork quilt up under her chin. The fire burned low and the clock on the cupboard ticked on. Jennie dozed fitfully.

All at once, Mama cried out "Dalton!" Jennie bolted from the rocker, startled. Lula struggled to get up and it took all Jennie's strength to hold her.

"Mama, what is it?" Lula stared blankly, wrapping her arms around herself. "Dalton, hold me" ...and then she was weeping... "Hold me." She swayed back and forth as though she were enclosed in her husband's arms. Suddenly she clutched Jennie's arm. "So frightened."

Jennie cried. "Don't be frightened, Mama, I'm right here."

Lula's body shook. She looked directly at Jennie with unseeing eyes and whispered hoarsely, "I need... I need Dalton."

Lula fell back amidst the tangled blankets, eyes closed, breathing deep and raspy.

Jennie was numb. What did Mama say? *Dalton, hold me!* She looked down at the worn, lined face of her mother and understood.

Jennie tenderly straightened Mama's blankets and tucked them around her. In one unguarded moment, Mama had answered all Jennie's questions. Like a school girl... like Minnie... Mama loves Papa. She doesn't want to hear how irresponsible he is or how much he drinks. What Mama yearns for is what they had when they were first married... and Papa can no longer give her that.

She felt ashamed. *I've been thinking of Mama as old, too old to need that kind of love. Who am I to judge?* She smoothed the hair back from the fevered brow. It doesn't matter I see Papa as no-account and worthless. Mama sees him as someone worth loving and it's what Mama sees that's important.

She felt chilled and went to the woodbin next to the stove and replenished the fire. Slowly she picked up the quilt, wrapped it around herself and fell into the rocker. Sleep wouldn't come. She whispered aloud into the darkness. "I promise, Mama, I'll never fight with you about Papa again."

⊠

The next morning again dawned cold and bleak, with gusty winds swirling the snow about. The roads were still impassably choked with snow.

Mama's fever fluctuated. Jennie dissolved the aspirin in water and managed to get some past Lula's parched lips. When her fever broke they rejoiced only to be discouraged when it returned. Jennie and Minnie took turns coaxing Mama to sit up. While they rubbed her back she leaned on them helplessly as the deep ugly coughing rumbled in her chest. There was nothing more to do.

Clint stared morosely at the bleak countryside, Jennie by his side. "Wonder when Mr. Wooding's gonna bring his oxen through to clear the roads?"

"No place to go, anyway, Clint. There's no school."

"I wouldn't go to school if they wuz. You need me here."

She turned to look at his worried face. "Yes, I do need you here, Clint. Doc says there should be a crisis in a few days, and I think we should all be together..." Jennie left the sentence unfinished. Clint started to turn away, then turned back to Jennie. "By the way, Jen, you know what today is?"

Jennie looked puzzled. "Today...?"

"My birthday."

Jennie's face fell. "Oh, Clint, I'm so sorry. I forgot."

Clint managed a weak smile. "It's all right, Jen, I don't 'spect anybody'd 'member, time like this. Anyways, I'm twelve today."

As the day wore on they went quietly about their chores. The boys cared for the livestock and chickens and made sure there was plenty of firewood to feed the hungry stove and water for cooking. Clint and Hubie cleared a pathway through the snow to the cow shed, the chicken house and the spring. Helen, usually so ready to argue, bundled up and dug into the snow-covered root cellar for potatoes and cabbages for their dinner. She brought back apples, too, to help Jennie make a cake for Clint.

The grey day slid into dusk, and with night the winds died to a whisper. The clouds scattered and a bright moon bathed the snow banks in brilliance. The Wainwright house became an oasis in a sea of white. Despite Lula's illness, or perhaps because of it, the family took comfort in being together.

Before trooping up to bed, they all knelt by Mama's side and said their prayers. Minnie, holding the lamp, led them upstairs to bed, leaving Jennie curled up in Mama's rocker.

Jennie awoke with a start. A deathly silence, broken only by the ticking clock, enfolded her and she couldn't determine what, if anything, was wrong. She got up from the rocker, shaking her head to clear out the remnants of sleep. Moonlight flooded the room. Now she knew what it was. Mama lay perfectly still.

With her heart thudding, Jennie leaned over and laid her hand on Mama's brow. The fever was gone; Mama was sleeping peacefully.

In the morning, Jennie, grinning broadly, met her siblings at the foot of the stairs. "Mama passed the crisis in the night. She's going to be all right." They all crowded around Mama, who was peacefully sleeping, unaware of the haggard faces bending over her. They were all anxious to see for themselves. Helen began to cry.

Hube said with disgust, "Look at cry-baby. Dint you hear Jennie say Mama's better?"

"I'm cryin' cause I'm happy... and don't call me cry-baby."

They quietly left Mama's side and went to the table, joining hands and giving thanks.

While Mama had passed the crisis, she was still very ill. Between terrible bouts of coughing, she slept, and when she awoke she found one of the children by her side, holding her hand. She smiled weakly, took a little of the nourishment they offered and quietly slipped back to sleep.

In the late afternoon Baxter appeared at their door. Jennie went to him, surprised as tears sprung to her eyes. She hastily blinked them away.

"Hey, Jen, I been worried about y'all," Baxter said. He put his arms around her, and for a moment Jennie surrendered to the incredible comfort of being held close.

"Mama's fever broke for the last time in the night. She's been sleeping on and off all day."

Baxter sighed in relief. "Ever since Doc told me 'bout your Mama I been trying to get here." He smiled at Jennie. "But I knew she was in good hands."

"Take off your things, Bax, and come see for yourself."

She watched as he picked up Lula's limp hand and felt her pulse, then her brow. Her eyes were closed and she lay still, and except for the harsh breathing, was sleeping peacefully.

"Yer right. She's cool as a cucumber." Baxter dropped into one of the chairs.

"Your Mama'll be pretty weak for a long time. She's gotta stay put on the sofa."

Jennie agreed. "That will be the hardest part, making her stay put."

"I don't think so. She ain't gonna have much strength to argue with you, wait and see."

Jennie grinned. It felt so good to grin... "Well, you know Mama."

Soldier barked at the door and Hube scrambled to let him in. He fell to his knees and caught the dog's face between his hands. "Mama's gonna be good as new, Soldier... you hear me, dog?"

Min and Helen set platters of food on the table: ham biscuits, bowls of steaming green beans and kernel corn, and golden brown fried apples.

They all hungrily spooned the food onto their plates, relief giving them an appetite. Between mouthfuls, Baxter kept up a steady conversation. "Me and Doc's been runnin 'round the countryside. Pa let me take our hoss, and I been off in one direction and Doc in the other.

He stopped to take a bite of his ham biscuit. "This sickness is a worry all over the country and, 'cordin' to the papers, millions are dyin' in Europe. Folks in Washington are sayin' it might jest get that bad here."

Minnie asked. "How many cases in Zionville?"

He chewed for a minute and swallowed. "Over thirty so far. You know Mary Lee Martin, played the piano at the Baptist church? Well she passed on day 'fore yesterday. Mr. Dobbs that runs the saw mill, his Pa died and so did Pap Fenley."

Jennie said, shocked, "Otis Fenley's father died?"

"Yep. The old man didn't linger at all and Mam Fenley is still pretty bad. They buried the old man and Mam don't even know he's gone." Baxter reached for another ham biscuit. "Preacher Truall's down sick too, but he's on the mend. Doc tell you your Papaw is doing fine?"

Jennie nodded. "Nothing much gets Papaw down."

Baxter finally pushed his plate away. "That was mighty good and I thank y'all kindly."

Minnie got up from her seat. "You visit with Baxter, Jen. Me and Helen will clear the table." She turned to the boys. "We need water and more wood. You decide 'tween you who's gonna do what, you hear?"

As the boys got into their coats, Min came back with the coffee pot and refilled their cups.

Baxter said, "Jen, now your Mama is outta danger, Doc'll probably call on you to help out."

"I expect so. When I'm sure Mama is all right I'll be glad to help."
Baxter sighed deeply and rubbed his eyes.

Jennie said, "You must be so tired."

He reached over and took her hands. "Through all a this, Jen, I ain't forgot Christmas afternoon. You thought any more 'bout what I said? I mean it now more'n I ever did."

Jennie let her hands rest in his. "I've been too worried, Bax, to think about anything much, but there's something I should have told you Christmas day."

Baxter looked serious, but said nothing, waiting for Jennie to continue.

"James' letters have gotten a lot more than just friendly. He..."

Baxter interrupted, annoyed. "I told you that wuz gonna happen, didn't I?"

Jennie pulled her hands gently away. "I know, I know you did. He wants to come to Zionville and I haven't discouraged it. I really want to meet him."

"I see. So what are you sayin', you think maybe this James person..."

"I don't really know what I'm saying. His letters are special. He sounds special and I want to meet him."

Baxter nodded, unsmiling. "Does that mean I'll never be more than a friend?"

"I haven't said that either, Bax. It's too soon to make any decisions about anything," Jennie said firmly.

Baxter grinned. "Jest so's I'm not out of the running."

Jennie returned the grin.

Baxter got up wearily. "Guess I better go. I'll let Doc know your Mama's on the mend."

Jennie helped him into his coat at the door. "I'm glad you came tonight, Baxter. You always seem to come when I need you most."

Baxter looked into her eyes. "I hope you always need me, Jen."

It was late before Jennie could herd the children up to bed. Min, however, was determined to stay up with Jennie and settled into Lula's rocker, tucking the patchwork quilt around her. She fingered the frayed edges of the quilt. "I remember when Mama was working on this."

"It's hard to remember Mama *not* working on something."

"Tell me something, Jennie, why is it so important for you to go to nursin' school?" Min asked earnestly. "Doc says you're a good nurse right now. Ain't that enough?"

"There's a *big* difference in what Doc has taught me and what I could learn in school. It's not just the money I could earn. I want to be a real nurse. Isn't there anything *you* really want?"

Min squirmed to get more comfortable. "I guess what I want most in the whole world is to get married. And Jennie, me and Sherm decided we want to marry each other."

Jennie looked thoughtfully at Min. "That puzzles me, you being so young and having such grown up feelings. You really think you're ready for marriage?"

"Maybe not right this minute, but it's Sherm I want to marry some day."

"You'll have to wait until he can support a wife and home. Then there's children. Hope you've both thought of all that."

"We've done a lot of thinkin' and talkin'. His Ma and Pa would help us. Clara and Jeb Owen like me a lot."

"They think of you as the little girl next door. If they've thought about the two of you being in love, they've no doubt thought of it as puppy love," Jennie cautioned her sister.

Minnie said with exasperation, "Well, they're wrong. Maybe we are children in years, but we don't *feel* like children." She sat up in the rocker and looked earnestly at Jennie. "I know in my heart Sherm and me are meant to be together. I know there's more to marriage than kissin', but I know too that Sherm's gonna make a good husband. He's like his Pa, works hard and all. The fact that we're young has nuthin' to do with it."

Jennie sighed. "I'm not the one to give advice. It's your life, yours and Sherm's."

After a pause Min said, "Seems to me you got some decidin' to do yourself."

"About what?"

"Is it gonna be Baxter or James? I can see how Baxter feels 'bout you. I never fer a minute thought he wuz interested in Gayle. He wears his heart out in the open where you're concerned. And then, all them letters you been gettin' from James..."

Jennie said seriously, "Min, I know Baxter will make a steady, hardworking husband for someone. What I don't know is if I want that someone to be me. On the other hand, while James' letters are wonderful and exciting, I've not met the man."

"Think maybe James'll come to Zionville?"

"He may."

"S'pose he wants to marry you and take you away?"

"What makes you think James would want to marry me, or me him for that matter?" Jennie said in surprise.

"Oh, come on, Jennie. I see your face when you get a letter from James and how you run off to be alone when you read it, and how you get a kinda of silly expression on your face whenever you talk about him."

Jennie laughed, "Lordy, Min, you're a busybody."

"It's true, though, ain't it?"

"Well... I don't know what he'd find interesting in a girl from the hills. I hardly even wear shoes half the time."

"That might be what 'ud interest him most. Someone simple and good..."

"Simple and good, that's me, all right."

Minnie was indignant. "If James don't see you the way everyone else does, then he's the fool."

Chapter Eighteen
A Little One is Stricken

Jennie Girl,

I am writing aboard the troop ship that is carrying us home—no word in my vocabulary sounds sweeter. My hand is not steady due to the rolling of the ship, so I hope you will be able to read this.

Our unit will make port at Montreal and then we'll be shipped cross country by train to Vancouver where our unit is based. We'll be discharged from there. Pete's family lives in Vancouver and he is anxious to see them.

Towards the end of the war, even though negotiations were under way, fighting was ferocious. We were in a valley and the Germans were entrenched not 100 yards from us... machine guns every few yards... snipers in the trees. They stood us off for five days and during that time I guess I slept off and on maybe ten hours.

During the day we helped carry the wounded to the first aid station just behind our lines. The nurses gained our everlasting admiration, Jen, so caring and efficient. At night we stood guard duty, holding the lines, with the Boche within hearing distance...

"Irish... you awake?"

"We better be, laddie, we're on guard duty... and keep your voice down."

"Yeah, well, I find myself fallin' asleep if I don't keep movin'. Did you hear? The word is that peace is being negotiated, but it sure don't seem like the Boche know about it."

"Sure as hell doesn't. Just keep your head down. If the Boche are ready to call it quits, you don't want to end up being the booby prize."

"What's a booby prize?"

"It's the prize awarded to the loser."

"Oh... I'd give my right arm for a fag right now."

"You know there's no smoking..."

"I know, I know. I just meant..."

James saw the flash of the rifle a split second before the shot buried itself in the lip of the trench with a thud, sending out a spray of dirt. The shock sent Pete staggering backward, landing on the floor of the muddy trench, arms and legs askew.

In the confusion, James fell to his knees beside Pete, not completely sure the bullet had missed his friend. "Pete. For God's sake, Pete." He tore at the neck of Pete's uniform, ready to look for the wound.

Pete looked up, spitting mud. "Somebody oughta go over there and tell that stupid bastard the war's over."

The very next day our big guns began a barrage along the entire front that started at 3:00 a.m. and ended at 6:00 p.m. We advanced and established ourselves in the vacated German bunkers and were prepared to start all over again at sunup, but the Germans had retreated... They were gone. That was the end.

It was hard for Pete and me to leave our mates. It seems those befriended in cruel times burrow to the deepest spot in your heart. As it was with Edward. I'm anxious for word of him. We had just that short time in the hospital together, but thoughts of him have stayed with me. When next you write to him, tell him I look forward to seeing him in Zionville.

"My God, Irish, if you gotta eat, don't do it in front of me. Just seeing you push that food in your face is enough to make me heave... If only this damn ship would stop rollin'."

"Sorry, boyo. I'm all finished." James pushed aside his empty tray. "In a day or two you'll be able..."

Pete held up his hand. "I don't even want to talk about it."

"All right, all right, we'll talk about something else."

Pete said, "I'm sure looking forward to seeing Mom and Gloria. She's got three kids, Gloria has. All boys, Jerry, Henry and Peter. He's the youngest, Peter. Guess he's about five now. Looks a little like me, too... blue eyes. Gloria'll be able to put you up. You'll love Gloria."

"If she had the same sparkling personality as you, boyo, I'll no doubt fall in love wi' the lass at first sight."

Pete missed the sarcasm. "Yeah, Gloria's great. She's ten years older than me. Always seemed more like another mother than a sister.

God I gave Mom and Gloria a hard time after my Dad died. When Mom remarried I was all set to hate Bruce, that's my step-dad, but Gloria liked him right off. Me? I fought it like hell, but after a while I liked him too. Best thing ever happened to me, considering where I was headed."

James sat with his back against the bulkhead watching the horizon appear and disappear. He thought it best to let Pete ramble on. It kept his attention off the increasingly choppy seas.

Pete rolled on his side and propped his head on his hand.

"So, after we leave Vancouver we'll head down into the States, pick up jobs here and there and head east. Sound okay?"

James nodded. The ship gave a sudden lurch. "Say, Irish, is it my imagination or is this ship rolling more than it was?"

As if on cue, a voice came over the loudspeaker. "Attention. Now hear this. We're coming into heavy seas. All troops report below decks. Life jackets on. Check the location of your life boat station." The message was repeated several times. Reluctantly, Pete got to his feet and followed James.

"Boyo, your face is turning the loveliest shade of green."

"Go to hell."

I'll write no more for now as I have all I can do to stay in my hammock. I'll mail this letter when I get to Montreal.

My love to you, lass,
James

Jennie lay across her bed and reread the letter. It was hard to admit, because it was such a cowardly thought, that she was relieved their meeting wouldn't take place for some time yet. She'd been involved for more than a year with James' past, with his plans for the future, what he thought about so many things, but she had never allowed herself to think about James actually knocking on her door, her answering it, and finding them standing face to face.

She was filled with self-doubt. Suppose when they met they realized they had no more in common than the sun and the moon, and all the letters they shared were worthless dreams. Would they smile and say 'It was nice to meet you' and then goodbye?

Jennie rolled off the bed. She reminded herself the meeting was just postponed, not cancelled. Time enough to panic when he told her his time and date of arrival.

The cold spell held on. The wind continued to sweep furiously down the mountainside and whip the snow banks into a make-believe storm. Clint, worried about Lib and Lizzie, stuffed rags in all the chinks of the cow shed and made sure they had plenty of clean hay and feed. When he went to the spring he took along an axe to break up the ice and allow the water to run freer.

School was open but ill-attended; nor had the potbellied stove at the store drawn its usual crowd. Everyone agreed, this January was the coldest anyone could remember.

Jennie made poultices of onions and mustard, applying them to Lula's chest. Gradually the fierce cough diminished. As Lula healed, she moved, under Jennie's protest, to her rocker. After a day or two the mending pile appeared at her side, at which point Jennie acknowledged defeat. Minnie stood by the window watching Clint, Hube and Helen work on a snowman while Soldier, leaping in great bounds, disappeared from one snowbank to the next. "Mama, here comes Buelis Green."

Jennie wiped her hands on her apron and opened the kitchen door as Buelis came up the steps.

Lula called from her rocker, "Lands sakes, Buelis, come in by the fire and warm up. I 'preciate your comin' to set with me. The good Lord knows I could use some company."

Buelis stamped her feet and stepped into the kitchen. She handed a basket to Jennie along with her shawl.

"I know how partial y'all are to my molasses and apple cakes, Lu, so I brung ya one."

"Well, thank you kindly, Buelis."

Jennie shook out the heavy shawl and choked back a smile, remembering how Sarah had reacted to it. "This is a mighty handsome piece of knitting, Mrs. Green."

"Ain't it though? Used up ever scattered piece a yarn I could find."

Mama shook her head in wonder. "Looks like Joseph's coat of many colors."

"Lu, that's a good 'un," and Buelis slapped her well padded thigh, "I'll have to remember that 'un and tell Harley... Joseph's coat, I swan."

Still laughing, she settled herself on the sofa. " Well, now, we was right worried 'bout you, Lula. Harley says to me this morning, time you see how Lu is and so here I am. You look a mite peaked, Lu, but I guess that's to be 'spected what with all you been through."

"I'm healin' nicely, Buelis."

"We been lucky so far, me and Harley. I asked Doc yestiday at the store if it was too soon fer me to visit and he said to come ahead, that you was up in your rocker, so here I am. Poor Doc, he's gonna end up sick, the way he's been pushin' hisself.

"I heard a good story on Doc. This uz before the snowfall. Seems Jacob Wooding come on Doc's horse and carriage late one night just below Lije's store when he was walking home from visitin' with Emmaline. They do make a nice couple don't they, Emmaline and Jacob, well anyways Jacob looked in and there's Doc slumped over in the seat. Jacob had a start, thought the ole man uz dead 'til Doc started snoring. Seems Doc jest fell asleep on his way home from one a his calls and ole Penelope figured she would just nap a little herself. So Jacob climbed in the carriage, woke Pen up real gentle like as he didn't want to spook her, and drove the pair of 'em home."

Mama said, "Well, maybe in years comin' we can all laugh about that story, Buelis, but now's not the time. Poor ole Doc."

"I know, it's fearsome. We ain't had Sunday service in a while what with Prosper down. Ain't been any mail delivery neither and did you hear Pearl and all her young'uns is bad sick?"

Jennie gasped," Mrs. Green, you mean Aunt Pearl has influenza?"

"Fraid I do, Jennie, young'uns too. Doc sent for Luther to come home soon's he can, but it'll probably be a while afore he gets here. That ain't all. I hear Jeb Owen and one of his boys, don't know which, is awful poorly. I was feared to go in, so I left a basket on their front porch."

Jennie's eyes flew to Min standing by the sink. Her color was grey. In a choked voice Min said, "Mrs. Green, you say you don't know which of the boys is sick?"

Jennie went to Min and put her arm around her. "Min, now don't..."

"No, chile, don't know if it's Clayton or Sherman."

Minnie shrugged off Jennie's arm. "I got to go over there. If it's Sherm, he'll need me." She turned to the coats by the kitchen door.

Lula stopped rocking. "Min, you think that would be a good idea? Clara can handle..." Her voice trailed off, worry showing in her eyes.

"Mama, I *got* to go." Minnie frantically pulled on her coat and sat on the floor to pull on her galoshes.

Buelis shook her head. "Goodness, Lu, bad enough you been sick, you gonna let that chile go over there?"

Lula looked helplessly at Jennie. "Jen, what do you think?"

"I think it's too late." The kitchen door banged shut after Minnie. "What we think doesn't matter anyway, Mama. Min is in love with Sherm. If anything happens to him without her doing all she can to help, she will never forgive herself."

Buelis snorted. "Humpf, Lu, what does a child that age know 'bout love. That's nonsense."

Lula said. "I agree. Min's no mor'n a baby."

"Mama, call it baby love, puppy love, whatever you want, but to Min it's real."

"But that's jest young'un nonsense, them foolin' round together all the time." She seemed to be talking to herself. "Love... a child jest fourteen can't have growed up feelins' yet."

Jen said, "No use arguing, she's gone just like I got to go to Aunt Pearl's. You're on the mend now and Helen and the boys are here to do the chores."

Lula sighed. "I guess so, Jen. I kin take care of things here, you go. Aunt Pearl and her young'uns need you. As fer Min and Sherm..." Lula looked dazed, "guess I ain't gonna have much to say about it."

Though Tom Wooding and his oxen had cleared the road of snow, the ruts left in the mud beneath had frozen, making progress down the road slow and perilous. Jennie walked as quickly as she could, clutching her bundle of clothes in front of her for extra protection against the wind, while juggling the usual basket of food over the other arm. She pulled her chin down into her coat. *Lands, I don't remember ever being this cold before... and it looks like more snow comin'.*

She rounded the turn in the road and Luther's cabin came into view. The cabin was a picture with icicles edging the roof and snow piled high around it. As she got closer, she saw the snow hadn't been cleared from the porch or steps and with dismay noted there was no smoke rising from the chimney.

She ran the last few yards, mounted the steps and pushed open the door, closing it quickly behind her. Pearl had covered the windows with old blankets to help keep out the wind and the resulting dimness made the room already cold, seem colder.

"Pearl," she called softly. There was no sign of anyone. The table was covered with dirty dishes as well as an iron pot containing the remnants of something greasy and unappetizing. She made space on the table for her basket and turned to the stove. There was a feeble ember glowing in the ashes and she quickly fed in the last of the wood from the wood bin. With the draft adjusted, the fire caught and began to burn.

She tiptoed to Pearl's bedroom and peered in. The room was dark.

"Pearl?" She walked cautiously to Pearl's bedside and could see the grey hair spread out over the pillow. The unmistakable smell of sickness hung in the air and Jennie put her hand to her mouth while her heart thudded crazily. Just then the old woman moaned faintly and with relief Jennie whispered, "Aunt Pearl, it's me, Jennie."

Pearl opened her eyes and looked about, frightened and unfocused. Jennie sat on the side of the bed, took the old woman's hands in hers and squeezed them gently.

"It's all right, Aunt Pearl, I'm here to help you." She silently prayed Pearl would respond.

The old woman looked up blankly through sunken, red-rimmed eyes. A shaky breath brought on a fit of coughing and Jennie gently drew the frail body to her until the coughing subsided. Pearl smiled and Jennie was weak with relief.

"Jennie, my angel. I been prayin' so hard... and you heard me, didn't you?"

Jennie felt Pearl's forehead. "You don't have a fever, Aunt Pearl."

"Fever broke, I don't know, maybe yesterday. I can't remember."

Jennie would have been alarmed but for having been through the same thing with Mama. Pearl had passed the crisis but like Mama was left with the terrible congestion and wracking cough. Jennie was overwhelmed with guilt. Someone should have checked on the old woman.

Pearl gestured feebly to a bed in the corner. "That's Ada. She's been so bad sick, Jennie, I made up a bed for her over there so's I could take care of her, then I got sick." Great tears rolled down the withered cheeks. "I got no business tryin' to take care of these young'uns... an old woman like me."

Jennie crossed the room to the other bed and pulled back the covers. Ada was limp and sweaty, her flannel nightdress twisted awkwardly about her body. With a sick heart, Jennie remembered Ada in the beautiful bonnet with ribbons she wore at Christmas.

Was it just three weeks ago? The child's hair was pressed damply against her temples and her face glowed with fever, giving her a false look of well-being.

"Oh, Ada, my poor little one," Jennie whispered. She felt for her pulse and found it weak and erratic. With a feeling of dread, she pulled the covers up under Ada's chin and went back to Pearl. "She's sleeping."

"I been so weak, not good fer much, Jennie. Betsey, poor lamb, has been tryin' to care for the lot of us. Doin' a good job of it too." Pearl smiled feebly. "But I prayed every waking minute you'd come."

"Now I'm here. You rest. I'm going to check on the others, then I'll be back."

"Hurry, I'm fierce worried."

Jennie found the other children in the second bedroom, all four of them huddled together in one bed as much for comfort as warmth. Junior, Iva Lee and Abel were sleeping, but Betsey was wide awake, her eyes enormous in the small pinched face.

"Jennie." She lifted up her thin arms and began to whimper.

Jennie drew her close, prepared to find the child feverish, but her forehead was cool to the touch, her eyes frightened, but bright and clear. Quickly she felt the other three and was relieved to find them all free of fever.

She turned to Betsey and spoke softly so as not to wake the others. "You been playing nurse with Ada and Aunt Pearl?"

Betsey nodded solemnly. "Don't seem much like playin'. I been scairt."

"Now I'm here. I'll help you take care of them... are you hungry?" Betsey nodded.

"That's good, cause I have some delicious chicken soup and soon's the fire comes up, we'll heat it up."

Betsey managed a smile and swung her thin legs from under the covers. She whispered, "What do you want me to do first?"

"Suppose you find some warm clothes and get dressed?"

Back in the kitchen, Jennie found the room warmer. Won't stay warm long without firewood, she thought, and reached for her gloves.

The wind, howling down from Grandfather Mountain, had dropped the temperature several more degrees and Jennie gasped as the wind snatched at her breath. A quick search around the yard revealed a pile of logs stacked against the house.

She murmured aloud. "I knew Luther wouldn't leave them without firewood, but they'll have to be split." She struggled to pull the embedded axe free from the tree stump, then set a log on end and with a mighty swing, split it down the middle. After she had split several, she chopped them into pieces that would fit into the stove. By the time she had a large enough supply, she was sweating.

"There," she said, breathing heavily, "that should do for now."

Betsey was busily clearing the dishes from the table as Jennie, arms loaded with firewood, kicked open the cabin door and dropped the wood into the bin. The child gave Jennie a generous grin. "I'm powerful happy you're here."

Soon there was a good blaze going in the old iron stove and Jennie put the pot of chicken soup on to heat.

"That should stir some appetites, Betsey, don't you think?"

Betsey grinned and nodded.

"Now the water." Jennie lifted an old iron pail out of the sink and went into the cold again. The well was at the side of the house. She set her pail on the ground and carefully swung the well bucket out and down, turning the handle until she heard the bucket splash at the bottom. She waited a moment for it to fill, then brought the bucket up. After she'd transferred the water to her pail, she hauled it back to the house and put the iron pail on the back of the stove for the water to heat.

She heard Betsey talking to the other children in the bedroom, but figured that as long as they weren't sick, they could wait until she tended to Pearl and Ada.

She shrugged out of her coat and went into Pearl's room. The old lady had fallen into a restful sleep. "Good," Jennie whispered, "She just needed to know someone was looking after the children. Now for Ada."

She rummaged through drawers until she found some clean clothes. They weren't nightclothes and they didn't belong to Ada, but they were clean.

"Come on, little one," she said, "let's get out of these damp things, make you more comfortable."

Jennie talked as though the child could hear her. "Your arm goes in here, good girl. Now don't you feel much better?"

She crushed one of the aspirins Doctor Payne had given her and mixed it with some water. With Ada cradled in her arms, she tried to drip the liquid between her lips with little success. Jennie was frustrated. She lay Ada down and covered her warmly, the red gold curls lying in a tangled mass about her face. Jennie bit her lip. "Rest, little one. I'll be back."

All the children were standing in a line, waiting for her. Junior looked at her soberly. "Aunt Pearl and Ada gonna die?"

Jennie could see he was fighting tears. She reached for him and put an arm around his shoulders. Iva Lee pushed her way in beside him and Jennie held them both. "Nobody's gonna die."

Betsey struggled with Abel, trying to get his clothes on. "Abel's being bad, Jennie."

Jennie went down on her knees and held her arms out. With a cry, the child came to her. "You're not bad, are you, Abel, just scared?" After he was dressed she hugged him close and smoothed the blond curls from his forehead.

Jennie sat back on her heels. "Betsey, you and Iva Lee and Junior are big enough to understand and help me. At the same time, you'll be helping Aunt Pearl and Ada. Can I count on all of you?" They all solemnly nodded.

Everyone but Ada ravenously ate the chicken soup with thick slices of bread and butter.

Jennie fed Pearl, stopping each time as the cough rumbled up from her chest. Finally the old woman whispered hoarsely. "Good, Jennie, but I can't eat no more." She fell back on her pillow and closed her eyes.

Jennie went to Ada. The child still burned with fever, the congestion in her lungs plain to hear with each labored breath.

She tried again with the aspirin in water but the results were the same. Ada didn't respond.

Jennie went down on her knees beside the bed. She took the fevered hand in hers and closed her eyes. "Dear God, she's so little and frail. Give me the strength to care for her and help her to get well."

Outside the snow had again begun to fall and the children went restlessly from window to window. Betsey was doing her best to keep them occupied and quiet while Jennie kept vigil over Pearl and Ada.

Pearl followed the path Lula had taken. The fever was gone, but coughing wracked her body. Jennie made onion and mustard poultices and applied them to both Pearl and Ada's chests. Pearl responded, waking long enough to ask how her young'uns were before falling again into a fitful sleep. Ada's fever raged.

The afternoon darkened into evening and Jennie got all the children washed and into bed. They fell asleep immediately, even Betsey, who had been determined to stay up all night and help take care of the invalids.

Jennie sat by the window wrapped in a blanket, trying to ignore the cold air that seeped in through cracks around the windows and under the door. The snow fell, beating gently against the window pane. As Jennie watched, Baxter turned onto the pathway and climbed the porch steps.

She jumped to her feet, dropping the blanket in her haste to open the door. "Baxter." The lump in her throat wouldn't allow her to say more. Baxter opened his arms and Jennie fell into them, mindless of the snow covering his coat, and buried her head in his chest. Frustration and worry over Ada spilled out in great sobs. He held her tightly and laid his cheek on her hair.

He crooned to her softly, "It's all right, Jennie... it's gonna be all right."

After a few moments, Jennie drew back and looked up at him. "Ada isn't responding, Baxter, and I can't think what else to do." She took his coat and hung it over a chair, all the while talking. "I've been trying to get her fever down and get liquids into her... talking to her, to try and wake her up, you know..."

She stopped abruptly, her eyes huge and frightened. "I can't think what else to do."

Baxter took her gently by the shoulders and spoke to her soothingly. "You've been doing everything you can, Jen, God knows. I ain't never seen so much sickness. The worst is seein' the little ones sufferin'. They don't understand."

He dropped his arms and ran a tired hand over the stubble on his chin. "We've all been doin' everything possible. You, me, Doc, everyone and none of it is any good. Until this influenza plays itself out, people will keep on dying."

The haggard look in his eyes sobered Jennie. "I'm sorry, Baxter, you've had the brunt of it, you and Doc. I should be trying to comfort you, not the other way around."

He gave her a weak smile. "Ada?" He pointed to Pearl's bedroom. Jennie nodded and followed him into the room.

Aunt Pearl's ragged breathing filled the room. They crossed to the small bed in the far corner. The lamp was turned low, barely casting enough light, but enough to see the child lying motionless, not breathing, her eyes open and unseeing.

"Oh, my God," Jennie covered her face with her hands.

Strong arms were closing around her... holding her up... letting her sink into darkness.

Chapter Nineteen
A Final Goodbye

Aunt Pearl sat in her rocker by the stove wrapped snugly in a blanket, Iva Lee and Abel nestled in her arms, Junior at her feet. She was wan and weak and the coughing still rumbled in her chest, but she steadfastly refused to stay in bed. Jennie, sitting in a chair by her side, thought it was hard enough keeping her in the rocker.

"It was my fault Ada died. I ain't got the sense I wuz born with thinking I could care for these young'uns." The tears rolled unchecked down her cheeks.

"Aunt Pearl, please don't talk like that. You know how frail Ada has always been. You had no control over her getting sick."

"Mebbe not, but I wasn't there to comfort her at the end. I'll see her pitiful face in my dreams fer the rest o' my born days. Oh, Jennie, how am I gonna face Luther."

"He'll understand, Pearl. He surely will."

"I wouldn't blame the man if he put me out in the cold. I didn't take care of his baby." She leaned her head back in the rocker and closed her eyes, moaning softly.

Jennie patted Pearl's shoulder and rose from the chair. "I'm going to tend to Ada now."

Pearl came forward in the rocker and tried to lift the children off her lap. Jennie quickly put her hand on Pearl's shoulder. "No. You stay here and care for Abel and Iva Lee and Junior. That's the best job for you right now."

"Oh, Jennie, oh God, Jennie..."

"I know, I know. It's cruel, but she's in God's care now and out of pain." Pearl laid her head back, the tears flowing freely down her cheeks.

Jennie found a clean cloth in the cupboard and took it along with a small bowl of warm water and a bar of soap into the bedroom, closing the door softly behind her. Betsey was standing beside Ada, staring down at her.

Without her nightclothes on, Ada looked more like a child of six than ten. The illness had wasted away what little roundness there was to the tiny frame and left the bones jutting out sharply. Her skin was almost transparent and she looked for all the world like a china doll.

Jennie dipped the soft cloth into the warm soapy water and began to wash the quiet face and then the arms and legs. She found it hard to swallow the lump in her throat and more than once had to blink back tears. It wouldn't do to cry in front of Betsey. The child was having a hard enough time.

"She looks like she's sleepin', Jennie."

"Yes, she does. I guess you could say she is asleep, Betsey. That's all death really is. A quiet sleep."

"'Cept that Ada won't never wake up."

"No, Ada won't ever wake up."

Unconsciously, Jennie began to sing the lullaby Mama had sung to all of them so long ago.

> *"Sleep, little bitty baby, close your eyes*
> *The wee tiny song bird to his nest flies*
> *God in his heaven has called home the sun*
> *Now is for sleeping, the night has begun."*

Betsey watched Jennie's face as she sung the lullaby. "That was pretty, Jennie. I think Ada would like it could she hear it."

"I'm sure she would."

Jennie finished bathing Ada and gently dried her. "You can hand me Ada's dress, Betsey."

"This is Ada's favorite. The green one with the pretty bow for her hair. She has pretty hair, don't she Jennie?"

Betsey reached out a hand and hesitated a second before picking up a few gold strands of Ada's hair. She turned to Jennie. "Wait, Jennie." She scurried away and returned with Ada's hair brush.

"'Member I won this at the picnic?"

Jennie took the brush and began to brush Ada's hair. "I remember, Betsey. You were fast. You almost came in first."

Jennie saw that Betsey was tenderly fingering the hair bow. She gently turned the child to her. "Betsey, you know I think maybe Ada would like you to have that bow."

Betsey's face lit up. "You think so, Jennie?"

"I really do. As a matter of fact, I think I heard Ada say that someday she was going to give it to you." Betsey turned and carried the bow with great reverence out of the bedroom.

Jennie finished dressing Ada. She stepped back and surveyed the child, pleased that all traces of suffering were gone. Now she could let Pearl see the little girl.

"Jennie," Betsey whispered from the doorway. "Papa is home. He's jest now comin' down the road." She didn't wait for Jennie to answer, but raced ahead to open the door. Jennie followed and quietly closed the bedroom door behind her.

Luther was standing in the open doorway, Abel already in his arms, Iva Lee and Junior pulling at his coat. The remarkable red beard and moustache were badly in need of trimming and because of the weather, lightly coated with a wet sheen.

Surprise was written on his face to find Jennie there.

"What...?" His eyes went to Pearl and in a flash he knew. "Ada?"

Pearl put her face in her hands, her breath coming in great tearing sobs.

Jennie said softly, "Mr. Norris, I'm so sorry. Ada died last night."

Luther nodded, dazed. He pulled Abel close and buried his face in the golden curls, his shoulders shaking in silent grief. After a moment he said, "I got word from Doc Payne I best come home. Knew right off it was Ada, but I didn't think...:

He put Abel down and went to Pearl and fell to his knees beside the rocking chair. He put his arms around the frail body and they wept in each other's arms.

After a long moment he stood up and took off his coat and hung it up, then turned and opened his arms to his children

✉

The poor house was scrubbed clean and the table was laid with all manner of food brought in by good neighbors and friends. There were great slices of ham and wedges of cheese, several platters of fried chicken and patties of sausage meat, slaws and relishes, jams and fried apple pies, apple cakes and fresh baked bread and biscuits. Jennie fussed over the food, unwrapping packages and finding plates to put the food on. Betsey wouldn't leave her side.

The women busied themselves, competing with each other to see who could be the most helpful. The Norris children were well fed, rested and comforted by their elders while Pearl was made to stay in her rocker, protesting all the while that she was well enough to do her share of the preparations.

Luther stood at the cabin window, his hands resting on the sill, his face immobile. He watched while Tom and Otis and Harley worked to construct a coffin from the pile of pine planks stacked in the yard. Tom did the measuring while the others sawed and sanded. When enough boards were cut, Tom carefully fitted them together and nailed them in place. The men worked steadily.

Behind Luther the women were busy. They sat in a circle, each with a piece of white broadcloth across her lap. Their fingers moved deftly, the needles going steadily in and out. They were sewing the lining for the coffin.

Lula said, "You gettin' tired, Pearl? Maybe you want to rest for a bit."

"I thank ya kindly, Lu, but I'm fine. I need to do something." Pearl rocked steadily. "I need to do something for my Ada... this will be my last chance."

Cora Fenley looked over the rim of her glasses, her small birdlike features pinched with the effort to keep from crying. "Otis and me hurt bad when Pap Fenley passed on, but he were 84 and said often 'nuff he wuz ready to go to his reward. It pains me to see a young'un like Ada pass over. Don't seem right, the Lord takin' one so young."

Lula reached over and grasped Cora's hand. "Otis' Papa wuz a good man, Cora. This terrible sickness takes old and young alike, some of us spared while others..." She didn't finish. Heads nodded in agreement.

Lula asked, "How is Mam Fenley holdin' up?"

Cora said, "Poor ole soul don't know the time a day. A blessin' in disguise, I says, her not knowin' 'bout Pap." She bent her head to her sewing.

After a pause, Buelis changed the subject. "I wish the weather would warm up so's the men would have a easier time digging..." she stopped as Lula shook her head. "Oh, well, I mean, we would all 'preciate a let up of this weather. My fingers don't work right in the cold."

Buelis Green rose from her chair and set her sewing aside. "I'm gonna get some coffee made, the men will be nearly froze 'fore they get their job done."

Elsie Wooding said, "Doc says once the weather warms up this influenza will be done with. It being only January, though, we have a ways to go."

Lula asked, "How many has fallen to the influenza? Did Doc say?"

"Too many, I says." Clara answered. "It vexes me some they ain't more can be done. When Jeb got sick, alls Doc said wuz it ud hafta run its course."

Lula asked. "How's Jeb doin' now?"

"Still weak as a newborn. That's why he ain't here. 'Bout kills him ta hafta rest so much. I been tryin' to fatten him up, but his appetite ain't good yet. Can you imagine Jeb not bein' able to eat?"

Lula laughed. "Truth to tell, Clara, never did think I'd see that day, Jeb not eatin'.

"Well, I don't know 'bout y'all," Elsie said, "but I trust my poultices and camomile tea 'bout as much as I trust anything."

Heads nodded around the circle.

Pearl's hands fell idle in her lap. "Don't matter no how. Ain't no medicine can help Ada now." She looked over at Jennie.

"You know, Lu, I'll be forever grateful to your Jennie. I always called her my angel and she is in truth jest that. Don't know what I woulda done, if she hadn't a been here."

Lula reached over and squeezed Pearl's hand. "Jennie does have somethin'. She seems able to take charge in pitiful times like this." Their eyes went to the closed bedroom door where Ada's body waited for burial.

There was much stamping on the porch and Luther turned as the men entered. Harley carried in the coffin and laid it at Luther's feet "It's the purtiest little box we ever did make, Luther."

Tom gripped Luther's shoulder. "Come spring I'll carve out a headstone you'll be proud of."

Luther nodded sadly. "I thank y'all kindly."

Elsie rose from the circle and collected coats, while Buelis filled mugs with steaming coffee. The men gratefully cupped their frozen hands around the mugs and settled themselves, their job done.

Lula knelt by the coffin. "It is a pretty box, Pearl. Come see."

The women gathered around, padding the inside with layers of cloth and covering it all with the broadcloth lining, finally tacking it carefully in place. Luther and Pearl disappeared into the bedroom and after several minutes returned, Luther carrying Ada. He place her gently in the coffin. Pearl fussed over the little body, smoothing the dress and patting the hair. Betsey stood by, clutching the bow, and when Pearl started to reach for it Jennie caught her eye and shook her head. Pearl nodded in understanding.

Luther picked up the lid and held it in place while Tom fished a handful of nails from his pocket and hammered the coffin closed. Luther and Tom effortlessly picked up the coffin and carried it out on the porch, where it would remain until the burial next day.

Pearl settled herself in the rocker and Betsey came to stand by her side, solemn and still. Pearl drew Betsey on her lap and began to stroke the child's hair, the way she had so often done with Ada.

Friends and neighbors arrived, sheltering their horses and oxen in Luther's barn. Emmaline Fenley and Jacob Wooding arrived, Emmaline leading Mam Fenley along like a child. Mam's face was wreathed in a smile which didn't reach the vacant depths of her eyes. Cora got up and took Mam's coat and found her a seat.

Everyone ate and drank and the men disappeared from time to time to take a nip of the corn liquor someone had supplied.

Lije and Effie Proffitt and Sarah joined the mourners, bringing with them an enormous bag of coffee beans.

Sarah made for Jennie's side and put her arm around her friends's waist. "Jen, anything I kin do?"

"Nothing to do, Sarah, it's all been done."

The girls looked at each other in surprise as Luther greeted Lucy Glenwood at the door.

Sarah whispered, "Wonder what Miss Glenwood is doing here."

"It's because Ada was her student, I'm sure."

Everyone loved Lucy Glenwood. Her face was narrow with sharp features, but always alive and interested. In kindness she was described as slim, but she was actually gaunt and large boned, which she skillfully softened with loose flowing dresses and tastefully placed bows. The result was attractive. Lucy and Jennie exchanged smiles.

Jont Payne and Baxter joined the assemblage, weariness showing in their every move. The women made a great fuss of them.

Otis moved over on the sofa to make room for the doctor. "Come sit by the stove, Jont, warm yerself. Must be y'all are wore out."

Doc sank gratefully to the sofa as Clara put a heaping plate of food in his hands. "I kindly thank ya, good ladies, it looks mighty fine." Without further word he began to eat.

Baxter turned Jennie from the table. "How're ya doin, Jen?"

"It's not an easy time, Baxter, but I'm all right." She noted the dark circles under his eyes.

"Doc says if I'm ever gonna be a doctor, I gotta learn to put feelin's aside in times like this and just do a good job of doctorin'. He says it don't do no good to let the heart carry you away."

Jennie said, "That's easy said, Baxter, but don't know as I can do that. Maybe if it was someone I didn't know it would be easier, but even then...

Baxter shook his head in angry agreement. "I know. Nothin's ever easy. I'm wonderin' when the good Lord's gonna see fit to show some pity. Show He cares what happens to us. Life is hard enough in these mountains 'thout..."

It was Jennie's turn to comfort. She put a finger to his lips. "Ssh. You're just tired. What you need is some good food and rest. The food we can take care of right now."

Baxter put an arm around her shoulders. "Food and rest is least of what I need, Jen. Mostly I need you. In all this runnin' around tryin' to be in three places at once, you never been out of my mind. Thinkin' 'bout you is what keeps me goin'."

Jennie looked into his tired eyes. She felt deep pity mixed with love and admiration for his selfless giving and endless patience. She was close to tears.

She said softly, "Baxter, dear Baxter." She stroked his face and he took her hand and kissed the palm. Jennie drew away, conscious of the people surrounding them. She took him by the hand and led him to a chair in the corner.

"Now you sit here while I fix a plate for you."

As everyone relaxed in camaraderie, the sad aspect of the gathering softened, and subdued laughter could be heard, even that of Luther and Pearl. No one felt it should be otherwise.

"Last viewin' I was to," said Lije, "was when ole man Blackburn died. They was so many people come to the viewin' you could stand up in the corner and sleep."

"I remember that 'un," Harley said. He took his pipe from his mouth. "It was right blowin' up a hurricane that night. I 'member Zeb Perry sayin' as how he wuz walkin' by the cemetery.."

Buelis interrupted, "It weren't Zeb Perry, Harley, it were Earl Doudy."

Harley gave her a blistering look.

Buelis mumbled, "Well, come to think on it, it was Zeb Perry."

From across the room, Sarah caught Jennie's eye and Jennie felt the laughter bubble up in her throat. Would Sarah never miss an opportunity to giggle at Buelis Green?

"Anyways," Harley continued, "Zeb says he was passin' by the graveyard on his way home from the viewin' and felt someone or somethin' tap him on the shoulder. He whirled 'round and weren't a soul in sight, so he continues on. Little while later, another tap on the shoulder. Well sir, he took off like a untamed hoss, but couldn't shake whatever was reachin' fer him. Ran all the way home and when he finally got the courage to look back, he found his tie was thrown back by the wind and was rapping his shoulder."

After all were sated with the good food, they began to sing. 'When the Roll is Called Up Yonder' and "Crossing the Bar" and every hymn that came to mind.

The hour was late. Some left for home while others stayed and slept where they sat or lay. The lamps sputtered into darkness. There was no sound except the gentle breathing of the sleepers. Jennie drowsed in a chair with Baxter at her feet, his head in her lap. There was an occasional snort from Doc, who sat with his head thrown back, mouth open wide.

✉

Snow was gently falling. Jeb's wagon, with Bro and Sis in the harness and Sherman at the reins, carried the small coffin along Cemetery Road, over the bridge and up the hill on the far side to the graveyard at the top. Over all protests, Pearl insisted she was strong enough to see her baby buried. Now she sat in the wagon, swathed in blankets, between Sherm and Prosper Truall, with Iva Lee on her lap.

Luther carried Abel, while Betsey and Junior stumbled along by his side. The rest of the mourners, Pearl's and Luther's friends, followed behind.

Lula and Jennie walked beside the wagon, Lula's voice raised in song. After a minute or two the rest of the mourners joined in.

"Safe in the arms of Jesus, safe on His gentle breast.
There by his love o'er-shaded, sweetly my soul shall rest.
Hark! 'tis the voice of angels, borne in a song to me,
Over the fields of glory, over the jasper sea.
Safe in the arms of Jesus, safe on His gentle breast
There by his love o'er-shaded, sweetly my soul shall rest.

Clint and Hubie, below at the church, pulled the bell cord and the church bells rang out in tempo with the sorrowful singing.

The wagon stopped at the grave site. Luther and Doc on one side and Baxter and Tom on the other lifted out the coffin. It was covered with a film of snow. As Reverend Truall recited the 23rd Psalm, the men lowered Ada amid the swirling flakes into her grave.

Chapter Twenty
A Happy Surprise

Dearest Jennie

We are now officially mustered out of the army. I thank the good God in heaven, Jen, to be finally free of the army ...away from the scenes that filled my mind and soul for so long... back in civilian clothes, eating food that doesn't come out of a can. Our train ride across country was anything but comfortable, but it was far better than what we endured the past two years. The trip lasted five days and we ate and slept where we sat, exercising only briefly at little whistle stops where the train took on coal and water.

We have been staying with Pete's sister, Gloria, for four days and as anxious as Pete was to see her, he is now ready to leave. I understand his feelings as his sister treats him like one of her children. I find it touching, but Pete is growling under his breath like a bear. He is exercising admirable control, but I think it best we leave before he explodes. We've been picking up newspapers from the states and checking for job opportunities.

Today Pete came across an article about Mt. Elmore Logging Camps in Oregon. Neither of us have ever felled a tree, but the article promises employment stating only the strong and healthy need apply. Pete says that is us. We will be moving on tomorrow, taking a train to Victoria and from there a ferry across to Seattle, Washington. From Seattle we will have to find our way to Eugene, Oregon where the logging office is. My next letter will be from within the boundaries of the United States. Does that not sound grand?

There is an expression, 'the luck of the Irish', and it must be so. I've been fair lucky since I received your first dear letter. You were with me through all the drear days of the war and I cannot think of a future without you. Keep me in your prayers as I keep you in mine. You will soon have an address where you can write to me. I miss your letters. I close with all my love.

James

Now that Mama had her strength back and the influenza epidemic seemed to be slowing down, Mama talked of nothing else but going to visit Edward. His letters were short but cheerful, saying the doctors would have allowed him to come home but for the epidemic. With his lungs so damaged, they were afraid of putting his health in jeopardy by exposing him to the sickness and Mama agreed this was sensible. But now she was getting anxious, sure that something besides the epidemic was standing in the way of his release. No one could dissuade her of this idea, even Papaw, and finally it was easier to agree with her than to argue.

Jennie offered part of the money set aside for nursing school for Mama's train ticket to Washington, D.C., but neither Papaw nor Mama would hear of it. When the subject was broached to Edward, he said that though he would love a visit, it was foolish since he expected to be home soon, and why waste the money.

All of this discussion kept Jennie from thinking about Ada, but today was a rare interval of rest and visions of her little friend filled her mind. On top of that, the letter from James, which should have made her happy, made her blue. She wondered, despite his assurances, whether he was having second thoughts about coming to Zionville at all.

Then there was school. The money was at hand... Mama was in agreement that she should go... and a letter of acceptance to the North Carolina School of Nursing in Charlotte had been received. The epidemic had interceded and now she would have to wait for the new session to begin, which was not until September.

She moved morosely to the window. The great snow banks left in the wake of the storms had dwindled to small patches that dotted the pastures. She pulled the wooly grey sweater closely around her and... what is this? A hole in the sleeve? She took the sweater off and... sure enough, a big ragged hole. Tears filled her eyes... her favorite sweater... with a hole in the sleeve. This was too much. She buried her face in the softness of it and wept.

After a minute or two, the silence of the room mocked her and she straightened up and wiped her eyes. She looked again at the hole and this time it made her angry. She threw it across the room and it landed on the floor by the door. Who needed the stupid old sweater anyway?

She turned again to the window and saw Mama walking vigorously back from the Owen house. They were all concerned about Jeb's slow recovery, and Mama visited them often to help keep their spirits up. It had been Clay that had fallen ill the same time as Jeb, but he had recovered nicely.

Mama's head was bowed against the frigid wind and she clutched her shawl tightly around her head and neck. Soldier bounded up to her and she stooped to pet him. After the greeting, Soldier continued down Valley Road, running with a purpose, ears flattened to his head. The dog never missed. He was on his way to meet Hubie from school.

Mama came in the back door. "What is your sweater doing on the floor?"

Jennie turned from the window, feeling foolish. "Oh, I guess it just fell off the hook."

Mama tossed it to her. "Put it on, the house is chilly."

Jennie put it on and pulled it close around her. "Yes, it does feel good."

✉

"I can't believe it's snowing again." Jennie watched Clint moving around the cow shed, snow swirling about his red wool hat.

Mama said, exasperatedly, "Will you jest look at this?" She held up a pair of overalls that showed holes in both knees. "Even the patches have holes in 'em. That Hubie spends more time on his knees than his behind."

"It's the dog," Jennie said. "They're all the time wrestling with each other. As a matter of fact that's what they're doing right now. They're covered in snow... Helen too."

"They been out most the afternoon, time to get them in. 'Fore they do, Jennie, send Hube to see if they's any mail from Edward, and send Helen over to the Owen's to fetch Min. Seems every time I turn around she's over there, and don't come back 'less I send someone to fetch her. Don't know how Clara puts up with it." Jennie went to the door to do Mama's bidding.

Mama dropped her head and resumed her sewing. "In my last letter to Edward, I asked him to find out the directions from the train station to the hospital by bus. No sense taking a taxi if the buses run nearby..."

Jennie interrupted, "Oh, did you come up with money for the fare?"

Mama continued to inspect the mending, not looking at Jennie. "No, not exactly, but I thought they's a few things around here I could sell."

Jennie almost laughed. "Sell? Even if we had something worth selling, who would have the money to buy it?"

Mama dropped her hands in her lap and looked at Jennie with annoyance. "I need help in finding a way to get to see Edward, Jennie, not someone throwing shoes at my ideas."

"Mama, I wish you would be reasonable. Why don't you listen to Edward? He says he will be home soon. All this talk about trains and buses...and you'd have to have a place to stay in Washington as well. You surely wouldn't be able to stay at the hospital."

Mama picked up a shirt and inspected it closely. "God is working on it, Jennie. When he figures out a way for me to see Edward, he'll let me know."

Hube was back first. He shrugged out of his wet coat and hung it up. "Weren't no mail, Mama."

Mama looked disappointed. "I thought sure there would be a letter from Edward."

Hubie said, "Mr. Proffitt says two boys from Sugar Grove are back from the war. You s'pose Ed's on his way home too?"

"It would be nice to think so, Hube, but Edward's in the hospital. It's not the same thing."

Helen and Min stamped their feet on the porch and came in.

"Mama," Helen groaned, "I'm so cold." She hurriedly got out of her coat, ran to the stove and held her hands up to it.

Hube snorted. "You baby, it ain't that cold out."

"I'm not a baby, Hubie."

"Are too."

"I ain't... Mama."

"Stop teasin' your sister." Mama turned to Minnie. "Min, it's time we had a talk."

Minnie looked resigned. "Guess I know what you're gonna say."

"I think mebbe you better spend less time over to the Owens and more time at your own place. I can't think Clara 'preciates your being there all the time."

"Mrs. Owen don't mind... she likes having another woman in the house."

"Humpf... woman," Mama looked sternly at Min. "You got a lot to learn 'fore you can call yourself a woman. You jest spend more time on your school work and less time pesterin' Clara Owen."

"Mama, me and Sherm..."

Mama cut her off. "Now I said what I had to say and that's the end of it. I don't want to hear another word on it."

"I don't see why you won't talk about me and Sherm..."

Lula was angry. "Didn't I say not another word?"

Min turned to Jennie and shrugged.

Clint came in and hung his coat on the peg, then stood alternately on one foot, then the other to remove his galoshes. Lula said, "Get that rag hangin' behind the stove and mop up them puddles, Clint."

They all settled down. Mama returned to her sewing and Jennie and Min fetched their sewing baskets to help Mama reduce the pile of mending. Clint buried himself in the Farmer's Almanac and Helen and Hube pulled out their game of 'Fox and Goose', plumped themselves on the floor in front of the stove and scrambled to get the dice for first toss.

The afternoon wore on. Clint got up and wandered restlessly about the room, ending up at the window overlooking the front porch. He leaned on the window sill.

"Stopped snowin'," he said. He watched as the sun set. The stark landscape, softened by the new cover of blue-white snow, spread out in endless bumps and hollows. The icicles that had dripped steadily in the afternoon sun had begun to freeze again, rimming the eaves of the house with sparkling diamonds in the dying sunlight.

All at once Clint let out a whoop.

"Here's Ed. Here's Ed come home. He's jest gettin' outa Mr. Truall's buggy." He ran to the door and flung it open.

Ed ran up the porch steps, dropped his duffel bag inside the door and caught Mama in his arms. The rest of them crowded around, all talking at once, Hube and Helen jumping up and down squealing with excitement.

While everyone talked at once, trying to claim Ed's attention, the dog barking to add to the commotion, Jennie stood back and examined her brother.

He was taller, and terribly thin. When Mama stopped to take stock of him, that would be the first thing she would notice... how thin he was. There were other changes having nothing to do with the ordeal he'd been through. His shoulders... they were broader and he looked older, his face... matured? Beard stubble had replaced the boyish down that used to cover his chin. Only the curly dark hair, wide-set blue eyes and smile reminded her of the boy who had so suddenly enlisted to go to war. Jennie took a deep breath. *He's home... thank God, he's home.*

Ed shrugged out of his army coat. "I got into Boone on the train yesterday and managed to get a ride into Sugar Grove. I spent last night with Papaw. He woulda come on with me today, but he couldn't on such short notice. Said he'd be along in a week or two. I wuz gonna walk, but Papaw arranged for Prosper Truall to stop by the mill and pick me up. Just as well. Doctors told me to take it easy for a while."

He stopped, puzzled. They were all staring at him. "What's the matter?"

Minnie said, "Well, you look like our brother Ed, but you sure don't sound like him."

Ed laughed. "Oh, you mean my voice. It ain't come back right. Doctors say mebbe it never will. Sometimes I lose it altogether."

Lula said, nodding, "Come sit by the stove and tell us about it." She turned and led the way into the kitchen.

They all trooped after her and Ed sank gratefully onto the sofa with Min and Jennie on either side of him and Clint perched on the sofa arm. Mama sat in her rocker and Helen and Hube sat cross-legged at his feet. Soldier pushed his way in, sniffed at Ed's leg and began to bark.

Hubie pulled the dog into his arms. "This here's Soldier."

Ed leaned down and let the dog sniff his fingers. "You named him Soldier?"

"After you."

"I'm right honored." He scratched Soldier's ear and got his hand licked in return.

Mama said, "The doctor wrote us letters saying you were improving and doing nicely, but never a word as to when you could come home. I wuz startin' to suspect the lot of them, wasn't I, Jennie? Almost had it worked out to come see you."

"No need for it now." He looked around the room. "God, Mama, it's good to be home."

Mama said, "You sure you're all right?"

Ed nodded. "I'll have to go into Johnson City for a check up every month or so, and they give me some medicine to take when the pain comes on."

"You still have pain?"

"Some, but it ain't nuthing I can't handle."

"Doctor said you were fightin' with chlorine gas."

"*We* weren't, Mama, *they* were, the Germans. We called it mustard gas cause it kindly smelled like mustard. It does a God-awful job on your lungs. I wuz pretty lucky, though. I came through with the help of some good doctors taking care of me."

Mama said, "I see you're pitiful thin and that's somethin' I can take care of."

Ed laughed. "That's what kept me goin', thinkin' 'bout your cookin'... but Papaw said you wuz sick too. Said you had influenza. I wuz expectin' you to look poorly, but you look good."

Lula nodded. "By the grace of God."

Ed pulled Jennie and Minnie close in a hug. "Jest look at all of you. Hube and Helen each musta growed a foot since I seen 'em last. And Clint, he's 'most a man already."

Clint beamed. "I turned twelve last month."

Lula said. "Poor young'un didn't get much more'n a pat on the head fer his birthday what with all that wuz goin' on. The boy growed up in a hurry after you left."

Clint fidgeted. "I kin use some help with the chores."

"Oh for heaven sake, Clint," Min said. "First night Ed's home and you talk about him helpin' with the chores."

Clint reddened. "I didn't mean..."

Ed reached out a hand to Clint. "I understand, little brother."

Jennie was touched to see Ed remembered Clint sometimes had trouble finding the right words.

Ed turned his attention to Jennie and Minnie. "And lookit here. Jen and Min has growed out in all directions."

Minnie giggled. "I have a beau."

Ed turned to Mama. "And who is this pimply-faced, squeaky-voiced varmint been hangin' 'round our Min?"

Minnie squealed and playfully swung at Ed.

Hube shouted. "It's Sherm Owen. That's who ole pimple face is." Hube and Helen fell over backwards laughing.

"You mean that little runt from over yonder?"

Min was indignant. "Sherm ain't no runt, he's growed up."

Lula dismissed the subject with a wave of her hand. "None of us take the young'uns serious."

Ed turned to Jennie. "How 'bout you, Jen?"

Helen giggled. "Jennie's beau is James."

Ed grinned, still looking at Jennie. "Irish?"

"Says he's coming to Zionville. Then we'll see."

Ed smiled a little absently. "Yeah, James. He was a good friend. If it hadn't a been fer James..."

Jennie said, "Most every letter I've gotten he asks about you."

Ed nodded again. "Sometime I'll tell you about James..." He abruptly shook off his somber mood and changed the subject. "And how's Papa? You wrote he went off to the mines."

Mama nodded. "Yes, he left for the mines soon after you left for the army. He gets home every so often."

Ed was pleased. "So Papa is working." He looked at Jennie and nodded. Jennie could see he thought Papa had straightened out and was shouldering his responsibilities. Time enough for him to find out differently.

Ed said, "Papaw said y'all had a good Christmas."

Clint said, "Papaw gimme his rifle."

Ed clapped his brother on the back. "Hey, now we can do some real huntin'."

Lula pushed herself from the rocker. "Come along, girls. Let's get some food on the table. Clint, you light the lamps."

After the meal, Ed answered questions about the army, making Hube and Helen laugh with stories about going to sleep with his clothes on and cooking in his helmet. Hube turned serious. "Papaw and me wuz talkin' and he says... he says you probly got yerself a medal."

"Yup. It's somewheres in my duffel and first thing tomorrow I'll get it out and show it to you."

Mama yawned and got up. "That's enough for now, it's past bedtime. You can hear about the army tomorrow and the next day and the next. I spect you're plum wore out, Ed." She said to Helen, "You can sleep in your own bed now your brother's home. Tomorrow is Sunday meeting and won't everyone be surprised to see Ed?"

Hube cried. "I don't want to go to bed, not yet Mama, please, please..."

Ed smiled. "Mama's right, Hube, it's bedtime. We got all the time in the world now."

Lula adjusted the damper on the stove and said to Ed, "I guess I'll sleep best I slept in the past two years." She continued with a broad grin. "I won't be layin' awake 'til all hours tryin' to figure a way to get to that confounded hospital."

They all laughed, Mama loudest of all. She finally got the children on their feet and herded them ahead of her to the stairs, picking up one of the lamps on her way. "You comin' up, Jennie?"

"In a bit, Mama."

Quiet settled over them and with only one lamp left the room was in shadows. Ed laid his head back and closed his eyes.

"Was it bad, Ed... the war and the hospital and all?"

Ed remained silent and when the silence continued, Jennie was angry with herself for bringing up the subject. Maybe he wasn't ready to talk about it yet.

Finally he spoke without raising his head or opening his eyes. "Yeah, it was bad. Seemed like a lot of needless dying. God knows we all got to die someday, but thank the Lord he didn't let me die like that."

"Like what?"

"Without meaning, Jen. So many died... so many. I can't make sense of it." He sat up and looked at her. "We wuz all het up when we finished our training. All fired up to go over and beat the Germans. We thought we wuz somethin', dressed in uniform, carrying a rifle. We wuz ready to beat the enemy into the ground... hell, I don't think a one of us really thought about killing someone, or being killed.

"It wuz s'pose to be this noble thing we wuz doin', fightin' for our country and then, when we got in the thick of it, we wuz jest a bunch of scared kids.

"We trudged over roads tore up with shell holes, so tired we sometimes fell asleep walking, only waking up when we hit the ground. We marched through villages with houses all bombed out. And the people, Jen, the women and old folk caught in the middle with no place to run to. Young'uns hanging on their Mama's skirts, hungry and sick, eyes wide and hurting."

Jennie listened, speechless.

"One night we wuz stringing barbed wired, near a small village called Villers-Tournelle. I'll never forget that name. We were close to the front lines and could hear the big guns going off. The rockets and flares made it seem like a party 'steada what it was. During the night we got our orders to march to the front and the Germans started peppering us with mustard gas. We hurried to get our masks on and had to keep them on all that night, right through the fightin'. And the fightin' was fierce... bombs bursting, men screaming. I don't know how I missed getting hit. I could feel the heat from exploding shells all around me."

Jennie put her hand on his arm. She wanted to tell him to stop, but he kept on, his voice almost gone.

"Sometime during that night I couldn't breathe no more so I ripped my mask off. A lot of us did. The smell of the gas and burned flesh was enough to make ya puke. When the barrage stopped we jest started droppin' like flies. I woke up in a field hospital. Some of us never woke up... and that's what I meant, Jennie, dying without meaning."

Ed was lost, remembering. "I wuz burned black from the gas and they had to soak my body in oil and peel the clothes off me. The pain was so bad I kept passing out. I almost prayed I would die. I cried... jest like a baby, I cried for Mama. Only one ever heard me was James." Jennie's heart skipped a beat.

Ed sat slumped over, his hands open, palms up, on his knees. "I couldn't talk." He rubbed his chest as if remembering. "James was in the bed next to me. That first night he musta heard me crying. He whispered to me... soldier, you're alive, nothing better than that ... and then he started talking. Through most of that night he talked. I can't tell you a thing he said, but the sound of his voice was a comfort. Then Dora come and give me something that put me out."

Jennie had trouble swallowing past the lump in her throat.

"When I come to again, there was James smiling at me." Ed imitated James. "Well, laddie, in case you didn't get me name before, it's James B. Culhane and I'm pleased to meet ye."

Ed managed a small grin. "He really does talk like that, Jen. It's somethin' to listen to him. He was in pain, too, from a shoulder wound, but it didn't stop him talking. He knew I couldn't answer but he went on anyway, telling me 'bout Ireland and his brother Danny and his Da."

Ed fell silent. Jennie didn't speak. She couldn't think of a thing to say. Ed's voice was just a whisper. "I don't remember much about those first few weeks except for James being there, encouraging me. His buddy, Pete, was wounded too and when James wasn't around,

Pete told me if it wasn't fer James he'd still be out there in no man's land rotting away.

"I had to write everything down on a pad cause I had no voice and when James offered to write to Mama, I let him. When he saw your picture, he asked could he write to you, too."

Jennie finally spoke. "I'm glad you did, Ed. I love getting his letters. From the very first I felt like I knew him."

Ed nodded. "Me too. Then the doctors thought I needed better care than they could give me there at the front and sent me to the hospital in Paris. Hospital is another story."

He took Jen's hand and spoke with just a word or two. "Glad you kept in touch...if he died... would never a knowed."

Jennie wanted to say more. She wanted to tell Ed how close she and James had become through their letters, but his eyes were closed, his face grey with exhaustion. It could wait... it could wait.

✉

Jennie thought for the first time in months the house had a happy feel to it. Mama's eyes twinkled and there was color in her cheeks; and when Mama was happy, they were all happy. There was a change in Ed as well. After that first night, Jennie expected him to be somber and quiet, maybe a little awkward to talk to, but it wasn't so. His joy at being home infected them all and while they all loved the old Ed, they loved the new Ed even more. Mama cooked and baked and prodded him to eat 'jest another bite' and with all the love and concern heaped on him, he slowly relaxed.

After the first few days, he began to help with the chores. He and Clint spent hours going over the repairs to be made around the farm. They even talked of adding a few more cows to the cow shed. Mama stood in the background shaking her head.

When Jennie and Ed found a quiet moment, she told him about Papa, and that he hadn't changed at all. She related the incident of how she had managed to shout at Papa and how it had stopped him from taking the strap to Hubie. Ed was angry and disgusted.

Jennie asked him, "He'll be coming home one of these days. Think you'll be happy to see him?"

Ed looked thoughtful. "I don't know. One thing I do know. Things won't be like they wuz when I left. No more bullying. He won't bully none of us ever again."

234

Jennie felt a surge of relief. "Suppose he makes a fuss about me going off to school in the fall?"

"I don't think he will, Jen. I'm here to handle things, now. That's all he's worried about. Now he can go off and take care of hisself and leave everything else to me, and you going off to school won't matter to him anymore. There's somethin' else, but we'll keep this from Papa. I'm gonna be gettin' a small sum of money each month from the government 'cause of my injuries. Won't be much, but it will help keep us goin' 'til I kin find me some way to earn a little money."

At the end of the week two letters came. One was from James.

Dearest Jennie,

I am fair bursting with excitement. I am on American soil at last. I think of all the dreaming I've done, first in Ireland and then through all the bleak days of the war and now I am here.

We had a grand crossing from Victoria, British Columbia to Seattle, Washington which took us five hours by ferry, and when we arrived at customs, we passed right through with no trouble. I'm pinching myself to make sure I'm not dreaming...

"Good God, Irish, will ya wipe that grin off yer face? People will think I'm travelling with an idiot."

"Sorry, Pete, I can't help it. It's a grand feeling to finally be here."

"Yeah, well... we ain't got time to waste. We gotta get movin'."

"Movin' to where?"

"The freight yard. The guy in customs give me the directions."

James shifted his duffel bag to his other shoulder. "And is it a freight train then we're going to use for transportation?"

"That's the plan."

"Isn't that against the law?"

Pete stopped in his tracks and faced James who was obliged to stop walking too. "We ain't got much money in our kick, Irish, you got a better plan let's hear it."

James thought for a minute. "No, I guess I haven't got a better plan. You lead, I'll follow, laddie."

When they arrived at the freight yard, it was late in the afternoon.

James said. "Since I've not had any experience hopping a freight, boyo, I'm hopin' you know how to go about it."

"Trust me."

"That's what I was afraid you were going to say."

Pete ignored the remark. "There's a bunch a guys over there. Let's see what they can tell us."

"They're a pretty sorry looking lot."

"We don't exactly look like upper crust either. Just do like I do."

"Lead on, MacDuff."

Pete gave him a look. "I wouldn't bring up no MacDuff if I was you. Not everyone is understandin' like me."

Three men hovered over a fire. One was stirring something in a rusty can with an old wooden spoon, the can hanging on a tripod over the flame. Their clothing was worn and dirty and seemed to be held together by ropes and safety pins, but a closer look showed the clothing to be layers of shirts and jackets and sweaters, which fortified them pretty well against the cold. The men looked up with suspicion as Pete and James approached.

"Hello," Pete said. He let his duffel bag fall from his shoulder.

No one answered. No one even blinked.

Pete went on, "Me and my buddy, Irish here, was wondering if you could give us some information." No answer.

"Look," Pete said with some irritation, "we ain't lookin' for trouble. Irish and me are fresh outta the army. We're headin' for Portland. Ain't got much in the way of car fare and thought catching a freight would be the way to travel. Problem is, we don't know how the freights are runnin' or the ones headin' for Portland. Thought one of you might know."

Pete and James waited. The three men exchanged looks. Finally, the one tending the tin can said, "Sit... take a load off."

James threw his duffel down and sat on it. Pete sat down as well. "Much obliged," he said.

The one that told them to sit asked, "What's in Portland?"

James thought it was time he entered the conversation. "Actually, gentlemen, we're heading for Eugene by way of Portland. Our purpose is to seek employment at the Mt. Elmore Logging Operation, the main office of which is in Eugene."

The man's somber face broke into a grin, showing a mouthful of brown-stained teeth.

"Guess that's why they call you Irish. You talk funny."

They all laughed and the tension was broken.

"My name's Gabe," and he gestured with the spoon. "That's One-Eye and that's Jersey Joe."

One-Eye squinted from under a thatch of grey hair. "You kids hungry?"

Pete looked at James and they both looked at the can. The aroma hit them at the same time. Pete said, "God, that smells good."

They had something cooking in an old tin can over the fire and, Jen, it was the best stew I've eaten since leaving Ireland. I didn't ask what was in it. There are some things best not known.

It is here by the fire I am writing this letter. Gabe told us which freight is due to leave the yard tonight for Portland and Pete and I have staked out an empty freight car, but there is a wee problem. Seems the railway police frown on freight hopping and carry billy clubs to discourage passengers. If caught, we could land in jail.

It is growing dark and we will soon be trying our luck. I dearly hope I am as fleet of foot as when I was a tad. I am leaving this letter with Gabe and he promises to mail it tomorrow. Sorry I can't write more, but time does not permit. You will hear from me again when, be the good Lord willing, we arrive in Portland.

Love to my dear Jennie.
James

Jennie finished the letter and continued to stare at the pages. Eating out of a rusty can, sneaking a ride on a freight car with the police breathing down his neck, good God in heaven, will I ever get to meet the boy?

She got up from the bed and walked around in frustration. If he got into trouble he'd be sent back to Canada and not be allowed to cross the border again. She sighed in resignation. Worrying won't help.

She stuffed the letter into her pocket and headed down the stairs. I'll show Ed the letter. He'll be happy to hear the news. I just hope that Irish luck holds up.

As for the other letter, Jennie was resigned to the fact that Papa was coming home.

Chapter Twenty-One
Tater Hill

"Come on, Jennie. Today's your birthday, let's celebrate." Baxter stood in the open doorway of the Wainwright kitchen. "I got Pen waitin' on us, and Ma fixed us a picnic lunch. Thought mebbe we'uns could go up on Tater Hill."

"I can't, Baxter, Papa came home last night."

Baxter stood silent for a moment. Then in a soft voice he said, "All the more reason you come with me, Jen."

Jennie smiled at his understanding. "I'd like to, believe me Baxter, but..."

"No buts, Jen. Everyone gets to do what they want on their birthday... come on." It was March and the air was warm in the valley. A deceptive feeling of spring filled the air.

"We'd freeze up there, Bax."

Baxter was grinning. Jennie couldn't resist his infectious good humor. "Well... guess it might be fun at that. Come on in and wait 'til I get ready."

She whirled from the doorway and left Baxter to come into the kitchen and close the door.

Tater Hill was an outcropping of rocks atop Rich Mountain. From the valley it looked like a lumpy potato, hence the name. In the summer months, it was a popular picnicking spot. Penelope wound her sure-footed way up the mountain trails, and as they climbed higher spring disappeared. Snow began to appear in spotty patches and what little heat the sun held was lost to the March winds that swirled and eddied among the bare branches of the trees. Out of the valley, winter held on.

Jennie straddled Penelope behind Baxter, her arms wrapped around his waist. She wore a pair of Ed's old levis and a double layer of sweaters, the outer sweater being her comfortable grey one. Clint's red wool hat was jammed down over her ears but still allowed wisps of hair to curl around her face.

Baxter was warmly dressed as well but his head was bare and the wind whipped his hair about in all directions. Behind him Jennie giggled and leaned up to his ear. "You look like the madman of the mountains."

His hand went up to his hair and he tried unsuccessfully to smooth it down. He looked back at her and smiled. "I don't care, it feels good."

A canvas bag holding their lunch swung from the saddle. The forest was silent but for the steady clumping of Pen's feet on the mossy ground.

Baxter pulled up on the reins and turned his head to face Jen. "This is as far as we'll take Pen. The trail gets pretty rugged ahead."

He reached around, swung Jennie down, dismounted and pulled the reins over Pen's head.

"This looks like a good spot to leave ole Pen fer an hour or two." He tethered the horse to a tree, retrieved their lunch bag and slung it over his shoulder. "If ya get tired, Jen, jest let me know."

"And what will you do, Bax, carry me?"

He turned and started off at a brisk pace. "Like a sack a corn meal... over my shoulder."

Jennie hurried to catch up with Baxter as they followed the trail through the woods, climbing steadily upward in sunlight filtering down through bare branches. After a half hour they broke out of the forest.

Baxter surveyed the mountain of rocks before them that gave Tater Hill its name. He turned and grinned at Jennie.

"What are you grinning at?"

"Nothing special, jest happy to be here with you. Come on."

He led the way onto the rocks, finding the footholds, then turning to give Jen a hand up. They were both breathing heavily when they finally stood on the highest knobby rock. The air was cold, and Baxter pulled Jennie close as much for warmth as to steady them against the buffeting wind. They surveyed the awesome panorama in silence.

The sky was an endless expanse of blue, dotted with puffy clouds that streamed recklessly along on the high winds. In the misty distance the blurred outlines of mountain peaks blended with the sky and far below, the ground showed up bleak and grey with trees still bare of leaves. The rocks with the sun beating down sent up a measure of warmth but still Jennie shivered. Baxter pulled her closer.

Majestic hawks rode the thermals, gliding in ever widening circles with an eye to the ground searching for prey.

Suddenly Jennie pointed. "Over there, Baxter, see that hawk diving?" They watched as the hunter swooped down out of sight and in an instant returned to the air, something in its talons.

"He must of caught a mouse."

Baxter laughed and pretended he was going to throw her off the ledge. "You want to go down and catch a mouse?"

Jennie squealed. "Ugh... not my idea of lunch."

"It ain't too far to the bottom. Sides, you could jest float back up like that ole legend 'bout the Indian maid."

"The Indian maiden didn't jump off Tater Hill you dunce, it was Blowing Rock."

"Blowin' Rock, Tater Hill, don't make no never mind, when you're hungry, you're hungry."

Jennie giggled. "And she didn't throw herself off Blowing Rock to catch a mouse, it was for love of her Indian brave."

"You think you're so smart, Miss Jennie, I happen to know she saw them ole hawks comin' up with them juicy mice and she thought 'mmmm, they look mighty good I'll jest go down and git me some.'"

"Baxter, you're hopeless."

They turned their gaze back to the mountains.

"As often as I see these mountains, Jen, they still take my breath away. Look over yonder, Grandfather Mountain... looks peaceful lying there on his back."

Grandfather Mountain was called *Tanawha* by the Cherokee Indians long before the white man came to the valley. An unusual arrangement of rocks along its rim resembled the profile of an old man lying on his back. A heavy brow overslung the indentation of the eye, followed by an outcropping of rock that became a prominent nose. The chin was lost in a scraggly rock beard spread out over his chest.

Jennie followed his gaze. "Makes you realize how insignificant we all are, doesn't it? The mountains have been here long before any of us living now, and they'll be here long after we're gone... You love the mountains, don't you?"

"Mmmm. I love the mountains and trees and the creeks full of trout... and the people."

"But you don't love farming."

"Right, I don't love farmin'. I ain't saying anything 'gainst farmin', Jen. Look at Ed, ever since he got back he's been doin' nuthin' but talkin' bout all that has to be done on your place. I respect that. I respect my Pa too for his love of the land. But it ain't fer me. I'll be happy to come back to the mountains as a doctor."

He turned his serious brown eyes to her. "And if I knew you would be here waiting for me, Jen, there wouldn't be another thing in the whole world I'd need."

She met his eyes. "Baxter, any girl would love to be here waiting for you..."

He was almost angry. "I'm not in love with just any girl, Jen, you know that. I'm in love with you and sometimes I think you are in love with me."

Jennie nodded her head slowly. "I know, and sometimes I think I'm in love with you too. Then I think..."

"Jennie, don't think. Just be in love with me." He suddenly turned her to face him and instinctively her arms went around his waist. He pulled her close and she nestled her head on his chest.

It felt warm and safe to be in his arms with the sun beating down and the wind whipping around them. His lips brushed her hair. She raised her head and the look in his eyes started her heart pounding. He kissed her. After a long moment they came apart, both of them breathless.

"Like now, Jen. Right now I think you are in love with me."

Jennie was shaking. He was right. When he kissed her like that she didn't want him to stop.

"Baxter, you said you'd be patient. There's James..."

"I know, I know. There's always James." He dropped his arms and turned away from her. He dug his hands in his pockets.

Jennie felt frustrated and angry; angry with herself because she hated hurting Baxter. He was honest with her and so good in so many ways. She respected him. Like Papaw said, respect is just about the most important thing between a man and woman. He didn't drink like a lot of the young boys did and he had ambition. He was handsome, too, in his own gangly rough way. Any girl would be happy to have such a man in love with her.

If I were fair, I'd tell Baxter to find someone else. Not keep him standing around shuffling his feet. But if I do tell him to find someone else, suppose he does and then James comes and we feel nothing for each other. She thought about that for a moment. What I'm doing is keeping Baxter in reserve in case it doesn't work out with James... that's contemptible. She reached for his hand. "Baxter, let's talk. I think there are a lot of things need saying."

He turned. "I know. I'm just afraid of what you want to say. Let's open Ma's lunch first and talk after."

They climbed carefully down from their rocky perch, walked back out of the wind and found a large flat rock in the sun. Jennie pulled the wool hat from her head and ran her fingers through her tousled hair. When they'd settled themselves comfortably on the rock, sitting cross-legged facing each other, Baxter opened the canvas bag. It contained thick slices of ham on homemade bread, four hardboiled eggs, two pieces of apple cake and a jug of grape juice.

They ate in silence, enjoying the tranquility of the mountain, the warm sunshine laced with the sharp tang of the forest and their feeling of contentment in being with each other. They smiled often, not needing a reason. Baxter handed her the jug of juice. After she drank some, she handed the jug back and wiped her hand across her mouth. They stretched out on the rock and were quiet for a long time.

"You ever think about Gayle?"

Baxter didn't answer and Jen was almost sorry she brought up the subject. There really wasn't much more they could discuss about Gayle. Why did she bring up her name?

Finally Baxter said, not looking at Jennie. "Yeah. Have to admit I do, but I don't long fer her. Know what I mean? I don't wish we were together. I try to think what it was about her that made me think it was love. She played up to me, made me think I wuz the greatest man ever come her way and now I think she was stringin' me along, like I wuz jest there to amuse her."

Jennie had to bite her tongue to keep from telling Baxter how right he was. But she'd protected Baxter this long, no sense blurting it out now. Better for Baxter to come to the truth in his own way, in his own time. "Your Mom ever hear from Aunt Serina? Gayle ever get in touch with her?"

"We ain't heard and I don't much care... Enough about Gayle. How are Min and Sherm doin'?"

Jennie frowned. "I know they sneak off together a lot. I've tried talking to her but she won't listen to me, says I don't understand. Even Ed got Sherm aside one day and tried to talk to him bout them being young and maybe they shouldn't spend so much time together. When Min found out, she jumped all over Ed. She's only fourteen and thinks she should be treated like an adult."

Baxter said. "Some people are more adult at fourteen than others at thirty. Them two think like adults..."

"Well she hasn't been acting like an adult. Snappin' at everyone, cranky all the time. She's just no fun anymore."

Baxter turned his face to Jennie. "I think I can understand how she feels."

"You understand?"

"Yeah I do, Jen. Cause I'm in the same place Min and Sherm are. Wantin' somcone so bad and not bein' able to do a darn thing about it."

Jennie rolled over on her side and propped her head on her hand. "Maybe we should have our talk, Bax."

Baxter looked up into her face and suddenly Jennie felt an overwhelming sadness. What is missing? She thought. Why can't I love him? Hc's ambitious. I would always be able to count on him and most important, he loves me... so what is missing? Aloud she said, "What I'm doing is not fair to you."

"Jest what is it you're doin'?"

"Well, to start, I don't know what it will be like when I meet James. I can't explain why but I'm drawn to him. I know so little about him and maybe it's the not knowing that is so exciting." She wanted him to understand, yet she hardly understood it herself.

"And you think 'cause you know me so well, that somehow I'm not exciting enough?"

Jennie let that sink in. She slowly nodded. "Sounds awful, Baxter, but maybe that's it. I'm so comfortable with you... there are no surprises left." Jennie could see the hurt in his eyes.

She continued. "At the same time, a few letters and a feeling isn't much to base your whole life on."

Baxter reacted to that. He rolled over and propped his head on his hand so that they were facing each other. "As long as you can scc that, Jen, I feel I have as much chance as James. You know right here and now how I feel. I've loved you from the time we was in fourth gradc. There's somethin' to be said for knowin' everything about someone."

"I guess," Jennie agreed, "but what I'm trying to tell you is that it's not fair of me to expect you to stand around and wait."

"What do you mean, stand around and wait?"

"You spend all your spare time with me. You don't give yourself a chance to know any other girls. When you go away to school you'll meet lots of new people and it just makes sense you give yourself a chance..."

"Jennie, Jennie. That ain't no answer." He said almost angrily, "I don't have to go nowhere to know what I want. Look, let's just leave things the way they are. You said often 'nuff we're best friends. Well, friends don't just stop being friends, do they?"

Jennie looked long into his eyes. With a deep sigh she said, "I guess I would miss not seeing you."

Baxter grabbed her hand and squeezed it. "Why don't we jest wait 'til James comes and see what happens?"

"Bax, that's more than I deserve."

He laughed. "I know it is, but we got the whole summer. Anything can happen."

"What if we don't have the whole summer?"

"All the better, Jen. I'm ready to face James."

"Suppose I'm not ready?"

Baxter tried to hold back laughter. "Then James and me'll settle it between us who you end up with."

Jennie sat up straight. "You and James..." She suddenly saw he was teasing. "Oh you..." and pushed him down again on his back. He pulled her to him so their faces were inches apart.

"Girl, I love you."

She kissed him lightly on the lips. "You did say you'd be content to wait?"

Baxter sighed. "Do I have a choice?"

"Neither of us do."

Jennie lay down again beside him. The sun felt good on her face. After awhile her thoughts moved to another problem. She sighed.

"What was that for?"

"Papa."

She felt him grip her hand tighter. "Last time he was home, what was it, Christmas? you had words. He say anything more?"

"No, and I don't think he will, now Ed's home."

"Then what's the problem?"

"Papa is going to put everything on Ed's shoulders, I just know he is, and Ed isn't well enough yet to handle it. As far as school is concerned, I am enrolled and will start with the fall semester, same as you. Ed won't hear of me postponing it again, and he says if Papa says anything, he'll handle it."

"Jen, you got to stop tryin' to change your Papa. It's the way he is and it's the way he's gonna be fer the rest of his time on earth. You keep thinkin' all of a sudden he's gonna be concerned about your Mama and all of you. It's jest not gonna happen."

Jennie nodded, sadly. "Of course you're right, Bax. But hope dies hard."

The combined warmth of the rock beneath them and the peaceful aura of the forest added to their contentment. They drifted off to sleep.

After a time Jennie opened her eyes. The sun was dipping towards the horizon and a chill had settled over the forest. She turned to look at Baxter and saw his eyes were still closed. She nudged him gently. "Come on, wild man of the mountains, time to head for home."

Baxter opened his eyes. "This is nice, Jen, wakin' up and findin' you lying next to me."

She got to her feet. "Won't be so nice once the sun goes down."

He stood up and stretched. "This's been a good day."

They threaded their way back along the trail and found Pen patiently waiting for them. "Such a good old girl, Pen." Baxter stroked the side of her head and she nuzzled him in return.

"She's as fond of you as she is of Doc."

"We got to know each other these past months. I've been on her back 'most as much as Doc." He drew the reins over the horse's head, mounted and reached a hand down to Jen.

She pulled herself up behind him. "Animals can tell when people like them. Take Lib and Lizzie. I swear when Clint is around they nuzzle and push against him just about asking for attention. Lizzie especially, cause she's the orneriest and Clint gives her the most attention. Same with Hube and Soldier... poor Hube. Mama says he has to keep Soldier locked in the Owens barn while Papa is home. I don't know who I'm sorrier for, Hube or the dog."

"Why d'ya hafta keep 'em locked up?"

"Cause Papa hates the dog. Mama says Soldier better be out of his sight."

"You got a strange Papa, Jen."

"You just now noticed?"

The sun was gone by the time Jennie slid off Pen's back at the Wainwright gate. "It was a wonderful day, Baxter. Thank you."

"We won't wait 'til your next birthday to do it again. Next time we'll go to Blowing Rock and test that ole legend."

"See this ad in the *Democrat*, Lu?" Dalton sat at the kitchen table, the paper spread out before him. "It's fer one of them dang automobiles.

A hoss can't hardly pull a wagon down the road in a spring thaw, don't know how they think one of these contraptions can make it."

Lu sat in her rocker sewing buttons on a shirt. She looked up. "Didn't I hear somewhere Doc Payne is thinkin' on buying one?"

Dalton snorted. "Doc give up on Pen? Why'd he do a fool thing like that? Now I could see mebbe Lije gettin' one. You'd need to know somethin' 'bout repairin' it. They break down a whole lot and Ev's a pretty good hand with machines. Yeah, I could see Lije, but not Doc."

Jennie and Ed sat at the kitchen table, Jennie writing a letter as Ed leafed through the almanac.

Ed said,. "Papa's right. Doc would be foolish to trade Pen for an automobile. Right now, anyway. In the future, maybe. The world's changin'... Speakin' of changes, Papa, Jen's goin' to school in the fall."

Jennie looked up, startled; Mama stopped sewing and looked at Papa. Ed caught Jennie's eye and winked.

Ed continued, "She's been accepted at The North Carolina School of Nursing in Charlotte and Papaw has the money for her, so she'll be leaving for school come September."

Papa didn't lift his eyes from the paper. Both Jennie and Mama fixed him with a steady gaze, waiting for a comment, but he casually turned the page without looking at either of them and continued his absorption in the paper. Jennie knew it was a pretense. Finally he said, from behind the paper, "I don't give a good God-damn what Jennie does."

✉

Jennie sat cross legged on Ed's bed, watching him pack his duffel bag. "What did Papa say when you told him you were going back to the mines with him?"

"Funny. I thought he would be all fired up 'bout it. I could swear he don't want me goin' back with him. Asked me wuz I sure it wuz what I wanted. Course it ain't, but I can't get any work 'round here."

"Well it doesn't sound like Papa, being concerned about your health. But if *he* isn't *we* all are. It isn't a good idea, you goin' down in the mines."

Ed was irritated. "My lungs is all right." He stopped and turned to Jennie. "You know as well as I do, Jen, we need the money. It's plain Papa ain't gonna provide it, so it's up to me." He turned again to his packing, discouraging further discussion on the subject. "It won't be my life's work. I'm gonna see we get some of the things needed around here, like glasses for Helen and mebbe even a sewing machine for Mama."

Jennie said in surprise, "A sewing machine?"

"Yep, 'bout time Mama got some help, what with all the sewin' she does."

Jennie watched him in silence, a smile on her lips. "I sure was proud of you just up and telling Papa about me going to school. Did you see Mama's face? She didn't know whether to laugh or run for her Bible."

Ed laughed at that. "You're right. That's Mama's line of defense, her Bible. Well, Papa had to know. I kinda enjoyed telling him, too."

Jennie was struck by the change in Ed. It was plain he no longer considered himself a child. "I was kinda hoping you would be here when James comes."

Ed looked at her with a grin. "How do you feel about meetin' James?"

"Scared."

"Really? He ain't someone to be scared of."

"Maybe I don't mean scared. Maybe just nervous he won't like me."

Ed looked solemn. After a moment he said, "I ain't never met anyone kind as James, or easier to talk to. Same can be said of you, Jen. Can't think a two people more suited." Jennie dropped her head to cover her embarrassment. Ed continued, "But that does make fer a problem, don't it?"

Jennie met his eyes with an innocent look. "What do you mean?"

"Come on, Jen, you know what I mean... Baxter."

Jennie breathed out a long troubled sigh. "Sometimes I think I'm in love with that boy."

Edward said, "I allus thought a body'd know if they wuz in love. Mebbe you should ask Min. She seems sure 'nuff."

Jennie smiled. "She sure does." The smile faded and Jennie turned serious. "But Min is thinking of how she feels right now. I'm thinking of a lifetime."

Ed picked up a shirt, rolled it into a ball and stuffed it in his duffel. "Wish I could help, Jen, but I don't know anymore'n you do."

Jennie pulled the shirt out of the duffel and began to fold it. "I always thought the way Mama and Papa acted with each other was the way all married folks behaved."

Ed watched her thoughtfully and began to fold his other shirt. "What started you thinkin' different?"

"It was what Mama said when she was sick... when she was delirious. Mama is in love with Papa the way she was when they were first married and it's plain Papa isn't. It's hard for me to think Papa ever was in love with Mama the way he treats her now."

Ed carefully packed the folded shirt into the duffel, drew the cord tight and stood the bag on end. "If it will make you feel any better, Jen, I don't know two people more different than Papa and James... or Baxter for that matter. I can't picture either one of them turning out like Papa. But they is one thing I can give Papa credit for. He showed me how *not* to treat a woman. Right now I gotta get movin'."

Jennie climbed off the bed. "We'll miss you. Make sure you get home to visit as often as you can. Mama will be worried about you... we all will."

He hefted the bag to his shoulder. "Ain't like the war, Jen, I won't be that far away."

"If you can manage to write once in awhile..."

"Yes, Jennie, I'll write once in awhile."

Chapter Twenty-Two
Two Lumberjacks

James whispered. "Look at that moon, laddie, is it not the most glorious one we've seen yet?"

Pete snorted in disgust. "That's about what I'd expect you to say. Here we are trying to sneak aboard a freight car and the damn moon comes out making it like daylight. Leave it to you to think that's *glorious*." Pete hurried their pace.

"Peter, me lad, I'm a firm believer in what will be, will be. If we are meant to safely board a freight car, we will. If not... Shhh. I hear voices." They scurried to a nearby water shed and stood in its shadow. Two men approached. They were in uniform and each carried a billy club. The policemen were in lively conversation and didn't look right or left as they strode past the two shadows.

James held his breath until he could no longer hear the men talking. "Close, laddie, close..." They continued walking.

Pete whispered. "Remember the plan, Irish. We wait 'til the cars start to move. Then we both take off like a shot for the next to last box car in the line, the one we staked out. With luck the police won't notice the door open a crack. I'll be able to get a handhold and slide the door open enough for me to throw my duffel in and climb in after it. You throw me your duffel and then I'll give you a hand up. We got to work fast."

James nodded. "And if you make it and I don't, you wait for me in Portland. I'll be asking the kind policeman to hold the next freight for me."

"Damn it, Jim, be serious. Either we both make it or we wait for the next opportunity."

"Keep your voice down, laddie, or there'll *be* no next time. Pity we can't board the car now, before it starts movin'."

"You heard what Gabe said. The bulls almost always check each car just before the freight moves out. We can't take a chance that tonight they won't check. I'm just hopin' they don't notice the door we left open and secure it."

They made their way along the length of cars towards the rear of the freight train. Suddenly the engine came to life, huffing loudly. They looked to the engine and saw sparks from the engine's fire box leaping into the night sky and without a word they began to run.

They were almost to their car when suddenly whistles shrilled and shouting erupted. This time there was no shed to give them cover. They looked frantically around. Jim threw his duffel to the ground and fell beside it, pulling Pete down beside him. They curled up in a ball and froze just as several men came stumbling around the rear of the train with several more men close on their heels. Midst the commotion, the heap of clothes on the ground went unnoticed. As the shouting faded away James and Pete sat up and grinned at each other.

They had no time to congratulate themselves. The train came to life, jerking forward a foot or two, causing the cars all the way down the line to crash into each other. Pete and James scrambled to their feet, grabbed their duffels and ran. As they reached their car, the train was moving laboriously forward.

There was no time or breath for words. Pete threw himself at the door, dug his fingers into the open slot and tugged at the sliding door with all his might. The huge door slid open. He threw his duffel in and James gave him a leg up. Pete fell forward into the car as it began to pick up speed. He turned and leaned out grabbing Jim's duffel and heaving it over his shoulder.

"Gimme your hand," he shouted. James ran alongside, trying to keep his footing on the gravel. He reached up. Pete caught his hand and with one frantic yank heaved him aboard. They fell back panting on the floor of the box car as the freight gave a mournful wail and rumbled off into the night.

After he caught his breath, James sat up and ran his two hands through his hair. "Lord love us, laddie, we made it."

Pete grunted from a prone position. James could almost see him smiling in the dark. "Ain't my favorite way to travel, but it being free makes all the difference."

James got up and cautiously moved his arms and legs. "Nuthin' broken." He moved to the sliding door and stood at the opening. The train had cleared the freight yard and was now chugging slowly along the outskirts of the Seattle suburbs. The landscape was silent and bright with moonlight.

Pete joined him. The slow pace of the freight train lulled them into a sense of peace and security.

After they'd stood in silence for a time, James said, "You never been in the States, Pete, why?"

"Always meant to see what it was like, but I never got the chance."

"It's been my dream for so long it's almost like I've lived here."

"You mean it looks familiar?"

"Not exactly familiar. I haven't seen that much of it yet, but I've read every book I could get my hands on about the United States of America. It's pretty much what I expected. Grand and beautiful."

"So is Canada."

"Aye, it is, but... I never felt at home in Canada. Here, for some reason I can't explain, I feel like I'm comin' home."

"You think maybe Jennie has somethin' to do with it?"

"Oh, yes, but that's not it entirely."

James turned to Pete. His earnest grey eyes shining in the moonlight. "From early on I've felt my future is here. We can go to Pennsylvania and look into the steel industry, or to Michigan and find out about Ford cars. The opportunities are endless."

Pete stared solemnly at the moving landscape. "You got education, Irish. That'll take you far. I left school in the eighth grade. After Dad died, there was no way Mom could keep me in school, so I ain't got much education."

James put his hand on Pete's shoulder. "You didn't turn out badly, Bucko."

Pete continued, "Was a time I was pretty wild... traveled with the wrong crowd... ended up in reform school."

"You were doin' fine when I met you."

Pete grinned. "Yeah. By that time I was. When I got out of reform school Mom was keeping company with Bruce and he was a brakeman on the railroad. He straightened me out. Got me on as a fireman when I was old enough."

"Is that what you want to go back to?"

"I don't know. I kinda liked bein' a fireman."

James turned back to the moonlit landscape moving steadily by. "I don't exactly know meself what I want, but I have the feelin' the findin' out will be as gratifyin' as the end result."

"How does Jennie figure in all that?"

"Well, now, from what I read in her letters, she's much like me. She's not content with her life as it is now. She talks about getting an education, being a nurse and she's not going to be able to do that buried away in a little mountain town."

"That's what she says in her letters."

"Aye. When it comes down to it, we'll have to see."

"S'posin' she don't want to leave her home after all."

After he'd thought about it, James said, "That's a hard one, Pete. All I've ever been able to think about was seeing the States. I mean really traveling, finding the place I want to settle down. At the same time I have this uncanny feeling that Jennie is the one I want to settle down with." He flashed a sudden grin and his teeth gleamed white in the moonlight.

"Who knows, boyo, maybe Zionville will be that place."

Pete grunted. "Nuthin's ever that easy." He turned away from the open door, knelt down on the floor of the box car and fumbled for his duffel bag in the dark. "We'll be needing our blankets. The wind whistling through them cracks is gonna make fer a long cold ride. We'll be freezin' our ass off."

"Ya know, laddie, this is not unlike the ship what with the swaying and all."

Pete muttered. "That's all you had to remind me of. I think I'm gonna be seasick."

$$\boxtimes$$

The sign read '**Mt. Elmore Logging Co.**' and in smaller letters beneath, MGR. JOSEPH MCNULTY.

James and Pete entered the small office. A waist high divider ran right to left through the center separating the front of the office from the back. A gate allowed access to either of the two sections. A second door in the back led, presumably, into another office. Behind the divider a woman, perhaps thirty years old, sat at a desk with a large ledger open in front of her. She was attractive despite large horn-rimmed glasses with thick lenses which magnified her eyes, giving her face an owlish look. Her hair was pale blond, bobbed and marceled in the latest fashion, and her dark blue wool suit with the trim white blouse looked expensive.

Before she acknowledged their presence, Pete whispered to Jim. "Leave the talking to me, Irish, I'll score us some points."

James said with a grin, "I bow to the expert."

Pete sauntered to the divider and sat atop it, swinging one leg. "Morning, little lady."

The young woman looked up and gave Pete a businesslike smile. "Good morning. What can I do for you?"

"Anybody ever tell you you have a beautiful smile?"

She replied matter of factly, "Yes, I'm told that every day. Now what can I do for you?"

Undaunted, Pete tried again. "I been all over the world and I ain't never seen a prettier smile."

The young woman nodded seriously. "Now that we've established I have the prettiest smile in the world, what is it you want?"

Pete pulled in his stomach and stood tall. "Well, little lady, understand you're looking for lumberjacks. Me and my buddy here come to apply."

The door at the back of the office opened and a man, as tall as Pete but outweighing him by at least a hundred pounds, lumbered in. His expression was businesslike, neither scowling nor overly friendly.

The young woman kept her eyes on Pete and said, "Then I guess you want to talk to my husband." She turned her gaze to include the big man. "He does all the hiring for the camps."

James hurriedly stepped forward. A husband such as this meant dangerous waters. "Aye. We saw your ad in the papers."

Pete added nothing at all.

The big man brought his hand out and James took an involuntary step backward. "Name's McNulty, gentlemen, Joe McNulty." They shook hands all around. The man grinned. "Everyone calls me Mac."

The grin showed teeth so white they looked polished. "We got four camps spread throughout the forests of central Oregon and the turnover is pretty constant. It ain't an easy job and we need men that can handle themselves... men with a bit of muscle."

He stopped and pointedly looked James and Pete over. He said to Pete, "You're a good prospect." He turned to James. "Have you ever handled an axe?"

Pete interrupted. "Irish here has book learning. Maybe you have something..."

Joe, his eyes still on James, said, "Book learning? Irish?"

"Aye, back in Ireland...

Joe clapped James on the back. "Irish, are you? My Dad was from Ireland, County Cork. I've never been to Ireland myself, but one day... say listen, we have a spot at Camp Geronimo. Doc MacIntosh runs the office and he's been crying for help. Think you could handle the ledgers, Irish?"

James nodded. "I'm a quick learner."

"All right then." He turned to the girl. "Nan, get the papers ready." He turned again to James. "Pay is two dollars a day and board. Be here at the office, let's see, today is Tuesday... Thursday morning at 5:00 a.m. Buckboard leaves on time. See you don't miss it. You'll be needing some stout brogans." He looked down at their feet. "See you're wearing army boots... they're good, and warm shirts. It's still cold in the woods. Report in to Doc MacIntosh when you get to the camp and give him the papers."

He stopped and smiled. "Guess that's about it." He held out his hand and they shook hands all around again. "Welcome to the rolls of Mt.Elmore Logging Company. Good luck to you." He smiled again and disappeared into the back office.

...and so, Jennie girl, we're to leave for the camp on Thursday. The pay is two dollars a day and since there's not much a body can spend money on in a logging camp, I'll be saving most of it... and that is what this is all about, saving money to make my way east and to finally meet the girl of my dreams.

I will write as soon as I arrive so you will have an address to write to. It's been so long since I last had a letter from you. I need to hear from you....

Love,
James

Chapter Twenty-Three
Minnie and Sherm

Jennie finished reading the letter and looked up at Mama, a smile on her face. "Mama, they actually hitched a ride on a freight car without getting caught. Did you ever hear of such a thing? I wonder if I would have the nerve to do that."

Mama opened the oven door and slipped the two loaves of bread in to bake. "Let's hope when you get to ride on a train, it will be as a passenger. That should be excitement enough for anybody, never mind a freight car."

Jennie went back to the letter. "Says here they got work in a lumber camp. Looks like I'll be able to write to him soon."

"'Bout time."

A knock sounded at the back door and Mama wiped her hands on her apron as she went to answer it. "Well, Clara, come along inside, and set a spell." Lula opened the door wider and smiled at her neighbor.

Clara came inside and took off her shawl. She looked distracted, smiling at Jennie without really seeing her. "Is Min here?"

Lula turned from hanging up Clara's shawl. "Min? Why no. Matter of fact, I thought she was over to your place. You know, Clara, I cautioned that child 'bout spendin' so much time over there. Seems like you'd get tired having her underfoot all the time. When she gets to be a bother, jest tell her to come on home." Lula went to her rocker and sat down.

Clara sank to the sofa. "I wuz hopin' Min would be here and me and Jeb wuz wrong." Jennie sat down beside Clara.

Lula looked at Jennie and then back at Clara. "Wrong? 'Bout what, Clara? Don't be skittish, tell me? Is it somethin' 'bout Min?"

Clara continued, "I thought Min and Sherm might be over here. But you say you ain't seen them? Either one of them?"

Jennie felt a hint of foreboding.

Lula said, "No, we don't see much a Sherm at all. Jeb keeps the young'un busy, don't he? Min's been gone since early on. Didn't come home fer dinner. Figured she took dinner over to your place." Lula waited patiently for Clara to explain.

Clara took a deep breath. "Jeb and me think they's run off, Lu."

Lula's smile faded. "What do you mean..." She stopped rocking. Jennie caught her breath.

Clara went on, "Jeb sent Sherm out to the barn early this morning to do some chores. Min, of course, went with him. She's a good hand at helpin'."

Lula was impatient. "Yes, yes, Clara ... go on."

"Come dinner time I sent Clay out to fetch them in and they wasn't there. Sherm ain't never missed dinner a day in his life. What's more, Bro is gone from his stall."

"Maybe they jest took Bro riding," Jennie said, not believing it even as she said it.

"The young'uns never take the horses 'less they ask their Pa. Clay and me looked all over but wasn't hide ner hair of them."

Clara got up from the sofa and began to pace. "I shoulda knowed this was gonna happen. I shoulda seen it comin', but I thought the two of them wuz jest playing at being in love. They is so young. It's my fault." She continued to pace.

Lula said, "No it ain't your fault, Clara. If they's any fault it can be laid on my doorstep. Every time Min brought up the subject of her and Sherm, I'd shush her. She's been trying to tell me somethin' fer a long time and I wouldn't listen."

Jennie got up from the couch. "We have to find them before they do somethin' foolish."

Clara stopped pacing. "If you mean get married, Jennie, I'm sure that's what they's aimin' to do. Jeb and me talked 'bout it 'for I come over here. All we want is to have them come back. We're scared they might get married and take off fer some place thinking we'uns might make trouble and not let them stay together. We agree being married so young ain't the best but we can handle that if they jest come home. Jeb needs his son." Clara was close to tears.

Lula was angry. "I told that young'un she had more growin' up to do..."

Clara interrupted. "No sense gettin' mad, Lu, they's gone. Jeb can't do no runnin' after them, you know he ain't never got his strength back, and Clay and Clint's too young." She turned to Jennie. "I thought mebbe you could try and find them, Jennie. You can take Sis and go lookin'."

Jennie nodded. "They're more'n likely in Boone. I'll head for Papaw's first, and if they're not there I'll go on to Boone and look for them."

Lula said to Clara, "I don't s'pose they's any mistake. We ain't jest jumpin' ahead of ourselves?"

"No, Lu. More I think on it, the more sure I am. Last few days Min and Sherm's been whisperin' and gigglin' more'n usual. I shoulda knowed somethin wuz up." She started to wring her hands. "Jeb's been leanin' heavy on Sherm. He'll be lost without the boy."

Clara hugged Lula. "I don't know as it's a bad idea, Lu, them two gettin' married. They's crazy fer each other, that's a fact... and you know we love Minnie. If they jest wasn't so dern young." She took her shawl from the peg and said over her shoulder as she went out the kitchen door, "Jeb will saddle Sis, Jennie. Come over soon's yer ready."

Lula was numb. "Lord, Minnie," she said, "what have you gone and done?"

Jennie had Sis at a gallop. She was a strong young horse and Jennie was light on her back. They were almost to the Combs farm. Jennie spotted Baxter coming down his road and she reined the horse in and waited for him. Baxter was all smiles. "This is a surprise, Jennie, you comin' to see me?" His smile faded as he saw her face. "What's the matter?"

She said breathlessly, "It's Min and Sherm. The Owens think they've run off to get married and I'm gonna see if I can stop them. I'm on my way to Papaw's, if they're not there I'll go on to Boone."

Baxter held on to Sis's bridle. "Jen, you can't go alone. Let me go with you."

Jennie felt a surge of relief. "Could you?"

Baxter was already turning back to his house. "I'll jest tell Pa where I'm goin' and leave word for Doc too. I'll be right back."

It wasn't as easy for Sis to carry the two of them, but seeming to sense the urgency of the trip, the horse kept up a steady pace and the distance to Sugar Grove was covered in record time. They reined in at Papaw's house and Jennie slid down without waiting for help. There was no sign of Bro. "Oh Bax, they aren't here." She was halfway up the walk before Baxter dismounted. There was no one in the house.

Jennie looked at Baxter. "The mill!" The two of them hurried out the back door.

Papaw was filling grain sacks when they burst in. "What in tarnation... ain't no one sick is they?"

Baxter put his hand on Jennie's arm and with a look told her to calm down. He smiled at Papaw. "No one sick, Mr. Miller. Jennie and me are out lookin' fer a couple a runaways. Least we think they's runaways."

Jennie reached up and gave her grandfather a peck on the cheek. Papaw looked from one to the other. "Who's run away?"

Jennie said, "We think Min and Sherm Owen have run off." She waited for a reaction. Papaw just nodded.

Jennie tried to sound calm. "Mama and the Owens are worried so Baxter and me set out to find them."

"They ain't been here, have they, Mr. Miller?"

Papaws expression showed neither shock nor surprise. "No they ain't." He slapped the dust from his clothes and headed out of the mill. He said over his shoulder, "Come along to the house."

Papaw and Baxter sat at the kitchen table while Jennie paced. The old man took out his sack of tobacco and began the familiar ritual of packing his pipe.

Papaw said, quite unruffled, "Jest settle down, Jennie, this ain't no matter a life and death. What makes you think they run off to get married?"

Jennie said, "We don't know that they have, but they haven't been seen since about eight o'clock this morning. They're gone and so is Bro. It sure looks like they run off." Jennie ran a hand through her hair. "What are they thinking? Sherm's only seventeen and Min will be fifteen in a couple of months."

Papaw tamped the tobacco down. "You think mebbe they's a reason for them to run off like that?"

"I have no idea what reason... oh." Jennie stopped pacing. "You mean maybe she's pregnant?" Papaw was busy lighting his pipe. "Somehow I don't think so, Papaw, but you may be right."

Papaw had his pipe going. "Would be a good 'nuff reason, but if she ain't then they's jest in a blamed hurry to play at bein' growed up. Seems like I had this argument with your Mama when she was your age. Didn't do no good then and probably won't do no good now. Don't matter a hoot ner a holler what anyone says. They's gonna do what they please. Your Mama did."

Papaw leaned comfortably back in his chair and blew a long stream of smoke toward the ceiling. "Being ready fer marriage ain't a matter of age anyways. Comes down to common sense and responsibility. That sound like Min and Sherm?"

Jennie was impatient. "I don't know, I guess....."

Papaw interrupted. "More important is respect... they respect each other? I know young'uns don't generally think long those lines, but love is a passing thing. Respect on the other hand lasts fer a lifetime."

Jennie realized Papaw was talking about Mama and Papa but she couldn't think about it now. She began pacing again. "I can't stay and argue, Papaw. We got to find them. If they're already married, well we can't do anything about it, but if we can stop them I think it would be better all around."

"Better fer who? Ya can't stop a rock rollin' down hill once it's started. Now they got the idea, they won't be put off. Might's well go long with it, otherwise your Mama might lose Minnie altogether."

Jennie hesitated. "You're probably right, but I need to talk to Min. I want her to tell me it's what she wants and that Sherm isn't pushing her into it."

Baxter said, "There's another thing, Mr. Miller. Mr. Owen is still ailing and he's been leaning on Sherm to run his place. They're afraid Min and Sherm will be too scared to come back home."

Jennie stood up. "I should have been there for Min. I should have seen the signs."

Papaw took the pipe from his mouth. "I agree. Shoulda been talked out long ago. Well, if you'uns are gonna go to Boone I think you best have a plan. If Min and Sherm are of a mind to get married they got to have a license. What you do is go to the city hall and ask to see Calvin Hemsley. He's the clerk issues the licenses. If they been there then leastways you'll know they do plan on marryin' 'stead of jest off playin' fer the day." Jennie nodded.

Papaw continued, "They'll be wantin' a preacher too. They's any number of preachers in town, but mebbe Calvin will know which one they wuz plannin' to go to." He pushed away from the table. "I think you best take my horse. Sis looks to be plumb wore out. Come along, Baxter, we'll saddle up Lazarus."

Lazarus was a large, strong horse and easily held Jennie and Baxter, but he was old and Jennie had to refrain from prodding him to speed up. She was angry with herself. I should have known what Min was planning, she thought. When Mama wouldn't listen to her I should have been there for her to talk to. Despite herself, Jen smiled. Min had certainly made a grown up decision.

Boone was a busy place. People walked purposefully in and out of the shops and offices that lined King Street, the main thoroughfare. Any other time Jennie would have enjoyed the bustle, but the runaways drove all other thoughts from her mind.

The city hall was an old wooden structure and showed up shabbier than it might have if not overshadowed by the new brick courthouse with four shining white pillars that stood next to it. Jennie and Baxter hurried up the wooden stairs, pushed open the double doors and entered a small, dimly lighted foyer. On the wall was a plaque that gave the office designations and where they were located.

Jennie pointed, "There it is, Baxter."

They walked quickly down the long hallway to the License Bureau.

"It's almost 5:00 o'clock," Jennie whispered, "I hope Calvin Hemsley is still here." They stepped into the office.

A long counter divided the office in two. Behind the counter were three desks, only one of which was occupied. A middle aged man got up without enthusiasm from the desk and approached the counter. His straight black hair was brushed sideways across a bald spot on top. Glasses, perched low on a long thin nose, looked as if they would drop off with a sudden movement. He wore a rumpled long sleeved white shirt with a colorful tie. Red arm bands pulled his sleeves taut.

Unsmiling, he addressed Baxter. "What can I do for you?"

"Uh, we wuz hopin' we might speak with Mr. Calvin Hemsley."

"Well, best speak fast, son, it's 'most closing time."

Baxter grinned in relief. "You Mr. Hemsley?"

"Yep. State your business."

Jennie spoke up. "We're looking... that is, did you issue a license today to a Minnie Wainwright and Sherman Owen?"

The man was impatient. "What kind of license... fishing, business, building, marriage... what?"

"Oh, ah, marriage." Jennie thought the man was rude.

Mr. Hemsley went back to his desk, pulled a black ledger toward him and began to rifle through the pages. "Names were Wainwright and Owen? Yep they were here this morning." He snapped the ledger closed and returned to the counter, folded his arms and looked at them without speaking. Finally Baxter said, "Well, did you give them a license?"

"The girl didn't look eighteen to me, but they were determined, so against my better judgment I gave them a license."

Jennie was exasperated. "Look, Mr. Hemsley, we're sorry to bother you so late in the day but my Papaw, Mylart Miller, said you would be able to help us."

A smile spread over Mr. Hemsley's face and with it a change in attitude. "That a fact. Your Papaw's Mylart Miller is he?" He leaned on the counter ready for conversation. "I know your Papaw. A mighty fine gentleman."

"Yes," Jennie agreed. "He is a mighty fine gentleman." *I should have mentioned Papaw right off.*

Aloud she said, "Uh, so you issued them a license." Below the counter she crossed her fingers. "I wonder if they mentioned who was going to marry them?"

"They didn't know a preacher so I gave them the names of two. Don't know which one they went to. One was Reverend Dean Jennings, pastor of the First Baptist church right here on King Street. You can't miss it. You go left as you come out of the city hall. The other name I gave them was James Birdwell, preacher of the Methodist Church on Queen Street, one block over."

Baxter asked, "Can you remember what time that was, Mr. Hemsley?"

"Well, now let's see. I was just about to go get my dinner when they came in. After I issued the license and we talked about the preachers they left. Must a been 'bout 12:30."

Jennie was disappointed. "If it was that early they must be married by now."

Mr. Hemsley said, "Said they were going to do some shopping first. They sure were nervous. Hung on to each other for dear life." He frowned at Jennie. "You know for a fact how old they are? Said they were both eighteen."

Jennie backed away from the counter, smiling. "Well, we thank you kindly, Mr. Hemsley." They walked briskly to the door.

Calvin called after them, "I'll be telling your Papaw I saw you."

The door banged shut behind them. Outside, Lazarus waited patiently. Baxter mounted and gave Jennie a hand up. He turned around with a grin. "Eighteen, huh?"

Jennie couldn't help grinning too. "I know. Eighteen is stretching it a bit."

"Baptist church is closest, we'll go there first."

Jennie nodded. Baxter dug his heels in and Lazarus started off at a brisk trot.

There was no sign of the Owen horse as Baxter reined in at the church. "I don't see Bro, Baxter."

"Me neither, but we better check inside anyways. You wait here."

He tried the church with no luck and gestured to Jennie that he was going to try the parsonage next door. In a matter of minutes he returned.

"Mrs. Jennings says they were here earlier." He hurriedly mounted. "But her husband is out of town for the day. She don't know where they went."

Baxter prodded Lazarus and the old horse carried them along King Street, then down a block to Queen Street. They were almost to the outskirts of town when the Methodist church came into view. The sun was dipping low. Jennie said with relief, "There's the church."

It was a neat white clapboard structure set far back off the road. It nestled comfortably in a grove of maple trees. The walkway that led to the big double doors was made of slabs of grey slate neatly embedded in the ground. Tied to one of the maples was a big chestnut horse placidly nibbling the grass. It was Bro.

The church wasn't locked. Jennie and Baxter silently pulled open the heavy doors and slipped inside. Stained glass windows reflected the late afternoon sun and bathed them in shafts of colored light. An aura of peace and quiet filled the church and Jennie felt herself relax.

There were two figures sitting in the first pew and a man stood before them speaking so softly that neither Jen nor Baxter could hear what he was saying. They hurried up the aisle and the man looked up as they approached. Min and Sherm turned around. Min looked shocked as she jumped to her feet. "Jennie...how...?"

Jennie ran the last few feet and threw her arms around her sister. "Min, I'm so glad we found the two of you."

Sherm found his voice. "Preacher, this is Min's sister Jennie and our friend Baxter Combs." He turned to Jennie and Baxter. "And this is Preacher Birdwell."

Jennie nodded, and with her arm around Minnie, said, "Preacher, I wonder if you would excuse us for a moment while we talk privately."

Preacher Birdwell was a round little man. His hair was abundant and the color of the slate walkway in front of the church. His cheeks were so full that his eyes almost closed as he smiled at them.

"Not at all, child, happy to see the young'uns here have some kin present." He walked to the rear of the church and settled into a pew to wait.

Minnie pulled away from Jennie. "There's no use makin' a fuss, Jen, Sherm and I have come this far and we are gonna get married."

Sherm stood beside Minnie. "There ain't nuthin you kin say, Jennie, ner you either Baxter, we made up our minds."

Jennie looked at the two of them standing side by side. Sherm's hair was neatly combed and he wore a clean white shirt with a black string tie. His levis were clean and his boots were polished to a high sheen.

Minnie was dressed in a pale blue dress Jennie had never seen before. It fit her waist snugly and fell in soft billows to mid calf. The neckline was scooped and trimmed in lace. Her hair was a mass of black waves that fell softly around her face and shoulders and nestled in the waves was a blue satin bow. She wore her Sunday meeting high buttoned shoes.

They looked so grown up. Jennie could barely speak for the lump in her throat. "Min, I know you and Sherm love each other, everyone can see it, but..."

Min held up her hand. "It's all been said before, Jennie. Waiting three, four years won't change the way we feel one bit, so why wait? We only know we have to be together." She turned her face to Sherm and the look they exchanged excluded everyone from their world. "Sherman knows it and I know it."

Jennie took a deep breath, not knowing how to ask what had to be asked. She took Min's hand and held it tight. "I have to ask, Minnie, are you and Sherm, that is, are you..."

Minnie grinned. "No, Jennie, me and Sherm ain't gonna have a baby, if that's what you mean, but that's why we wanna get married..." She looked at Sherm. "We wuz afraid, like Mama said, to bring down the wrath of the Lord."

Jennie couldn't help but grin. Mama and her Bible.

Baxter turned to Jennie and smiled. "Guess there ain't nuthin' more to say."

Jennie's eyes had never left Minnie. "Yes, there is. I don't know when I've seen a more beautiful bride. Min, would you like me to stand up for you?"

⊠

Jennie slumped tiredly against Baxter, her arms wrapped around him for warmth. Lazarus lumbered steadily along through the dark, knowing the route. After several attempts to speed the horse up, Baxter gave up and let Lazarus find his own pace. They plodded along in comfortable silence.

Min and Sherm's happy faces kept coming up in Jen's mind, making her grin. Then she thought of Mama. Mama was going to have a fit. But Mama should be grateful at least that her Bible training had paid off. There would be no baby in less than nine months to be embarrassed about. Jennie snuggled closer to Baxter and decided she was too tired to worry about it. In time, Lazarus turned onto Papaw's log bridge, without direction, and plodded up the road.

Jennie slid down and Baxter followed. "I'll see to Lazarus, Jen, you go in and tell your Papaw. He must be worried."

Jennie nodded and hurried along the path to the house. Papaw was already at the door, his figure lit from behind by lamplight. "So, did ya find 'em?" Papaw opened the screen door and stepped aside to let Jennie enter. Jennie nodded wearily. "And....?"

"She isn't pregnant, Papaw, and I could have done something to stop it, but I chose not to." She dropped into a chair by the kitchen table. Papaw joined her and waited patiently for Jennie to tell her story.

"We did like you said. We went to the city hall and found Mr. Hemsley. He told us he issued a license to Min and Sherm around noon, and also which churches he sent them to. When we got to the Methodist church, there was old Bro tethered in the yard."

Jennie suddenly grinned. "You should have seen them, Papaw, Min decked out in a beautiful blue dress and Sherm, hair all slicked down and boots polished... I've never seen either of them looking so good."

"Well, them's two good lookin' young'uns ta begin with. What happened next?"

"They right away said nothing would change their minds, that we might as well turn around and go home. By that time, nothing could have made us leave, so we stayed and stood up for them."

They turned as Baxter came through the kitchen door. "Jen tell you the news, Mr. Miller?"

"Yep, and it's jest as well you didn't make no fuss. We'll sit tight and see how they take to being' married." He got up and brought a pan of cornbread and a jug of milk to the table. "Get them mugs from the cupboard, Jen... Yessir, they'll find out soon 'nuff it ain't all huggin' and kissin.'"

Jennie came back to the table with mugs and plates and cut big wedges of corn bread from the pan, while Papaw poured the milk.

"They're gonna spend the night in Boone. They got a room over Aunt Maudie's restaurant."

Baxter said with his mouth full, "They wuz sure happy to hear Sherm's Ma and Pa wuzn't mad, jest worried 'bout mebbe they wouldn't come home."

Jennie said, "Sherm said they planned all along on coming back home. Said he wouldn't run off knowin' how much his Pa needed him."

"Well then," Papaw said, "mebbe we ain't got as much to worry 'bout as I thought."

Baxter poured another mug of milk. "Jeb and Clara Owen ain't the problem as I see it."

Papaw and Jennie looked at each other and said in one breath, "Mama... Lula."

The next day Minnie and Sherm returned to Zionville. Clara caught them both in her arms, laughing and crying at once while Jeb stood by smiling. "I should spank the two of you worryin' us like you did." She drew away from them. "But Jeb and me are just happy you come back."

Minnie said. "Sherm and me never would've run off if we thought we could convince you to let us get married, but..."

Clara interrupted. "I think Jeb and me woulda understood, but your Mama..."

Minnie flinched. "Mama's mad, isn't she?"

Clara nodded. Minnie said to Sherm, "You wait here. Best I see Mama alone at first." Sherm nodded with relief.

Lula rocked furiously, arms folded across her chest, and refused to look at Minnie.

Min smiled uncertainly. "Mama, we're sorry if we hurt you, but we couldn't think of any other way. I tried so many times to talk to you, but you wouldn't listen."

Lula remained silent. Minnie pulled a chair over and sat down in front of her. "More than anything, I wanted you to be there, but you wouldn't a never give your permission and we jest couldn't stand to be apart. Mama, look at me.... please."

Lula grudgingly shifted her eyes to Minnie... no hint of forgiveness in them.

"Now I gotta go live over at the Owens. I know how you must feel... like I'm deserting you or something, but I'll only be down the road. I'll come over every day to see you... Mama, I can't leave with you mad at me."

Lula remained stubbornly silent.

Minnie sighed and got to her feet. "I'm gonna have to pack. Won't you at least say goodbye?"

Lula's face broke up. Tears welled up in her eyes.

Minnie kneeled beside her mother and put her arms around her. "Please don't cry. I love you Mama."

Lula stroked Min's hair. She said in a choked voice, "Never thought you would be first to go. You're jest a baby yet."

Minnie gently pulled away. "I never felt more growed up than I do right now."

Lula sighed. "Guess there ain't no sense to fightin' it. Won't change anything." She lifted a corner of her apron and dabbed at her eyes and with a tentative smile said, "Lordy, Min, I can't believe it. You're a married lady."

Chapter Twenty-four
Another Wedding

Jennie Dear,

I am writing you from the midst of a glorious forest in the State of Oregon. Camp Geronimo sits in a clearing surrounded by the most magnificent trees I have seen in my lifetime. They stand hundreds of feet tall. It seems a crime and a shame to cut them down.

Hard to believe that just four months ago I was finishing my stint as a soldier and now I'm to begin work in a logging camp in the United States of America and the best of it all is now I have an address you can write to. Life is good.

The trip to camp took five and a half hours and a rugged trip it was. We rode in a buckboard, pulled by a yoke of oxen, so loaded down with supplies there was barely room for me and Pete. Our driver was a short skinny bloke named Buck Harper and I wondered what he did at the camp. I asked if he was a logger...

"Me? A logger?" Buck started laughing which turned into a hacking cough. It was several seconds before he was able to talk. "I ain't got the build for lumberjacking... but cook? I kin outcook anyone. Me and two other guys cook for the camp and every third day I drive my rig into Eugene for supplies."

Pete asked, "What kinda cookin' ya do?"

"Lotta stew, sides of beef, lotsa potatoes." He started to chuckle. "Then, a' course, when the oxen get past their prime, they end up on the table."

James stole a look to see if he was serious. "You really eat the oxen? Isn't the meat pretty tough?"

"Loggers ain't fussy. Matter a fact, the other night we cut into a roast and danged if the knife didn't hit on something hard. Turned out to be a yoke buckle. Ole Burt Crowder picked up the buckle and gnawed it clean like it was a bone."

James shook his head. "Guess it can't be any worse than army food."

Buck looked miffed. "Ain't nobody starvin'."

Pete said, "And you make this trip every third day?"

"Yup. The other two cooks and me take turns. With more'n 150 men in camp we need a lot of supplies." He looked sideways at James who sat between him and Pete. "You fellas greenhorns?"

James answered. "We've never felled a tree, bucko, so I guess that makes us greenhorns."

Buck snorted. "An Irish greenhorn at that."

"But I'll be working in the office. It's Pete here that will be learnin' the trade of the lumberjack."

There were no roads, Jen, only pathways through the woods, and four or five times we got stuck on the muddy trail. Thank the good Lord for Pete. It was his brawn that saved the day, him and the oxen. Along about 3:00 in the afternoon we pulled into the camp. It looks like a wee town in the heart of the forest...

"Whoa...whooah." Buck brought the tired oxen to a halt in front of a rough two story building. "The camp office is in here. You report in and I'll catch up with you later."

"Righto," James said, "and thanks. The boys jumped stiffly from the buckboard, pulled their duffels from the rear and gave Buck a casual wave as he hauled his rig out of sight around the rear of the building.

They surveyed their surroundings. Besides the camp office, there were four low, one story, barrack-type buildings and two small log cabins. "This is home for the time being, laddie."

"Don't look like much."

"Aye, but better than a bloomin' tent and a lot better than a freezing boxcar."

They picked up their duffels, mounted the steps and entered the building. The room they stepped into was makeshift; exposed beams, unpainted walls and rough-hewn floor boards. The two desks and three filing cabinets along one wall were scarred and battered and the long bench that lined the opposite wall was no more than several boards nailed haphazardly together.

A young woman, standing by the window, looked up as James and Pete entered. James was sure she had been watching them. She was small and fragile-looking with long, straight, lustrous black hair pulled back from her face with a narrow red ribbon. Her eyes, which immediately settled on Pete, were pale green and her mouth, opened slightly, showed small even teeth. She was dressed primly in a full grey wool skirt and white high-necked, long- sleeved blouse that buttoned down the front. The sombre effect was lightened by the red satin bow nestled at her throat.

They all stood perfectly still for a heartbeat and then Pete walked forward, lifted the girl by her slim waist and swung her around. His words were joking, but his face was serious.

"Where have you been all my life?"

James thought to himself... *here we go again.*

Before the surprised girl could answer the door opened and a wiry little man, no more than 5'6", came in, stopped dead in his tracks and let out a bellow.

"What de ye think yer doin?"

Pete set the girl on her feet, turned and grinned. "Just my way of saying hello."

The little man was indignant. He marched up to Pete, who stood almost a foot taller than he, and jabbed him in the chest.

"I would say, laddie, it's more likely yer sayin' goodbye. I'll not stand for any man-handlin' of my daughter. You can pick up yer gear and head back to where you come from." He turned to James, "And you too."

Pete's face went blank. James held up both hands. "Sir, my friend here is a bit boisterous, I'll admit, but he meant no harm. We're fresh out of the army and our manners are somewhat rusty. We apologize." He looked at Pete. "Don't we, Pete?"

Pete came to life. "Uhh, yes, I apologize...sir. It's jest your daughter is so beautiful..."

James groaned. He knew immediately Pete had thrown more fuel on the fire. From the corner of his eye, he could see the girl, hand clasped over her mouth trying not to laugh. The angry little man pointed a finger at Pete and opened his mouth. Pete realizing his blunder, threw up his hands and said, "But you're right, sir, I apologize for acting like a barbarian. I was out of place and I hope you will forgive me."

The girl giggled. "Oh father, don't be such a boor. He didn't hurt me."

The man had a hard time swallowing his anger. He glared at Pete. "All right then, but in the future, you will stay out of this office and away from my daughter. Is that clear?"

Pete dropped his eyes and nodded without a word.

The little man continued to glare. "What are the two of you doing here anyway?"

James rummaged in his pocket and brought out their papers. "We were hired by Joe McNulty in Eugene and just arrived with Buck Harper."

The little man held out his hand and James almost shook it before he realized a handshake wasn't being offered, it was the papers he wanted. "Sit," the man said, and they hurriedly sat on the bench.

After a few minutes, the man looked up and without smiling said "I'm Doc MacIntosh," and then reluctantly turned to his daughter. "This is Laura. She helps me in the office and I don't brook any nonsense where she is concerned. I hope that is understood."

Pete and James nodded without saying a word. Laura stood behind her father and James saw that she was no longer laughing.

She was staring at Pete, and when James turned to Pete he saw the same look. He looked again at Laura and her eyes were downcast, but a smile lingered at the corners of her mouth and she was blushing. James looked quickly at Doc MacIntosh and was relieved to see Doc was busy examining their papers and had missed the exchange...

It was something to see, Jen, Doc who is 5'6", giving Pete who is 6'3", a tongue lashing and Pete not saying a word in return. But we understand Doc's concern, seeing as how the camp is naught but men with a handful of women.

The camp has a small store where items like razors and soap and such can be bought. We sleep in one of the barracks, each one of which holds about forty-five men. It's quite comfortable with a large stove in the center and the cots arranged along the walls. We gather to eat in the main building where the logging office is as well. All the buildings are pretty much makeshift, because the camps move to different locations as the trees are depleted. It doesn't look to be an easy life. Buck says the turnover is great. The men constantly taking knocks, some serious enough to send them back to the city for treatment. Man last week lost a leg. We decided Buck was letting us know that to be careless could lead to a disability or even death.

270

Pete is the one who will be taking the chances. As for me, I'll be working side by side with Doc in the office and that job may be the more difficult. Doc is the camp manager and takes over when there is an emergency. I'm not sure he's a true doctor and I'll not ask, as I don't think the man is partial to either me or Pete, but then again, I'm familiar with the dour disposition of the Scots.

We are an island in the wilderness and I'll be more than happy to leave when my purse is full. Then I will head east. Now you have my address I'll be waiting to hear from you. You must have a lot of news for me. Write as soon as you can. The day has been a long one. As I finish my letter night has fallen and I've had to light a lamp. It is the only one lit in the entire camp. Despite the chorus of snoring that assails my ears, it is peaceful. Though it is April, the cold is penetrating at night and the stars in their brilliance are a wonder to behold. How I would love to share all this with you.

Take heart. I feel closer to you each day.

With my love, I remain
James

With May the days warmed. White bell-shaped lily of the valley and shy bird's-foot violets covered the forest floors. Delicate white thimbleweed and nodding yellow trout lilies sprung up in the mossy woodlands. White and pink dogwood trees spotted the hillsides, and the white ungainly blossoms of the tulip trees stood out among the green foliage of the oaks and maples. Gardens sprouted and cows grew fat on the new grass.

Spring spread its balm, smoothing the rough edges left by the long sad winter. Though the deaths and sickness would never be forgotten, the pain slowly faded, taking its place in memory.

For the first time in her life, Jennie had a room of her own. Helen was back in Ed's room for the time being, ready to vacate if he came home. Min was gone, living with her husband at the Owens. Jen desperately missed Minnie, especially in the morning when she awoke expecting to see her sister beside her in the bed.

Jennie sprawled on her bed. The evenings were still too chilly to sit on the porch and school was over, so Clint didn't need her to help with his homework. She was tired and cranky from spending the day in the garden.

She stared at the ceiling. In four months she would be at nursing school, going to classes with other girls like herself, maybe even being a little ahead of the others because of her training with Doc. She was looking forward to it.

But what would happen when she met James? What if... suppose they... then what would happen to her plans for school? She got off the bed and began to pace. Would James be content to stay in one place? He talked of seeing the United States. But that's what he was doing now, wasn't it? Seeing the country? Maybe he would be content to settle in Charlotte near the school. But how can I ask him to do that?

The pacing found her in front of the mirror and she stared closely at herself. It won't happen. James will take one look at me and say, what was I thinking? This girl isn't for me. She's a country girl. She moved away from the mirror, went to the window and rested her hands on the sill.

The twilight was deepening into dusk and the first stirrings of summer could be heard in the soft tentative whirring of insects. Her thoughts turned to Papaw. All at once she longed to see him. *I'm going to Sugar Grove.*

✉

The church was filled to overflowing. Most of Zionville had followed the courtship of Emmaline Fenley and Jacob Wooding for the past three years and with a collective sigh, they were now gathered to witness the result.

Cora Fenley had gathered huge armfuls of early wildflowers, artfully arranged them in large wooden buckets and placed them around the freshly scrubbed church. The light spring breeze that wafted through the open doors mingled the fragrance of the flowers with the smell of soap and polish.

Cora sat stiffly in the first pew, her hands folded over the Bible in her lap. Her strawberry blond hair was tightly curled and an inverted flowerpot shaped hat perched becomingly on her head. Jennie recognized her yellow print dress with the high neckline as the one Mama had helped her sew. Mam Fenley sat vacant-eyed by her side, in a clean cotton print dress with a sash of a different print altogether and an uneven hemline.

In the pew across the aisle sat Elsie and Tom Wooding. Tom looked uncomfortable in a brown suit and striped tie, his neck bulging around the tight white shirt collar, his great hands locked in his lap. Elsie wore a pale green cotton dress with a tiny clutch of flowers decorating her hair. She smiled nervously, looking around at everyone.

Jennie, Baxter, Min and Sherm sat together. Jennie wore her blue and white print dress with the full white starched collar and Min wore her pale blue wedding dress. Baxter whispered in Jennie's ear, "You're prettier'n anybody here, includin' the bride." She smiled and squeezed his hand in response. Jennie turned to Min. "I wish we could have had a wedding like this for you and Sherm."

"It woulda been nice, Jen, but I'm jest as happy." She gave Sherm an adoring look and giggled. "I don't think Sherm woulda lived through what Jacob is going through now."

Sherm hadn't heard the entire exchange. "Lived through what?"

"Standin' up there in front of everybody and gettin' married."

Sherm nodded. "I woulda felt like a fool."

"S'pose I wanted to get married like Emmaline?"

He smiled at her. "I woulda jumped through a hoop if you wanted."

Clara Owen sat between Jeb and Helen in the pew in front of them. Clara, pretty as ever in her soft pink flowered dress, sat very close to Jeb. By straining her head just a bit, Jennie could see she was holding his hand.

Jeb had begun to use a walking stick. He claimed his old leg injury was acting up. Somehow, Clara told Lula, it shamed him that his strength was gone and the use of the cane was easier explained as a help to his old injury than to admit he hadn't been able to recoup after his bout with influenza. After all, Lula and Pearl had both made good recoveries.

Clara turned around to Jennie. "Where's your Mama?"

"Hubie was up all night with a toothache. Mama took him to Doc Payne to see if it had to come out."

Clara frowned. "Poor young'un. He ain't gonna like that."

Jennie spotted Aunt Pearl and her brood. Sitting beside Aunt Pearl was... Betsey? Can't be she thought. Where is the little mouse that stood in Ada's shadow? Betsey's face seemed fuller and her eyes were as bright and interested as ever, but the biggest change was her long, glossy hair pulled back with a pretty green bow.

Luther was there too, neatly dressed, his hair and beard trimmed and slicked down. Jennie leaned forward a little to see who was sitting next to him. Just as she thought, it was Lucy Glenwood, dressed becomingly in a long-waisted filmy dress with a pleated skirt. Ada would be pleased.

Prosper Truall walked up to the altar. Frenda Combs, at the piano, began to play "The Wedding March". Everyone stood, and all eyes went to the back of the church. Emmaline and Otis Fenley stood for a moment in the open doorway and then began their march down the aisle. Jennie felt a lump in her throat.

No one thought of Emmaline as a beauty but today, dressed in a simple white poplin dress trimmed at the neckline with lace and a short veil softening her sharp features, the bride was indisputably beautiful. She smiled demurely to the right and left, acknowledging the good wishes of the townspeople. When she and her father finally reached the altar, there was Jacob in his navy blue suit with a sparkling clean white shirt and starched collar, smiling broadly, holding out his hand to her.

Otis stepped back and joined Cora and his mother in the pew.

Emmaline and Jacob took their place, side by side, in front of Prosper Truall. There was a scuffling as everyone resumed their seats.

Jennie stifled the impulse to laugh, picturing Jacob doing an angry dance in front of Prosper, threatening to throw him off Emmaline's front porch. Now here he was officiating at their wedding.

Prosper began the service. "We are gathered here, in the presence of God, to join this man and this woman in holy matrimony..." Her thoughts wandered back to the visit with Papaw.

Jennie sat in the rocker on Papaw's porch, her feet tucked up under her. "Papaw, I think I may have a problem. But maybe not. Then again..."

Mylart had concentrated on the block of wood in his big hands, turning it from side to side and shaving off a bit here and a bit there with his pocket knife. It was shaping up nicely into a horse.

He stopped and looked at Jennie. "If somethin's botherin' you, young'un, just spit it out."

Jennie slumped. "Now I feel foolish. I came all this way for nothing really."

The old man went back to his whittling. "When a body's as riled up as you are about nuthin', then nuthin' is, generally speakin', somethin."

"Well, I kinda think it's maybe foolish for me to think this, but, well... suppose James comes, just suppose now Papaw, he might not... and he and I..."

Papaw didn't look up. "You mean suppose James asks you to marry him, which would interfere with your plans to go to school."

Jennie nodded, close to tears.

"Child, don't you think that's puttin' the cart afore the horse? Unless somethin' definite was said in your letters back and forth, ain't no reason to assume marriage is in the picture, is there?"

"Of course, you're right, Papaw, no reason to think that at all, but just suppose. What would I do?"

Papaw stopped whittling and rested his hands on his knees.

"Well, Jen, that would be some decision, seein' as how all you ever wanted was an education, but on the other hand, there ain't nuthin' in the world like a good marriage. Who's to say you can't have both?" Papaw's eyes held a twinkle.

"Papaw, don't make fun, I'm serious."

"I *am* serious, child. If we're talkin' about love here, then all sorts of accommodations can be made. Put it the other way around. Suppose James is bound and determined to work in say, Timbuktu? Ain't your idea of a place to live, but you'd go, 'cause love is a wonderful glue. It binds two people together under the worst of conditions."

"Yes, Papaw, I understand that, but... you're talking about a good marriage, one like you had with Mamaw."

"Well, Jen, I wouldn't expect you to settle for less."

"How would I know... how would I know if James..."

"Is the right one? Well, that's a tough one. A body can be fooled into thinkin' cause a box is wrapped pretty with a big bow, that what's in the box is gotta be a quality item. Your Mama and Papa are a case in point. Lula took one look at that handsome Papa of yours and made the biggest mistake of her life."

"That's exactly what I mean."

"Then just be smarter than your Mama."

She stopped rocking and planted her feet on the porch floor. "I think I know what a good marriage would be. I would certainly want to have my say about things and he would listen to me. Maybe we wouldn't agree, but he would at least listen and take into consideration what I say. And then... and then he would put his family first, always, making sure the children didn't want for anything. And he would be ambitious, working hard and looking ahead and planning...

"Whoa, Jennie, whoa. Seems to me like you ain't leaving any room for simple human weakness. Ain't a one of us in the whole dang world is perfect. Yer talkin' 'bout the ideal, chile, ain't that way in real life. Best thing you can hope fer, Jen, I think, is a kind man. One with ambition. One you can respect. And you wouldn't want a man you could lead around by the nose. If he's as strong-willed as you that ain't such a bad thing. You argue things out. Your Mamaw and me, we argued all the time."

Jennie fell back in the rocker. "You know what I'm doing, Papaw? I'm describing a man the very opposite of Papa."

"Only natural, chile. Guess your Papa done you a good turn after all. He set an example of all the things you want to steer away from when you get serious about marrying."

"You've been a good example. You and Mamaw."

"Your Mamaw and me argued all the time, and sometimes I won my point, and then again sometimes she won hers. And sometimes we argued for the pure joy of arguing and then making up." Papaw looked off into the distance and said out loud but to himself,

"That's always the best part, the making up." After a pause, he looked back at Jennie. "Now with your Mama, seems the only way she can keep your Papa comin' home is to agree with everything he says. It ain't right, but that's the only way she can show him she still loves him."

Jennie sighed. "That's not the kind of marriage I want."

Papaw shrugged. "Everyone needs somethin' different, Jen. You just gotta be smart enough to know what's right for you... You heard from James lately?"

"Oh yes, he's still at the logging camp clear across country."

Papaw put down the block of wood, closed up his knife and pocketed it. The pipe and tobacco came out. "Well now, I think a lot more of that young'un fer the very reason you seem miffed at him. That is to say he don't want to show up here 'thout some money in his pocket."

Jennie stopped rocking. "You think that's the reason he hasn't come east yet, Papaw?"

"What else could it be? Less, of course, he's heard what an almighty firecracker you are an is scairt outta his britches."

Jennie was sober all of a sudden. "Papaw, you think..."

Mylart looked up from packing his pipe and grinned.

"Oh Papaw, you tease..."

Jennie straightened up and returned her wandering thoughts to the wedding at hand.

"Do you, Emmaline Charlotte Fenley, take Jacob Thomas Wooding to be your lawful wedded husband?"

"I do."

"And do you, Jacob Thomas Wooding, take Emmaline Charlotte Fenley for your wedded wife?"

"I do."

"Then with the powers vested in me, I now pronounce you man and wife."

Hubie came home minus a tooth.

Dearest Jen,

I got your long letter yesterday and sat up most of the night reading and rereading it. For a wee town nestled safely in the mountains, Zionville has had its share of joy and sorrow.

Now that the weather has taken a turn towards spring, you can leave winter behind with all its sadness. I find it strange that your Papa can't see what a wonderful nurse you would make by the way you took care of your Mama... and Ada. You've a strong character, lass, just one more trait for me to love about you.

So it is settled that you will be going to nursing school in September...

James stopped writing and stared at what he had written. It would be quite a complication if when they met, they decided they should be together. What happens to nursing school then? But no. Why should Jennie give up what she has struggled so long for? If she wants to be a nurse, I'll help her any way I can. There are nursing schools all over the country...

*Your description of Minnie's wedding and all that led up
to it read like a story. It is hard for an Irishman to understand
a lad of such tender years taking on the responsibility of
marriage. The Irish are famed for holding off the wedding date
until they are sure of the proper moment. My own Da didn't
take the vows until he was close to forty, and claimed he was
too young at that. I'll not say seventeen is too young, nor will
I say forty is too old. The telling time for marriage is in the
heart to be answered as the call is heard. It is only a sorrow
when the call never comes.*

*Speaking of the call, Jen, for the first time since I met
Pete, I find him serious in the game of love. I call it a game,
for that is what it has always been to Pete, at least up until
now. He is altogether smitten with Laura MacIntosh and she
with him...*

"Pete, you're wasting your sweet talk on Laura. She's already convinced. It's Doc you should be working on."

"I know that, Jim, but you see how he treats me. He won't give me the time of day."

"It doesn't endear you to him when he suspects you and Laura are sneaking off together."

"So far it's just a suspicion."

"That's not going to last long."

Pete grinned. "Yeah, it was close the other night, wasn't it?"

"It was just dumb luck I caught Doc before he barreled into the office and found the two of you."

Pete's face sobered. "Honest, Irish, we wuz just talking, not doing a thing wrong. Doc has a fit if he even catches Laura talking to me."

"I think it is time you have a heart to heart talk with him, then, Pete. Tell him how much you love his daughter and how you will work hard to be a proper husband..."

"Hold it, Irish, hold it. Who said anything about marriage?"

James looked long and hard at Pete. "Then I think Doc has a perfect right to worry about you. If your intentions aren't honorable..."

Pete looked pained. "Marry. God, that's a big step."

"Pete, I remember one night you telling me you would never find anyone to be close to. You envied what Jennie and I have, be it only in letters. Do you remember?"

Pete nodded absently. "But marry, Jim..."

"If you can walk away from the girl and not think of her ever again, then you're right, laddie, marrying would be the wrong step. But if Laura means something to you, marriage is the only step."

Until such time as Peter can admit to being in love with Laura (something, incidentally, that is as plain to me as the nose on his face) I must play the part of watchman, diverting the suspicious Scotsman to another path when he wanders too close to their rendezvous. If ever there was a Romeo and Juliet it is these two. Only time will tell the outcome.

It was good to read your news of Ed, but I was sorry to hear he is off in the mines. Like you, my concern is that his health may suffer for it. I'm sure, having his own farm will win out in the end, but in the meantime, having the extra money from the mines is important. I am doing much the same thing myself.

Life in a logging camp is an education. The trees are a hundred feet around and more, immense. Imagine the time and muscle it takes to bring them down. Sometimes, after a tree is down, it has to be abandoned as it can't be brought out of the canyon... like a fallen deer shot by a hunter who discovers he can't pack out the meat.

We have a small mill in the woods for roughing out 'the big sticks' as the lumbermen call them. Then we send them down the flumes, which are like wooden canals through the steep woods, to the big finishing mill below by the river.

It's a hazardous life. Loggers are a breed alone. On a Saturday night after they pocket their pay, it is off to town for some drinking and brawling, and back of a Sunday morning with more cuts and bruises than they get on the job. I have earned the reputation of being a tightwad... no Saturday night brawling for me. Doc MacIntosh is much impressed with my frugality, him being the typical thrifty Scot. Pete is earning a little respect from Doc as well, since he is foregoing the carousing though I know it puts a strain on his fun loving nature. The lad is trying.

The camp lights are low, lass, but my spirits are high.

All my love to you.

James

Jennie sat with her back against a tree, Baxter stretched out with his head in her lap, his hand holding hers. They listened to the crowd shouting in the church field. Baxter said, "Wonder if Min and Sherm are going to enter the egg toss again."

"She better not miss. Now they're married, Sherm won't be as understanding as when they were courting."

"Probably not... Remember last year, Jen? Gayle missed the egg and it got all over her dress?"

Jennie smiled with satisfaction, remembering. "Yeah."

There was a long pause. Finally Baxter sat up and faced Jennie. "Speaking of Gayle, been meaning to tell you something."

Jennie waited but when Baxter didn't immediately begin, she said "What, Bax, you've got my curiosity up?"

"Ma got a letter from Aunt Serina."

Jennie sat a little straighter. "And?"

"Seems Gayle come home."

"Alone?"

Baxter nodded, surprised at the question. "Of course, alone."

Jennie spoke before she thought. "So, I guess it didn't work out."

Baxter looked at her quizzically. "What didn't work out?"

Jennie bit her tongue. "Oh, you know, being unhappy, running away. Did she say where she'd been?"

"No. Just that she ran outta money and didn't know where else to go, so she came home."

Jennie thought, so she came home alone, no Josh Cummings. Obviously Aunt Serina is still in the dark too.

"Aunt Serina kinda hinted to Ma that Gayle wants to come back here." Jennie was dumbfounded. Would the girl have the nerve?

Baxter continued. "Yeah, Ma asked me what I thought about Gayle coming back."

Jennie was almost afraid to ask. "And what did you say?"

Baxter gave Jennie a broad grin. "I told her Gayle could go jump off Blowin' Rock."

Dear Jennie,

I woke up yesterday with the feeling that it was time to move on. With that thought in mind I cornered Pete for a heart to heart talk. When I told him I was leaving he fair jumped for joy, as the lad's first instinct was to come with me. But after a moment his face fell and I could tell by the look in his eyes that it was not to be. Laura has a stronger hold on him than I and so it should be. I suggested she come with us, but Laura isn't the roaming sort, more a nesting lass, and so...

"Can't believe I'm lettin' ya go without me, Irish."

"It's not the end of our friendship, boyo." James gave Pete a soft punch in the shoulder. "We'll keep in touch and when I'm settled, you and Laura can come for a visit."

Pete nodded morosely. "Yeah, maybe. Looks like we'll be movin' on too. Laura don't want to stay in the camp, neither, so we'll more'n likely leave here soon too. All three of us."

James caught the pained look on Pete's face. "You mean you and Laura... and Doc?"

Pete said. "Laura says her father needs her to look after him. I says does a rattlesnake take lookin' after?"

James grinned. "What did she say to that?"

Pete squirmed. "Didn't like it much. I feel a little sorry for her. She's always havin' to come between Doc and me. That man's got a tongue that don't quit."

James turned and picked up his duffel. "Well, laddie, I'll keep in touch in case you want to join me."

Pete looked sorrowful. "Yeah, do that, Jim..."

Since I am an old hand at riding the rails, after I got to Eugene, I headed straight for the freight yards. I searched for my old friends, Gabe, One-Eye and Jersey Joe, but had no luck in finding them. I would have liked the company since I missed Pete. It's the first time in five years we haven't traveled the same road together. I could always count on Pete, just as he could count on me.

Anyway, there were plenty of freights heading east and I hopped one en route to Boise, Idaho where I waited two days for another freight eastbound. When I couldn't connect, my patience gave out and I caught a freight south to Salt Lake City, Utah and from there, east again to Denver, Colorado. Heading out of Colorado, we hit the wheat fields of Kansas. It was instant fascination, Jen. I couldn't believe what I was seeing... wheat stretching as far as the eye could see, swaying and waving in the wind like the waters of the sea. The freight slowed down for a crossing near a small town called Hays and on impulse I heaved myself from the car, rolled head over teakettle and come to my feet all of a piece. I had a kind of empty feeling watching the train disappear, wondering if it would be easy for me to catch another. I chided myself for acting on a whim, but since there was nothing I could do about it, I hiked into town.

Hays is unlike any town I've seen so far. Not like Victoria or Vancouver, and surely not like Eugene or the camp towns. It is dedicated solely and completely to the farming industry. Even the small restaurant I headed for, talk centered around the harvest, the price of wheat, the search for hands to help in the fields and the weather...

The farmer's overalls were soiled and his long sleeved shirt sweat stained. He pulled a red kerchief from his rear pocket, lifted his wide brimmed straw hat and wiped the sweat from his brow. The three farmers sitting at the counter, alongside James, greeted him.

The newcomer said, "God Almighty, hot enough out there to set fire to the soles of yer boots." He came to the counter and took the stool next to James. "Give me a cool one, Louise, I'm so parched I could spit dust." He looked side ways at James. "New in these parts or just passin' through?"

James couldn't determine if the tone was threatening or just curious. There was no smile on the farmer's face. James decided to play it safe. "Just passing through, I guess."

Louise set a tall, icy glass of lemonade on the counter in front of the farmer. "This do ya, Mr. Laws?"

"I thank ya, Louise, this'll do fine." He took a long drink from the glass, set it down, and turned his attention again to James. "Where ya from?"

James chewed, swallowed and said, "Well... guess you could say I'm from all over but I started out in Ireland if it's my accent you're referring to."

The farmer nodded, neither smiling nor frowning. He picked up the glass and took another long drink, finished it and motioned for Louise to fill his glass again. "Lookin' for work?"

James pushed his empty plate away and swung around on the stool to face the farmer, "Aye, but I'm on my way east, so it's not for long I'll be needin' employment."

"Your employment will last long enough to help with the wheat harvest. Then you can be on your way."

So I signed on with Farmer Laws. The pay is $3 a day and meals. Should be about a week to bring the harvest in, then I'll pick up my travels east again. From logger to farmer, lass, quite a leap and each a world apart.

Mr. Laws took me back to the farmhouse and I stayed the night, sleeping in the barn on my bedroll. Early next morning, after eating a breakfast big enough to choke a horse, we (there are eight of us) were driven by wagon out into the wheat fields. We went to work at once, following the horse drawn reaper, gathering the wheat into bundles and tying them off. The knack of it came back to me from days spent by Da's side at our own harvests in Ireland, but the Irish wheat harvests can naught compare with the scale of the harvesting in the fields of Kansas. The meals are good. The cook, Ruthie, is a young lass with a babe. The babe cries a good bit and spends much of his time perched on her hip. I wonder sometimes how she manages. Her husband, Robert, works along with us in the field.

The cookhouse is a grand invention. It is a wee house on wheels, horse drawn, and follows the workers from field to field. It is open on one side with a counter and benches to the outside, and that's where we are served our meals. On the other side of the counter is the cook stove and shelves to hold the provisions. A cow provides fresh milk and butter. The water, needed for drinking and watering the horses, is carried in barrels lashed to the back of the cookhouse. If we get a splash or two for washing we consider ourselves lucky.

I am writing this letter by the light of the cookhouse as Ruthie does the washing up. Mr. Laws promised to mail it when he goes into town tomorrow for supplies.

Ruthie came to the counter where James was writing. "Must be someone special, you writing a letter when you look like you're ready to fall asleep where you sit."

James looked up and smiled. Ruthie was young, fairly tall and very slim. The long hours she worked left her pallid and exhausted. The skin below her eyes was smudged and tired lines drew her mouth into a frown. Several strands of hair had escaped the carelessly tied bun at the nape of her neck and she absentmindedly tucked them behind her ear. She leaned tiredly against the side of the cookhouse.

"I'll be finishing up me letter in a minute and be out of your way."

"Don't hurry. I need a moment to relax before I pick up L'il Rob. He's finally asleep on his blanket over there. I think the poor mite is teething. Been meaning to ask you James, you seem to have a bit more education than most around here, what are you doing harvesting wheat? Robert and I have been wondering."

James looked up again from his letter. "To be honest, Ruthie, I didn't give a thought to the harvesting when I hopped off the freight. I was entranced by your beautiful wheat fields, so when the freight slowed down at the crossing, I just hopped off."

Ruthie said as a statement rather than a question, "Beautiful, you're calling the wheat fields beautiful."

"Aye. You see, I've just come from the forests of Oregon where the trees grow as tall as mountains. I didn't believe anything I ever saw again could be as inspiring, but when my journey took me past your wheat fields, I was struck by how they looked all the world like the sea, rippling and waving, stretching as far as the eye could see... just as beautiful, in their own way, as those magnificent trees. I guess it was a rash act, but I hopped off the freight, with a few bumps and bruises to show for it, and here I am."

Darkness was slowly settling over the fields. "Strange," Ruthie said, "to be able to come and go as you please... no responsibility, no one to answer to. Strange and a little sad too."

James felt defensive. "But there is someone. She is waiting for me back east."

"Ah... then you are writing to someone special. Better not waste *too* much time on these wheat fields. The girls worth having have a way of slipping away. I hope you can count on her waiting. Good night, James." He smiled weakly and went back to his letter.

I'll soon be turning in. After the sun goes down, the night winds come up. 'Tis a mixed blessing. The winds bring cool relief from the blistering heat of the day but also biting dust and bits of the chaff from the harvested fields. Our only refuge is our bedrolls with the covers clear over our heads.

It is an ever wonder to me, lass, that the same moon and stars that shine down on the giant redwoods of Oregon gleam just as brightly over this vast sea of wheat. I am ever impressed.

You are in my thoughts. Soon, Jennie, soon.

My love,
James

As he sealed the envelope, he thought of what Ruthie had said. Hope you can count on her waiting. The wind blew across the fields and chilled him. It was true. How can I expect Jennie to wait forever? Suddenly he was anxious to be free of the wheat fields and on his way.

Chapter Twenty-Five
James Meets Papaw

The August sun washed over the town of Boone. Rainwater from the previous night's thunderstorm had King Street running in a sea of mud, and pedestrians crossed with mud sucking at their boots, prepared to dodge the wagons that had to keep rolling or become mired down in the middle of the street.

The train depot platform on the outskirts of town was peopled with travelers waiting for the 9:00 am from Johnson City. Three workmen, dressed in bib overalls, long-sleeved shirts rolled up to their elbows, and misshapen felt hats pushed far back on their heads leaned against a low-slung wagon piled high with freight to be loaded on the train's boxcars. They were relaxed, smoking.

A lonely whistle echoing off the surrounding mountains brought workmen and travelers to attention and as the train chugged and puffed into the depot, they ground out their cigarettes and shielded their eyes from soot and dirt. The engine, which hauled three passenger cars and two boxcars in its wake, came to a halt, expelling great clouds of steam, and sat hissing and rumbling softly like a giant black cat.

The conductor leaped off shouting, "Boone!" followed by his passengers. The first off was a young man balancing a duffel bag on his shoulder. The conductor turned and clasped his hand. "I wish ya luck, young'un. Hope to see you agin one day."

James nodded. "Aye, ya never can tell."

James walked a few feet from the train, dropped his bag, stretched and looked around eagerly at his surroundings. His eyes darted everywhere, taking in the depot, the people and finally settled on the surrounding mountains. He said aloud, "Jennie, lass, in all your letters ya never once told me how beautiful your mountains are."

A young woman hurrying to the train stopped, thinking James' remarks were directed at her. "I beg your pardon?"

James smiled. "I was just remarkin' at the beauty of the mountains."

She nodded and returned the smile. "Oh, yes, the mountains," and continued on her way.

James spied the workmen, busily unloading supplies from the freight car. Hefting his duffel again to his shoulder, he walked over to them.

"Top o' the mornin to ye, lads. I just arrived in your fair town and I've a thirst and hunger gnawin' at me innards. I was wonderin' if ye could tell me where I might find something to eat?"

The muscled man in the boxcar was sweating with exertion, hefting boxes and bags to the front of the car where the other two lifted them off and stacked them on the ground. They continued to work but looked curiously at the stranger.

The man in the car said, "Well now, what be that accent o' yourn? Don't sound like nuthin' from 'round here."

"Me name is James B. Culhane and I'm from County Sligo, Ireland." He let the bag slide from his shoulder, took off his cap and bent over in a mock bow.

The man laughed aloud. "Dang, don't that beat all. Isaac's my name. 'Pears you be a long ways from home."

He disappeared into the dark of the boxcar and emerged again, pushing the last of the cartons to the doorway. "Like to set and visit with you, Irishman, but we got some freight to load aboard 'fore this train takes off on us."

The two on the ground were already transferring the freight from the wagon to the lip of the boxcar, where Isaac pulled it into the car and stacked it. James stepped forward to help. When everything was loaded, Isaac jumped from the car and waved to the conductor, who turned and signaled the engineer. They hurriedly pulled the sliding door shut as the train, straining and spewing steam, gained momentum and slowly chugged out of the station.

Isaac put out his hand and James grasped it. "We thank ya kindly fer the help young'un." He turned to the two men. "This here's Willem and this be Lawton." Each man acknowledged James with a nod.

"So yer lookin' fer a place to eat," Isaac said. "They's a small place middle o'town called 'Maudies'. Aunt Maudie Grimm makes 'bout the best biscuits and grits you ever did set yer tongue to, and if ya need a place to sleep, she has rooms over top of her restaurant."

James gave a small salute and shouldered his bag again.

"What brings ya to Boone?" Isaac asked.

James turned back, warmed by the man's friendly tone. "I'm of a mind to look up me mate from the army. Name is Edward Wainwright. Lives in Zionville. Maybe you know the lad?"

The man took off his hat and scratched his head. "No, don't know as I do." He turned to the other two. "Ever hear of a Wainwright these parts?" They shook their heads and Isaac turned back to James. "I'm bettin' Prosper Truall will know him. Prosper carries the mail to Zionville and he's minister of the Methodist church there too. Anyone knows, should be Prosper."

James thought to himself. *Ah yes, Prosper Truall.*

Isaac pushed back his hat and surveyed the empty platform. "Don't see him 'round yct, but he's got to pick up this mail right soon. Tell you what—You go get yerself some vittles and when I see Prosper I'll tell him to wait on you. Don't be long, though. Mail's gotta go through."

James nodded. "You think Mr. Truall can give me a lift to Zionville?"

"Don't see why not."

"I'm much obliged. Now if you'll head me in the right direction to town I'll be payin' me respects to Aunt Maudie."

The town was already bustling. Shops were open and people crowded the sidewalks. James didn't look out of place in his short jacket, levis and boots, but he was a stranger and people turned curiously to smile at him. "Top o' the mornin' to ye." He smiled broadly and tipped his cap in response. A group of young girls stopped in their tracks, their gazes lingering on the tall tanned stranger whose mass of unruly auburn hair glinted like copper in the morning sunlight.

James again surveyed the mountains and felt the fresh morning breeze, clean after the rain, sweeping down from their great heights. He felt a sudden rush of excitement. *So this is where fair Jennie lives.* His heart beat a little faster and his step quickened.

✉

Prosper Truall was transferring the last bag of mail from the low wagon to his buckboard as James approached.

"Might you be Prosper Truall?" James inquired, stretching out his hand. "Name's James Culhane." The horse stamped and snorted and threw her head back.

Prosper caught the horse's bridle and steadied her. "Whoa, Fanny girl." He took James' outstretched hand and shook it. "That's my name." With a puzzled look, he went on, "You the one lookin' fer Ed Wainwright?"

James nodded. "Had the good fortune to meet up with the lad in the army and he said if ever I came to his part of the country I was to be sure and look him up." The Irish lilt in his voice was unmistakable.

288

Prosper's face lit up. "You're the Irishman. Isaac didn't say no more'n that a young feller was lookin fer Ed Wainwright and mebbe I could tell you where to find him."

Prosper grabbed James' hand again and shook it vigorously. "I remember Ed's Ma sayin' you and he met in the hospital. Well now, this is somethin'." Prosper finally released his hand.

"I didn't know exactly when I'd be getting in, so Edward isn't expectin' me. Hope that won't be a problem. Is there a chance, Mr. Truall, you might give me a lift to Zionville?"

"Call me Prosper and y'all are welcome to ride along. First have to deliver mail to Sugar Grove and... say, Ed's grandfather, Mylart Miller, runs the grist mill in Sugar Grove. Long as we have to stop there anyway, mebbe you would like to meet him?"

James drew in his breath and let it out slowly. "Yes, I'd like to meet him." He pictured the tall man with white hair that Jennie had written so much about. Papaw, she called him. He felt they had already met. "Ed talked a lot about his Grandfather."

"Well then, James, hoist yourself right up there in my rig. Throw your bag on top of the mail back there. I'll just check out before we take off." Prosper turned and headed for the depot office.

James tossed his bag in the wagon and pulled himself up in the passenger seat. Well, Jennie lass, he thought, looks like I'll be meetin' Papaw before I'm meeting you.

✉

Fanny clopped down the muddy road, sure-footed, with the buckboard bumping along behind. Prosper slapped the reins gently on her rump, but Fanny did no more than flick her tail and continue along at the same pace.

Prosper said, "Say, ya know, I just happen to think. Ed's been off in Virginia working the mines with his Pa. You probably won't find him at home."

"Yes, I know he works at the mines, but I thought there might be a chance I'd catch him at home." James thought. *It might be awkward without Ed there...*

Prosper was saying, "Never been much in the way of work these parts, you know..."

How will their Mama feel about my showing up on their doorstep?

"...it being mostly farm country."

289

The sun rose higher in the sky as they continued on to Sugar Grove. Sweet-smelling honeysuckle vines grew to the top of fences. Delicate Queen Anne's Lace and pokeweed, with its dark clustered berries, dotted the fields and wild elderberry shrubs, heavy with ripened fruit, showed through tangles of grass and weeds. Cows meandered about, feeding on the sweet pasture grass, swatting at the flies and gnats with heavy tasseled tails.

"Guess we should be grateful for what we got, though," Prosper continued. "Had us a lot of rain this summer so far, you can see by the gardens. Be plenty for cannin'. Look yonder at that corn. It's a pretty sight, isn't it?"

James nodded. "Not too different from Ireland."

"Grow corn in Ireland, do you?"

"Our main crop is potatoes, but we plant corn too." James paused for a moment caught again by the beauty of the mountains. "Da's farm lies in a valley such as this, surrounded by hills that stretch as far as the eye can see."

Prosper snorted, "This is a pretty valley, but you can't see much beyond the mountains."

James agreed again. "And grand they are."

Fanny's hooves beat a steady monotonous rhythm on the road bed. The sun was directly overhead. The buckboard rounded a curve in the road and suddenly they were riding down the middle of Sugar Grove.

"The Miller home place is just down the road a piece on the left there. You can see it... that stone house."

James had the eerie feeling of having been here before. Jennie's description of the old stone house with the mill behind it was perfect. They bounced over the log bridge spanning the creek, continued up the hill and pulled up to the gate.

"Mylart's probably at the mill 'round back. Come along, I'll introduce you."

They jumped down from the wagon, tethered Fanny to the fence and proceeded up the walk. They rounded the house and headed toward the mill. James wondered how much Papaw knew about him from Jennie.

As they neared the mill he said, "if I didn't know na better, Prosper, I'd say we were coming up to Tad O'Hearn's mill in Tubercurry. Looks much the same."

They paused for a moment, admiring the mill.

"That a fact?" Prosper said.

Papaw, in shirt sleeves and old stained overalls, came out of the mill and watched the two men approach.

"Hey Mylart," Prosper called, "Brought someone for you to meet."

"I see ya did." Papaw scrutinized James as they drew nearer.

Prosper turned to James. "Like for you to meet Mylart Miller."

James extended his hand. "Tis a pleasure, sir."

Prosper turned to Papaw, "and this..."

"Is the Irishman," Papaw finished, shaking the younger man's hand firmly. "James, isn't it?"

James smiled and nodded. "Yes sir."

"Well now, dang it, Mylart," Prosper said, "thought we could surprise you. Anyway, James here come to visit with Ed and I was tellin' him Ed is off to the mines with his Pa."

"Yep, since 'long about April, but it won't do no harm fer you to go on to Zionville. We'll get word to Ed yer here."

"I guess you two got things to talk about." said Prosper, "I'd best get over to the store. They'll be waitin on the mail."

Papaw put out a restraining arm. "I was jest fixin' to eat some dinner, Prosper. Mebbe you and James would like to set down with me?"

Prosper said, "I kindly thank ya for the invite, Mylart, but I best get the mail delivered. I'll get something to eat at Grundy's store." He turned, calling over his shoulder, "I'll be back after dinner to fetch you, James, and carry you on to Zionville." He disappeared around the house.

James felt awkward. "I'm afraid you have a dinner guest whether you want one or not, sir."

"Don't make no nevermind to me, young'un. Got plenty and 'sides, I like the company. Come along." They stopped at the spring house, and as Papaw rooted around gathering what he needed to make a meal, he kept up a steady flow of conversation.

"What are your plans, young'un, aside from visiting Ed and Jennie?"

James swallowed a few times. He hadn't missed Papaw's inclusion of Jennie's name and until he talked with Jennie, he had no idea what his plans were. He couldn't exactly tell the old man that, could he?

Aloud he said, "This is a big country, Mr. Miller. In the past six months I've seen quite a bit of it and my plan is to see it all."

They reached the house, each with their arms loaded, and Papaw held the screen door open with his foot for James to enter.

After they set the supplies on the table, the old man went to the sink and began working the pump handle until the water splashed out. He caught some water in his cupped hands and splashed it over his face and neck. "That feels mighty good. Come along here, son, and get some of that road dirt off ya."

James gratefully stepped up to the sink and followed Papaw's actions, using the towel the old man tossed to him.

"Have yourself a seat while I rustle us up somethin to eat." He motioned James to a chair by the table and handed him six ears of corn. "Husk them fer me, son."

Papaw turned to the stove, stoked the fire and then began to open cupboards and rattle pans. Into a skillet he put a large dollop of bacon fat and placed it on the stove to heat. "So what do you think of this country?"

"It's amazing, sir, just amazing." James picked up an ear and began to husk it. "I spent a good deal of the past few months at the Geronimo logging camp in Oregon. I worked on the camp ledgers. That's a beautiful area."

"Loggin' camp, eh. Tell me somethin' 'bout loggin' in the west. It's pretty much finished in these parts."

"Well, to begin with, the trees, Douglas Firs, are immense. Some grow a hundred feet around."

Papaw came to the table with a knife and four large potatoes, sat down opposite James and began to peel them. "We have us some good size trees in these parts, but none big as that. How do they bring 'em down?"

"It must be much like felling a tree anywhere, sir, except the trees are so immense you have to first build a platform above the boles of the tree for two men to stand on while they cut in the notch." James forgot the corn he was shucking and used his hands in his explanation.

"Well sir, they begin sawing on the opposite side of the notch and believe me, when they hear the first crack that the tree is going, they leap off that platform like a shot outta hell and if they're not quick enough, the trunk catches them as it snaps off. They call that operation the widow maker. Smaller trees are brought down crossway on the path so's to skid the giant along."

Papaw nodded, understanding. James continued.

"It takes five to ten yoke of oxen, hitched in tandem to get the tree moving along the skid to the mill. I tell ya, sir, it is a sight to see... and smell. The skid greasers run along in front and daub dogfish oil on the skid to reduce the friction. I'll not soon forget that smell. Tis foul and clings to your clothes."

Papaw said, "I'm familiar with the smell."

James was afraid he was talking too much, but Papaw encouraged him to continue. Warmed by the older man's interest, James leaned forward on his elbows. "I'm sure the mills are the same as here, sir. After they are dressed in the mill, the logs are loaded on the flumes... you know, the huge wooden troughs that are banked at the curves so the logs won't jump off?"

Papaw nodded and continued to whittle away at the potatoes while James husked the last of the corn.

"Some of the lads thought it a good way to get into town on a Saturday night. After being paid, they'd climb on the flume and ride it down to the river. T'was a dangerous feat and many a splinter had to be extracted come Monday morning."

Papaw grimaced at the thought. "You ever ride the flume?"

"Well I'll tell you, sir. I did it but once, just to see what it was like. It was a fast ride to the bottom, but I didna enjoy the trek back up the mountain."

Papaw reached over and clapped James on the shoulder. "I can see it didn't do no damage." He went to the stove and began to slice potatoes and onions into the hot bacon fat. The aroma made James' mouth water.

James went on talking. "After I left the forests on my way east I passed through Idaho, and then south into Utah and then east again into Colorado. Stayed a few days in Denver to catch my breath. On my way through Kansas I was fascinated by the wheat fields and when the freight slowed for a crossing near a small town called Hays, I jumped off and ended up helping with the harvest."

Papaw rattled more pans on the stove. "Them wheat fields, anything like what you see round here?"

"Yes, except that they stretch as far as the eye can see, there being no mountains to interfere. In a wind the wheat bends and sways and looks like the waves of the ocean. A grand sight."

Papaw nodded. "Must be. I been readin' in the papers at the store 'bout these big combines takin' down the wheat. Any truth to it?"

"I didn't see any. The farmers do the harvesting by hand, but there was talk of forming a cooperative, each farmer paying a fair share, and buying one combine that would service all their farms."

Papaw said, "Mighty good idea."

"Trains only run once a week out of Hays, so I waited two days and paid a proper fare into Kansas City. Felt strange I tell you after riding the rails. Anyway, at Kansas City I signed on a barge going down the River to St. Louis.

"By that time, I'd had my fill of freight trains and barges and I was pretty anxious to get here, so I cleaned my self up and paid my fare into Nashville. From Nashville I caught a train to Johnson City and from Johnson City to Boone."

Papaw, fork in hand, had turned from the stove, listening intently. "That's quite some travelin'. Can't say I envy you, young feller, it sounds too exhaustin' fer me, but it 'pears you're quite an authority on this country. You seen more of it than I have. Now I have a question for you. I'm puzzled why so many o' the young folk are leaving Ireland to come to America. They's comin over here by the boatload."

"Well, sir, I don't think most people living here are aware a lad can be anything he wants to be. There is so much opportunity and enough work for anyone who is willing to put his mind to it...or his back. In Ireland unless you inherit from your Da there is nothing for you... nowhere to go. If you are born poor, poor you remain until you die."

Papaw turned back to the stove to stir the potatoes. "So you think there are opportunities in America? I think if you talk to some of the folk in these parts you'll find yerself an argument. Ed, fer instance. Couldn't get a lick a work here once he was outta the army. He had to go work in the blamed mines with his Pa. Work ain't easy to find these parts."

"So Prosper said, but you're talking about the small towns, sir. In the cities there is ample work for those willin' to look for it. In Ireland although my Da has a good working farm there is naught for me unless I want to be a farmer, which I don't. I wouldn't stand a chance of becoming anything else. Bankers spawn bankers, doctors spawn doctors, and so on."

"I thought Jennie said you have some university schoolin'," Mylart Miller said.

"True, I had two years at university. I guess I could have found something to my liking, but to be honest, I had me sights set on coming to America. Nothing else would do."

"So, you're sayin you plan to stay and find work in the States?"

"That's me plan so far."

"But not in these parts, I spect, since you don't like farmin'." Papaw turned again from the stove to look at James.

James squirmed under his gaze. He would liked to have said that so much depended on Jennie, but he wasn't going to bring her name up if Papaw didn't. He hesitated.

"No, I've had me fill of farmin' on me Da's farm. Me brother Danny, now he loves the life and is happy to spend the rest of his born days tending the fields, but as for me I want to try me hand here in the big cities."

Papaw looked about to say something, changed his mind and turned back to the stove. He said no more and concentrated on the cooking. James tried to think of something clever to say, could think of nothing and decided to remain silent.

Finally Papaw turned from the stove with two plates, "Now young'un, let's see what you can do with that."

James stared at his plate. There was a thick steak sending up a mouth-watering aroma, home fries, corn on the cob and tomatoes.

"Well, sir, one thing can be said for a farm. The food is better than anywhere else on earth."

For the next few minutes all that could be heard was the clink of forks and knives. James looked up several times at the man opposite him but Mylart's full attention was on his plate and James was just as glad for it.

In time Papaw pushed his plate away and rose from the table. He brought two cups and a steaming pot of coffee back from the stove, pouring for both of them.

James drew his hand across his mouth. "That was food for a king, Mr. Miller, and I thank ye for it."

Papaw blew on his coffee and took a sip. "Don't mean to ask yer business, young'un, but just what kind o' opportunity you lookin' fer?"

James poured cream in his coffee and stirred it, adding two teaspoons of sugar. "Well sir, I haven't exactly made up my mind, but gasoline cars are the coming thing and with cars, they'll need mechanics and, of course, roadways. I've read in the papers already, that the government is planning a cross section of roads to crisscross the country." He sipped his coffee. "And then ...airplanes. Both England and America made great strides in air power due to the war and I'm sure it will carry over into civilian use. The opportunities are endless."

Papaw stared at him for a long minute. "Hmm... gasoline cars and airplanes... well," he took another sip of coffee, "I'm sure you'll find something."

James felt himself flush. *He must think I'm a bloody fool. I sound like a schoolboy.*

"How long you plannin' on stayin' in these parts?"

James stared into his coffee cup, avoiding the piercing blue eyes. He knew exactly what Papaw was fishing for, and damned if he knew what to answer.

He sipped his coffee. "I, um, really can't say. I'll wait to see Ed, of course. After that..."

There was a knock at the door and Prosper poked his head in.

"Y'all finished with yer dinner? If so, we best be on our way, James. Got to get on to Zionville with the mail."

James heaved an inward sigh of relief and took a last gulp of coffee to cover the smile that threatened. Over the rim of the cup he could see that Papaw was smiling too. He thought to himself, I bloody well like this old man.

Papaw squinted from the porch as the buggy pulled away from the gate. James waved and Papaw returned the farewell. He was still standing on the porch as they rounded the turn towards Zionville.

✉

Prosper flicked Fanny's rump lightly with the reins. They rode on without conversation for a while and James felt drowsy from the heat of the sun and Papaw's meal. Fanny's hooves drummed on the roadbed and Cove Creek gurgled along beside them.

James was thankful for the silence. Jennie's description of her grandfather was accurate enough, his looks and physical strength, but he wasn't prepared for the old man's depth of interest and sharp understanding. He couldn't tell if Papaw liked him or not. Sure hoped so. He could almost hear Papaw say—you hurt Jennie and you'll have me to answer to. James thought, I don't plan on hurting Jennie but if I did, I don't think I could run fast enough.

Prosper broke the silence. "I was wonderin', James, it's gonna be late in the day before we get to Zionville. Where you plannin' to stay?"

"Well, there was no way for me to plan ahead, guess I just thought I'd solve the problem when I arrived." He turned to look at Prosper. "Have you an idea?"

"Well, now, I was thinking you might wanna talk with Ben and Frenda Combs. They got room ever since their young'uns moved on, except' Baxter. Matter o' fact I been boardin' and takin' my meals with them myself. About three years now. Right nice folks."

James knew the name Baxter. He was the one Jen talked about wanting to be a doctor. "Sounds good."

"All right, then, I'll introduce you to them."

"Whoa, there Fanny," The horse had picked up speed. Prosper chuckled. "Fanny starts kickin' up her heels when we get close to home. That's the Methodist church I preach at coming up on your right and across from it is the Combs farm.

James barely listened. *Must be close to Jennie...*

Down the road aways is Doc Payne's place. We had us a pretty bad time with sickness this past winter. Was sick myself. Influenza. Had a lot of deaths right here in Zionville. Doc Payne and Baxter... Baxter is Doc's apprentice and Ben and Frenda's youngest, well Doc and Baxter had them a busy time."

Prosper pulled on Fanny's reins and she turned onto the Comb's road. Prosper continued, "Ben, he don't like it much that Baxter's more interested in doctoring than in farming. He's getting on in years and there's no one left to take over the farm. There's Ben on the porch."

Fanny slowed and pulled into the yard without direction from Prosper, "Come on, James, I'll introduce ya to Ben and then I gotta run this mail to the store." He jumped from the wagon and headed for the porch with James following.

Ben slowly heaved himself out of his rocker as the two men climbed the porch steps. James' first impression was that the man was old and frail. There was a stoop to his shoulders and his body seemed lost in overalls several sizes too large.

"Hey, Ben. Here's someone I want you to meet." Prosper turned to James. "James Culhane, meet Ben Combs."

Ben held out a gnarled hand and James was surprised at the strength of his grip.

"Tis a pleasure, sir," James said.

"Likewise, young'un." Ben backed up and groped for the arm of the rocker, lowering himself painfully into it.

Prosper noticed. "Your back out again, Ben?"

Ben made a disgruntled noise and gave an annoyed wave of the hand. "Yep, throwed it out yestidy."

"Whyn't you get your son the doctor to give you some medicine?" Prosper smiled at his joke.

Ben snorted. "My son the doctor... he's over to Doc Payne's as usual, steada out helpin' his Ma in the garden."

Prosper motioned towards James. "Reason we're here, Ben, James come in from the city to visit with the Wainwrights. Thought maybe you could rent him a room while he's here."

Ben turned to James, this time giving him a more thorough examination. James unconsciously straightened under the scrutiny. Finally Ben spoke.

"You the Irishman?"

James stifled a sigh. "Yes sir."

Ben said, "Guess we got room fer ya. Frenda takes care of all that. She'll be up from the garden soon." He gestured to the other chairs on the porch. "Meantime, come set a spell."

"Can't," Prosper said. "Got to get the mail to the store." He headed back down the porch steps. "I'll jest go along... see ya sometime this evening Ben... you too, James."

"Aye, Prosper, and thanks for all your trouble."

"No trouble." He gave a final wave, climbed into his buckboard and was soon back on the road.

Chapter Twenty-Six
At Last

James stood at the foot of the Combs porch. "I'll just be goin' then to the Wainwrights, Mrs. Combs, before night sets in. I appreciate you allowin' me to leave my duffel here. It's a nuisance having to carry it around."

Frenda said, "The door will be open. You kin come right on in. I showed you your room already. Bed's made up ready fer sleepin.'"

Ben said, "Come back and eat with us, young'un."

James started to back away. "No thank you, sir. Mr. Miller was kind enough to feed me a proper dinner. Me innards are still fair to bursting." He turned around and almost collided with Baxter, standing in the path.

Frenda said from the porch, "James, this is my son Baxter."

James smiled and put out his hand. "Och, yes, Baxter. Jennie mentioned you often in her letters. James Culhane here. Pleased to meet you."

Baxter stared, taking the outstretched hand reluctantly. "Oh... yes. Heard about you, too." Baxter shook his head as if to clear it. "You're the Irishman."

James grinned. "Aye. Seems everyone in Zionville knows about the Irishman."

Baxter didn't return the grin, and James felt a little uncomfortable. The boy actually seemed unfriendly. Suddenly Baxter took him roughly by the arm, turned him around, and steered him back up the stairs to the porch. James was too surprised to resist.

Baxter all but pushed him into a rocker, "Come on and set. It's right nice o' you to take some time to visit." He turned to Frenda and asked with a decided edge to his voice, "We got somethin' cool to drink fer James here?"

Frenda looked from Baxter to James and back again. "I'll bring some cider out fer you'uns." She turned to Ben. "Come get yer supper, Pa. We'll leave the young'uns to visit." She held out her hand to help him from the rocker.

Ben looked puzzled. "Ain't it some early fer supper?"

Frenda was determined. "I said, it's time fer supper."

"Well, I guess if you say so..."

James held up his hand. "Really, Mrs. Combs, I thank you kindly, but..."

Baxter interrupted. "It's no trouble."

Frenda kept her hand on Ben's arm, and when they got to the door, he called over his shoulder, "See y'all later, then." He seemed bewildered at the speed with which he was being steered into the house. The screen door banged shut behind them.

James was anxious to get away, but he couldn't be rude. Baxter sat on the porch railing in front of him, his arms crossed over his chest. "So, you come to visit the Wainwrights. Ed is off workin' the mines with his Pa, ya know."

James nodded. "Yes... so Jennie said in her letter."

Baxter continued to stare, solemn and tense. James felt the animosity directed at him and he decided to wait and see what it was all about. Couldn't do much else, with Baxter standing over him like a jailer.

Baxter said, "But you're goin' on down to the Wainwrights anyway even though Ed ain't home?"

"Actually, Baxter, I want to visit with Jennie as well." James felt his anger starting to build, and he struggled not to let it show. "Prosper introduced me to Ed's grandfather on our way through Sugar Grove and Mr. Miller said he would get word to Edward at the mines that I'm here. Hopefully, Ed will be able to get home for a visit." He added innocently. "I'm in no hurry to leave."

Baxter nodded his head and was about to say something when his mother came out carrying a tray with a pitcher of cider and two glasses. She stole a glance at Baxter and he stared back with angry eyes. James thought, *Seems he's angry with his mother... maybe that's what it is. There is something between the two of them and it is just spilling over on me.*

"I'll jest put your cider here on the table. Y'all help yerselves." She glanced again at Baxter and hurried into the house.

James was resigned as he took the glass Baxter handed him.

"So," Baxter continued, "You met Ed's Papaw."

"Aye, and a fine gentleman he is too."

The two young men stared at each other as they sipped their cider. One easily the man of the world, travelled and sure of himself but awkward in his present surroundings, the other not as polished but at ease as he sat on his own porch railing, one foot dangling.

Baxter stared into his glass and twirled the liquid around.

He suddenly said, "Say, James, I feel like I'd like to stretch my legs some." He pushed himself away from the railing and set his glass on the tray. "Whyn't I jest go 'long with you to the Wainwrights. I ain't seen Jen or her Ma in a day or two. Wouldn't mind seein' how they's doin'."

It took a moment for James to realize Baxter was ready to go. He fumbled, setting his glass on the tray, almost spilling the contents, and struggled out of the rocker. "Oh... well, yes... let's go then."

Baxter led the way off the porch, through the gate and started off at a fast pace down the road. James ran a step or two to catch up. He was disappointed. It wasn't exactly the meeting he had planned with Jennie, but he was certain there was no way he could have kept Baxter from coming along.

If James was surprised by Baxter's actions, it didn't take him long to figure out the problem. In all Jennie's talk about Zionville and the people that lived here, she never once mentioned that Baxter was in love with her.

He stole a look at the boy out of the corner of his eye. Baxter was kicking angrily at the stones as he strode along, his mouth a forbidding line. James almost felt sorry for him... almost. This should prove quite a meeting. Baxter broke the uneasy silence. "So, how long you plannin' to stay in Zionville?"

"Depends."

Baxter didn't break stride, but cast him a black look. "Depends on what?"

James met his look. "On a lot of things, Baxter. On a lot of things." He wasn't giving an inch. Let him sweat a little. On the other hand, he thought, maybe I should be doing the sweating.

In a few minutes the Wainwright house came into view.

Jennie sat in the porch swing, the lazy action deterring her from going to the creek for a bath. She was relaxed, finally, after a full day of canning and the late afternoon breeze felt good after the kitchen's stifling heat.

This year there was no help from Min with the canning. She was busy in Clara's kitchen with the beans and tomatoes from the Owen garden, which was only right, but Jennie missed her. They use to make fun out of the tedious chore of canning. Mama and Helen were over to the Owens now and Jennie guessed the reason was, Mama was anxious to know if Minnie had proven a help to Clara. Mama should know better.

Min was married five months already. Jennie recalled the panic they'd all felt thinking the girl was too young for marriage, but Min had settled right into it.

Her thoughts drifted to James, as they so often did. The wheat harvest. Papaw would be interested in it, and would like that James wasn't afraid of hard work. That was something Papaw most admired, a hardworking man. James said he would be on his way east soon. What did he mean by soon? She wondered.

She dropped her gaze to the short note from Ed open in her lap. He and Papa expected to be home in a day or two, maybe in time for the church homecoming. It would be the first visit since Ed went back with Papa to the mines.

Poor Ed. All those long withering months in the army, then his injury and the stay in the hospital. It seemed a punishment to come home and have to spend his days under the earth. She shuddered.

Her gaze wandered over the pasture, her eyes caught by a hawk gliding low, hunting. The sun was sinking. Time for a bath. She made a move to get up, wondering if Hube and Clint were finished playing in the creek.

Two people came down the road and she strained to see who they were. One was unmistakably Baxter, she would know his gangling stride anywhere... who is with him? 'Pears to be a stranger. They drew closer. Jennie's hand flew to her throat... it can't be, she thought. No it can't be... I'm not ready. I look a sight. She looked down at her work dress, stained with sweat and tomato juice. Her hands flew to her hair and she tried to smooth back the limp strands clinging to her face.

James and Baxter reached the bottom of the steps and paused. Jennie stood shakily and came to the top of the steps. She smiled nervously and peered down into the face of the stranger who was not a stranger after all.

She forced herself to smile. "It's James, isn't it?"

James returned her smile and said softly, "Aye, Jennie lass, it's James." He came up two steps and stood below her.

She stuttered, "I, er, I... well this is a surprise," feeling herself flush at the stupid words.

James reached for her hands and held them firmly. He seemed to know what was going through her mind. "I'm sorry I couldn't give you some notice of my coming, Jennie, but it was a sudden thing."

He climbed the last two steps and turned her to face him, still holding her hands. He lead her to a rocker and gently sat her down, dropping into the rocker next to her. "It was just by chance I got a ride from Prosper Truall this morning from Boone."

Jennie couldn't concentrate. *He's much more handsome than I had imagined. That copper-colored hair. I pictured him with bright red hair and freckles... and his wonderful grey eyes. It's been such a long wait and now he's here and he's so beautiful and I'm... Oh, God, I'm a mess.* Her hand went again to smooth her hair. Finally, some of what he was saying broke through her daze.

"When I spoke with your Papaw, he said..."

"You spoke with Papaw?"

"Aye. Prosper had to drop off the mail at Grundy's store and while he did so, I visited with your grandfather. We had a lovely visit... and a great dinner, I might add."

"Baxter cleared his throat and came up the steps to the porch. "James is gonna stay at our house, Jennie, we already settled it with Ma."

Jennie didn't take her eyes from James' face. "That's nice." Baxter stood awkwardly shifting from one foot to the other. It was plain he felt out of place on this familiar porch. Finally he came to lean on the porch rail in front of them, misery plain on his face.

Jennie finally got hold of herself. "It's good to see you, James. After all this time, it's good to have you sitting here next to me. I've been expecting you." She blushed and looked down at her dress. "Of course I expected to be a little more presentable when we did meet."

"No worry, lass, I'm a bit travel worn meself."

Baxter cleared his throat again and this time got Jennie's attention. She looked up at him. "It's generous of your Ma and Pa to put James up, Baxter."

"Well it wouldn't be fittin' him stayin' here with your men folk away." He cast a smug look at James.

James was quick to answer, "You're absolutely right, laddie, I'm beholden to your Mum." Baxter gave him a bleak look.

Jennie said, "Speaking of our menfolk, Ed and Papa are due to come home in a day or two." She picked up Ed's letter to confirm her words. "It's fate, isn't it? Ed arriving the same time as you?"

James' face lit up. "Fate it is, Jennie. I was wondering how I would get to see Ed." He turned to Baxter. "Last time I saw Ed he was in the hospital and in pain." He turned back to Jennie. "His voice come back?"

"Not altogether, but we've all gotten used to it."

Jennie thought, this stilted conversation. Is it going to be difficult to talk to him? It was so easy to say anything I wanted to in letters, but face to face... she searched her mind for a subject. "Your friend, Pete. You said in your letter he didn't want to come east with you?"

James laughed, "Oh, the lad would have come with me in a trice, but the lass, Laura, wouldna hear of it. Pete was fair put out I left without him. I told him he had to choose either the road with me or life with Laura. I guess you know who made the choice for him."

James abruptly sobered. "I missed him on the road with me. I relied on him like a brother, especially after all we'd been through in the war. But Laura had other plans and I can't say as I blame her. Pete will make a fine husband."

Jennie said, "I hope it's not all Laura's idea."

"Oh no, Pete just needs a bit of tamin'. He loves the lass I'm sure... but he loves the roamin' life too. He'll settle down."

With a sense of relief, Jennie said, "Here come Mama and Helen."

Helen held the gate open for Mama. They came up the walk, Helen skipping ahead. "It's James, Mama, I'll bet it's James."

James stood up as Lula climbed the porch steps. He held out his hand. "The lass is right. James Culhane, Mrs. Wainwright. It's pleased I am to meet you."

Helen couldn't stand still. "Finally, now Jennie can stop moping around waiting for you." Jennie sent Helen a withering look.

"Why you looking at me like that, Jennie? You know it's the truth." Helen looked at James. "Everyone knows Jennie's been jest sick waiting on you."

Mama restrained Helen first, "That's enough, Helen, you're embarrassin' the young man... Well, now James, it's a pure pleasure to meet you at last. Come along. Let's everyone set down and get acquainted." Helen grabbed the swing and Lula plumped down in the rocker James had hastily vacated, leaving James and Baxter to stand uncomfortably side by side at the railing. "See you're here too, Baxter."

"Yes ma'am. James is gonna be stayin' at my Ma and Pa's place."

Lula nodded. "Good... good." She turned to James. "Jennie tell you Ed's expected?"

James nodded. "Aye, she did that."

"Ed... and Jennie.... have talked so much about you, seems like we know you already."

James smiled. Jennie couldn't believe he was as relaxed as he seemed. *This has got to be as awkward for him as it is for me.*

Hube banged out the screen door followed by Clint, their hair wet and plastered down from playing in the creek. They both stopped short when they saw the stranger.

James smiled, "And this has to be Hube and Clint."

Jennie said to the boys, "This is James."

Hube smiled shyly and went to stand by Lula. Clint mumbled, "Pleased ta meet ya."

Lula continued, "We'll always be obliged to you, James, fer your kindness to Ed while he was so sick."

"Wasn't just me, we all felt bound to help each other."

Lula said, "He don't tell us much about it. I know it was a painful recovery and I was worried 'bout him goin' to the mines, but none of us could talk him out of it. And about your injuries, young'un, you fully healed?"

James flexed his arm. "Good as the day I was born." They all fell silent. *Oh God,* thought Jennie. *I wish everyone would leave. This isn't at all the way I pictured our first meeting.* She looked at James and caught him staring at her. *Does he feel the same way?* As if somehow they had communicated, James rose.

"Well, I guess maybe Baxter and me will be getting back to his Mum's." Jennie felt a surge of relief.

Lula said, "Y'all stay fer supper."

Baxter mumbled, "Well, maybe..." Jennie glared at him.

James said, "No, thank you, ma'am. We're not hungry." He turned and smiled at Baxter. "Are we, Baxter?"

Baxter looked dazed. "No, guess not."

James stood in front of Jennie. "I'll be coming over in the morning if it's all right with you, lass."

Their eyes met and Jennie saw the laughter in them. For the first time she truly recognized the boy she had been writing to for almost two years.

She nodded. "Yes... yes, that's fine."

"Right then. Come along, Baxter me lad, and good evenin' to ye all." He went down the steps, leaving Baxter no alternative but to hurry after him.

Baxter turned and gave a feeble wave.

Jennie hardly waited for them to go through the gate before she dashed into the house, grabbed her soap and towel and made for the creek.

✉

Jennie waited impatiently on the porch. Tired as she'd been last night, she couldn't sleep. The bath in the creek hadn't helped. By the time she got there the sun was gone and the water was icy. She came back to the house shivering with her hair wet and spent most of the evening trying to get warm.

The meeting with James rankled. She kept thinking of things she should have said. She was a little put out with Mama. It pleased her that Mama made James feel welcome, but did she have to take over the entire conversation? And then Baxter! It was unforgivable of him to come with James. He knew how anxious she was about James' visit... yet under the circumstances, how could she blame him?

When sleep finally came it was a restless one, ending with a dream of James walking out of her life as quickly as he'd walked in. But this morning she arose determined to change that first impression.

She was up early and got the irons on the stove to heat and when they were hot enough she ironed the wrinkles out of the blue and white print. Her hair was brushed and glossy and hung in soft waves around her face. She settled on the porch swing. Mama had orders to keep everyone in the house lest there was a repeat of last night's visit.

She peered down the road and there he was, walking toward her. Her heart began to thump wildly. He was dressed as he'd been the night before... clean white shirt tucked into his levis, copper hair neatly combed and shining like the sun.

He stopped at the gate. "And shall we forget about last evening and begin again?"

Jennie felt a surge of relief. He had felt it too then, the disappointment of their first meeting. "I think that would be a good idea."

He opened the gate for her and held out his hand. Softly he said, "Jennie girl, you look beautiful."

She laughed. "A little better than yesterday, I hope."

He was very serious. "When I first saw you yesterday I thought what a lucky lad I am to be knowin' you... and how much I want to be knowin' you better. And now this mornin' you fair put the roses there by the porch to shame."

She squeezed his hand. "And is that the blarney Irishmen are famous for?"

He laughed. "How do you know so much about the Irish?"

"I read a lot."

They started down the road.

"Where shall we go then?"

"Maybe just for a walk. If we stay on the porch, it will be like last evening all over again." She looked over her shoulder.

"No Baxter today?"

"He wanted to come, but his Da had other plans for him. Can't say I'm sorry." He turned to look at her. "You didn't tell me he was in love with you."

Jennie hesitated. "Did he tell you that?"

"No, but that's not something a lad can hide. I feel sorry for him. I know how I would feel if a stranger showed up on my doorstep and threatened to change all me well laid plans."

Jennie flushed. "Baxter is my best friend."

"No more than friend then?"

Jennie felt the urge to lie, but couldn't. "I'm not sure."

James nodded with a weak smile. "Aye, well he seems a good lad... and I like your Mum and Helen and your brothers too."

"It was a lot to handle all at once."

"No, it was fine. I mean they made me feel welcome," he laughed, "even your Mum."

"Oh, Mama softened a long time ago. She calls you 'the Irishman'."

"As does just about everyone I've met so far. You know, Jen, I will always have me roots in Ireland, but from now on I hope to be thought of as American too. I love this country. The more I see of it, the more I think of it as home."

They strolled quietly along.

"So you don't expect to ever go back to Ireland?"

"I will one day... for a visit, but I've first to make my way here in America."

"Have you thought what you want to do?"

"I was discussing some ideas with your Grandfather."

"And what were they?"

"Well, we talked about all the opportunities there are in the big cities. Things I plan to look into."

"I hope you have more luck than Ed. He ended up going to work in the mines."

"That's because he wants to stay in a small farming community. There's more than enough work if you don't limit yourself and go where the work is."

Jennie stopped abruptly and turned to James. "I know. That applies to me too. Papaw is going to provide me with a way to explore what is beyond the mountains. I'll be forever grateful to him."

"I know. All of that you wrote in your letters. Big cities have teaching hospitals, automobile industry, and since the war, machines of all kinds are being invented. Anyone good with machinery will be in demand. There's room out there for everyone."

Jennie decided it was too soon to be serious. "At this moment I'm not worried about everyone... just us. Come on, I'll show you where you can put your foot in Tennessee."

She pulled him to the fence at the side of the road. "First we have to climb Jeb Owen's fence and go across his pasture to the creek." For a moment she was sorry she'd worn her good dress but the next moment she gathered it up around her and was over the fence, James close behind. She started running and called over her shoulder, "We have to keep an eye out for Herman."

"Who's Herman?"

"Jeb's bull... and he's not exactly friendly."

She laughed at the stricken look on his face. They ran across the pasture with no sign of Herman and climbed the fence on the far side. James caught up with her at the creek.

Jennie said. "We have to cross the creek here."

"And then we will be in Tennessee?"

"No, we have to climb the hill on the other side of the creek, come on, follow me." Jennie jumped deftly from one rock to another and landed lightly on the other side.

James began to follow, missed his step and plunged one foot into the creek. The water came up over his boot. He lifted his foot out and looked up at Jennie with a pained expression. "Saints preserve us, that water is cold."

Jennie started to laugh. "How would you like to take a bath in it?"

He jumped to her side and Jennie laughed all the harder as the water squished out of his boot. He found a stone to sit on, pulled his boot off and with great ceremony poured the water from it. "Care for a cup of tea, Jen?...I'm pouring."

They both laughed as he peeled his sock off. "You say you bathe in this water?"

Jennie tried to control her laughter. "Yes, we do in the summer. In the winter we have to haul the water to the house and heat it on the stove. I don't know which is more of a bother."

"I know what it is like to bathe in a creek, we did it whenever we had a chance in the army... but the water was never as cold as this." With elaborate actions he wrung the sock out, put it back on and pushed his foot into the soggy boot.

James got up from the rock, staggering. Jennie sobered immediately. She hurried to him and caught his arm. "What is it, James, your ankle?"

He quickly turned her to him, closed his arms around her and kissed her soundly on the lips. He drew back without dropping his arms and said with a laugh, "Not me ankle, Jen, I've just been thinking, I've not given the lass a proper greeting."

Jennie allowed herself to be held. She smiled, "Yes, I know."

He bent to kiss her again but she laughed and dipped under his arm. Too soon, she thought, too soon.

She caught his hand and pulled him after her. "We go up this hill and on the top, over the fence, is Tennessee."

He stared at the steep incline. "This, dear Jennie, is not a hill."

She dropped his hand and climbed swiftly ahead, sure of her footing. After a minute or two she stood beside the fence on top, hands on hips, waiting for him to catch up.

He struggled up and stood beside her. "And now it's over another fence?"

She laughed, turned quickly and climbed the fence. James followed. They stood side by side and looked down over a field of wild flowers gently swaying in a light breeze. Jennie ran down, stooped to pick a flower and threaded it into her hair.

James stood transfixed.

She turned to him. The breeze caught her skirt and billowed it around her. She held it down with one hand. The other she held out to him. "Come wade in the flowers with me."

He walked slowly towards her. "You're my picture come alive, Jennie. The picture I carried with me all the long days of the war. Jennie with her hair blowing in the wind in a field of flowers... waving to me."

She stood perfectly still, a smile on her face. When he took her into his arms she didn't pull away, and the kiss was long and sweet and tender.

Chapter Twenty-Seven
Homecoming

"It's called homecoming, James. Anyone's ever had anything to do with our church... people that have moved away, ministers gone to another calling... even visitors, are welcome to come to Sunday morning worship and then join us for a covered-dish dinner afterward."

They were walking through the store, Jennie with a list in her hand, stopping periodically to pick up an item.

James nodded, interested. "Homecoming. Sounds friendly. In Ireland religion and socializing are two separate things. It is a fair shame, too, as I can see the benefit in mixing the two. When I was young Da insisted Danny and me go to church and though we never argued, t'was dreary and boring for us. If a little fun were added to the mix, going to church wouldna be such a burden."

"Yes, I see what you mean." Jennie said. "We have cake walks, too. They are always fun and the money that is raised goes to the church. The single women of the church bake cakes and decorate them as fancy as they can, then the cakes are laid out on a table and the boys go round and round and bid on the cake that attracts them the most. The girl that baked it must then be his partner for the fun that follows."

"And if a lassie likes a particular lad, she can let him know beforehand which is her cake?"

Jennie grinned. "You catch on fast."

"And this homecoming covered-dish supper is to be this Sunday and you want me to come with you?"

"Yes, you will be my guest. It will be a wonderful opportunity for you to meet all the people I've written about in my letters. I know they are all anxious to meet you."

James nodded. "Yes. And I them."

"Ed said in his letter he and Papa would be home in time for homecoming. Of course Papa won't go, he never does, but the rest of us are looking forward to it."

Jennie frowned at the look of concern on James' face. "James, if you don't want to go..."

"Oh I want to go, lass... it's just... I don't want to make a spectacle of meself by doing the wrong thing."

Jennie squeezed his arm and grinned. "James you are going to be the biggest spectacle Zionville has ever seen and whatever 'thing' you do will be perfectly all right with everyone."

James nodded soberly. "But there's somethin' I haven't told you, lass. You see I have this tic that contorts me face something fierce when I get nervous and it is very embarrassing."

Jennie's face fell. "A tic?"

James, still solemn, said, "Yes, like this..." and he started to twitch.

Jennie was aghast.

James, still twitching, said, "The only thing that will stop it is if you put your arms around me neck and kiss me soundly."

It was a moment before Jennie realized it was a joke. "Oh James," she laughed and gave him a shove. "I'll put my hands around your neck instead."

"Hey, Jennie," Sarah leaned over the counter and beckoned to them.

"James, I want you to meet someone. Sarah, this is James. James, Sarah, my best friend."

James grinned. "Ach, and this is Sarah, the one you wrote about, Jennie. The one wi' the grand sense of humor."

Sarah blushed. "Jennie, what all you been tellin' James?"

Jennie said, "To start with, I wrote him all about the last tent meeting, and then..."

Sarah put her hands to her face. "No more, don't say no more."

James put his hand on Sarah's arm. "Don't be embarrassed, lassie. If it will make you feel easier, I have this tic..."

Jennie giggled. "I can see the two of you are going to get along just fine."

A sudden shower fell on the meadows, driving the cows to shelter under the trees and chickens to run squawking to the chicken house. Thunder rumbled down the mountainside. Mama, Helen and Hube were caught in the garden when the rain started and Mama, her apron overflowing with beans, ran to the shelter of the back porch. Hube and Helen, in a state of bliss, ran around in circles, arms outstretched and faces lifted, enjoying the downpour.

Mama shouted from the back porch. "If it starts lightnin', young'uns, you come straight in the house, you hear?"

Baxter sat balanced on the Wainwright porch rail, his back against the post and his feet stretched out along the railing in front of him, protected from the deluge by the roof overhang. Jennie and James sat side by side in the swing.

"Remember, Bax," Jennie said, "we use to do that? Run around in the rain?"

"Yeah. And after the storm let up, we'd play in the creek 'cause it would be all swole up from the rain."

James interrupted. "And where's the wee dog, Soldier? I would have thought he'd be out playing in the rain wi' Hube and Helen?"

Jennie said. "Seein' as how we expect Papa, Soldier's not here. For some reason Papa hates him. Can't understand why, he's such a funny little dog and Hube loves him to death."

"Where's he hidin', then?"

"Hube took him over to the Owen's barn."

The sound of a wagon coming down the road could be heard over the rolling thunder. They watched as Prosper's wagon pulled up to the gate.

The wagon barely stopped moving before Ed and Dalton jumped out, hunching their shoulders in the downpour. Prosper, protected by his oilskins, reached into the wagon bed and tossed Dalton his bag and then Ed his duffel. Ed waved his thanks to Prosper as the wagon rolled off. The two men bounded to the shelter of the porch. James was waiting at the top of the steps.

"Hey, everybody," Ed shouted. Then he and James came together laughing and punching and pummeling each other. After a few minutes they stood back.

"Gawd, it's good to see you agin', Irish."

James gave him a final punch. "Let's get a good look at you, laddie." They grinned foolishly at each other.

"I wouldna recognize ye out of uniform, but with that croaky voice I couldna miss."

Ed laughed, "And same with you. Ain't too many people I know speak like a foreigner." They fell on one another again, slapping each other on the back.

Jennie grinned, enjoying the exchange while Dalton and Baxter watched silently. Finally the two came apart.

Ed turned to Dalton. "James Culhane, meet my Papa."

"Pleased ta meet ya."

"Me pleasure, Mr. Wainwright."

Ed turned to Jennie and Baxter. "So what do ya think of my Irishman?"

Before either could answer, Mama appeared at the screen door. "You'uns look like two drowned rats, best you go 'round back."

They all trooped around to the kitchen door and after much stamping of feet, entered the kitchen. Lula hugged Ed and smiled broadly at Dalton. "Come along and set yerselves at the table."

Ed said to Mama, "We stopped fer a minute at Papaw's while Prosper dropped the mail at Grundy's. Papaw thought he might come along but the rain clouds was buildin' up and he says no sense courtin' a chill."

Mama asked, "Did he 'spect to be here Sunday fer the homecoming?"

"Said he'd try."

Dalton ran his hands through his wet hair. "We rode aheada the rain most all the way from Sugar Grove 'til jest about Combs farm and then it caught up with us."

Lula headed for the stairs. She called over her shoulder. "Jennie, go call the young'uns out of the rain. I'll go get everyone somethin' dry to put on."

Ed asked James, "Where's Pete? Didn't he come with you?"

"Lad was all broke up trying to decide. A lassie from the camp caught his eye and he couldn't bring himself to leave her."

Ed looked dumbfounded. "You mean a woman got Pete t' stand still long 'nuff to put a ring through his nose?"

James grinned. "Aye... and changed the course of history. I don't think the lad minds one bit. As far as marrying the lass, I'll believe that when it happens... But what about you, Ed, how do you like working in the mines?"

Ed shrugged. "Pay is good, but that's 'bout all. Bent over double, wadin' in water up to your knees and breathin' coal dust ain't no way fer man ner beast to live. You know what I want, Jim... some land of my own. After I give Mama a hand here on the farm for a time and get a little money ahead I'll think 'bout a place of my own. Ain't nuthin' better than workin the land. All I could think about them months in the war and later in the hospital, was a piece of land of my own."

Baxter said, "Guess it's all in what yer lookin' fer in life. Can't say it's farmin' fer me, but then agin' my Pa wouldn't be nuthin' *but* a farmer."

Papa snorted. "Farmin'. Only a fool would spend his life working sunup to sunset and have nothin' to show fer it in the end. In the mines least you get some money fer yer effort."

Ed looked steadily at Dalton. There was an awkward silence. Finally he said, "Farmin's kept this family in food and shelter. Something the mines ain't been able to do." Jennie looked from one to the other. Something's not right, she thought; I wonder what's happened between them.

Dalton's face was flushed and unsmiling, but before he could answer Ed's remark, Lula came back into the kitchen and handed Ed and Dalton each a shirt. The awkward moment passed. "Jest you get outta them wet things. Like Papaw said, no sense courtin' a chill." She looked around the kitchen. "Where's the young'uns?"

Jennie said, "Couldn't see them anywhere, Mama. They're probably in the creek."

"They'll likely end up sick, mark my words." She turned to Ed. "You're lookin' peaked agin, Ed, you been eatin'?"

Ed shifted his gaze from Dalton. "Don't have much hunger fer any cookin' but yours, Mama."

"Then I best get somethin on the table fer you'uns."

Dalton stood up. "Not fer me, Lu. Rain's let up. I'll be back later." Jennie and Ed exchanged looks.

✉

Jennie, Lula, Aunt Pearl and Buelis sat in the shade at one of the long wooden tables set up by the side of the church. The remains of the homecoming meal had been cleared away and now the congregation and guests were scattered under the trees enjoying the lazy afternoon.

Jennie let her gaze drift over the church grounds. Luther Norris and Lucy Glenwood sat with Prosper, Luther looking rested and handsome with a little more weight on him, and Lucy, her thin pointed face alive and interested in the conversation. Abel stood close by her side and Lucy's arm was around his neck, her fingers absently smoothing the blond curls. There was James, chatting easily with a group... Ed and Ev Proffitt, Baxter, Tom Wooding and Jeb Owen, all listening attentively to what he was saying.

At one of the tables Lije and Effie Proffitt chatted with with Cora and Otis Fenley and Emmaline and Jacob Wooding. Emmaline looked soft and round and happy. She and Jacob hadn't wasted any time in getting pregnant. It was obvious that *all* the Fenleys were in a high state of expectation, especially Mam, who hovered over Emmaline, smiling her faraway smile. A baby in the family was going to be good for Mam, poor soul.

Min and Sherm lounged comfortably beneath a big maple, Sarah sitting cross-legged in front of them. All around, in and out, the children ran and played.

Jennie sat with her elbows on the table and chin in hands.

Pearl was saying, "I swan, I jest I can't abide a busybody."

"What can you do, Pearl," Buelis said, "short of tellin' the woman' she ain't welcome... it's Luther's place after all."

"But the woman acts like she knows everything there is to know 'bout raisin' young'uns and she ain't never took care a nary a one and..."

Lula interrupted. "You can't rightly say Lucy don't know how to do fer children, Pearl, she is a teacher after all."

Pearl snorted. "Ain't the same thing. She ain't never held a pukin' child over her shoulder ner changed a dirty diaper in her whole life." Pearl looked to Jennie for support. "Ain't that true, Jennie?"

Jennie smiled at Pearl, recognizing the real problem. Pearl was jealous. "You know how to take care of feeding the young'uns and what to do in case they get sick, and that's very important, but a teacher has something to give too, Aunt Pearl."

Lula asked, "What does Luther have to say?"

Pearl let her gaze drift to Luther. "I think the fool is love-struck."

Lula leaned over and patted Pearl's arm. "Now, Pearl, we all feel fer Luther and you should too. Mary's been gone most three years."

"You know that's right, Pearl," Buelis said. "Time Luther had a little joy in his life."

Pearl was stubborn. "I jest don't think Lucy Glenwood is the right one."

"Ain't fer you to say, Pearl."

"I know, I know." Pearl heaved a giant sigh.

Lula leaned over and took Pearl's gnarled hand. "Sides, I think the children are gettin' to be too much fer you. You with yer rheumatism and all. Time you took life a mite easier."

Pearl looked indignant. "That ain't true, Lu. I kin still outwork anyone half my age and you know it."

Lu shook her head. "Ain't entirely true. You been leanin' more and more on Jennie these past months."

Before Pearl could answer, Jennie said, "Mama's right. You've done what was asked of you and a wonderful job, at that. Now if Miss Glenwood has stepped in to help you, why not let her?"

"But the woman don't know beans, Jennie, an..."

"Then you have to teach her. The children won't forget it was you opened your arms to them when their Mama died... and Mr. Norris won't forget it either."

Pearl studied her folded hands. "You really think so? Cause I'd like ta die if I had to give up my young'uns."

Jennie said, "I'm sure it won't come to that. None of them can do without you."

Pearl nodded, a smile at the corners of her mouth. "Can't picture Lucy Glenwood cookin' a meal... and if she did I can't picture Luther eatin' it."

Buelis slapped her knee and laughed loud enough for several people to stop their conversation and look over at them. "So, Pearl, you gotta stay and do the cookin', else they's all gonna die of hunger."

Pearl laughed, her melancholy gone. "Yer right." She leaned over and whispered, "The woman can't bile water."

Clara strolled towards them. "Hey y'all. She sat down beside them at the table. "Your father didn't make homecoming, Lu. I was sure he would be here."

"Papa will be here later today. He just couldn't make homecoming."

Clara said, "Mylart wants Jeb to go to Boone with him to record the sale of the property."

Lula said, "You think Jeb'll be able to make the trip, Clara?"

"Oh yes. Mylart said they'd spend the night at his place, and come back the next day. That will make it easier on Jeb."

They all turned to the group where James was the center of attention. At that moment James threw his head back and laughed and the rest joined in. "I have to say, Jennie," Clara said, "You picked yourself a right handsome beau."

Jennie blushed. Before she could say anything, Mama said, "Pretty is as pretty does, Clara, and I said as much to Jennie. I'll hold my judgment 'til he proves he's more'n what we see on the surface."

"I agree," Pearl said, "We all want what's best fer our Jennie here."

Clara nodded, "Oh I allow, it's too soon to judge the boy and even with time it's never certain a body's ready for marriage, be it man or woman. I hope our young'uns made the right decision, Lu." They all looked to Min and Sherm, giggling at some nonsense they shared.

Lula snorted. "I still say they's too young, but what's done is done."

"Me and Jeb'll help them grow up."

Lula nodded at Clara. "Everyone knows you have a good marriage, Clara. Anybody can help them over the rough times, it's you and Jeb."

Jennie stood between James and Baxter and tried to concentrate on the conversation around her. It was difficult. James was comfortable, answering questions about Ireland and the war and laughing with Ed and Jeb and Tom Wooding. Mama had warned her often enough not to make James a hero, that he was a man and no more, but it wasn't possible to read his letters and know his thoughts and not imagine the kind of man he would be. *It's a small wonder he is so much more than I expected.*

She turned to Baxter who was listening intently to the stories, a small smile on his lips and thought, you are no less wonderful than James. I know exactly the kind of husband and father you'll make... gentle, patient, loving. You are secure and steady and a person would be crazy not to want that kind of life, but... Baxter turned at that moment and smiled fleetingly at her. He took her hand and held it casually as he'd done so many times down through the years. The feel of his hand holding hers was as natural as the breeze that swept over them.

James reached for her other hand and squeezed it. She thought, this is ridiculous standing here holding hands with both of them. A nervous giggle worked its way up her throat and threatened to explode. She looked around to see if anyone noticed, caught a mischievous look from Sarah over Emmaline's shoulder and quickly averted her gaze. That's all I need, she thought, Sarah to start giggling and then I'm lost.

"Aye, Mr. Owen," James was saying. "I can see it is hard for you, a farmin' man, to understand my not wantin' to go back to Ireland and my Da's farm. But it's been six years since I left and I've had a taste of roaming the world what with the war and my travels in Canada and the States. With no offense intended, I canna go back to farmin'."

Jeb said, "It must be a hard on yer Pa, you not wantin' to go back. Speakin' fer myself, I don't know what I'd do without my sons. What will it be then, more travellin' round the country?"

"I think so, before I settle down." Without turning to look at Jennie, he squeezed her hand again. She looked down at his hand covering hers. Strong, bronzed by the sun, a smattering of freckles across the back; a forceful hand.

Her eyes, seemingly with a will of their own, turned to Baxter. He wouldn't be able to hold the attention of a group. He was much too shy, too unsure of himself. Maybe that's what made him so compassionate, sympathetic of other's needs. It was the very thing that allowed his Pa to make him feel guilty about going off to the Academy.

Dear God. Tell me what to do.

Jennie looked over her shoulder and searched the crowd for Doctor Payne, dropping James' hand and waving to get Doc's attention. When she did, they exchanged nods. Jennie gently backed away from the group and pulled Baxter along with her. Doctor Payne joined them and took Baxter's other arm. "Let's us find your Pa, Bax, and have a little talk."

Baxter shook his head. "Won't do no good, Doc, Pa's a stubborn man. He jest don't see the good a me bein' a doctor, regardless of what I want. To him the only life is farmin'. Even Ma can't budge him... and I'm finding it hard to go against his wishes. He *is* my Pa."

Jennie said, "Baxter, I'm sure if you just left, even though your Pa is angry, he'd get over it in time, and probably end up being prouder of you than anyone."

"He might just, Jennie, but he'd never admit it. It's hard fer Pa to back down."

Doc was determined, "Ben's had a lot of time to think about it, son. Let's see if we can give him a little help in reversin' his position." They found Ben relaxed against the trunk of a tree, his legs outstretched, but his eyes turned steely as they approached.

"Hey Ben," Doc said agreeably, fully prepared for a set-to. They sat down on the ground in front of Ben and Doc came right to the point. "Time we had a real serious talk about Baxter's schooling."

Ben came away from the tree and Doc could see he was ready to argue. Doc held up his hand and smiled, "Whoa, Ben, this ain't gonna be a battle. We're talkin' about a boy we all love, you as a father,

Jennie as his closest friend and me as a... well, what would you call me, a benefactor?"

Ben threw an angry look at Baxter. "Ain't fair you throwin' your weight around, Doc. I say the boy's got no business goin' off. I need him on the farm." Ben lost a little of his anger. "Don't he realize I'm keepin' up the farm jest fer him? I'm gettin' on in years. Neither me or his Ma is gonna be around much longer and then the whole dang business will be his. I worked hard all my life to see my boys ended up with somethin' and I'm offerin' Baxter the home place as his share. He wants to throw it away like all my work and time and energy over the years has meant nothing." Ben fell silent.

Jennie felt sorry for him. She could understand his frustration, while at the same time Baxter was just as frustrated.

Doc said, "Ben, we all know there ain't no more honorable way of life than farming. You've given your wife and three sons the benefit of your labors and you've all lived well. Your farm is one of the best in the county. No one denies that. Not me ner Baxter ner no one. But they's other things in life to love.

"You've got a boy here you can be proud of, smart, with a real leanin' towards medicine and what's more, the boy loves it. All them things makes for a first class doctor."

Baxter was studying his father's face as Doc talked. He interrupted. "Pa, what you do is something I'll never be able to do. Doc's right. You made a success of farming, but I don't love it like you do and I think it's pretty hard to be a success at something if your heart ain't in it. My heart's in medicine." His head drooped to his chest. "But I won't go to the Academy, Pa. I'll stay on the farm and do like you want." He raised his head and tried to smile. "And maybe, who knows, I'll get good at farmin' like you."

Jennie and Doc knew when to be quiet. They watched Ben struggle with Baxter's words. Finally Ben said, "Had no trouble with your two brothers. From the time they was knee high it was all I could do to hold them down, they was so het up to helpin' in the fields. But you... always wantin' to read and study. Never could understand it." He paused, staring long at Baxter, no one daring to break the silence. Finally he swallowed hard and said, "But hell, Bax, I guess two outta three ain't bad."

Baxter met his father's eyes and the two of them smiled. Doc and Jennie stood up and quietly walked away.

Chapter Twenty-Eight
Papaw Speaks Up

It was late afternoon. The threat of rain had cut short the homecoming, sending everyone scurrying for home.

Heat lightning flickered and shimmered within the menacing black storm clouds that blotted out the last of the sun's rays. The muttered approach of the rain mixed with rolling thunder slowly advanced down the mountainside until it finally fell with fury on the fields and pastures. A whipping wind accompanied the rain and swept away the hot sticky air trapped in the valley.

Jennie and James watched the display from the porch.

Jennie shivered. "That air is cool."

He looked at her curled up in the rocker, her arms wrapped around her legs. "You got a chill, lass?"

"Just a bit, but it feels good after all the heat." After a pause, she said. "Why so somber? Didn't you enjoy the homecoming?"

"The truth, Jen, I don't know when I've enjoyed meself so much."

"You look so sad."

He didn't answer but came to her side and sat down, taking her hands into his. "I've been debating with meself, lass. These last few days the words have been piling up inside bursting to come out. Sure and I'll explode if I don't say them."

She smiled encouragingly but said nothing.

James continued. "I've been here a week tomorrow. In truth I thought it would take time to know if what I felt from our letters would be what I felt meeting you face to face."

Jennie uncurled her legs and sat up straight. She started to interrupt but James shook his head.

"Let me finish, Jen. I knew from our first letters we would be friends and when I saw your picture I fair lost me senses. But can friendship and being smitten with a picture be called love?" Jennie nodded, understanding, since these were the same thoughts she was having.

James went on, "For all my life I've set challenges for myself and I know I will meet and conquer them one day. I've always pictured doing it alone and I can, I know I can, but after all our letters, I thought how much sweeter the game if it is shared with someone."

" I was so sure when I started east that you would be the one and the closer I got to Zionville, the more unsure I became. Then I walked down the road and met you and after just a week I know for a certainty that you *are* the one I want to share these challenges, and my life, with. Don't ask how I am so sure, I just know there is something inside that says if I let you go I'll forever call myself the fool. Jen, marry me. Come away with me."

"James ... I ... you..." She pulled her hands from his, got up and stood at the railing facing the storm. "I've been battling the same feelings but I've been trying to be sensible too. A week... to decide a lifetime." The rain swept in and dampened her face. Without turning she said, "It's just too soon to decide."

"Jen, you remember I wrote in one of my letters that the tellin' time for marriage is in the heart to be answered when the call is heard. I hear that call, lass, with every beat of my heart."

Still she didn't turn from the railing.

James spoke again, "If we had grown up together, I would have been sittin' on your porch swing whisperin' in your ear from the time we were school mates. Instead we wrote letters. I think I know you well. Your feelings for your Mum and sisters and brothers and yes, your Papa too. I know what you want to do with the rest of your life."

Finally she turned to face him. "Yes, to be a nurse. How will that happen if...?"

"That's your challenge, Jen, and we would work on it together." He got up and joined her. "Our dreams, yours and mine, are waiting to be fulfilled and if we are together how much sweeter the challenge."

Why am I waiting? she thought. Isn't this what I've been dreaming about? To have James in love with me? Every night I prayed he would come safely through the war and one day come to me. Now he's here and saying all the things I've been waiting to hear. Why can't I say yes?

James studied her face. He could almost read her thoughts. He dropped his hands. "Jen... I'm sorry. Here I am going on telling you my feelings and I've not asked for yours. All these dreams are for naught if you don't love me." He waited for her answer.

Jennie felt a lump in her throat. It was hard to speak. "I know it feels right to be with you. When you're not here I feel empty and alone. You make the future sound wonderful and exciting. But is it love, James, or the opportunity of a wonderful adventure? Tell me, is it?"

She turned back to the rail, closed her eyes and held her face up to the rain. Still with her eyes closed she said, "I see what being in love has done to Mama. It scares me. I want to be sure."

"Jennie lass, when two people first come together there's no way they can be absolutely sure. Some things have to be taken on faith. You must believe I'll never hurt you."

She turned her face to him, wet with rain. "I think I know that. I want to say yes but something holds me back."

James held her eyes with his. He finally nodded and said, "You may be right. I know it's not too soon for me, but maybe it is for you. Tell me, does Baxter have anything to do with your doubts? I guess I could understand if he does... someone you've known all your life and..."

"I have to be honest with you as well as myself. I can't disregard Baxter. I know he loves me, and before you came I was almost convinced I was in love with him."

"You said almost, Jennie. You're not sure then."

"No... I'm not sure."

James put a finger to her lips. "Well then, I'll not push. I'm willin' to wait and if it's time you need you'll have it. But I'll not go away... until you tell me to." He opened his arms, and without hesitation Jennie moved into the circle, lifting her face to his kiss.

When they parted James said, "Somehow, lass, I don't think I'll have long to wait."

She nodded, unable to speak. He pulled her close again and she laid her head on his shoulder. They rocked gently back and forth, the sound of the rain a steady drumbeat on the metal roof.

The next day Papaw, astride Lazarus, cantered into the Wainwright yard. The big horse and his rider alike were splattered with mud.

Clint, coming out of the chicken house, ran to his side. "Hey, Papaw." He took the reins from his grandfather and held Lazarus steady as the old man dismounted. "It's like a holiday, Papaw. Ed and Papa come for the homecoming, and James being here, and now you."

Papaw ruffled Clint's hair. "Holiday, huh? See you can get some o'this muck off Lazarus. Poor ole hoss looks like he's been wallerin' in a mud hole."

"I'll clean him up good, Papaw."

"Good boy!"

"Hey, Papaw." Jennie came through the yard with a bucket of water from the spring. It sloshed around her ankles as she tried to hurry. "We missed you at homecoming."

"Couldn't make it, Jen. Was it a good day?"

"Till the rain." Papaw took the bucket and the two of them mounted the porch steps. Mylart kicked off his muddy boots before following Jennie into the kitchen.

Dalton sat at the table, a cup of coffee in front of him. "Sit down, take a load off, Mylart."

"You want a cup of coffee, Papaw?"

"Thank you, Jennie, don't mind if I do." He sat down, rested his elbows on the table and stared, unsmiling, at Dalton, his eyes unwavering. The look caught Dalton by surprise, with his cup half way to his mouth. "Somethin' eatin at you, Mylart?"

"You might say so."

Jennie set a mug of coffee in front of Papaw and looked curiously from one to the other of the two men. *Something's bothering Papaw. I wonder if it's the same thing that's bothering Ed. Am I imagining it?*

Mylart kept his eyes on Dalton. "You and me has got some talkin' to do. Now's not the time, but 'fore you go back to the mines, make sure you find the time fer us to have a little chat."

Dalton nodded, puzzled. "I'm always ready to do some jawin', Mylart, you know that."

They both turned as Lula and Helen came into the kitchen, Helen jumping up and down with nervous energy. "We seen you comin' up the road, Papaw. Mama says looked like you wuz ridin' a different horse cause Lazarus wuz so covered in mud, but I said it was ole Lazarus all right, I could tell."

Papaw smiled. "You're a right smart young'un."

"It's a shame you couldn't make the homecoming, Papa, we all looked for you."

"Couldn't get away, Lu. They was some things I had to tend to."

The meal was a boisterous occasion. There were ten in all counting Minnie and Sherm, who came in as they were all sitting down to the table.

"Mother Owen sent over a platter of ham biscuits, Mama, said maybe you could use some extra."

"That's good of Clara. Just set it on the table, Min. Papaw, will you say grace?"

After grace was said, the business of passing food and filling plates took over and everyone settled down to eat.

Ed said, "Did you tell Jennie 'bout nurse Dora, James? Umm, she wuz sure beautiful. Had everyone doin' handstands jest so's she would take notice."

James caught Ed's wink. "Yes, I think I mentioned Dora. Didn't I, lass? Would you please pass the biscuits?"

"Dora?... yes. You said she was a good nurse."

Ed said, "But did he say just how good she was? James was her favorite. The rest of us jest stood 'round kickin' our heels, waitin' to be noticed."

Jennie felt her face flush and she dropped her eyes to her plate.

Sherm, who had caught the wink also, said, "Heard a lot 'bout them English nurses...heard they wuz real obligin'."

Minnie gasped. "Sherm, you ain't heard no such a thing."

Hubie looked up from his plate with his mouth full. "What does obligin' mean?"

Mama said with half a smile on her face, "Jest you tend to cleanin' up yer plate."

"Obligin' means," Helen said with a self-satisfied look, "you do a lot of favors for people."

Sherm choked on his food and everyone laughed, even Jennie, who realized she was being teased. She looked up and caught James smiling at her.

"I appreciate the good meal, Lu, you never disappoint your old Papa."

James said, "Yes, Mrs. Wainwright, being a lad on the move doesn't give a body time to sit down and enjoy a good meal. I thank you."

Lula pushed away from the table. "It weren't much, but I kindly thank y'all."

Ed followed Mylart out to the cowshed where he found the old man fitting a feed bag on Lazarus. Jennie, her curiosity aroused, was close on Ed's heels.

Ed said, "Jennie, you mind goin' back in the house? I have to talk private-like with Papaw."

"Yes, I do mind, Ed. There's something going on, I feel it and if something's happening that affects the family, I think I should know."

Ed was exasperated. "Jennie..."

Jennie stood her ground. "I'm old enough, Ed, and maybe I can help."

Ed looked to Papaw and the old man nodded. "She ain't going away, Ed, you might jest as well spill it out. Guess mebbe I know what it is you want to talk about anyway."

Ed looked puzzled. "You do?"

"Have anything to do with your Papa?"

Ed made circles in the dirt with his foot. "Nothin' much gets past you, does it?"

"It ain't that I gossip, son, it's just I got good friends tellin' me things they think I ought to know. In this case, it was Luther Norris."

Ed nodded. "Yes, Luther would know. Him bein' at the mines and seein' what everyone else is seein'."

Jennie looked from one to the other. "Seeing what?"

Ed ignored her and looked at his grandfather with troubled eyes. "Papa is makin' a damn fool of hisself and he don't seem to care who knows it, not even me. This widow woman, Carrie Crane, that runs the boardin' house where we're stayin', and Papa are carryin' on. It's like Papa is a free man to do what he wants."

Papaw listened, shaking his head. "Makes me wonder what the man can be thinkin'. That's why I come. I aim to have a talk with your Papa."

Jennie was aghast and angry. "You mean..."

Ed looked at Jennie, annoyed. "Hesh, Jennie, I want to hear what Papaw has to say about it."

"Well, to start with," Papaw said, "we'll see what the man has to say fer hisself."

✉

Sherm sat on the porch steps in the twilight, Minnie in a rocker, while Jen and James swung lazily in the porch swing. The evening air was cool and a gentle breeze ruffled the leaves in the buckeye tree. The pastures were alive with blinking fireflies competing with the winking stars above. The moon was on the rise.

Min said, "Did you do much fishing in Ireland, James?"

"Aye. Me and me friend Jimmy Armstrong used to fish. We'd get on our bicycles early morn and head out for Aclaire, a small town close by. The River Moy ran through the town and the banks were grass to the river's edge. We'd spend the entire day fishing, that is, when Da could spare me."

Min asked, "What did you catch?"

"Salmon mostly, but trout too."

Sherm nodded. "Trout's good eatin', don't know about salmon. Tell me somethin' 'bout farmin' in Ireland. Is it much different than here?"

"Farming is farming wherever you are, but we don't grow as many crops. We have some 1800 acres and raise cattle, sheep and some horses."

Sherm sat up in surprise. "Did you say 1800 acres? God, James, how do you tend a farm that size?"

"Some of the land is peat bogs. We use peat in the fireplaces for heating the way you use wood. Most of the rest of the land, except for some pasture, is rugged terrain not good for farming and not much better for grazing. Isn't too bad in the summer. The cattle can find enough grass in the pastures and the sheep climb 'way up in the hills to feed. But when the snows hit and there is no more grass for the sheep, they are too dumb to come off the hill. We never find them all. The cattle have a bit more sense and head for the barn when the weather turns grim."

"Don't you grow crops that will feed them come winter?"

"Like I said, we do the best we can with the land we have, but it isn't fertile land, not like here."

Sherm nodded gravely. "Sounds a hard life."

"One I'm not of a mind to go back to."

"We're glad of that," Minnie said. "We want you to stay here."

"But it's not here I'll be staying, lass."

Jennie caught the look that passed between Sherm and Minnie and read them like a book. Farming was all they knew and all they ever wanted to know and she envied their dedication, wondering, in some corner of her mind, if she would ever find the same contentment.

Twilight had gradually drifted into night and Minnie said into the dark, "You and Jennie make a good pair. Neither of you are satisfied to stay put. You both want to be off making things happen... you to travel, James, and Jennie to get an education. I sometimes wonder if Sherm and me are missing something. Like maybe we should be wantin' more."

James said, "Nothing wrong with being satisfied with your lot in life, Min. When, or if, I get to the point where I feel content to stay put, I will have achieved what you and Sherm have already."

Sherm got up from the steps yawning and stretching. "Don't know as I agree with all that, James. Ask me how satisfied I am with my lot in life when that dang rooster starts crowin' at the crack of dawn. Come on, Mrs. Min," he reached for Min's hand and lifted her out of the rocker.

Min and Sherm turned at the bottom of the steps. "Night y'all."

Jen and James said in unison, "Goodnight."

Someone inside lit a lamp, and its glow reflected faintly on their faces as they sat comfortably silent, gently swinging. James pulled Jennie to him and kissed her softly on the forehead and each eye, the tip of her nose and finally her mouth.

The screen door banged and Papaw and Ed came out on the porch.

Papaw teased, "Doin' a little spoonin'?"

Jennie was glad they couldn't see her face. She sat up quickly. "No, we were just enjoying the cool evening, is all."

Papaw eased himself into the rocker. "Thought we'uns ud do the same. Lu and the young'uns is already abed."

Ed said, "You and Jeb Owen are takin' off tomorrow for Boone, that right, Papaw?"

"Yep. Gotta go see the county clerk and sign fer the transfer of the property. Be stayin' at my place over night seein' as how Jeb ain't fit fer a lot a travellin'. We'll be back day after tomorrow."

Ed said, "Papaw, uh, when you gonna talk to Papa?"

"Tonight. Ain't gonna put it off... and I think you and mebbe James here better stay close by while I'm gone."

"You think maybe Papa...?"

"Don't rightly know what the man might do."

James saw the concern on the old man's face in the faint lamplight and felt the stirring of alarm. He decided to get Ed aside and find out what the problem was. He stopped the swing and stood up. "Guess I'll head up the road. You want to walk with me, Ed?"

Ed got up too. "Sure."

James took Jen's hand and squeezed it. "I'll see you come morning, love."

After they were gone the silence grew, until Jennie could stand it no longer. She finally said, "Tonight, Papaw? You gonna talk with Papa tonight?"

Papaw took his time answering. "It ain't somethin' you should be concerned with, Jennie."

"But I am concerned with it, Papaw. I have a right to be. Does Mama know about this... this other woman?"

"Don't know. She ain't said."

Jennie kept the swing moving and the squeaky hinge sang a monotonous song. "And you're waiting on him right now?"

"Yes and I'd be obliged if you would make yerself scarce so's me and your Papa can talk in private."

Jennie stopped the swing. "Yes. I guess it's better that way, but you have to let me know what happens."

"I guess it will all come out in the wash anyway."

"Papaw, I'm not just being curious. You know how hurt Mama is going to be. I want to be able to help."

Papaw sighed, "When you get aholt a somethin' you hang on like a pup with a shoe."

Jennie stood up, "All right. I won't badger you anymore." She leaned over the rocker and kissed him on the cheek and without another word went into the house.

She paused inside the door and after a moment or two of indecision, went through the kitchen and slipped out the back door. Careful not to make a sound, she went around to the turn of the porch, sat down with her back against the house and waited. She was keeping Papaw company whether he wanted her to or not.

She clasped her arms around her knees and shivered in the night chill. Even though she knew Papaw could handle most any situation he put his mind to, it worried her that if Papa came home drunk, he might be a problem. What would she do then? Papaw was, after all, seventy-five years old and Papa was pretty strong. Well, she thought, I can yell pretty loud.

$$\boxtimes$$

"I guess I don't have to ask how you feel about Jennie, Jim, it's plain as the nose on your face."

"I'm not a man can hide me feelings, Ed. I knew long before I met her I wanted her to be me wife."

"You wuz takin' a chance. S'posin' she turned out a nag?"

James laughed. "No chance o' that, laddie. No one could write the kind of letters she did and be anything but a wonder."

They walked silently up the road towards the Combs farm. Ed said, "Can't think of another soul I'd rather have for a brother-in-law."

James poked him in the arm, "Aye, goes for me too, but there is the matter of the lady sayin' yes first."

Ed said with surprise, "You mean she ain't said she'll marry you?"

"Hard to figure that one out, isn't it, me being the perfect catch, but it might not be me you're gettin' as a brother-in-law."

"Guess you're talkin' bout Baxter."

"And he is a formidable adversary. The lad has a wonderful purpose in life, one that appeals greatly to Jen. I'm not about to count him out."

"Hard to think of Baxter as anything but a family friend, he's hung around the house so much, but I guess I don't look at him the same way Jen does." He kicked at a few stones. "Irish, from what I see, standin' back watchin', it's you Jennie is in love with. I'm almost sure of it."

"I hope you're right, bucko. I promised her I'd not push, I'd leave her to make up her mind, but in truth I plan to push as hard as I can, subtly of course."

Ed laughed. "Now that sounds like the stubborn Irishman I know."

They walked on in comfortable silence. Finally Ed asked, "What does Jen say about nursing? You know, when you set your mind on one thing for as long as Jen has 'bout being a nurse, it's kinda hard to change direction."

"I've already told the lass there's no need to forsake the idea of being a nurse. I'm willin' to help her."

"Papaw will be glad to hear that. I told our Papa that Jennie is going to get the education she wants, and his answer was he didn't give a damn. But when it comes right down to her going, I don't know what he'll do. Papa works underhanded."

"With me and you and your Papaw all protecting Jennie's interests, I don't think the man will stand a chance of interfering... and speakin' of your father, Ed, I get the feelin' he is engaged in some mischief and I see something in your Papaw's face and in yours too, that spells trouble."

They walked along in silence for a moment or two, then Ed said, "Seein' as you are almost family, guess I can tell you. When I talked to

Papa about going back to the mines with him, it didn't seem like he wanted me to, and I found out pretty soon why. He's been carrying on with the woman runs the boarding house there... Carrie Crane..."

James could feel his anger.

"...and they don't care who knows about it. Papa earns good money and he gives it all to this woman while Mama is back here tryin' to do for the kids, making all kinds of excuses for the man, and all the while he's spendin' time in this woman's bed. I tell ya, James, we all of us put up with shit from this man for all our lives, Mama especially, and now this on top of all those rotten years."

✉

Jennie caught a whiff of Papaw's pipe and was almost lulled to sleep by the creaking of the rocker. She heard the gate swing open... Papa... her heart came up in her throat as she quietly peeked around the corner of the house. It was Ed. He fell into the rocker beside Papaw.

"He ain't come home yet?"

Papaw didn't say anything and Jennie assumed he must have shook his head because Ed said, "You want me to be here?"

The old man continued to rock quietly. "Nope. Chased Jennie up to bed and I'm chasin' you, too. I can handle Dalton."

"S'pose he tries to deny it, Papaw. I know what I know and if he tries to deny what's been goin' on..."

"Don't you worry. Like I said, I can handle the man."

She heard Ed get up. "I'm sure you can, Papaw. Tell you the truth, I wouldn't wanna be in his shoes." The screen door closed softly.

The porch was uncomfortable without even a pillow to sit on and the air chilled her to the bone. She thought of sneaking in for her sweater, but was afraid of making a noise... there was nothing wrong with Papaw's hearing. She peeked around the corner again and saw that Papaw's head was down on his chest with his pipe, unlit, still clutched in his hand. Jennie dozed off too, her head cradled on her knees, coming awake abruptly when she heard the gate creak.

The figure stood inside the gate, swaying slightly. "See ya waited up fer me." Papaw didn't answer. Dalton came up the walk and climbed the steps halfway then promptly sat down. "Whyn't you jest spit it out, Mylart, steada making a big ta-do bout it. I can guess what you're gonna say anyhow."

"That so," Papaw said, "Then you'll know my concern."

Dalton said. "Your concern... hogwash, it ain't any a your damn business."

"Anything to do with my family is my concern. You been foolin' 'round with a widow woman, name of Carrie Crane, back at the mines. Ain't it time you acted like a man? Bad 'nuff you don't do for your wife and children, but to carry on publicly with some woman... I'm givin' you fair warnin'...

Dalton laughed. "You threatenin' me? I say you're scratchin' up the wrong tree, Mylart. Guess mebbe you don't know Lu like I do. You raise a hand to me and she'll come flyin' at you like a wildcat. Don't you know I got Lula wrapped 'round my little finger? Anything I say is law 'round here. Carrie don't care I'm married and tell ya the truth, old man, I don't neither." He laughed, "Don't pretend ya ain't never dipped yer foot in the pool. You ain't no saint." Jennie held her breath.

Mylart got up slowly, moved to the edge of the porch and glared down at the figure sprawled on the steps below him. His voice was just loud enough. "Mebbe Lu is weak where you're concerned, but being weak don't mean she'll put up with the public disgrace of your actions. I'm willin' to bet when she hears 'bout this widow woman, she'll send you packin' so fast your feet won't touch the ground."

Dalton scrabbled to stand up and swayed precariously on the steps. His voice was a coarse whisper. "Don't bet on it, old man, cause you'll be the loser. What can she do anyhow? This house is mine and this land too. I ain't givin' up what's mine. Lula is putty in my hands. She's pathetic. She never wuz much and now she's older, she ain't worth a tinker's damn. Carrie is more woman than most men would even tackle, and she wants me. Think I'm gonna give that up... think again. You jest keep that damn Miller nose outta my business."

Papaw took the steps slowly, finally facing Dalton halfway down. He reached out, took a handful of Dalton's shirt, lifted him off his feet and dropped him down the rest of the steps to the ground where he landed in a heap. "Lula don't take care of this situation, then I will."

Jennie clasped her hand over her mouth to keep from cheering. *Oh what a man is my Papaw!*

Dalton scowled up at the huge figure looming above him. "Well now, we'll jest see who Lula believes... I wouldn't plan on it bein' you."

A shadow moved in the dim light behind the screen door.

Chapter Twenty-Nine
A Solution for All

Jennie and Papaw stood at the gate, waiting for Jeb Owen and his wagon. Papaw was preoccupied and Jennie knew why. She couldn't rightly let Papaw know she'd heard the confrontation with Papa, as he might chew her out for eavesdropping. She asked, innocently, "Did you have your talk with Papa last night?"

Papaw said, "Yes."

"What did he say?"

Papaw looked exasperated. "Jennie, girl, until I have a long talk with your Mama, I think we should just let it lay for the time being. Your Papa for sure isn't going to discuss it with her and it can all wait until I get back from Boone. It's unfortunate I made this arrangement with Jeb right now, but since I did, we'll take care of our business in Boone and be back tomorrow."

"You don't think Mama knows anything about it, then."

"It's been your Mama's history to back off of anything unpleasant where your Papa is concerned, so if she knows, she ain't about to say."

He looked at her sharply. "And I don't want you nor Ed sayin' anythin' to her either. I'll take care of it in my own way. You promise me, girl?"

"I promise, Papaw. I won't say anything to Mama."

Papaw said, "Your Papa ain't 'bout to mend his ways, Jennie. Only thing left is to tell your Ma and fact is, I don't know as she will believe me. Even if she does, she might turn a blind eye to what's goin' on. That's pretty much been her actions in the past."

He put his arm around her shoulders, and his angry blue eyes bore into hers. "But you can mark my words, child, Dalton Wainwright has caused his last bit of mischief where Lula is concerned."

They both heard Jeb's wagon moving up the road and there was no more time for conversation. Papaw pulled himself up beside Jeb and with a wave, they moved off. Papaw called over his shoulder. "We'll be back tomorrow sometime, Jen. Tell your Ma."

Jennie waved her acknowledgment.

✉

Soldier continued digging. The hole was almost big enough for him to squeeze through and then he would be free of the Owen barn.

His snout was caked with mud and he panted with exertion, but he ignored his drinking water, nor would he take the time to rest. He kept digging furiously.

$\boxtimes$

Dalton sat sprawled in a stupor in the porch rocker, his head thrown back, mouth open, snoring loudly. Lula sewed quietly in the other rocker.

Jennie looked away from her father in disgust. After the confrontation with Papaw, you would have thought Papa would at least have stayed sober. But, thinking it over, Jennie was sure it was Papa's way of letting Papaw, and all of them, know he was in charge and could do anything he pleased.

But Mama knew. Papaw said he hadn't said a word to her, but looking at Mama's somber expression, Jennie was sure she knew.

"Mama," Helen intruded on Jennie's thoughts. "My arm's bout to fall off. I can't do this ole churn no more."

Jennie, sewing basket open by her side, mending in her lap, was absorbed with threading a needle. She said without looking up, "We agreed to take turns, Helen, and it's your turn."

Helen whined, "How come Hubie and Clint don't get a turn?"

Mama said, "Cause they ain't here, that's why."

Baxter sat balanced on the porch rail. "I'll work it for a while, if you want." Helen stopped with a grin on her face, already halfway out of her seat.

Jennie, still engrossed with the needle said, "No thanks, Baxter, it's Helen's turn."

He dropped his legs to the porch. "I don't mind..."

Jennie cut him off with a look.

Baxter grinned and resumed his seat.

Helen looked indignant. "Mama..." Lula looked sternly at Helen and the child, pouting, sighed loudly and took up the dasher again.

Lula said, "Where *are* the boys, anyway? It's 'most time for supper."

Jennie said, "Ed and James took them out squirrel hunting. Clint needs the practice with Papaw's rifle."

It was late afternoon and the sun was near setting. Over Dalton's snoring and the monotonous clunking of the butter churn could be heard the noisy chatter of birds from the treetops as they settled down to nest for the night.

Hubie and Clint ran across the field, rounded the corner of the house and clattered breathlessly up the porch steps. Clint propped the rifle beside the screen door. "Ed says the rifle sight is off a bit. He's gotta fix it." He sat on the porch rail beside Baxter.

Lula asked, "Where're the other two?"

"They're comin'," Hubie said. He pushed Helen off her seat at the butter churn, grabbed the dasher and without missing a beat said, "It's my turn." Helen looked at Lula in surprise and they exchanged smiles.

James and Ed walked into the yard and climbed the porch steps. James stopped beside Jennie and sat down. Ed, with a sigh, fell heavily into the rocker.

Jennie asked. "Get any squirrels?"

Ed laughed. "No, but Clint killed a pretty good size tree limb."

Clint said with good humor, "You didn't do no better."

Lula said, "You jest never mind, Clint. Ain't much meat on a squirrel anyway. I got to say again, you boys did a good job in shorin' up the chicken house. I'm right pleased. I won't have to worry about it collapsing on the chickens anymore."

Clint turned to Ed and grinned. "I bet it's the most work they done since they got outta the army."

Ed jumped from the rocker with a hoot and took a playful swipe at Clint. Trying to avoid Ed, Clint grabbed Baxter and the two of them swayed precariously on the railing. James came up quietly behind Clint and grabbed him in a bear hug while Ed pretended to punch and box his ears.

Ed said, "That all the thanks we'uns get fer helpin you with your chores?"

Hubie came to Clint's defense and the roughhousing continued down the porch steps into the yard.

Baxter grinned from the porch rail watching the free for all.

All of a sudden a white bullet leaped into the middle of the scuffle barking and snapping. He grabbed Hubie's pant leg and backed off, snarling and shaking his head.

"Soldier, what are you doing here, dog?" Hube quickly looked up at Dalton, saw that he was still snoring away and with relief turned back to Soldier. He reached down and grabbed the dog around the middle, drawing him onto the heap of wrestling bodies.

Lula shook her head. "Yard's all puddled up from the rain. They's gonna be mud from here to yonder."

Dalton stirred. "Whas all the damn ruckus?" He came halfway out of the rocker, then fell back again. "Yappin' dog." He turned his bloodshot eyes to Lula. "Din I say git ridda that dog?" His voice was drowned out by the shouts and laughter.

Hubie squealed, "Dog, leggo my pants."

Ed grabbed Soldier and James grabbed Hubie and a tug of war developed. Lula cried, "Let 'em be, Ed, that dog'll tear Hubc's pant leg clean off."

Dalton mumbled, louder, "Din I say get ridda that dog?"

No one paid any attention.

Laughing, Hubie made a grab for Soldier and they all fell in a heap. "He's only funnin', Mama, he ain't serious."

"Serious or no, I'm the one has ta do the mendin'."

Dalton sat up grumbling.

James, Ed and Clint sat back on the grass breathing heavily.

Ed leaned over and roughed Clint's hair. "Gettin' some muscle little brother... soon you'll be able to wrestle me good."

Hubie and Soldier chased each other around the yard.

Dalton swayed to his feet, picked up the rifle by the door and put it to his shoulder. "Don no one listen I say somethin? I said that dog's a pest." They all looked up in surprise. Before anyone could make a move, Dalton fired. The sound of the shot echoed through the hills.

Soldier flew into the air, yelped and fell to the ground. In the silence that followed, they all stared, bewildered, at the bleeding dog. Soldier tried to get up but collapsed again, blood pouring from the wound in his side. He lay unmoving on the ground. Hubie, not sure what had happened, looked down at him in dumb surprise.

Dalton raised the rifle again.

James was the first to move. "Enough," he roared and stormed toward Dalton, his body between the stricken dog and the gun.

Jennie leaped from the steps and reached her father's side at the same time James reached the bottom of the steps. At that point, Jennie remembered later, the rifle was no longer aimed at the dog, but at James. She lunged for the gun as James flew up the steps, the loud report echoing again off the mountains, but this time the shot went wild. Dalton, confused, fell back. James wrenched the gun from his hands and in one motion turned, plunged down the steps and threw the gun to Ed.

"Take charge of your father, Ed."

James ran to the dog and gently pushed Hube aside. Stooping, he cradled the unmoving dog in his arms and took off, half walking, half running, down the road toward Doc Paynes. Hubie, sobbing, stumbled along by his side.

James called loudly over his shoulder, "Baxter... Baxter, come on, man, we need you."

Jennie stood, shaking, watching them disappear down the road.

✉

James and Baxter, with Soldier limp between them, did a running walk down Valley Road. Their gait was awkward and surprisingly, the little dog was heavy. Soldier showed no signs of life and James was afraid their efforts would be futile, but for Hubie's sake, he intended to make a good show of trying to save him. As they approached Doctor Payne's house, they saw it was dark.

Baxter said, "Oh no. I forgot. Doc is down at the Fenleys' tonight seeing to Mam. We'll have to take the dog to my place." He looked at Hubie, wide-eyed and frightened. "It's all right, Hube. I got some instruments Doc gave me; I know what to do. Come on, James, faster."

They turned onto the Combs road and burst into the yard, and with all the commotion, Frenda came out on the porch, "Land sakes, what on earth happened?"

"Dog's been shot, Mama, where can we take him?"

Frenda was all business. "Round to the wash shed." She came down the porch steps and ran ahead, opened the shed door and was already pulling a rickety table to the center of the shed when they got there. "Here's an old sheet to lay him on. That's Hubie's dog, ain't it?"

Baxter grunted. "They's a lamp over yonder, James, light it, will ya?" James sprung to do his bidding, recognizing Baxter was in charge.

"Get me a bucket of water, Mama, and any antiseptic you can find... and my instruments, Mama. The case Doc give me. James, tear some of this sheet into pieces."

Hubie laid a hand on Soldier's head and whispered, "Y'ere gonna be all right, dog."

A dim circle of light fell from the kerosene lamp James held aloft. Hubie stood as close to Soldier as he could, stroking one limp paw, tears streaming unnoticed down his face. "He's gonna be all right, ain't he, Baxter?"

"Don't know, Hube. That shot come close to his heart." Without turning from the dog he said, "Ya gotta hold that lamp in closer, James, it's comin' on dark."

James obeyed. It seemed the search for the bullet went on endlessly and they all stood motionless and quiet while Baxter worked deftly, probing gently into the wound. Frenda stood by with the strips of cloth James had torn off the sheet and stanched the flow of blood as best she could.

Finally, Baxter heaved a sigh of relief. "Got it." His bloody fingers held up the bullet. Without wasted motion, he poured the antiseptic over the wound, then quickly and carefully wrapped the small body round and round with bandages. He straightened and arched his tired back.

"That's 'bout all we can do, Hubie." He stooped down to be on a level with the boy. "The bullet come close to his heart. It hit a rib, and I don't know what else it did." He put a hand on Hube's shoulder. "You got to be prepared, Hube, Soldier might not make it."

Hubie nodded slowly. His eyes went to the dog lying quietly on the table. "When will we know?"

"We'll jest have ta wait an see. Right now he's in shock and we have to keep him warm. Fetch that ole quilt over yonder and cover him up."

Frenda came up behind Hube and dropped her arm around his shoulders. The boy's dark curls were a mass of snarls and his face dirty except for the clean pathways left in the wake of his tears. "Come along, young'un. 'Pears like Soldier is restin' quiet. We'll wash your face and hands and then find something to eat." Frenda herded Hubie in front of her and headed for the house. She turned at the shed door. "Come along inside, the two a you, when you're ready."

James and Baxter set about cleaning up the wash shed and Baxter's instruments and after Baxter checked his patient again, they both slumped to the ground, their backs against the shed wall.

"You were a wonder to watch, bucko. When we didn't find Doctor Payne at home I thought the dog would surely die. You have a real talent, Baxter. You'll make a fine doctor one day."

Baxter had a tired but satisfied smile on his face. "It's gonna happen, James. Doc and Ma... and Pa too, are all behind me. When I'm done with schoolin' I'll come back and practice right here in Zionville."

"You're a fortunate lad to know what you want. I'm not sure what the future holds for me."

After a silence Baxter said, "You say I'm fortunate, James, but I guess maybe you're the best off." Flickering light from the lamp probed the dark corners of the shed. "And I guess maybe we both know why."

James didn't answer at once. He looked at Baxter and found him waiting.

James said softly, "You mean Jennie."

Baxter sighed, "Yes, I mean Jennie."

James remained silent, waiting for Baxter to go on.

"Jennie and me's been friends since we started school. We grew up fightin' each other's battles. Never fightin' each other. Life wuzn't always easy fer either of us and when it was real bad we always had each other to turn to. Guess I always been in love with her. I never told her how I felt 'til jest recent. Stupid me, I thought she felt the same way."

Baxter took a deep breath. James remained silent.

"I knowed you wuz writin her letters. Didn't give a thought that maybe she was fallin' in love with you 'til one day when she was talking 'bout you it was plain on her face. Even then I wuz sure it would be me in the end. That is, 'til you come."

James broke his silence. "Jen says she isn't sure how she feels..." He struggled to think of something more to say but could think of nothing.

Baxter got up and brushed the dirt from his levis. James got up after him. They faced each other. Baxter said. "Maybe she says she ain't sure, but it's plain to everyone she's in love with you. Ain't nuthin' more ta say. I ain't holdin' it against you. I wuz mad at first but I kin see she's different with you and if it's you she wants ain't no way I can change it."

James put out his hand and Baxter took it. "I'm only hopin', Baxter, you'll let me be as good a friend to you as Jennie is."

✉

In the Wainwright yard, everyone stood in shock as James and Baxter, carrying the limp dog between them, and Hubie, too shocked to cry, ran down the road together.

Ed, still holding the gun in his hands, turned to his father. Dalton had slumped back into the rocker, mumbling and cursing, seemingly unaware of what he had done.

339

Helen sobbed in Mama's arms and when she had calmed down a little, Mama said to Clint, "I want you to take Helen and go over to the Owens and stay with Min til I send for the two of you."

Clint opened his mouth, but Mama held up her hand. "Boy, just do as I say."

Clint, seeing Mama was not to be argued with, put an arm around Helen and gently led her away towards the Owen house.

Mama turned to Jennie and Ed and gave them a look that said as plain as day... I'll handle this. They stayed rooted to the spot as she marched up the porch steps and stood before Papa. He was slumped over in a stupor and Mama prodded him with her foot.

"You better wake up, Dalt, and hear what I have to say."

He roused himself. "I don't want to hear nothin' 'bout that damn dog. If you got ridda him way I asked I wouldn't a had to shoot him. It's your fault."

Lula glared at him. "Yes, a lotta things has been my fault around here. Not standin' up fer Hubie so's he could have his dog is only one thing."

Dalton leaned back in the rocker and waved his hand dismissing Lula like a bothersome fly. When she didn't go he looked up at her with annoyance. "What?"

Ed walked up and stood behind her and Jennie followed. If Papa was going to get ugly, he would have to handle the three of them.

Lula stood ramrod straight, arms at her sides and Jennie saw that her face was cold and unsmiling. She'd never seen Mama like that towards Papa. Mama always had an apologetic look when she spoke to Papa... not now.

Mama said, "I didn't go right to bed last night. I was behind the screen door when you come home." *So. Mama does know.*

Dalton started rocking his chair. He looked up at Lula. "So?"

"I heard your conversation with Papa."

Dalton's smile started to fade. "You wuz listenin' to my private conversation...?"

Lula went on, "Lucky I did. I coulda gone on bein'... what was it you said... putty in your hands? I coulda gone on lettin' you think whatever you do I hafta put up with."

Her anger was beginning to show. She paced up and down the porch. "I heard all about Carrie Crane and what you been up to at the mines. That's where all your money goes, isn't it? That's where you spend your time when you should be home with your wife and children. All along I been pitying you, thinking you work so hard you deserve whatever you take fer yerself. I never once thought of another woman." She stopped and turned and stared at him.

His smile was gone, but he was still cocky. "A man needs someone to tend to him, cook and the like..."

"But that's not all she's doin'... she's in your bed, isn't she?"

"Wal, not..."

Lula stiffened. "Don't deny it, Dalton. I guess I could forgive you most anything. You always could josh me inta thinking things your way, but not this..."

Dalton tried to take control. "Now you just wait one minute, Lu, you're my wife, you're supposed..."

"I'm supposed to what? Suppose to forget you're sleeping with another woman? You said I'm pathetic, not worth a tinker's damn. Well, you're right about that. I *am* pathetic... for putting up with your drinking. All those years I done that, but another woman..."

Dalton, realizing he was close to losing the game, stood up and held out his arms, a simpering smile on his lips. "That woman means nothing to me, Lu. You're the only woman I ever..."

"Don't say love to me. Jest don't say that word. I know now you never loved me. 'Bout time I realize jest who it is you do love... yourself."

His arms dropped to his sides. He said, a little desperately, "Well, if that don't take all. Here I been bustin' my gut at the mines and that's all the thanks I get."

Lula studied his aging, handsome face. She said quietly, completely in control, "There has been nothing for years that I can thank you for. I guess maybe you better go back to the mines and—and—I don't want you comin' back here ever agin."

Now he was angry. "Jest you hold on a damn minute. This is my house and land. You ain't throwin' me out. If anything, I kin throw you out."

"That so? We'll jest ask Papa about that. This is no more your house than mine. Papa never turned over the deed to your name. Who do you think has been payin' the taxes all these years? Papa. That shoulda been a clue."

Jennie couldn't see Lula's face, but the satisfaction was plain in her voice. "You don't own nary a piece of this house."

Dalton stared dumbly back at her. "I don't believe you."

Lula stood up a little straighter. "You can believe what you want... the truth is you don't own one shingle, one windowpane, one doorknob. Nothing."

There was great sadness in her voice. "We coulda been happy. We coulda made a good life fer ourselves and the young'uns. I loved you so much, Dalt. I don't guess you'll ever know jest how much. I woulda gone through the fires of hell fer you, but none of it was enough, was it?" She shook her head. "So now you kin go to your Carrie Crane and never have to worry 'bout comin' home again." She walked to the screen door and turned to face him once more. "I packed your satchel. It's sitting outside the back door."

There was silence on the porch after the screen door banged shut behind Lula. Jennie, surprisingly calm, waited for Dalton to turn back to them. When he did, his anger was frightening to see. He looked squarely at Jennie. "This is your fault, you meddlin' little bitch."

Ed took at step towards Papa and Jennie put a restraining hand on his arm.

"Meddling bitch?" she said. "Oh, how I wish I were. Nothing would give me more pleasure than to think I caused Mama to finally open her eyes. No, Papa, you did this all by yourself. And isn't it sad? Not one of your children finds it in his heart to stand up for you."

Dalton gave her a wicked smile. "Well, now, dont'cha know, girl, I don't need nobody? Least of all this mealy-mouthed bunch. Y'all will be sorry 'thout a man around..."

Jennie lifted her eyebrows in surprise. "Until Ed came home, there never *has* been a man around here." She turned her back on him and started to walk away, then as an afterthought turned back and with her voice dripping sarcasm said, "Oh, Papa, do you want me to fetch your satchel?"

Dalton Wainwright, his face flushed with anger, walked to the back porch, picked up his satchel, and walked out of their lives.

✉

Lula sat with her hands tightly clasped in her lap. "Guess it's time I admitted your Papa is no-count." Her lips trembled and tears slid down her cheeks.

Jennie said, "You did good, Mama. Ed and I are proud of you and Papaw will be too when he comes back."

Lula didn't hear her. She was talking to herself. "And I woulda gone on puttin' up with it all, except he found him another woman. I woulda kept on sharin' him with the drink and his selfish ways, but no woman with any pride would share her man with another woman." Lula wiped at her eyes angrily. "I'm so ashamed."

Jennie said, "No reason for you to be ashamed, Mama. Everyone knows you've done your share and more."

"That's just it. Everyone knows... and the dog... Hubie's Soldier. That dog dies I don't know if the young'un'll ever forgive me." Fresh tears started. Jennie patted her mother's arm and waited patiently.

"Somethin' else, Jennie." Mama took Jennie's hand and held it to her face. "All them years I turned my head away when he beat all you young'uns. You especially. Use to tell myself it was cause y'all needed a thrashin' now and agin, but that wuzn't so. I wuz afraid. You wuz the only one had gumption nuff to stand up to him. God knows I didn't. Steada takin' your side I looked away." Jennie couldn't find the words to comfort her. "How am I ever gonna make it up to you?"

"Mama, you don't need to make anything up to me... I just... I just never understood how you could love a man that gave you nothing in return."

"What can I say, Jen? I don't understand myself. All you gotta know is not every man is like your Papa."

Finally Lula picked up the edge of her apron and wiped her face. "No sense carryin' on. I know I done the right thing tellin' Dalton to leave. It's been a long time comin'."

Jennie said, "Maybe someday, Mama..."

"No. Someday's been and gone. I shed my last tear over your Papa."

✉

When Papaw returned from Boone he blamed himself for the events that lead up to Soldier being shot, saying he should have straightened Dalton out before he left for Boone. Jennie secretly thought what Papaw really regretted was not being here to kick Papa out. It was something he'd wanted to do for a long time.

"Lula," Papaw said. "I want y'all to come to the kitchen table for a meeting. That includes everyone, Min and Sherm too... the whole family."

Lula was puzzled. "What on earth...?"

"Never mind, Lu, just get everyone together. I'll tell you what I have in mind when we're all seated round the table."

⊠

"Sherm and me ain't had time to clean up. We smell like the barn. Hope no one minds."

Helen, holding her nose, said, "Jest don't sit by me, is all."

"Hubie won't be here," Mama said. "The young'un won't leave Soldier's side."

Clint said, "Dog's gonna be all right, though. I wuz there this morning and Soldier opened his eyes and wagged his tail, jest a little wag, but we all seen it. Baxter says we can bring him home maybe tomorrow."

Minnie said, "You should see the job that dog done on the barn. Father Owen says Soldier would make a fine posthole digger."

"That's the case, we'll hire him." Ed poked Clint. "Whatta ya say, little brother?"

"Here's Papaw." Jennie got up and gave him her seat, pulling another chair to the table. "Now maybe we'll hear what this is all about."

Papaw rapped on the table for them to be quiet. He cleared his throat. "Somethin' I been thinking about fer a long stretch. Now seems the time to say it." They all settled down and waited.

"Now that Dalton ain't in the picture, Lu, you might want to consider coming to Sugar Grove to live. You, Clint, Hube and Helen. I figured Ed might want to stay here and run your farm. Jennie, of course, will be away at school or" Papaw waved his hand and grinned, "Wherever".

"Other side of the coin..." Papaw held up his hand and bent down each finger as he counted. "One, I'm an old man, two, living alone, three, big house, and four, the responsibility of running the mill. Makes sense to me for us to join hands, so to speak.

"Now as fer the mill. I wuz hopin' Clint might take an interest in it." He looked at Clint and held up his hand when Clint shook his head. "Hear me out first Clint. "I know you think and feel like Ed does about your home place. Well, I got me some cows and heifers need tending and I got a garden too, so there's plenty of farmin' in Sugar Grove. We could even bring Libby and Lizzie. What I'm askin' is fer you to give the mill a chance. In the years to come, if you can't abide workin' in the mill, I'll see you get a piece a land of your own.

"Then we come to Hube and Helen. I'll see Helen goes on to the Academy if she's a mind to, Hube too, if it's his fancy. And so as not to leave Min and Sherm out in the cold, I'll go along with Jeb in helpin' them get a start in a place of their own." Papaw held up his hands. "I'm finished. Now. What do y'all think of my plan?"

For a split second there was complete silence, then everyone started to talk at once. Mama finally stood up and clapped her hands and they stopped to listen.

"Was a time nothin' in the world woulda made me give up my home. But now don't seem much point to stay on. Clint and Hube and Helen need some directin'. Lord knows they never got much from their father. But, Papa, you raised your own family, now you want to take on raisin' your grandchildren? Don't seem fair."

"Lu, I already told you the benefits of you and the young'uns movin' in. As fer raisin' my grandchildren... nuthin' on God's good green earth would make me happier."

Ed spoke up. "And me being on your home place, Mama, you could come back any time you wanted to."

Papaw looked at Clint. "What do you say, boy?"

Clint stared down at his hands, squirmed around in his chair and finally looked up at Papaw. "Why don't I stay here with Ed? He can't run the place all by hisself. He needs me."

Papaw nodded, seeming to give it some thought. Jennie could see right through the old man. There was no way Clint would be allowed to stay with Ed. Papaw knew it, but what would it hurt to let Clint think he was at least considering it. Papaw said, "If you wuz more'n twelve, young'un, I might could agree with that. But you got more growin' up to do." He looked at Lula. "What does your Mama say?"

"Like Papa says, Clint, twelve is a mite young to take on such a big responsibility. Best you wait until you're a bit older."

Clint grumbled under his breath, "Knew you wuz gonna say that."

Sherm spoke up. "Papaw, it's a generous offer you made Min and me and we 'preciate it, honest, but Pa needs me somethin' fierce right now. I can't jest up and go."

Jennie knew as well as Papaw, that Sherm would say exactly that. But in order not to leave Min out, he had to make the offer.

"Well, if and when you and Min need my help, it will be there. Ain't heard from you, Helen, anything to add?"

"I like your house, Papaw. You got a pump right in your kitchen. I won't have to go to the old spring for water anymore." Everyone laughed and agreed that moving to Papaw's house would be best for them all.

⊠

"You want to see me, Papaw?"

"Come here, Jen."

Jennie sat down in the rocker. Mylart brought out his pipe and Jennie, used to Papaw's ways, waited patiently while he tamped in the tobacco and lit it. When the pipe was drawing well, Papaw looked up and smiled. "You think you'll be goin' off with this young man?"

Jennie inspected her hands. "Just yesterday I thought I had all the time I wanted to make up my mind. If that second bullet had hit James, Papaw," she looked up at him, "he'd be gone and there would be no decision to make."

Papaw quietly drew on his pipe. "So. You've decided to marry James?"

Jennie grinned. "Yes, and I think you're pleased, aren't you?"

Papaw smilingly nodded. "I think so... but time will tell." He reached in his pocket, drew out an envelope and handed it to her. "I signed over the property to Jeb yesterday and he paid me for it. It's the five hundred dollars I promised you."

Jennie looked down at the bulging envelope. "Thank you, Papaw. James has all sorts of plans, but he says he'll make sure I go to school."

"The boy's ambitious. If I wuz to pick out a young man fer you, Jen, it would be someone like James... and that's all I'm gonna say, 'cept whether you use the money for school or for a wedding present, don't make no nevermind to me. It's yours... and James'."

"Papaw, that's generous of you. You worry about everyone."

"Nothing much left fer an ole man to do but sit and worry."

"I don't ever think of you as old."

Mylart drew on his pipe. They watched the smoke from the pipe swirl away on the breeze.

Jennie knelt by his rocker. "I love you, Papaw."

Mylart took a deep breath. "I love you, too, Jen."

Jennie wore her blue print dress with the wide cape collar. She wished she had a different dress to wear, but this was the best of them. Her hair was clean and brushed and shone in the last rays of the sun. It would soon be too cool to sit like this on the old porch swing of an evening, which saddened her. The evenings were so beautiful with the light slowly fading and the mountains turning black against the twilight sky.

She reflected on how much of her life she'd spent on this porch. How many springs had she watched come alive? Pale green buds spotting the naked trees followed by the summers changing everything into a deep lush green. How many gardens had come and gone, and how many nights had she run midst fireflies so thick they outnumbered the stars?

And autumn... stealing in and mystically changing the leaves into brilliant colors, filling the soul with a sense of a job well done. Could she wake up and feel this peace in a strange bed in a strange place? Yes, she smiled, with James.... yes, she could.

A cool breeze ruffled the collar of her dress. A change was on the way.

She left the swing, went to the steps and peered up the road. Her melancholy left when she saw a figure walking toward her. In another moment she realized it wasn't James. It was Baxter. The ache in her throat made it hard to swallow. Baxter. How can I be so happy when I know how hurt Baxter is?

He walked through the gate and pushed it shut behind him, looking up at Jennie.

"Don't know mebbe you'll be mad or not, Jen, but I asked James if he would let me come and talk to you alone. He seemed to understand... hope you will."

Jennie knew this conversation was due. She owed it to him. She turned to the rocker. "Come on up and sit here by me."

He climbed the steps slowly and sat in the other rocker.

"You gotta say it, Jen. Guess I know already but I have to hear you say it."

Jennie nodded. "Guess it's been pretty plain to see."

"I'm all tore up inside, Jen, but the worst of it is I like him." He gave her a weak smile. "He's the kind of man I wish I could be... easy talkin', smart..."

"Oh, Baxter, what am I going to do with you. You are all of those things and, oh, so much more. You're going off to college in a few weeks. It will make all the difference in the world."

She reached for his hand. "I'll never have another friend like you."

"And I you. Guess that's something."

"We go back a long way, Baxter. None of that can be erased. It will always be there."

"You promise if ever you need me..."

"I promise."

347

"You still ain't said it, Jen, not right out."

"I've said it to myself, Baxter, but you're right. I haven't said it out loud."

James paced nervously. He'd promised Baxter he would wait, but the waiting was taking its toll. Finally, his patience at an end, he went quickly down the Combs steps, out the yard and headed up the road. He talked aloud to himself as he strode along. "I know Jennie loves me, I feel it in me heart. Baxter says he knows it too. But until Jennie says it... God, I didn't know how much I was counting on taking the lass with me. All my talk about seeing the world and finding my place in it means naught if Jen isn't by my side."

He hurried his pace and as he neared the Wainwright house he saw Jennie come out the gate and run up the road to meet him. He caught his breath. They met in the middle of the road and stopped and stared solemnly at each other. He reached for her and she went willingly into his arms.

"I love you, James," she said.

THE END

Epilogue

At first, Jennie and James planned to take a train from Boone and marry in Johnson City, but Mama would hear nothing of that. In the end a small wedding was planned.

Mama made Jennie a simple white, soft cotton dress, with a long satin sash tied in the back in a bow. The round neckline was adorned with tiny satin rosebuds and the veil (borrowed from Emmaline Wooding) was tucked in place with fresh flowers from the garden. Min stood beside her, dressed in her own wedding dress, smugly content that Jennie wasn't going to waste her life being "just a nurse."

The groom wore a pair of blue serge, store-bought trousers from Ev Proffitt's general store and a clean white shirt and tie. His boots were polished and his hair combed neatly off his forehead. Ed, the best man, shuffled nervously by his side, immensely happy at the thought James would be his brother-in- law.

The gathering at the church was both joyful and sad. Papaw proudly walked the bride down the aisle while Aunt Pearl sobbed noisily. Clara and Jeb were in the first pew with Mama, Clara holding fast to her hand. Hubie, with his watered-down curls beginning to stand out in all directions, stood beside Helen and Clint, subdued for the first time in his life.

Luther Norris held hands with Lucy Glenwood and Sarah Proffitt disguised, as best she could, the longing that showed clearly in her eyes. Doctor Payne was absent from the gathering as Grady Sykes had once again arrived at his house in a panic with news his Pa was dying.

Baxter stood at the back of the church with a smile pasted on his face, sure the pain he felt in his heart would be with him forever.

As Prosper Truall pronounced them man and wife, James turned Jennie to him and took her face in his hands.

"I love you, Jennie, and promise I will all the rest of my life."

Jennie looked into the earnest grey eyes and the words she'd found so difficult to say came freely to her lips.

"Oh, James. I love you, too."

Acknowledgements

Shirley Nikolaisen gave me the courage to begin; my husband, Robert, put up with all the hours I spent on my computer; my sister, Regina Kasmin, and my good friend, Joyce Borup, displayed their unflagging faith in me; my young friend Heather Monteith insists that I write another book about Jennie and James; Robert's relatives, especially Aunt Delia, furnished information about Jennie in particular and life in the High Country of western North Carolina in general.